THE CHILDREN'S HOUR

Volume One
FIRST STORY BOOK

Volume Two
FAVORITE FAIRY TALES

Volume Three
OLD TIME FAVORITES

Volume Four
CARAVAN OF FUN

Volume Five
BEST-LOVED POEMS

Volume Six
STORIES OF TODAY

Volume Seven
FAVORITE MYSTERY STORIES

Volume Eight
MYTHS AND LEGENDS

Volume Nine
FROM MANY LANDS

Volume Ten
SCHOOL AND SPORT

Volume Eleven
ALONG BLAZED TRAILS

Volume Twelve
STORIES OF LONG AGO

Volume Thirteen
ROADS TO ADVENTURE

Volume Fourteen
FAVORITE ANIMAL STORIES

Volume Fifteen
LEADERS AND HEROES

Volume Sixteen
SCIENCE FICTION – GUIDE

Roads to Adventure

A BOOK TO GROW ON

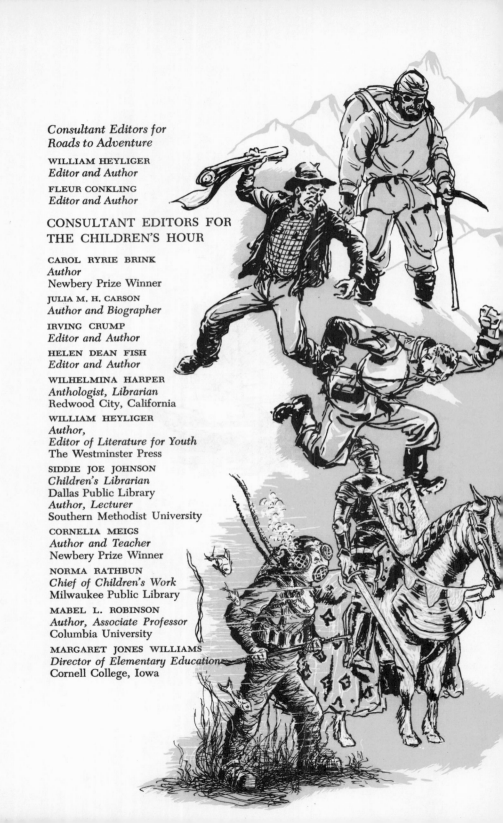

MARJORIE BARROWS, *Editor*

Roads
to Adventure

MATHILDA SCHIRMER
Associate Editor

DOROTHY SHORT
Art Editor

THE CHILDREN'S HOUR

PRINTED IN THE UNITED STATES OF AMERICA

Acknowledgments

The editor and publishers wish to thank the following publishers, agents, and authors for permission to use and reprint stories, poems, and illustrations included in this book:

GEORGE ALLEN & UNWIN, LTD., for Canadian permission to reprint "A Kon-Tiki Adventure" from *Kon-Tiki* by Thor Heyerdahl.

APPLETON-CENTURY-CROFTS, INC., for "Gorillas and Lions" from *On the Gorilla Trail* by Mary Hastings Bradley, copyright, 1922, D. Appleton & Company.

COLLINS *YOUNG ELIZABETHAN* and the authors for "The Mystery of the Bay" by Kenneth M. King and "Follow Your Leader" by S. T. James.

DODD, MEAD & COMPANY for "Climb High" from *Barnum's First Circus* by Laura Benét, copyright, 1936, by Laura Benét.

E. P. DUTTON & CO., INC., for "The Third of June on Annapurna" taken from *Annapurna* by Maurice Herzog, published and copyright, 1952, by E. P. Dutton & Co., Inc., New York; and "Secret in the Snow" taken from *Snow Treasure* by Marie McSwigan, published and copyright, 1942, by E. P. Dutton & Co., Inc., New York.

HARPER & BROTHERS for "Tom Chist and the Treasure Box" from *Howard Pyle's Book of Pirates* by Howard Pyle, copyright, 1921, Harper & Brothers. Copyright, 1949, Margaret K. Johnson.

HOLIDAY HOUSE for story and illustrations from *Whitey and the Rustlers* by Glen Rounds.

HENRY HOLT AND COMPANY, INC., for "Down in the Wolf Pit" from *Understood Betsy*, (Elizabeth Ann Fails in an Examination), by Dorothy Canfield, copyright, 1917, 1946, by Henry Holt and Company, Inc. Copyright, 1945, by Dorothy Canfield Fisher.

ALFRED A. KNOPF, INC., for "Little Red" by Pearl Buck, from *Youth Replies, I Can*, edited by May Lamberton Becker, copyright, 1945, by Alfred A. Knopf, Inc.

LITTLE, BROWN & COMPANY for "The Pearl Diver" from *I Turn Pearl Diver* by Charles Nordhoff, copyright, 1924. by the Atlantic Monthly Press.

THE MACMILLAN COMPANY for "A Power-Plant" from *Selected Poems* by Harriet Monroe.

McINTOSH AND OTIS, INC., for "Understudy" by Noel Streatfeild from *Children's Own Treasure Book* published by Odham's Press.

RAND McNALLY & COMPANY for "A Kon-Tiki Adventure" from *Kon-Tiki: Across the Pacific by Raft* by Thor Heyerdahl, copyright, 1950, by Thor Heyerdahl. Published in the United States by Rand McNally & Company.

RINEHART & COMPANY, INC., for "Oliver at the Circus" from *The Saturdays* by Elizabeth Enright, copyright, 1941, by Elizabeth Enright Gillham.

CHARLES SCRIBNER'S SONS for passages in "Understudy" by Noel Streatfeild from *Dear Brutus* by James M. Barrie, published by Charles Scribner's Sons.

STORY PARADE, INC., for "Alligator up the Bayou" by Steve Benedict, copyright, 1952, by Story Parade, Inc.; and "Storm Tide" by Willis Lindquist, copyright, 1950, by Story Parade, Inc.

THE VIKING PRESS, INC., for story and illustrations for "The Round Up" from *The Good Master* by Kate Seredy, copyright, 1935, by Kate Seredy; and story and pictures for "Pippi Acts as a Lifesaver" from *Pippi Longstocking* by Astrid Lindgren, translated by Florence Lamborn, and illustrated by Louis S. Glanzman, copyright, 1950, by The Viking Press, Inc

JANET NORRIS BANGS for "Down in Davy Jones' Locker" from *Heroes and Hazards* by Margaret Norris, published by The Macmillan Company.

VIVIAN BRECKENFELD for "A Touch of Arab" by Vivian Breck, first published in *The American Girl*.

HOWARD M. BRIER for "Fools Walk In," first published in *Boys' Life*.

LAVINIA R. DAVIS for "Why Bother with Ladders."

MAX EASTMAN for "At the Aquarium."

HUBERT EVANS for "A Trust Fulfilled," first published in *Child Life Magazine*.

WILLIAM HEYLIGER for "Steelman's Nerve," first published in *Boys' Life*.

WILLIS LINDQUIST for "Yukon Trail," first published in *The American Junior Red Cross Journal*.

CLAY PERRY for "Guides with Wings," first published in *Boys' Life*.

Contents

YUKON TRAIL	WILLIS LINDQUIST	1
CLIMB HIGH	LAURA BENÉT	8
WHITEY AND THE RUSTLERS	GLEN ROUNDS	16
OLIVER AT THE CIRCUS	ELIZABETH ENRIGHT	26
DOWN IN THE WOLF PIT	DOROTHY CANFIELD	38
STORM TIDE	WILLIS LINDQUIST	51
ALLIGATOR UP THE BAYOU	STEVE BENEDICT	60
LITTLE RED	PEARL S. BUCK	68
THE ROUND UP	KATE SEREDY	80
PIPPI ACTS AS A LIFESAVER	ASTRID LINDGREN	94
SECRET IN THE SNOW	MARIE MCSWIGAN	101
A TRUST FULFILLED	HUBERT EVANS	125
WHY BOTHER WITH LADDERS?	L. R. DAVIS	134
STEELMAN'S NERVE	WILLIAM HEYLIGER	144
GORILLAS AND LIONS	MARY HASTINGS BRADLEY	158
A TOUCH OF ARAB	VIVIAN BRECK	178
THE MYSTERY OF THE BAY	KENNETH M. KING	190
UNDERSTUDY	NOEL STREATFEILD	200
GUIDES WITH WINGS	CLAY PERRY	228
TOM CHIST	HOWARD PYLE	247
TRIAL BY BATTLE	HOWARD PYLE	278
DANTES' ESCAPE	ALEXANDER DUMAS	291
FOOLS WALK IN	HOWARD M. BRIER	302
FOLLOW YOUR LEADER	S. T. JAMES	315
THE THIRD OF JUNE	MAURICE HERZOG	322
DOWN IN DAVY JONES'S LOCKER	MARGARET NORRIS	334
THE PEARL DIVER	CHARLES NORDHOFF	347
A KON-TIKI ADVENTURE	THOR HEYERDAHL	354

Part I: FOR YOUNGER READERS

Willis Lindquist

YUKON TRAIL

ILLUSTRATED BY *Rod Ruth*

UNDER the lowering Alaskan sky, young Steve Woodford stepped from the train at the snow-covered outpost of Nenana. He looked anxiously around for his Uncle Jim, the famous "Flying Doctor" of the Yukon of whom he had boasted so much at the orphanage.

For years he had dreamed of going to the Yukon. Now he was on his way and he was happy. He was going to have a real home and belong to a family. He hoped Uncle Jim and Aunt Bess would like him.

The young Indian who came up grinning, couldn't have been over sixteen. "You're Steve?" he asked in perfect English. "Well, I'm Sam Ketchum. I've got a letter for you. There's been a lot of sickness up in the Yukon, and your uncle couldn't fly down for you."

Steve's heart sank as he took the letter. It was short. Uncle Jim wrote about how busy he was and that he might not be able to fly down for two or three weeks.

"Sam Ketchum is a young Indian guide who works for me," the letter went on. "I've told him to make you comfortable at the hotel. In a day or two he will be starting back for the Yukon with my new dog team. You could go with him if you wish, but I would not advise you to do so. It is a 350-mile mush through wilderness and tundra, and it would be a hardship for a boy accustomed to the soft life of civilization."

1

Steve read the letter several times at the hotel. It disturbed him that his uncle should think he was soft.

When he joined Sam for a dinner of venison roast, he said, "I wanted to come up here last year, Sam. But Uncle Jim wouldn't let me. He wrote that I was too young. He said the Yukon was a man's country, and it was no place for a boy. So he made me wait a year. And now he still thinks I'm soft. I'm going to show him, Sam. I'm going with you and the dog team."

Sam laughed. "It won't be easy," he warned. "But you have to learn about dogs sometime if you're going to be of any help to your uncle. We'll start at dawn."

It frightened Steve to think of the trip when he went to bed. He had never seen the big sled dogs. Some were part wolf and said to be dangerous.

It was still dark when the hotel man came with a set of fur breeches and a hooded parka, fur boots, and a fur sleeping bag.

Sam was waiting for him at the sled, with eleven mighty huskies straining at their harnesses, anxious to be off.

"Better meet some of your dogs," Sam said. "This first one, your leader, is Mutt. He's been to the Yukon before, and he knows the trail."

The tawny big brute lowered its head and watched Steve with suspicion. Steve fought down his fear and leaned over to pet the dog. Its fangs bared in a snarl.

"Not too close," Sam warned. "Mutt doesn't know you yet. And you better stay clear of Kooga—this big Malemute. He's a real trouble-maker."

"Why is the sled tied to a tree?" Steve asked.

"Because otherwise they'd be off like a flash, and we couldn't stop them," Sam explained. He pointed to an iron rod suspended above the ground at the rear of the sled. It looked like a narrow rake. "That's your brake. You step on it and the prongs dig into the snow and stop the sled."

They packed, and Steve got on top of the sled.

"Hold on!" Sam warned as he untied the rope from the tree.

The dogs were off, eleven big brutes harnessed in pair except for Mutt who took the lead. They raced over the snow

2

in full gallop. The sled bounced and flew, and it took all of Steve's strength to hold on.

Standing on the runners in back, Sam gave a hearty laugh. "Dogs are always wild to get started. They'll soon slow down."

They did. For hours they went, skirting great slopes of spruce and Norway pine, and on and on into the still white wilderness.

At midday they stopped for a few minutes' rest and a bite to eat.

"Now you drive," suggested Sam. "I'll run behind for a while to get warm. But whatever you do, don't fall off the sled. You'll not be able to stop the dogs and you'll lose them and the sled and all your food. It's not a good way to die."

Steve leaped on the runners. "Get going!" he shouted. Mutt turned his head back and looked at him, but nothing happened.

"Holler MUSH," Sam suggested. "When you want to go right, holler GEE, and for left UP. And swing the sled around corners so it doesn't tip."

Steve nodded. "MUSH!" he screamed. It worked. He stood proudly on the runners. He was driving a dog team!

There was real work to it, he soon discovered. Keeping the sled upright at curves was tricky, and he had to carefully avoid stumps and rocks that might smash the sled. On the down slopes, he stood on the brake to keep from running over the dogs.

But suddenly it happened. He made the mistake of looking back too long at Sam who was jogging half a mile behind them. He hit a slope, and his feet slipped from the runners. But he held on, dragging as the sled gathered speed downhill until it pushed the dogs forward into a wild scrambled heap. Then the sled tipped.

It started one of the wildest dog fights Steve had ever seen. Each seemed to be blaming the others for what had happened, and they snarled and slashed with white-fanged fury.

"Stop them! Stop them!" yelled Sam.

Steve stood frozen with fear. He didn't move. He didn't dare venture close.

Sam came up full speed, screaming at the dogs. He pried them loose one by one with a snowshoe and straightened their harnesses, which had become badly tangled. Then he mopped the sweat from his face.

"You'll have to learn how to do that quick," he gasped. "If you don't you'll lose a dog or two before you know it."

For five days they went on, and then Sam began to have chills and fever. "I was in the hospital for a week before you came," he explained. "Maybe I left too soon. It's coming back."

By noon he was groaning with pain and could not leave the sled. "There's a settlement over on Carlson Creek," he whispered. "You better get me there fast."

Steve reached the hollow among the bluffs in three hours, and only the women and children were there to meet them. The men were out on a week-long hunt.

"This one needs the doctor," said an old woman.

Steve went cold with dread, but he knew what had to be done. "Sam says my lead dog knows the trail well. I'll go get the doctor."

Sam rumbled in protest. "You'll stay here," he gasped. "Your uncle flies to this settlement every so often for a check."

"It might be weeks," said the old woman. "There is much sickness."

"I'll go," said Steve. He had no choice. Soon he found himself alone on the trail with a fierce pack of Malemutes and

4

Eskimo huskies, and he felt panic rising within him. He began to wonder if he could handle the team.

He began talking to the dogs, calling them by name as Sam had told him to do. He stopped for the night under a sheltering cliff near a staggering thicket of birches. Now the moment he dreaded most had come. He had to handle the big dogs.

Steve tried not to show his fear. The big leader dog watched with yellow eyes as he approached, its ears flattened to the massive head. As Steve reached down to unfasten the harness, the wolf-dog snarled.

"Easy, Mutt!" Swiftly, Steve unharnessed the dog and led it to the nearest birch tree and tied it up. He came away weak, but bursting with a happiness he had never known. HE COULD DO IT! The other dogs, even the big Malemute Kooga, were easy after that.

One day followed another with perfect weather. The dogs were beginning to know him, some even licked his hand. But Mutt, the leader, remained sullen.

Then he saw the plane in the sky one morning. It circled above him, his uncle waved, and Steve, forming big letters in the snow, told him to go to Sam at Carlson's Settlement.

5

A howling Arctic blizzard started that night and kept him in his sleeping bag for two days. The third morning dawned clear, and he looked out on a white world. No dogs were in sight. They had all been buried by the snow.

As they mushed north that afternoon, he became careless. He did not see the low branch until it struck him a stunning blow in the face. He was falling. "Don't lose your sled or you die!" Sam's words came roaring back to his ears.

With all his strength he tried to hold on. But it was no use. His fingers slipped and he lunged headlong into the snow. He floundered. He tried to rise to his feet, but the earth seemed to tilt on end, and he couldn't tell which side was up.

The dogs and the sled were speeding away. He could see them vaguely. In a few moments they would be gone. There was nothing he could do to stop them. His food, his sleeping bag, even his snowshoes were on the sled. A man couldn't live very long on the lonely white tundra without them.

In that reeling instant of terror, he seemed doomed. His mind cleared a little, and instinctively he cried out at the top of his lungs.

"Gee! Gee! Gee, Mutt!"

He held his breath. For a terrible instant nothing happened. But suddenly the big lead dog swung to the right. He waited until the whole team had turned. Then he screamed again. "Gee! Gee, Mutt!" Once more the lead dog turned.

They were coming back now. Steve got to his feet and stumbled to meet them, waving his arms. He tripped over a snowdrift and sprawled before the onrushing team. That was all he could remember for a time.

When he opened his eyes finally, it seemed that a miracle had happened. Mutt, towering over him, was licking his face.

He threw his arms around the big dog, buried his face in the heavy fur and let the tears come. Even a man could cry in Alaska if there was no one to see his tears.

From that day on his uncle paid daily visits to watch his progress and to drop sandwiches and food from Aunt Bess. In the first of these packages, he found a note.

6

"I have seen Sam," wrote his uncle. "He's doing fine, thanks to you. If you keep up your good speed you should reach home in three days. We'll be waiting."

Steve felt a deep inner excitement. Home! In three days! He could drive a dog team now and he felt sure that he could be of real use to his uncle. They would not find him soft and useless. They would like him.

Near sunset, three days later, as he came down the slope into the small settlement of Unison in the Yukon, his uncle and half the village came out to meet him. They were cheering and waving and smiling. His tall uncle wore a large smile and threw an arm over his shoulder.

"Good boy, Steve," he said warmly. To the people of the village he said, raising his voice, "I'm mighty proud to introduce you to my nephew, Steve. He mushed all the way from Nenana in fifteen days and that's a record for any of us to shoot at."

When they entered the log cabin which was to be his new home, there were gifts from almost everyone in the village—snowshoes, parkas, beaded reindeer pants, a beautiful Malemute pup, a carving from a walrus tusk, and bows and arrows.

Steve mumbled his thanks to the smiling villagers who stood before him. They were a strange mixture of old sourdoughs, Eskimos, Indians, and boys and girls.

One young man spoke up. "The Flying Doctor has cared for us and saved many of us from death. We love him as a father, and we are glad to welcome another of his blood."

It was not until later when Aunt Bess and Uncle Jim and Steve were alone, that Uncle Jim spoke.

"I want to confess, Steve, that I've been very worried about having you here. I wanted you to be happy, but I knew that a soft white boy from civilization would soon be looked upon by these people with contempt."

He smiled and took Steve firmly by the shoulders. "But I see now I was wrong. I need not have worried. You did what had to be done. You've got the makings of a real Yukon man."

Steve turned quickly away to play with the pup—and to hide the mist of happiness that had come into his eyes.

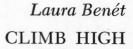

Laura Benét

CLIMB HIGH

ILLUSTRATED BY *Matilda Breuer*

WAS it really necessary for his father to sell their pony, pondered young Jon Vekelof. He was crouching over the warm fire while his father smoked his pipe at the other end of the long, low farmhouse room. Besides the rude wooden chairs there was a white-washed table with benches and a cushioned settle. It was a pleasant room, but tonight it seemed dreary as he thought about the pony. That shaggy pony was their link with the world outdoors, the world of free motion and soaring birds and wide skies. Often gray and harsh, it was still Iceland, his homeland. His love for it ran in his blood and was part of him. But if the pony, his companion, were gone . . . Hark! What was that whirring sound outside?

Jon leaped up from his knees and ran through the outer passage to the door. Thick fog hung outside, blanketing the hills, and the ground was hard frozen. Directly in front of his eyes was a sight that made him blink and look again. A strange thing was resting on the ground a stone's throw away, a thing of metal and wood with wings on either side of it and a blunt snout in front. Standing beside it were two men dressed like strangers. One of them began to speak. He was a tall, splendid fellow with dark, keen eyes. His companion, a little, wiry man who knew the Icelandic language, interpreted. Jon quickly grasped their meaning. They had had to land from this boat that flew in the air on account of the fog. They wished to spend the night at the farmhouse.

8

Jon had once seen a picture of an airplane in his schoolbook and had been told its name. Oh, if he might only see it rise and dip in the air! Meanwhile his father came to the door.

"Sleep here and be welcome," was his reply to their questions. Jon ran to build up the fire with more logs. In front of it he set two armchairs and then hastened to the loft to heap his bed with sheepskins. He would sleep by the fire tonight. When the strangers tramped in, there were mugs of hot tea ready for them, and dark rye bread and sausage, all there was in the cupboard. The boy wished, while they were eating, that he might creep out and touch the plane. What was their errand that they had come in such a strange way?

The taller of the Americans—they were Americans—soon answered Jon's thoughts. He spoke through his friend, adding to the interpreter's words by friendly nods.

"I am here to collect rare birds' eggs," he said, "and must find the nest of a golden eagle. Tell me, boy, is there one to be found near here?"

Jon screwed up his eyes. Like one who knows where a box of money is hidden, he could not part at once with his secret. "Yes," he finally stammered, "yes."

"Will you take us to it? We could go tomorrow in the plane," said the smaller man.

What a proposal! Jon's face grew red with delight but he answered honestly. "I'm afraid, sir, the strange machine flying in the air would startle the eagles. Then they would fly up in a rage and perhaps trample on their eggs. It's best for me to go by myself and climb the rocks quietly. I might be able to steal up to the nest while they're away. But if more than one goes, it makes too much disturbance. I'll go on Ingeborg," he added doubtfully, looking at his father and wondering how soon the pony might be sold.

But his father lifted his head. "My son will go," said old Jon, indicating that they might make the farmhouse their headquarters during the search.

"Good enough," said the tall man. "But how will you get up those tall cliffs?"

9

"Watch and see," laughed Jon. Many times he had wanted to bring down the eagles' eggs, but had always feared the fierce birds with their powerful flapping wings and beaks that could peck out a boy's eyes. Even the hoarse cry they gave was terrifying, and an attack from one was something to be dreaded. Yes, climbing cliffs was dangerous sport, but now. . . .

"We will pay well for these eggs. My collection will be incomplete without them."

These words settled and sealed the bargain. Joy lightened Jon's heart as he went out to tell the farm boy to fish for salmon. If he could earn kroner enough to pay their debts, then Ingeborg, the pony, might stay! Bad weather held up his trip for two days. On the second afternoon Jon went on foot to their nearest neighbor half a mile away to get some oats for the pony. She must be fed well or she would not be equal to the hard trip. The cliff where the eagle nested was near the hot springs, miles away. Nor was early spring a good time to go. Snow might fall.

On the morning he started, Ingeborg seemed to know that they must make double-quick time. Food and a flask of coffee were fastened to the saddle in a little wooden chest, called a *kaffort*. At first, under dusky though clear skies, their journey was a pleasant one. The path led them past a birch wood and around a group of dark hills, until they came to a river, a deep swirling stream. They crossed a slight wooden bridge and descended safely into a grassy valley watered by this same river. Here Jon halted to eat his luncheon and let the pony graze on the good grass.

He had started while it was yet twilight, for, in the land of the midnight sun, there are few hours of daylight except in midsummer. While these hours lasted he must travel quickly.

Ahead of them lay a bare, desolate stretch covered with slippery gravel and rock fragments. There were snowfields here and there at the foot of the towering mountains. If a storm should come up suddenly. . . . Suppose the two eagles had deserted that nest built on the cliff by the hot springs! Jon stroked his pet's ears and urged her on, "Ingeborg, hurry!"

10

On and on they went until he almost napped in the saddle and one hour of the precious daylight was gone. But, at last, he was rewarded by sight of the bleak-looking cliffs that guarded the springs. The steam that rose from them like smoke could be spied a long way off.

Then Jon saw something else that he dreamed for an instant was the airplane in which he longed to ride. But no, though it floated in the air so steadily, it was a bird, one of the eagles, soon followed by another. He could see the tawny neck-feathers and brown body that mark the golden eagle. The boy quivered all over with eagerness. No doubt the birds had scented a dead sheep in some far away pasture and were going after it. Now,

11

indeed, was his chance, a marvelous chance to climb up to the nest, secure the eggs, and get down before they returned.

He trotted the pony to the foot of the highest cliff, marking carefully with a practiced eye the direction from which the eagles had started. Hitching Ingeborg in a corner, Jon strapped on his back the basket for the eggs and put on his feet his rough climbing sandals of untanned cowhide. He longed for a comrade who would have stood on an overhanging ledge of rock and hauled him up on a good stout rope. But he must do this work alone. It was better.

Cautiously and skilfully he began to climb. He whistled between his teeth as he struggled up the rock's face and wished for a fairy or a troll to help him. Up and up, around a narrow point of rock, up and around another he went, occasionally clinging to a wild bit of scrubby bush. He placed his feet, one after the other, as carefully as if he were treading glass steps to a giant's castle. Above all he did not allow himself to lose his wind, stopping every few minutes to rest. But he did not pause longer than necessary for, at any moment, he feared the eagles might return and unite in a fierce attack.

At last he reached the final, dizzy ledge. Peering half-blinded into a gap between the rocks, he saw a loose nest of sticks. Lying in it were four eggs, white mottled with red, and they were still warm. Able now to steady himself, Jon stretched out a hand and, one by one, drew those eggs from their shelter. He wrapped each one securely in the thick bits of felt and cloth he had brought, and put them carefully in the basket. Triumph! His heart pounded happily as he rested flat for a while, lying on his stomach on top of the cliff. Ahead of him lay the ride home, but his father would certainly have the farm lad make hot pancakes . . . and the travelers would be pleased . . . and . . . he woke, sharply. Something was falling on his face and the pony was whimpering down below. Snow!

He started down. Several times he almost lost his footing and was only saved by bits of shrubbery. The wet flakes made the rocks more slippery and the deeps below them, terrifying. But his pony called continually and that gave him hope. Poor

12

beast, she was lonely and frightened. Brave old Ingeborg. Jon was almost down the cliff when a sweep of shadowy wings darkened the clouded sky above his head. He shivered. The eagles were already beating their way home! They would be sure to see the unfamiliar form against the rock and suspect that their nest had been robbed.

Should the eagles attack, a stumble, a slip even, on his part, would mean broken eggs as well as broken bones. Something must be done to protect the hard-won eggs. In his despair Jon had a sudden inspiration.

Reaching around with his left hand he unhooked the basket from his back. Searching with his eye for a tuft of grass where the fall would be made easy, he hurled the basket down, down and out into the air. He was barely in time, too, for in another instant the larger of the angry eagles swooped down on him. Sharp claws tore at his shoulders. Frantic to save his eyes, Jon shut them in desperation, and went whirling down the cliff after the basket.

When at last he opened his eyes, he thought they were the only part of him that would ever move, so bruised and sore and battered he felt. He was lying at the cliff's foot and close beside him stood Ingeborg. The pony, worried and distressed, had broken her tether and was whinnying beside him, licking his face with a rough tongue. Jon stroked the pony's nose and a dreadful surging pain shot through his left arm and shoulder. Turning his head slightly he saw his basket lying not far away, covered with snow. He turned over, groaning, and realized now that his left arm was broken. He crawled over to the basket a few inches at a time. He unfastened the cover, trembling to think what he might find. By some miraculous luck only one egg was broken. The other three had been protected by the wrappings of felt.

What should he do now? The dark was almost upon them, dark that was helping to ward off the eagles whose cries of rage he could still hear. Clutching at his precious basket, Jon managed to crawl back to the lee of the cliff and huddle under a shelf of rock, clinging close to his horse for warmth. There was

14

food left in the pack but he felt too ill to taste it. The many hours of the night seemed endless.

When he woke from a long uneasy doze, Jon put out his hand for the basket. Yes, there it was, but how was he to ride Ingeborg home? It must be late in the morning, much later than he usually woke. A fearful thought entered his mind. The enemy eagles! They must be at hand. His quickened ears heard whirring wings, saw a dark shadow floating in the sky outside the little barrier of rock. Well, he would turn Ingeborg loose. The pony could canter home without him and give the alarm.

Then a strange dream took possession of young Jon. He dreamed that the great, golden eagle came down to earth, alighting with a buzzing noise near him at the cliff's foot. Two small beings riding on its back dismounted and came over to him with loud cries. They worked at his arm, bound cool bandages on his head, and gave him a hot drink. How good it tasted, how sweet! His fevered fancy broke. He opened his eyes to see the two strangers by his side and his father with them, looking gray and troubled.

It was old Jon Vekelof who rode the pony home, the pony who dropped her head and whinnied sadly as she saw her master borne off in the thing that looked something like an eagle. Young Jon did not leave his bed for many days and a doctor, summoned from the town, said his escape had been a narrow one. The first day he was able to sit in an armchair by the log fire, Wilfrid Green, the naturalist and collector, spread kroner all over the white-washed table for Jon to see.

"These are for you," he said.

"That is too much," said the boy, flushing. "I could not take all of it."

The tall American touched his shoulder. "Take it for your father's sake, and your pony's," he said, gravely. "You had the courage of an eagle, boy. You were willing to take a chance in the face of certain danger. That is a fine thing."

Jon thanked him and grinned warmly. Who wouldn't have taken a chance for a pony like Ingeborg?

15

Glen Rounds

WHITEY AND THE RUSTLERS

ILLUSTRATED BY THE AUTHOR

I T WAS a fine spring morning in Lone Tree County, with the prairie beginning to turn green, and the wild chokecherry and plum thickets smelling sweet. Magpies and meadow larks were talking big about the business of starting new nests.

Whitey was headed for Cedar Spring to see if the windmill was working, but along the way he was looking for his two beef steers, which he ran with Uncle Torwal's cattle. He hadn't noticed them around for several days, and was worried.

Old Spot jogged along at his special ambling trot and thought about the days when he'd been a first-class cow horse. Whitey sat up straight and thought about the fine new saddle he'd buy in the fall when he sold those two steers of his.

He didn't really mind wearing a hand-me-down Stetson of Uncle Torwal's, especially when it had such a fine rattlesnake hatband, for most cowboys wore battered old hats. And for the same reason he didn't mind the old boots with the run-over heels and the fancy butterfly stitching on the tops, that he'd been given by a puncher with small feet who'd got a new pair of Fort Worths.

But this old saddle was something else again. It was an old Cogshell with a flat Texas horn. It was so old the corners of

16

the skirts were curled up tight, and the strings had long ago been chewed off by calves. Everywhere the stitching was coming undone, leaving great corners of old leather sticking up to give the whole affair the look of a molting hen. Furthermore, the stirrups were the clumsy iron kind, when the style hereabouts was a neat wooden oxbow pattern. For a long time Whitey had felt that it made him look more like a homesteader than a cowboy.

Of course, when he'd been smaller and first come to live with Uncle Torwal and help him run the Lone Tree Ranch, it hadn't mattered so much. But now that he was practically a top hand he had to think more about the looks of his equipment. People set a lot of store by such things.

So last summer Uncle Torwal had given him two Whiteface calves. Together they'd figured out a brand for him and sent it off to be registered, after they'd put it on the calves with a running iron. It was a fine big squiggle on the ribs with three dots at the end.

The Rattlesnake brand, they called it. Whitey figured it was about as fine a brand as he knew of. He saw no reason it shouldn't some day be as famous as the old "101." And Rattlesnake Ranch sounded good no matter how you said it!

So he rode on for a while, thinking about the time when the Rattlesnake brand would be on thousands of head of good beef cattle instead of only two, and he'd be able to have a new saddle every week if he felt like it.

But just when he had started thinking about how fine a Sunday saddle would look, decorated with silver in the Mexican fashion, he came on a calf bogged in the mud around an old water hole, so he had to stop thinking about saddles for a while.

The old cow near by was in a nasty humor, bawling and swinging her tail, so he didn't feel it was safe to get down off Spot. That meant he'd have to rope the calf and drag it out.

As calves will do, that one had gotten out into the middle of the softest patch of gumbo, so that if Whitey missed his first cast, as he usually did, he was bound to get his rope all muddy. That never did a throw rope any good, and was espe-

17

cially bad for a brand-new one like Whitey was carrying. He finally urged old Spot out onto the mud until he could reach down and drop the loop square on the calf.

After that he took a hitch around the saddle horn and in no time at all dragged the calf out onto solid ground. After he'd shaken the loop loose and the cow and calf had gone, he found his rope was muddy after all, so he had to get off and find some dry grass to clean it with.

It was then he noticed the fuss a bunch of magpies were making in a little gully not far off, so he decided to go see what it was they were doing.

The rain the day before had washed deeply into a pile of dirt that had caved off the cutbank, exposing some corners of what looked to be green cowhides, fresh enough to attract the magpies.

After some tugging and digging, Whitey uncovered three hides which had been carelessly buried by caving part of the bank onto them. Two hides carried his Rattlesnake brand and the other Uncle Torwal's Lone Tree!

He sat down on the bank, and if he hadn't been almost a man grown he'd have bawled like a kid, for there went his hopes of a new saddle. The two Rattlesnake steers he'd counted on so much were now in some rustler's truck on the road to a butcher shop far off.

18

He knew how the rustlers operated, going out at night with a truck and butchering two or three steers quickly, destroying the hides to prevent identification, and leaving to sell the meat before anyone knew they were about.

There'd been talk for some time that they must be operating around here, for ranchers all up and down the valley had been missing beef.

When Whitey rode into the ranch and up to the horse trough Torwal saw he looked mighty glum.

"Truck rustlers been getting our cattle," Whitey said, as Spot was drinking.

"There's been talk of such," Torwal said. "But nobody knows for sure."

"I found three fresh hides over by Cedar Spring this morning," Whitey said. "They was buried in a washout."

He brushed dust off his hat and waited for Uncle Torwal to ask him some more. He was trying to talk as any cowboy would instead of being excited like a kid.

Torwal saw there must be more to the story, so he said, casual-like, "Was the brands cut out?" For usually the rustlers cut the brand out of the hide and burn it.

"Reckon they must have been careless this time," Whitey said. "One was a Lone Tree steer and the other two were Rattlesnake brand."

19

Torwal whistled. "That was tough goin', cleanin' out your whole spread."

"Yeah, that's a fact," Whitey said. "Looks like I'll ride this old hull awhile longer." He led Spot away so Uncle Torwal wouldn't see how badly he felt.

They didn't say much as they cooked and ate dinner, but afterwards, as they sat on the porch, Torwal spoke up. "Reckon we might as well ride in and see the sheriff. Now that we know for sure that rustlers are workin' around here, maybe we can figure out something."

"I sure hope so," Whitey said. "They did me out of a new saddle, and I wish I was old enough to swear!"

When they got to town they tied their horses and walked into the sheriff's office. Mr. Hairpants Hagadorn, the sheriff, shook hands with them while Mr. Fort Worth Wilkerson, the deputy sheriff, dragged out chairs.

After some polite talk of this and that, Torwal told the sheriff what Whitey had found.

"Was them hides fresh, son?" the sheriff asked Whitey.

"Yessir, they looked to be only a day or two there."

"This is the first time we've had any proof," the sheriff said, "but there's been a lot of complaints of missin' beef critturs all up and down the valley."

"How you reckon they get in and out of the valley without anyone knowing?" Torwal wondered after a little.

"I been considerin' that myself," the sheriff told him. "They have to come through here or through Hill City to get in or out, and we've been watchin' both places close, yet nobody has seen any strangers or strange trucks."

"I wish we could catch them," Whitey spoke up. "I was going to get a new saddle with the money from the steers they got of mine!"

"Maybe you can figure how to catch them and use your share of the reward money for that saddle," the sheriff said.

At the mention of REWARD, Whitey brightened right up. "You mean there's a reward for those rustlers?" he asked.

"Sure," the sheriff told him.

After some more talk they shook hands with the sheriff, the deputy sheriff, and a man who had just wandered into the office looking for a place to sit down, and rode off towards the ranch.

As they rode along Whitey thought about that reward. It seemed to him that getting a new saddle by trapping rustlers was even better than by selling cattle.

"Uncle Torwal!" he said, suddenly. "A time or two lately I've noticed car tracks up in that little limestone canyon the other side of Cedar Spring. I just figured it was somebody building fence, but it might be where those rustlers are getting into the canyon, do you suppose?"

Torwal thought awhile. "It could be, maybe," he said. "There used to be an old road through there that went down into the Boxelder road. We might as well drop by and take a look at things."

They found that the old trail, which had for years been overgrown and washed out in places, did now show signs of use. The worst holes had been filled, and it was plain that a truck could travel over it.

"Looks like this might be it, all right," Torwal allowed.

21

"This trail comes out on the Boxelder road where nobody would think of watching for them."

"Why don't we lay for them when they come back?" Whitey asked, thinking of the reward and his new saddle.

"Well," said Torwal, "they might not come back. Those dudes are pretty smart and don't often work the same place twice." After seeing how Whitey's face fell, he went on, "On the other hand, with a trick road like this they might feel safe for a while longer. From all the talk of missing cattle in the valley, they must have made several trips already.

"Tell you what," Torwal said after they'd started home. "We might take turns watchin' that canyon evenings for a while, just in case they did come back."

"Yessir!" Whitey agreed. "We'll catch 'em coming in and collect the reward!"

"We don't want to bother them comin' in," Torwal corrected him. "We jest want to know when they come in so we'll have time to call the sheriff and catch them goin' out with the meat."

Whitey still favored capturing the rustlers without the sheriff, but he said nothing about it. He was bound he'd get that saddle the rustlers had done him out of, and even part of the reward would be enough.

"I'll take my blankets and go out right away to watch for them," he said.

"You won't need any blankets," Torwal told him. "Those fellers usually figure to come in just about sundown so they'll be able to locate the critturs they want before the dusk is gone. So if they aren't in sight by full dark they'll probably not come."

After Whitey had eaten an early supper and was leaving to watch the canyon, Uncle Torwal spoke up. "If they don't show up tonight, we'll take turns with the neighbors for a few nights."

"I don't want anyone to take turns," Whitey hollered. "I'm the one they cleaned out, and I'll watch every night!"

So every night for almost a week Whitey rode out to a small butte where he could watch the canyon. Every night he carefully hid Spot in a plum thicket and then crawled Indian fashion to the top of the butte, where he lay hidden in the sagebrush like some oldtime scout. But nothing happened, and he was beginning to believe the rustlers had deserted the valley.

On the seventh night, he'd just started down to go home when he thought he heard a truck motor. He hurried back up the hill, and the sound was plain there. It was a powerful motor, and working hard. Soon he could see the dimmed lights as they moved to the mouth of the canyon, where they were switched off and the motor stopped.

It was the rustlers, sure enough!

Whitey had been complaining to himself because Uncle Torwal wouldn't let him bring his rifle and capture the rustlers singlehanded, but tonight he thought of nothing but getting back to the ranch as soon as possible to tell Uncle Torwal and get word to the sheriff. It seemed to him now that it was the sheriff's business to deal with such people.

Spot got the surprise of his life when Whitey clapped spurs and quirt onto him! He couldn't remember the last time he'd traveled faster than a trot. But as this seemed to be in the nature of a special occasion he did his best, and before long Whitey and Torwal were sitting out by the road waiting for the sheriff and his deputies to come by and pick them up.

The word had spread, and by the time the sheriff got there, ranchers and cowboys from up and down the valley had gathered. Most of them carried rifles on their saddles, or pistols in their belts. Whitey was looking forward to a right exciting time when they caught up with the rustlers.

When the sheriff came they all went along to the little canyon. Whitey had been afraid someone would tell him to stay behind, but no one did.

The men had all been hidden in the plum thickets for what seemed a mighty long time to Whitey, when they heard the truck coming back.

"This is when the bullets start to fly!" Whitey thought, as the sheriff stepped out into the light of the truck and held up his hand. But the truck stopped without protest.

Deputies and ranch men flashed on flashlights and swarmed all round it. Four weaselly-looking men climbed carefully out and stood with their hands raised while they and the truck were searched.

"There's plenty beef in here!" a deputy hollered.

"All right!" the sheriff answered. "One of you drive the truck along behind me, and we'll haul these gents down to our jail for a spell."

The rustlers didn't say anything, except to sort of mutter to themselves. They didn't look like the tough guys Whitey had been picturing in his mind. They weren't wearing gun belts, and they didn't talk tough to the sheriff. Worst of all, they wore bib overalls, like farmers, and one even had on plow shoes! Whitey was mighty disappointed in them.

Early next morning Whitey and Uncle Torwal went to town, and Mr. Bugeye Beasly, editor of the *Lone Tree Eagle*, interviewed Whitey.

The reward turned out to be only fifty dollars, and that divided six ways, so there was not enough to buy the saddle with. Whitey had built his hopes so high on that reward that he felt mighty bad for a few days. But after reading what Mr. Beasly wrote about him in the paper, how his alertness had helped make Lone Tree County free of rustlers and the like, he sort of got used to the idea of getting along with the old saddle another year.

Then one morning Torwal told him, "We gotta go to town

24

this morning, Bub. Sheriff said something about wantin' to see you."

All the way into town Whitey wondered what the sheriff could want. Maybe he wanted to make him a deputy or something. He imagined this and that, but never thought of the real answer. For after some talk the sheriff pointed to a grain sack on the floor and told Whitey, "Feller left that here an' told me to give it to you."

Whitey opened it up and inside was a brand-new saddle. The decorations were hand-tooled, the whangleather tie strings shining bright yellow, the sheepskin lining bright and clean, and the whole thing smelling of neat's foot oil and new leather. It was the most beautiful saddle Whitey had ever seen.

On the back of the cantle was a small silver plate he'd missed at first. It was engraved:

To Whitey for Service in Ridding
Lone Tree County of Rustlers
From the Lone Tree Stockmen's Ass'n.

Whitey couldn't think of anything to say, so he just grinned and carried the saddle out to try how it looked on Spot.

THE four Melendy children, Mona, Rush, Miranda, and Oliver, live in New York with their father and Cuffy, their housekeeper. So that they can have more exciting Saturdays they decide to form the Independent Saturday Afternoon Adventure Club. By putting their allowances together, each Melendy can take a turn and afford to do something he has always wanted to do on a Saturday. This is the story of Oliver's Saturday.

Elizabeth Enright

OLIVER AT THE CIRCUS

ILLUSTRATED BY *Janet Smalley*

AFTER a while, very slowly, it began to be spring. There were rust-colored buds on the ailanthus trees, and one day Mona heard a blue jay in the backyard sounding countryfied and out of place. Pretty soon it would be time to go to the valley; back to the rambling old wooden house that the Melendys rented every summer. Mona was homesick thinking about it and got all her summer clothes out of their boxes to see if she had outgrown them (which she had, and Randy was glad because now they would descend to her) and forgot to put them away again until Cuffy got after her. Rush took his baseball bat to school, and Randy wrote a poem. Oliver spent hours in the backyard digging fortifications in the mud. The seats and knees of his overalls were a constant source of despair for Cuffy.

The Independent Saturday Afternoon Adventure Club had so far been entirely successful. Randy had spent her second Saturday at the Ballet Theatre and was now able to walk on her toes quite easily, and had made a ballet skirt out of five

26

pairs of muslin curtains that couldn't be darned any more. Rush had gone to hear Rudolf Serkin play the piano and had been practicing furiously ever since in the hours that were not occupied by school or baseball. Mona had seen Katharine Cornell in a play and was very hard to live with as a result. She now moved queenlike and distant through a world of her own.

But this particular Saturday was Oliver's, and they had agreed to stay home. Not that he could go out by himself, of course, as they could; but in order to make him feel like a proper member of the I.S.A.A.C., they respected his Saturday and stayed at home. Also, besides giving him back the three dimes he had lent them, each added a dime of his own. "That'll be almost half what we have to spend on our Saturdays, and it will look like a million dollars to him," Rush said; it was his idea.

The day passed pleasantly enough. There was lemon pie for dessert at lunch, and afterwards Rush and Randy gave Isaac a bath in the basement washtub. He was philosophical about this ordeal by now and stood passive, though loathing every minute of it. When he was dry, they took him for a walk to show him off. Mona didn't want to go because she had borrowed some of Cuffy's big steel hairpins and was doing her hair in a pompadour just for an experiment.

The walk was a great success, and so was Isaac. People stopped them frequently to admire and pat him; and every time they asked what kind of dog he was, Rush gave them a different answer in a polite, serious voice. A Bronx beagle, he might say, or a Central Park setter, or an Interborough Rapid Transit retriever. Randy almost died.

When they came back to their own block, they could see Mona hanging out of the second-story window of their house. "Where's Oliver?" she called, when they drew near.

Rush and Randy looked at her blankly.

"I don't know. Where is he?" shouted Rush.

"Isn't he home?" cried Randy.

"We can't find him *any* place," answered Mona, withdrawing her head and closing the window with a bang.

They ran up the steps and into the house. Cuffy looked pale

and distracted. "Rush, you go down the street to the Potters' and see if by any chance he's gone to play with Petey, though goodness knows he's *never* done such a thing before. Randy, you run round the block. Maybe he's trying out his roller skates."

"Maybe he's just hiding," suggested Randy.

"His coat and cap are gone," Mona told her. "And anyway I've looked everywhere. In all the closets and underneath the beds. Even in the trunks in the basement."

"Where's Father?"

"Gone to Philadelphia to lecture. He won't be back till five, and we don't know where to get him. Hurry up, Randy, run along."

At that moment the object of all this concern was seated comfortably at Madison Square Garden. His knees were crossed, he was leaning back with a bottle of pop in one hand, and watching a lady in spangles hanging by her teeth to a rope fifty feet above the ground.

It had all been very simple, but it was also a well-thought-out campaign. Four weeks ago Oliver had received seven dimes which he had prudently concealed in one of his last summer's sandals. Today he had received seven more, which together with the sandal money made fourteen dimes. Untold wealth, but he did not let it go to his head. Everything proceeded according to plan.

Today when he was supposed to be resting he had got up, put on his coat and cap, and walked, faintly jingling, right out of the house. There was no trouble of any kind. When he got to Fifth Avenue he went up to a policeman and said, "Where is the circus, please?"

And the policeman said, "Madison Square Garden. Aren't you kinda young to be out alone?"

Oliver simply said, "No, I don't think so," and went his way. When he came to another policeman some blocks farther on he went up to him and said, "Where is Madison Square Garden, please?"

"Going to the circus, eh?" said the policeman. "It's at Fiftieth Street and Eighth Avenue. You all alone?"

Oliver simply said, "Yes, I am," and proceeded on his way, leaving the policeman with his hands full of traffic.

At Fiftieth Street he went up to another policeman and said, "Which way is Eighth Avenue, please?"

"That way," said the policeman, jerking a white cotton thumb westward. "'Bout three blocks over. Ain't nobody with you?"

Oliver simply said, "No, nobody," and crossed the street with the light.

It was easy when he got there, too. He just stood in a long line of grownups and children and held tight to his dimes and listened to what the people in front of him said when they got to the window. So when he got there he was able to say, "One, please. The kind that costs one dollar," and counted out ten dimes slowly and carefully. The man behind the window had to peer down in order to see him at all. Then holding his ticket tightly he followed close behind a large family and tried hard to look like one of them.

"Like to hold your own ticket, eh, sonny?" said the ticket man.

"Yes, I do," replied Oliver, and entered the magic portals. It was wonderful. It smelled of elephants the minute you got in, even before you came to the real circus part. Breathing the smell deeply, Oliver climbed some steps that a uniformed man told him to, and then walked along a corridor that another uniformed man told him to. He thought he heard a lion roar some place, and his feet crunched on peanut shells. It was very exciting. Finally he came to the right door, entered it, and found himself in another world. It was a vast world, carpeted with blue sawdust and walled with thousands of faces. A complicated web of cables and rope ladders and nets rose from the huge arena to misty regions high overhead. On the blue sawdust at the bottom there were three large caged rings, and in each of these rings the most extraordinary things were happening.

"This way, Bud," said the usher, steering the bedazzled Oliver to a seat. Oliver sat down without knowing that he did so. After a long time he removed his coat and cap blindly, never taking his eyes off the ring nearest him. In it three lions, two bears, and a black leopard were climbing ladders, while on high

30

gold stools seven other lions sat and snarled and batted with their paws at their trainer, who was the bravest man in the world and wore a red coat. He could make those animals do anything. Before he was through, one of the bears was pushing the other in a huge baby carriage while all the lions, on a bridge overhead, sat up on their hind legs and begged. Oliver sighed deeply: it was almost too much. His only regret was that he was too busy watching his ring to pay attention to the others. The air rang with the crack of whips and the sharp commands of the trainers.

As the cages were dismantled and the animals taken away, Oliver began to notice the men who were going up and down the aisles selling things: jeweled canes, and clown hats, and things to eat. They called their wares hoarsely like a lot of crows. "Hot dogs, hot dogs!" cried one, and "*Get*cha roasted peanuts here," cried another, and "*Ice*cole pop," still another. But the one Oliver was most interested in was the man who kept saying "Cotton candy, Cotton c-a-a-a-n-dy," as he went by with what looked like a lot of pink birds' nests on sticks. Oliver finally bought one. It was interesting; you bit into a cloud of pink spun sugar, and it instantly became nothing in your mouth. He ate it lingeringly, to make it last. All the time fascinating things were going on in the huge arena before him. Clowns came out and did their stunts, a man jumped over three elephants, ladies in spangles rode standing up on the backs of broad white horses, and dozens of tiny taffy-colored ponies, with plumes on their foreheads like the frills on lamb chops, pranced delicately about the rings and performed the most astonishing tricks. Oliver bit into his pink cloud and stared dreamily.

"I want some of that candy," said a sharp little voice at his side. Oliver turned a startled glance on the occupant of the next seat. He had forgotten there was anyone else in the world besides himself and the circus people.

"Don't bother the little boy, Marleen," said the little girl's mother in the kind of weak, uncertain way that no self-respecting child pays any attention to.

"I *want* some," repeated Marleen through her nose. She

31

meant business. She was a very little girl and she had a pointed chin, dark eyes, black curls as stiff as cigars, a blue hair ribbon, a gold ring, and pink stuff on her tiny fingernails. Oliver detested her. He looked coldly away and went on eating his candy.

"Now, Marleen," said her mother.

"I want some. I *want* some of that boy's candy!"

"I'll get you some when the man comes by. Now you be a good girl and look at the pretty horsies."

"I want some of his. You give me that candy, boy!"

Oliver swallowed the last of it at a gulp and Marleen uttered a piercing scream of frustration. Heads in the row turned and looked at them. "Now, Marleen, now Marleen," said her mother helplessly. But Marleen continued to scream like a steam whistle until her mother had consoled her by buying her a cotton-candy stick of her own, and a fancy cane besides. Even then she stared unblinkingly at Oliver. She could not be persuaded to look at the arena, and after a while the consciousness of that baleful scrutiny spoiled even Oliver's enjoyment. He couldn't pay the proper attention to the jugglers. A few rows away, on the aisle, he noticed a vacant seat and after some deliberation made his way to it without a backward glance at Marleen.

After this unpleasant episode the performance progressed blissfully without a flaw. The procession was magnificent beyond description; from zebra-drawn coaches to elephants wearing tasseled capes and jeweled howdahs. Oliver watched it raptly while eating a hot dog with mustard. He surveyed the acrobats (whose muscles seemed to stretch like garters) while eating another hot dog, this time with sauerkraut. It was forbidden Paradise. Cuffy didn't believe in hot dogs or mustard or sauerkraut, but Oliver believed in them all. By the time the aerial artists had come along he was quenching a violent thirst with a bottle of pop. (It was at this moment that his entire family was in an uproar about his disappearance.) The act was so exciting that he couldn't finish the pop till it was over, because it made his stomach feel so queer when one of the glittering creatures high overhead leaped from her fragile swing and arched through the air like a bird to the next glittering creature. The climax came when one of the creatures stood on her head on a trapeze without holding on and swung to and fro, shimmering like a dragonfly, far above the arena. It was breathtaking. Oliver felt so weak after watching her that he quickly finished his pop and purchased a bag of peanuts to fortify himself.

What a circus it was! One continual blaze of glory from beginning to end; from the flashing, bounding acrobats to the trained seals clapping their flippers; from the daring tightrope walkers to the fat clown who kept finding live ducklings in his pockets. Oliver did not want to believe it was over and sat for quite a while with people climbing over him and pushing past him, in the hope that they were all mistaken and something new was about to begin in the arena.

"Whatcha waitin' for, Bud?" said the usher, coming up to him. "Don'tcha know you'll get swept up with the trash and fed to the elephants if you wait *too* long?"

Probably he doesn't mean it, Oliver thought, but he got up hastily. At first he couldn't find his coat or cap, but then he remembered he had left them in the seat from which Marleen had driven him. There they still were luckily, though littered with peanut shells and a piece of chewed chewing gum, doubtless the work of the vindictive Marleen. Oliver cleaned them

33

off as well as he could, put them on, and after quite a lot of blundering about in the wrong direction (owing to the fact that he didn't understand the meaning of the word "exit") he found himself out on the street. Already it was dusk, and he began to hurry. For the first time the probable consequences of his adventure began to trouble him. It made him especially uncomfortable to think of Cuffy, for some reason.

And now the streets kept turning out the wrong way, and he found himself on Tenth Avenue instead of Fifth. The place looked strange; full of high, dark buildings, and big noisy boys who went bowling by him on roller skates and shouted at him hoarsely to get out of the way. As if that weren't enough, he began to have a terrible stomach-ache. Though he was a calm and resourceful person, Oliver was only six years old after all. So the next move seemed to be to cry. He stumbled and banged along the street, sobbing quietly and wiping his nose on his sleeve, wishing with all his heart that he was at home with Cuffy, and that he had never heard of hot dogs or cotton candy. Dimly he was aware of a clopping of hoofs on pavement but he was too miserable to look up until he heard a voice say:

"Whatsa matter, sonny?"

Oliver saw a big square policeman seated on a big square horse, magnificent as anything at the circus. All his buttons and two gold teeth glittered richly in the light of the street lamp.

"What's eatin' you?" repeated the policeman kindly.

"I'm lost!" wept Oliver, "and I'm sick at my stomach, and I want to go *home!*"

"What's your name?"

"Oliver M-Melendy."

"Know where you live?"

Oliver told him.

"Okay. You quit crying now," said the policeman. "You and me will take a little ride to your house. Think ya can hold out?"

"I guess so," replied Oliver dubiously. His stomach felt awfully unreliable. The policeman got off his horse and hoisted Oliver up on it as if he had been a kitten. Then he got on himself, behind Oliver, clucked at the horse and away they went.

34

Oliver thought gloomily that it was probably the only time in his whole life that he was ever going to ride with a mounted policeman, and he felt so sick he couldn't appreciate it.

"I guess I'm going to get a scolding when I go home," Oliver told the policeman. "Maybe I'll get a spanking too." All the shine was gone off the day.

"Why, what did you do?"

"Will you promise not to arrest me?" said Oliver cautiously.

"I doubt if it will be necessary," said the policeman, so Oliver told him.

"Well, I'll let your family take care of the penalty," the policeman decided. "It's a very serious offense all right, but it seems to me you've been punished almost enough as it is."

The traffic cop at Fifth Avenue looked at the mounted policeman and Oliver and said, "You've run in another big-time gang leader, I see."

"You'd be surprised," replied Oliver's policeman, and gave Oliver a pat on the shoulder.

At the Melendy house all was confusion. Randy was in tears. Father (who had returned from Philadelphia) and Rush were still out searching, and Cuffy was saying into the telephone, "Six years old. He has blue eyes, blond hair, and he weighs—" when the doorbell rang, and she dropped the receiver.

"Oh, Oliver darling, where were you?" cried Mona's voice, and Cuffy arrived to see her on her knees beside Oliver, who looked smaller and paler than ever before. Behind him stood the largest, most solid policeman she had ever seen in her life.

Aching with relief, Cuffy hugged Oliver, then she looked up at the policeman and said, "That's the quickest response I ever got from anything. I hadn't no more than just finished describing him to the police this minute—"

"The police force is never at a loss, ma'am," replied the officer with a wink.

Cuffy held Oliver away from her:

"Where in the world have you been?"

"To the circus," replied Oliver wanly.

"To the circus! Alone?" Cuffy was horrified.

"I wouldn't be too hard on him, ma'am," advised the officer.

"Go ahead and spank me if you want to," Oliver said, and was sick on the doormat.

Long, long afterwards, when all the thunder and lightning in his stomach had subsided, and the danger of a spanking was past, Oliver lay in his small bed with his hand in Father's.

"Why did you go without telling us, though?" asked Father. "You could have gone to the circus. Rush or Cuffy would have been glad to take you. I would have taken you myself if I could have stolen the time."

Oliver sighed. "I did ask Cuffy about it once, but she said oh, no, there's too much measles around. And everybody else was going out alone on their Saturdays, so I just thought I'd go alone too. I did want to see the circus so badly."

"Didn't you know we'd worry?"

"I guess I didn't think about it till afterwards," Oliver admitted.

"Well, you'll never give us a scare like that again, will you?"

"No, I never will, if I can help it," promised Oliver.

"All right then. That's that. Now suppose you tell me what you liked best at the circus."

"Oh, everything was wonderful. I liked the man on the one-wheel bicycle, and the elephants, and that automobile with all the clowns and the donkey in it, and the lady who stood on her head on the swing, and I liked all the things I was eating, while I was eating them. But the thing I liked *best* of all wasn't in the circus."

"What was that?" said Father.

"It was when the policeman brought me home on the horse," replied Oliver.

For now, no longer overshadowed by stomach-aches or unhappy apprehensions, the memory of that ride had become a radiant thing. He remembered the horse's two pointed ears that could move independently of each other, and its brawny, arching neck with the tidy black mane; and its strong, healthy smell. It was sort of like riding on a boat, only better because it felt alive, and you were higher up. And behind, immense and gorgeous in his uniform, rode the officer of the law who had befriended him. Oliver remembered how he held the reins in white gloved hands the size of baseball mitts. The splendor of that ride would never die.

37

ELIZABETH ANN had lived with her Aunt Frances and Aunt Harriet in the city, but when Aunt Harriet became ill Elizabeth Ann was sent to Putney Farm in Vermont to stay with Cousin Ann, Uncle Henry, and Aunt Abigail. The Putneys were very different from her Aunt Frances. They assumed that she could do things by herself, and they didn't worry about little things. Elizabeth Ann, or Betsy as she was now called, liked the Putneys very much, for she found that she wanted to be independent. This story takes place one day after school.

Dorothy Canfield

DOWN IN THE WOLF PIT

ILLUSTRATED BY *Eleanor Campbell*

I WONDER if you can guess the name of a little girl who, about a month after this, was walking along through the melting snow in the woods with a big black dog running circles around her. Yes, all alone in the woods with a terrible great dog beside her, and yet not a bit afraid. You don't suppose it could be Elizabeth Ann? Well, whoever she was, she had something on her mind, for she walked more and more slowly and had only a very absent-minded pat for the dog's head when he thrust it up for a caress. When the wood road led into a clearing in which there was a rough little house of slabs, the child stopped altogether, and, looking down, began nervously to draw lines in the snow with her overshoe.

You see, something perfectly dreadful had happened in school that day. The Superintendent, the all-important, seldom-seen Superintendent, came to visit the school, and the children were

38

given some examinations so he could see how they were getting on.

Now, you know what an examination did to Elizabeth Ann. Or haven't I told you yet?

Well, if I haven't, it's because words fail me. If there is anything horrid that an examination *did*n't do to Elizabeth Ann, I have yet to hear of it. It began years ago, before ever she went to school, when she heard Aunt Frances talking about how *she* had dreaded examinations when she was a child, and how they dried up her mouth and made her ears ring and her head ache and her knees get all weak and her mind a perfect blank, so that she didn't know what two and two made. Of course Elizabeth Ann didn't feel *all* those things right off at her first examination, but by the time she had had several and had rushed to tell Aunt Frances about how awful they were and the two of them had sympathized with one another and compared symptoms and then wept about her resulting low marks, why, she not only had all the symptoms Aunt Frances had ever had, but a good many more of her own invention.

Well, she had had them all and had them hard this afternoon, when the Superintendent was there. Her mouth had gone dry and her knees had shaken and her elbows had felt as though they had no more bones in them than so much jelly, and her eyes had smarted, and oh, what answers she had made! That dreadful tight panic had clutched at her throat whenever the Superintendent had looked at her, and she had disgraced herself ten times over. She went hot and cold to think of it, and felt quite sick with hurt vanity. She who did so well every day and was so much looked up to by her classmates, what *must* they be thinking of her! To tell the truth, she had been crying as she walked along through the woods, because she was so sorry for herself. Her eyes were all red still, and her throat sore from the big lump in it.

And now she would live it all over again as she told the Putney cousins. For of course they must be told. She had always told Aunt Frances everything that happened in school. It happened that Aunt Abigail had been taking a nap when she got home

39

from school, and so she had come out to the saphouse, where Cousin Ann and Uncle Henry were making syrup, to have it over with as soon as possible. She went up to the little slab house now, dragging her feet and hanging her head, and opened the door.

Cousin Ann, in a very short old skirt and a man's coat and high rubber boots, was just poking some more wood into the big fire which blazed furiously under the broad, flat pan where the sap was boiling. The rough, brown hut was filled with white steam and that sweetest of all odors, hot maple syrup. Cousin Ann turned her head, her face red with the heat of the fire, and nodded at the child.

"Hello, Betsy, you're just in time. I've saved out a cupful of hot syrup for you, all ready to wax."

Betsy hardly heard this, although she had been wild about waxed sugar on snow ever since her very first taste of it. "Cousin Ann," she said unhappily, "the Superintendent visited our school this afternoon."

"Did he?" said Cousin Ann, dipping a thermometer into the boiling syrup.

"Yes, and we had *examinations!*" said Betsy.

"Did you?" said Cousin Ann, holding the thermometer up to the light and looking at it.

"And you know how perfectly awful examinations make you feel," said Betsy, very near to tears again.

"Why, no," said Cousin Ann, sorting over syrup tins. "They never made me feel awful. I thought they were sort of fun."

"Fun!" cried Betsy, indignantly, staring through the beginnings of her tears.

"Why, yes. Like taking a dare, don't you know. Somebody stumps you to jump off the hitching-post, and you do it to show 'em. I always used to think examinations were like that. Somebody stumps you to spell 'pneumonia,' and you do it to show 'em. Here's your cup of syrup. You'd better go right out and wax it while it's hot."

Elizabeth Ann automatically took the cup in her hand, but she did not look at it. "But supposing you get so scared you

40

"Wait a minute, Molly!" she called wildly down the pit

can't spell 'pneumonia' or anything else!" she said feelingly. "That's what happened to me. You know how your mouth gets all dry and your knees . . ." She stopped. Cousin Ann had said she did *not* know all about those things. "Well, anyhow, I got so scared I could hardly stand *up!* And I made the most awful mistakes—things I know just as *well!* I spelled 'doubt' without any b and 'separate' with an e, and I said Iowa was bounded on the north by *Wisconsin,* and I . . ."

"Oh, well," said Cousin Ann, "it doesn't matter if you really know the right answers, does it? That's the important thing."

This was an idea which had never in all her life entered Betsy's brain, and she did not take it in now. She only shook her head miserably and went on in a doleful tone. "And I said 13 and 8 are *22!* and I wrote March without any capital M, and I . . ."

"Look here, Betsy, do you *want* to tell me all this?" Cousin Ann spoke in the quick, ringing voice she had once in a while which made everybody, from old Shep up, open his eyes and get his wits about him. Betsy gathered hers and thought hard; and she came to an unexpected conclusion. No, she didn't really want to tell Cousin Ann all about it. Why was she doing it? Because she thought that was the thing to do. "Because if you don't really want to," went on Cousin Ann, "I don't see that it's doing anybody any good. I guess Hemlock Mountain will stand right there just the same even if you did forget to put a b in 'doubt.' And your syrup will be too cool to wax right if you don't take it out pretty soon."

She turned back to stoke the fire, and Elizabeth Ann, in a daze, found herself walking out of the door. It fell shut after her, and there she was under the clear, pale-blue sky, with the sun just hovering over the rim of Hemlock Mountain. She looked up at the big mountains, all blue and silver with shadows and snow, and wondered what in the world Cousin Ann had meant. Of course Hemlock Mountain would stand there just the same. But what of it? What did that have to do with her arithmetic, with anything? She had failed in her examination, hadn't she?

She found a clean white snowbank under a pine tree, and,

41

setting her cup of syrup down in a safe place, began to pat the snow down hard to make the right bed for the waxing of the syrup. The sun, very hot for that late March day, brought out strongly the tarry perfume of the big pine tree. Near her the sap dripped musically into a bucket, already half full, hung on a maple tree. A bluejay rushed suddenly through the upper branches of the wood, his screaming and chattering voice sounding like noisy children at play.

Elizabeth Ann took up her cup and poured some of the thick, hot syrup out on the hard snow, making loops and curves as she poured. It stiffened and hardened at once, and she lifted up a great coil of it, threw her head back, and let it drop into her mouth. Concentrated sweetness of summer days was in that mouthful, part of it still hot and aromatic, part of it icy and wet with melting snow. She crunched it all together into a delicious, big lump and sucked on it dreamily, her eyes on the rim of Hemlock Mountain, high above her there, the snow

on it bright golden in the sunlight. Uncle Henry had promised to take her up to the top as soon as the snow went off. She wondered what the top of a mountain would be like. Uncle Henry had said the main thing was that you could see so much of the world at once. He said it was too queer the way your own house and big barn and great fields looked like little toy things that weren't of any account. It was because you could see so much more than just the . . . .

She heard an imploring whine, and a cold nose was thrust into her hand! Why, there was old Shep begging for his share of waxed sugar. He loved it, though it did stick to his teeth so! She poured out another lot and gave half of it to Shep. It immediately stuck his jaws together tight, and he began pawing at his mouth and shaking his head till Betsy had to laugh. Then he managed to pull his jaws apart and chewed loudly and visibly, tossing his head, opening his mouth wide till Betsy could see the sticky, brown candy draped in melting festoons all over his big white teeth and red gullet. Then with a gulp he had swallowed it all down and was whining for more, striking softly at the little girl's skirt with his forepaw. "Oh, you eat it too fast!" cried Betsy, but she shared her next lot with him too. The sun had gone down over Hemlock Mountain by this time, and the big slope above her was all deep blue shadow. The mountain looked much higher now as the dusk began to fall, and loomed up bigger and bigger as though it reached to the sky. It was no wonder houses looked small from its top. Betsy ate the last of her sugar, looking up at the quiet giant there, towering grandly above her. There was no lump in her throat now. Although she still thought she did not know what in the world Cousin Ann meant by saying that about Hemlock Mountain and her examination, it's my opinion that she had made a good beginning of an understanding.

She was just picking up her cup to take it back to the saphouse when Shep growled a little and stood with his ears and tail up, looking down the road. Something was coming down that road in the blue, clear twilight, something that was making a very queer noise. It sounded almost like somebody crying. It

43

was somebody crying! It was a child crying. It was a little, little, girl. . . . Betsy could see her now . . . stumbling along and crying as though her heart would break. Why, it was little Molly, her own particular charge at school, whose reading lesson she heard every day. Betsy and Shep ran to meet her. "What's the matter, Molly? What's the matter?" Betsy knelt down and put her arms around the weeping child. "Did you fall down? Did you hurt you? What are you doing 'way off here? Did you lose your way?"

"I don't want to go away! I don't want to go away!" said Molly over and over, clinging tightly to Betsy. It was a long time before Betsy could quiet her enough to find out what had happened. Then she made out between Molly's sobs that her mother had been taken suddenly sick and had to go away to a hospital, and that left nobody at home to take care of Molly, and she was to be sent away to some strange relatives in the city who didn't want her at all and who said so right out. . . .

Elizabeth Ann knew all about that! Her heart swelled big with sympathy. For a moment she stood again out on the side-

44

walk in front of the Lathrop house, with old Mrs. Lathrop's un-
gracious white head bobbing from a window, and knew again
that ghastly feeling of being unwanted. She knew why little
Molly was crying! And she shut her hands together hard and
made up her mind that she *would* help her out!

Do you know what she did, right off, without thinking about
it? She didn't go and look up Aunt Abigail. She didn't wait till
Uncle Henry came back from his round of emptying sap buckets
into the big tub on his sled. As fast as her feet could carry her
she flew back to Cousin Ann in the saphouse. I can't tell you
(except again that Cousin Ann was Cousin Ann) why it was
that Betsy ran so fast to her and was so sure that everything
would be all right as soon as Cousin Ann knew about it; but
whatever the reason was it was a good one, for, though Cousin
Ann did not stop to kiss Molly or even to look at her more than
one sharp first glance, she said after a moment's pause, during
which she filled a syrup can and screwed the cover down very
tight: "Well, if her folks will let her stay, how would you like
to have Molly come and stay with us till her mother gets back
from the hospital? Now you've got a room of your own, I guess
if you wanted to you could have her sleep with you."

"Oh, Molly, Molly, *Molly!*" shouted Betsy, jumping up and
down, and then hugging the little girl with all her might. "Oh,
it will be like having a little sister!"

Cousin Ann sounded a dry, warning note: "Don't be too sure
her folks will let her. We don't know about them yet."

Betsy ran to her, and caught her hand, looking up at her
with shining eyes. "Cousin Ann, if *you* go to see them and ask
them, they will!"

This made even Cousin Ann give a little abashed smile of
pleasure, although she made her face grave again at once and
said: "You'd better go along back to the house now, Betsy. It's
time for you to help Mother with the supper."

The two children trotted back along the darkening wood
road, Shep running before them, little Molly clinging fast to
the older child's hand. "Aren't you ever afraid, Betsy, in the
woods this way?" she asked admiringly, looking about her.

45

"Oh, no!" said Betsy, protectingly; "there's nothing to be afraid of, except getting off on the wrong fork of the road, near the Wolf Pit."

"Oh, *ow!*" said Molly, scringing. "What's the Wolf Pit? What an awful name!"

Betsy laughed. She tried to make her laugh sound brave like Cousin Ann's, which always seemed so scornful of being afraid. As a matter of fact, she was beginning to fear that they *had* made the wrong turn, and she was not quite sure that she could find the way home. But she put this out of her mind and walked along very fast, peering ahead into the dusk. "It hasn't anything to do with wolves," she said in answer to Molly's question; "any-how, not now. It's just a big, deep hole in the ground where a brook had dug out a cave. . . . Uncle Henry told me all about it when he showed it to me . . . and then part of the roof caved in; sometimes there's ice in the corner of the covered part all the summer, Aunt Abigail says."

"Why do you call it the Wolf Pit?" asked Molly, walking very close to Betsy and holding very tightly to her hand.

"Oh, long, ever so long ago, when the first settlers came up here, they heard a wolf howling all night, and when it didn't stop in the morning, they came up here on the mountain and found a wolf had fallen in and couldn't get out."

"My! I hope they killed him!" said Molly.

"Gracious! that was more than a hundred years ago," said Betsy. She was not thinking of what she was saying. She was thinking that if they *were* on the right road they ought to be home by this time. She was thinking that the right road ran downhill to the house all the way, and that this certainly seemed to be going up a little. She was wondering what had become of Shep. "Stand here just a minute, Molly," she said. "I want . . . I just want to go ahead a little bit and see . . . and see . . ." She darted on around a curve of the road and stood still, her heart sinking. The road turned there and led straight up the mountain!

For just a moment the little girl felt a wild impulse to burst out in a shriek for Aunt Frances, and to run crazily away, anywhere so long as she was running. But the thought of Molly standing back there, trustfully waiting to be taken care of, shut Betsy's lips together hard before her scream of fright got out. She stood still, thinking. Now she mustn't get frightened. All they had to do was to walk back along the road till they came to the fork and then make the right turn. But what if they didn't get back to the turn till it was so dark they couldn't see it . . . ? Well, she mustn't think of that. She ran back, calling, "Come on, Molly," in a tone she tried to make as firm as Cousin Ann's. "I guess we have made the wrong turn after all. We'd better . . ."

But there was no Molly there. In the brief moment Betsy had stood thinking, Molly had disappeared. The long, shadowy wood road held not a trace of her.

Then Betsy *was* frightened and then she *did* begin to scream, at the top of her voice, "Molly! Molly!" She was beside herself with terror, and started back hastily to hear Molly's voice, very faint, apparently coming from the ground under her feet.

"Ow! Ow! Betsy! Get me out! Get me out!"

"Where *are* you?" shrieked Betsy.

"I don't know!" came Molly's sobbing voice. "I just moved the least little bit out of the road, and slipped on the ice and began to slide and I couldn't stop myself and I fell down into a deep hole!"

Betsy's head felt as though her hair were standing up straight on end with horror. Molly must have fallen down into the Wolf Pit! Yes, they were quite near it. She remembered now that big white-birch tree stood right at the place where the brook tumbled over the edge and fell into it. Although she was dreadfully afraid of falling in herself, she went cautiously over to this tree, feeling her way with her foot to make sure she did not slip, and peered down into the cavernous gloom below. Yes, there was Molly's little face, just a white speck. The child was crying, sobbing, and holding up her arms to Betsy.

"Are you hurt, Molly?"

"No. I fell into a big snowbank, but I'm all wet and frozen and I want to get out! I want to get out!"

Betsy held on to the birch tree. Her head whirled. What

47

should she do! "Look here, Molly," she called down, "I'm going to run back along to the right road and back to the house and get Uncle Henry. He'll come with a rope and get you out!"

At this Molly's crying rose to a frantic scream. "Oh, Betsy, don't leave me here alone! Don't! Don't! The wolves will get me! Betsy, *don't* leave me alone!" The child was wild with terror.

"But I *can't* get you out myself!" screamed back Betsy, crying herself. Her teeth were chattering with the cold.

"Don't go! Don't go!" came up from the darkness of the pit in a piteous howl. Betsy made a great effort and stopped crying. She sat down on a stone and tried to think. And this is what came into her mind as a guide: "What would Cousin Ann do if she were here? She wouldn't cry. She would *think* of something."

Betsy looked around her desperately. The first thing she saw was the big limb of a pine tree, broken off by the wind, which half lay and half slantingly stood up against a tree a little distance above the mouth of the pit. It had been there so long that the needles had dried and fallen off, and the skeleton of the branch with the broken stubs looked like . . . yes, it looked like a ladder! *That* was what Cousin Ann would have done!

"Wait a minute! Wait a minute, Molly!" she called wildly down the pit, warm all over in excitement. "Now listen. You go off there in a corner, where the ground makes a sort of roof. I'm going to throw down something you can climb up on, maybe."

"Ow! Ow, it'll hit me!" cried poor little Molly, more and more frightened. But she scrambled off under her shelter obediently, while Betsy struggled with the branch. It was so firmly imbedded in the snow that at first she could not budge it at all. But after she cleared that away and pried hard with the stick she was using as a lever she felt it give a little. She bore down with all her might, throwing her weight again and again on her lever, and finally felt the big branch move. After that it was easier, as its course was downhill over the snow to the mouth of the pit. Glowing, and pushing, wet with perspiration,

48

she slowly maneuvered it along to the edge, turned it squarely, gave it a great shove, and leaned over anxiously. Then she gave a great sigh of relief! Just as she had hoped, it went down sharp end first and stuck fast in the snow which had saved Molly from broken bones. She was so out of breath with her work that for a moment she could not speak. Then, "Molly, there! Now I guess you can climb up to where I can reach you."

Molly made a rush for any way out of her prison, and climbed, like the practiced squirrel that she was, up from one stub to another to the top of the branch. She was still below the edge of the pit there, but Betsy lay flat down on the snow and held out her hands. Molly took hold hard, and, digging her toes into the snow, slowly wormed her way up to the surface of the ground.

It was then, at that very moment, that Shep came bounding up to them, barking loudly, and after him Cousin Ann striding along in her rubber boots, with a lantern in her hand and a rather anxious look on her face.

She stopped short and looked at the two little girls, covered with snow, their faces flaming with excitement, and at the black hole gaping behind them. "I always *told* Father we ought to put a fence around that pit," she said in a matter-of-fact voice. "Some day a sheep's going to fall down there. Shep came along

to the house without you, and we thought most likely you'd taken the wrong turn."

Betsy felt terribly aggrieved. She wanted to be petted and praised for her heroism. She wanted Cousin Ann to *realize* . . . oh, if Aunt Frances were only there, *she* would realize . . . !

"I fell down in the hole, and Betsy wanted to go and get Mr. Putney, but I wouldn't let her, and so she threw down a big branch and I climbed out," explained Molly, who, now that her danger was past, took Betsy's action quite as a matter of course.

"Oh, that was how it happened," said Cousin Ann. She looked down the hole and saw the big branch, and looked back and saw the long trail of crushed snow where Betsy had dragged it. "Well, now, that was quite a good idea for a little girl to have," she said briefly. "I guess you'll do to take care of Molly all right!"

She spoke in her usual voice and immediately drew the children after her, but Betsy's heart was singing joyfully as she trotted along clasping Cousin Ann's strong hand. Now she knew that Cousin Ann realized. . . . She trotted fast, smiling to herself in the darkness.

"What made you think of doing that?" asked Cousin Ann presently, as they approached the house.

"Why, I tried to think what *you* would have done if you'd been there," said Betsy.

"Oh!" said Cousin Ann. "Well . . ."

She didn't say another word, but Betsy, glancing up into her face as they stepped into the lighted room, saw an expression that made her give a little skip and hop of joy. She had *pleased* Cousin Ann.

That night, as she lay in her bed, her arm over Molly cuddled up warm beside her, she remembered, ever so faintly, as something of no importance, that she had failed in an examination that afternoon.

Willis Lindquist

STORM TIDE

ILLUSTRATED BY *Matilda Breuer*

THE storm warnings and the rising wind seemed quite unimportant to Barney as he left the McMannus Island lighthouse and started slowly over the salt flats. Sea gulls mewed and wheeled overhead, and the sand was hot under his bare feet, but he knew that the storm would not strike before nightfall. It might even miss the island.

The scowl on his tanned young face came from thinking about the little seal that followed behind him like a trained dog. Minnie was her name, and she made pretty good speed until they came to the loose sand of the dunes.

Minnie belonged to Barney's uncle, the lighthouse keeper; Uncle Nels, everyone called him. He had found the baby seal abandoned among the rocks several months ago when the seals had passed on up the coast, and he had taken her home and fed her out of a bottle. Uncle Nels was like that. He loved everything that lived, and so did Barney.

Because Uncle Nels lived by himself at the lighthouse, he did not realize how strongly the fishermen in the village felt about seals. Twice a year the seals came in large numbers, stopping for a few days on the island to rest. That meant real trouble for the fishermen. The seals ate the fish right out of the nets and often tore the nets to bits.

Barney could understand that, but he still liked Minnie. She was such a smart little thing, so friendly and intelligent. He stopped at the top of a high dune and glanced back at the seal.

"Hurry up, can't you?" he called.

Minnie raised her sleek head, let out a friendly little yap.

51

Then flapping her flippers into the sand, she put on a burst of speed that made Barney laugh.

"You'll be all out of breath if you keep that up. Here, I'll carry you."

He caught her up and carried her under his arm. She reached up and touched his chin with her cool nose as if to thank him. How anyone could possibly hate Minnie, he couldn't imagine. Even his friend Tom, whose father was one of the head fishermen, didn't seem to like her.

Tom was waiting for them at the cove where the path turned into the village of white huts where the fishermen lived. Tom glared at Minnie. "I thought I told you to leave her at home," he complained. "Why do you always have to drag her along?"

"I like her," Barney replied. "What have you got against Minnie?"

Tom tossed his yellow hair out of his eyes. "If you were a fisherman's son, you wouldn't have to ask that," he said impatiently. "Minnie scares the fish away. She eats fish right out of the nets. She keeps tearing big holes in the nets."

A flush of anger stung Barney's face. "That's not so! The sharks are doing that. They've always done it before and now, just because Minnie happens to be around, you all blame her for it."

"It's been much worse since Minnie came."

Barney hugged Minnie close for a moment and set her on the ground. "Minnie couldn't have done it," he said firmly. "I've had her with me every minute of the day for the last month just to prove it. She's not scaring the fish away. It's just a poor season, that's all."

Tom looked at him and laughed. "That's the poorest proof I've ever heard. If you left her alone, she'd sleep all day. She goes out at night."

"No!" Barney shook his head. They had started walking over the dunes with Minnie flopping and sliding and rolling in her haste to keep up. "No. Uncle Nels keeps an eye on her then. He has to be up during the night anyhow."

Tom gave a grunt that meant plainly he didn't believe a

word of it. Barney kicked through the loose sand in hopeless anger. He felt so helpless. If he couldn't get his best friend to believe him, what chance would he have with the fishermen?

He stopped. "Wait a minute for Minnie," Barney said thickly.

"How will we ever get to the cave if we have to wait for her?"

Barney picked her up once more. "I'll carry her until we get to the beach. She'll swim the rest of the way faster than we can walk."

The shore they were following was on the lee side of the island, and the water, though higher than usual, was quite calm. At Barney's command, Minnie lunged into the sea and swam effortlessly, diving and coming up for air joyously as she kept abreast of them.

The blue horizon of the sea was dotted with fishing boats. Tom nodded to them. "They've got to get in all the nets before the storm," he explained. "That means less fish again this week. Dad says that settles it. They are not going to put up with Minnie any longer."

"What?" Barney gasped. "They—they don't blame Minnie for the storm too, do they?"

"Well," Tom shrugged, "everyone says she brings us bad luck."

Barney frowned. "What are they planning to do?"

"Dad and some others are going up to see Uncle Nels tonight. He's got to get rid of her."

"He won't," Barney gulped. "No one could ever get him to harm Minnie. And he won't send her to a zoo. He wants her to be free and happy." He looked out to where Minnie was blowing and gliding with beautiful ease, and tears stung his eyes. "Listen, Tom, when the seals come back from the north in three months Minnie will go with them!"

Tom said nothing. They walked in silence for a couple of miles. The beach narrowed as the cliffs came down to the sea, and presently they came to the dark mouth of a cavern.

The entrance was so low that the sea washed in a little at high tide and left dark, deep pools here and there.

A short whistle from Barney brought Minnie at top speed.

53

She entered the cave with them. It was cool and quiet and mysteriously dark, and Barney shivered with excitement.

They played follow-the-leader for a time, and Minnie seemed to enjoy it as much as they did. Once they became lost in a vast underground chamber that was knee-deep with water. It was ten minutes before they found their way back to the narrow passage by which they had entered.

"Funny we never found that cavern before," said Tom. "Let's eat soon."

They followed the main passage deeper into the cliff until they came to the small dry chamber where they kept the lantern. Barney fumbled for the glass bottle in which they kept their matches, and lit the lamp.

By its dim yellow glow, they unwrapped the wax paper from the lunch they had brought and wolfed down the sandwiches and apples. Minnie wanted a smell of everything, but she was not hungry, and she soon fell asleep with her head on Barney's lap.

Presently, a dark patch of water appeared at the entrance. It spread slowly over the floor in all directions, and the boys stared at it.

"That's funny," Tom said. "Water never came in here before."

Barney felt a cool prickle along his skin. "Do—do you suppose it's one of those storm tides?"

"What's that?"

"Uncle Nels says that sometimes a storm pushes the water ahead of it in a big flood tide. The water seemed awfully high this morning."

Tom jumped to his feet. "We'd better get going if we want to get out."

Barney and Minnie hurried after him. They were soon wading in water up to their chests, pushing against a strong current that came from the direction of the main entrance. Then they were forced to swim. But it was no good. The current carried them back.

"It's no use," gasped Tom finally. "The entrance is under water."

54

"But we can't stay here," Barney said. "Let's go back to the lantern. That's the highest place. Maybe—" He couldn't finish. If the water kept rising. . . .

When they reached the lamplight again, the water was already up to their knees and still pouring in. The sound of it rushing through the caves and passageways was a low and ominous rumble. There were weird whistling sounds, too, as the air of the cave escaped through crevices in the rock ceiling. The boys stared at each other.

The black water rose inch by inch until it had reached their hips.

"What'll we do?" Tom's voice wabbled with fright.

Barney took the oil lamp from the little rock shelf. Minnie yapped. She was darting and splashing around him as though they were playing some game.

Barney pushed her out of the way.

He knew only that they had to go. They had to get out of this chamber if they wanted to live. It was the highest spot in the whole cave, so far as they knew, but there was a narrow corridor beyond it, blocked by a deep pool across which they had never ventured.

"Come," he said to Tom. "We have to cross the deep pool. It might be higher on the other side."

"I—I hope there is another side to it."

They entered the narrow corridor and were at once up to their arm pits. Barney held the lamp high with his left hand and started a slow side stroke. He took a dozen good strokes and put his feet down. He could not touch bottom. Again he tried, after swimming a few yards, and this time his feet touched hard gravel.

The water became shallower as they walked ahead, and when they reached the small dead-end cavern at the end of it, the water was below their knees.

"This is as far as we go," Barney said. "It's better than the other place."

"Not much," said Tom with a flat hopelessness in his voice. He walked back and forth inspecting the chamber, testing the walls, trying to find the highest spot where they could stand together until the water became too high.

Barney watched him. The world outside where the air was clean and sweet seemed a great distance away, like something in a dream. They were sealed in a dungeon. The damp brown walls of rock seemed to close in until there was hardly a breath of air left for him.

The dark water kept rising. It climbed inch by inch until it it had reached their hips. It moved more slowly then, but it did not stop.

Barney did not dare to hope. A tide such as this might keep rising for several days until the storm had spent its force. There were no rules.

Time passed. It might have been hours. Barney could not tell. His legs were stiff and numb, painful to move. Though he held the lamp on his head, his arms ached from holding it there. The lamp oil was almost gone. He turned the wick lower and handed the lamp to Tom. It would not be long before the terrible darkness would close down.

The water was up to their chests now. The boys rarely spoke, and when they did, the cavernous depth threw back the echoes which rang unpleasantly in their ears as if they were speaking in a deep well.

Barney began to have difficulty with his breath. It came in short gasps. His racing heart seemed to pound his ear drums.

For a long time he had been aware of Minnie swimming peacefully back and forth between them. But suddenly she became excited. She yapped loudly. She dived and swam furiously about, coming up to blow and dive again.

"What's got into her?" Tom asked.

"Must be close to her feeding time. I think she wants to go home."

She kept the cave echoing with her yaps. But suddenly there was peaceful quiet. For a matter of minutes there was no sign of her at all, and Barney was puzzled.

He was startled when something brushed heavily against his leg. It was Minnie. She splashed water into his face as she came bobbing up. She swam around him, poking him with her nose, yapping excitedly. Then she dived and disappeared completely again.

Barney waited for what seemed a long time. He looked at Tom. "No seal ever stayed under water that long! Do you suppose she—"

Minnie was back, yapping into his face again. She seemed almost angry. He began to tremble as he watched her. He felt sure now that she was trying to make him follow her.

"All right, Minnie," he said. "Let's go home."

She seemed to go wild for a moment. He watched the direction of her dive. She went always the same way, toward the wall where the water was deepest. It was the one place they had not explored carefully. He followed after her as quickly as he could, diving deep. He found nothing but a blank wall and had to come up for air.

Again he dived, searching the bottom of the wall with his fingers. Then he found it, a yard-wide opening near the floor. He came up directly above it.

"Tom!" he gasped. "I think I've found it! If I don't come back, then try it yourself. It's right below this." He made a splash on the wall as a mark.

Once more he filled his lungs with air, dived, pulled into the hole. His back scraped the sharp rock, but he felt no pain. He was half crawling, half swimming.

His lungs seemed on the point of bursting. He let out a little air to relieve them and, clawing the rocky sides, pulled himself on and on in a frantic burst of speed.

For a terrible moment it seemed that the tunnel was getting smaller. Minnie could get through, but could he?

Frantic, desperate, he clawed on. His lungs burned. Air exploded from his lips, and he gulped in water. At the same instant, he saw the light. Somehow he reached it and came into the fresh air.

He was vaguely aware of Minnie clambering over him, of the trees and the twilight sky. That was all he could remember for a while.

After a time Tom was lying beside him in the rocky pool where they had often gone swimming. A full gale was blowing. It whistled and howled through the trees.

But when Tom and Barney sat up, they were not thinking about the storm. "It's Minnie's feeding time," Barney said.

Tom grinned. "Mighty lucky for us!" he shouted. He caught Minnie and gave her a hug. "If I know my father, he'll gladly feed Minnie right out of his nets until she leaves for the south."

Barney laughed. With Tom's father on their side, there was nothing at all to worry about—except that Minnie might get too fat.

Steve Benedict

ALLIGATOR UP THE BAYOU

ILLUSTRATED BY *Alexander Key*

TEE–PETE fell in love with the small .410 gauge shotgun almost at once. "What a gun to go hunting rabbits with, yeah," he said to himself ardently. He gazed with longing eyes at the boy-sized firearm in the showcase of the village's one general store.

He was rather small for his age, and that is why his friends called him Tee-Pete. Tee-Pete means Little Pete in the French-Cajun dialect of lower Louisiana.

Little Pete's home was at the mouth of the Mississippi River, where almost everyone is a hunter, trapper, or fisherman. The marshes, the bayous, the big brown stream, the salty windy Gulf —these gave Tee-Pete and his fellow natives their daily bread.

Down on the Delta no home is complete without a shotgun. No boy feels himself a true marshman until he owns a small one of his own. How Tee-Pete longed for such a gun! How often he had asked, "Buy me a .410, yeah, Pa?"

60

But the tall, dark-skinned man had only looked down at his son with black, half-Indian eyes. "You go out and earn the price of one, you," he had answered in a voice low-toned yet full of meaning. "That's the way I got my first shotgun, me. And I wasn't any older than you, no, Tee-Pete."

Luck, however, was against the boy. Two unusually cool summers had driven the crabs far out into warm Gulf waters. The big river catfish had been scarce lately, and so had the 'coons and muskrats last trapping season. As for rabbits, "How can a fellow hunt rabbits for the market without a shotgun?" Tee-Pete asked himself gloomily.

Instantly the vision of that long, double-barreled, steel-blue beauty in the showcase sprang before his eyes. He dropped the cast net he was knitting and began to pace the porch. "I wish it was winter so I could set traps, yeah," he said aloud. Down on the Delta, winter with its fur-trapping is always the money-making season.

Then, to add to his grief, Seraphine, his young schoolmate, had also set a longing heart on the .410. And Seraphine, with unexpected luck in finding a rare school, had just sent a barrel of catfish to the French Market in New Orleans, on the wide-beamed stern-wheeler that freighted up and down the river and came to Muskrat Island village once a week. Only this morning he had told Tee-Pete proudly, "Tomorrow, yeah, my check will come on the mailboat. Then I will buy that .410, me. Rabbits! Oh boy!"

A single day in which to earn ten dollars! In the summertime, too, the Delta's slowest season! That shotgun seemed far away indeed.

"With a miracle, yeah, maybe," sighed Tee-Pete as he picked up his long homemade knitting needle and resumed work on his net.

But miracles sometimes happen even down on the Delta. This one took the form of old Ciprean, a full-mustachioed trot-line fisherman. Tee-Pete opened the door of the screened-in porch to admit the gnarled old trot-liner, then closed it hastily, for the sunshine outside was buzzing with mosquitoes.

61

"Hallo, Mr. Ciprean," he said.

"Hallo," answered Ciprean. "Where's your father?"

"He's gone to Refish Lagoon, yeah, with a seining crew."

The old fisherman made a wry face. "Hmmm! Too bad, yeah. I saw a ten-footer up in Bayou Chauvie and came down to tell him about it. I don't hunt alligators, not me."

A ten-foot alligator! The price of that shotgun! A dollar a foot was what Old Man Lajoi, the storekeeper, was paying for alligator hides this summer. Tee-Pete's heart jumped. Alligators seldom traveled far, and Bayou Chauvie was only a couple hours of paddling away. That ten-footer would still be there tonight. And what a night for a hunt! No wind! And dark of the moon!

Boys grow up quickly in the marshlands that surround the Mississippi River. Tee-Pete had paddled for his father on more than one hunt already. He was small for his years but stringy, hardened, and an excellent paddler. Besides, the vision of that .410 was temptation indeed!

"Soon as it gets dark I'll start out, yeah," the boy said to himself. He clenched a small hard fist nervously. He could hardly wait.

So, even before sundown, he was busy getting ready. He worked stealthily, for he knew well that his mother would never let him sneak off alone. Ready at last, he sat down on the edge of the wharf to wait for night. He gazed idly at his native village. Muskrat Island was a tiny fishing hamlet of about fifty houses along the muddy river. Each house was raised on pilings above the marsh and had a wharf in front of it.

Tee-Pete adjusted his hunting light on his head. He rubbed kerosene on his hands and face to keep the mosquitoes away. He took down and loaded his father's single-barreled Long Tom alligator gun. The young Cajun began traveling with long slow strokes. His light ran along the bayou's shore, fell on the pink eyes of a rabbit, then on the silvery ones of a deer.

Tall canes rose over Tee-Pete's head on either bank. His carbide beam cut a bright gash in the moonless darkness as he paddled softly down the narrow, twisty bayou. His gun lay across the front seat, point ahead. His long alligator-grabbing

62

hook was at his side, and his keen-edged killing hatchet lay beneath his crossed legs.

The slender cypress canoe rounded a bend. The bayou straightened in its course. Tall canes became open marshland covered with waist-high sea grasses. Tee-Pete kept on paddling. An hour passed, then another. The bayou narrowed and trickled into stinking blue-black ooze, primordial, bottomless.

"The end!"

With a sad heart the young Cajun turned back his dugout. No ten-footer!

But before he left the headwaters of Bayou Chauvie, Tee-Pete stood up in his pirogue and let his light travel over the cut-grass. In the distance something reflected the stars—a pond!

There was his answer—and his alligator!

The lad's heart beat lightly once more. He stepped out of his canoe. The muddy water seeped into his shoes. He sank ankle deep though he was marshman enough to walk only on the thick clumps of salt-water grass. The pirogue was not light but the boy pulled and tugged until he got it over the quarter-mile-long drag into the pond. He sat down panting.

"Whew!" he blew out. "Some pull! I hope it's worth it."

After awhile he began paddling again, around the edge of the pond, keeping twenty feet or so from the shore. The night was pitch dark, eerie, and quiet. Only the garfish splashed. There was a dank fetid smell of shallow inland water.

Tee-Pete made a complete round, but his alligator never showed an eye. It was a discouraging task. The pond was not a small one, and he began to feel tired. But he gritted his teeth and kept on.

"I'll try the middle, yeah," he said to himself, steering his frail craft away from shore.

But the middle of the pond was no luckier than the shore or the bayou had been. And it was getting late. His water jug was empty, and there was a dull ache in his arms. That ten-dollar bill seemed as far away as ever.

Tee-Pete stopped and put down his paddle. He cupped his hands over his mouth and gave the call of the bull alligator.

"Uh! Uh! Uh!" Deep down, guttural, harsh, coming from below the throat, snapping out almost like a cough.

After a long time a tiny three-footer rippled the water's surface to stare defiantly into Tee-Pete's light. He winked an eye and with a splash was below the ripples again.

Sighing, Tee-Pete turned his canoe's bow. Weary of body and beaten of spirit, he returned over the drag and paddled back up Bayou Chauvie, back into the river.

Tee-Pete's dugout swung around the last bend, where the long bayou widened to flow into the giant stream. Although he had already given up hope, his hunting light was still shining.

The beam shone straight ahead and fell upon the brown water. It reflected the shimmering surface. It reflected two large, white, angry orbs that glared at Tee-Pete.

"Ten-footer!"

The huge bull began swimming leisurely toward the boy. A funny feeling came over the young hunter and oozed slowly down his spine. For a moment Tee-Pete wished that he had stayed at home.

The alligator was less than fifty feet distant. Tee-Pete kept staring, hypnotized, at the long knobby snout, halfway out of the water. The alligator stared back. The Cajun boy's breath came short and swift.

Then all at once the ten-footer was no more than two paddle lengths away. The boy was paddling automatically now.

Without thinking about it, Tee-Pete set down his paddle and reached for his gun. Pirogue and alligator were drawing closer. All at once the big reptile was right alongside Tee-Pete's canoe.

A tenseness had overtaken the lad's body. When his gun muzzle was almost touching the alligator's raised head, he pulled the trigger.

Flame cut the darkness and the crash made the marshy lowlands ring. Water splashed into Tee-Pete's pirogue. A moment later the boy felt himself rising into the air. A cold, scaly body slid along his leg. Cruel jaws snapped. The light went out. Hunter, alligator, gun, pirogue, all churned in one splashing pirouette. Tee-Pete had allowed the big beast to come too close before he fired.

The boy never knew how he got ashore. "Guess that alligator was even more frightened than me, yeah," he said afterward, smiling wanly.

A wet, bone-tired, and still pretty frightened boy tied his pirogue to the wharf that dawn. His father's fishing boat was there; the old marshman had just returned from his seining trip. He listened to Tee-Pete's story quietly.

At last he said, "Light ten dollars, gun twenty-five, hatchet one dollar, makes thirty-six dollars, yeah. No alligator. Not

66

such a good night's hunt, no, Tee-Pete. You can catch a lot of fish and make it up to me later, yeah?"

Tee-Pete drew in his breath deeply. He blinked. He did not see the silvery lining to his dark cloud.

That silvery lining took the form of old Ciprean, the trot-line fisherman who had brought the news of the big alligator up the bayou. That same evening Tee-Pete heard the dull putt-putt of Ciprean's little open-deck motorboat, which he called *Wimpy*. Barefooted, the boy ran out to the wharf.

"Hey!" he cried joyfully. He began to dance up and down on the rough boards, yelling loudly.

For on the tiny foredeck of the *Wimpy* lay a dead ten-foot-long bull alligator. And the old trot-liner was waving a shot-gun and a carbide hunting light over his head.

"I found the gun on the river bank, yeah," he was telling Tee-Pete less than five minutes later. "You must've hurled it there in your excitement, you. The light wasn't far from it. The alligator? Oh, it was drifting belly-up toward the Gulf of Mexico, yeah. It never lived long after you shot, no."

Tee-Pete's heart was singing with joy. A couple of minutes later he was busy whetting his skinning knife. He had just thanked the smiling old trot-line fisher for the half-dozenth time. Up the river, just abreast of the Gap Light, only a mile from Muskrat Island Village, old Captain Loring of the mail-boat was whistling for a landing. In fifteen more minutes the Captain would be at the Post Office wharf—with Seraphine's check! And Seraphine, Tee-Pete was certain, would be there to get it. Then off he would go to the store.

"Hey!" cried Tee-Pete excitedly to his younger brother. "'Poleon, you run down to the store, you, and tell Mr. Lajoi to be sure not to sell that .410, no. Tell him I'll be there with a ten-foot alligator hide in about fifteen minutes, me."

Pearl S. Buck

LITTLE RED

ILLUSTRATED BY *Hardie Gramatky*

LITTLE RED was called Little, because his father was Big Red, and he was called Red because, like his father, he always wore something red. Big Red and Little Red, father and son, had always lived, since they were born, in a village on the edge of a small lake in the mountainous country of Lu, in the province of Kiangsi, in China.

The reason the two, father and son, so loved the color red was a simple one. Big Red had been the only son of his mother, and for that reason she kept him dressed in red until he was too big, and then she gave him a red kerchief to wear around his neck.

"I can see you a long way off," she always said, "because of the red kerchief."

So Big Red grew up wearing the red kerchief.

When Little Red was born, he looked exactly like his father, and his mother, who was a sweet and gentle woman, was the first to see this. She loved Big Red, and as a sign of her joy in the little son, she kept him dressed in red until he was too big, and then she gave him a red kerchief, but a little one.

"I can always see where you both are, father and son, Big and Little, with your red kerchiefs," she said.

It was true that when the farmers were working in their fields she could see her two, and when they went to town, she could see them coming home, for when she looked out of the door, there were the two spots of red, which were their kerchiefs.

They lived happily in the village until the Japanese came,

68

and they never even imagined that some day an enemy would come and take their beautiful country. Some people might have called them poor, for no one in the village had ever seen an automobile, much less owned one, and the houses were small, and none of the fathers ever had much money in his pockets. On the other hand, some people would have called them rich, for they had good food to eat, rice and vegetables, and very fine fish, and chickens and pork, and certainly the best eggs. And they had clothes enough to keep them warm in winter, and in summer Little Red and his playmates went swimming in the ponds, or they climbed the mountains behind the village and spent the day exploring. In autumn they gathered chestnuts from the trees on the mountains and roasted them over charcoal. Altogether it was a good life.

When the Japanese came it changed so quickly that it was hard to believe that it was the same place. The village had been such a safe and pleasant one, where babies played in the street, and where mothers sat in the doorways sewing and watching and talking to one another and laughing at what their children did. As soon as school was over the school children played in the street, too, and Little Red was always one of them. They played hopscotch and shuttlecock and toss pennies, and then skipped home to early suppers, and if there were actors in town visiting, they might go to a play in the temple court afterward.

It was as pleasant as that one day, and the next day all was changed. The villagers had heard something about the war, of course. People in the village did not read newspapers, but they listened to other people traveling by, and they heard about the Japanese and how they wanted to take the whole of China. But almost as soon as they heard it, it really happened. For the next day, the whole village was in confusion. An army of men came tramping through. Some of the men were on foot, but some rode in the cars which the village had never seen. Little Red happened to be home from school for lunch, and he had taken his bowl to the door and stood eating as fast as he could because he wanted to get back to school in time to play before afternoon work began. He was pushing rice and cabbage into

69

his mouth with his chopsticks when suddenly he felt his father pull his shoulders, jerk him back, and slam the door shut and bar it.

Inside the house everything went wrong at once. His father dropped his bowl on the tile floor and broke it, his mother spilled the tea she was pouring, and the baby began to cry.

"The dwarfs are really here," Big Red gasped to Little Red's mother.

"You must run out of the back door up the mountain," she gasped back. "You should have gone yesterday, with the other men, when we first heard these dwarfs were near."

"I did want to get the cabbage planted before I went away," he groaned, "so that if I didn't get back you would have something to eat with the rice."

Before anything could be done, there was a great noise and clatter at the door.

"Shall I open the door, Father?" Little Red asked.

Before anyone could open the door, it crashed in, and there stood the strange men, who were the Japanese. Big Red and Little Red and the mother and the baby could only stare at them. They were all terrified, and the baby was so frightened that he stopped crying, his mouth wide open.

"You!" one of the men yelled at Big Red. He was an officer and he carried a sword as well as a pistol. "Come out here! We want able-bodied men to carry loads for us!"

The moment he spoke the soldiers behind him seized Big Red by the hands and legs and jerked him out in the street. There was already a long line of villagers tied together with ropes, and to this long line Little Red now saw his father tied, too. He ran and clung to his father's waist, and his father bent and whispered in his ear, "Get back into the house, bar the door, and take care of your mother!"

He dared not disobey his father, and yet how could he bear to see him go? He obeyed and he disobeyed. He ran into the house, barred the door, and ran out the back door again. There from a distance he watched what happened to his father. The line of villagers was driven down the road like oxen, and the

enemy soldiers whipped them if they went too slowly and pricked them with their bayonets. At the head of the line Little Red saw his father march steadfastly away, southward. Hiding himself in the bushes he followed, until he was sure of their road, and then he ran home to tell his mother.

You can imagine how his mother cried when she heard what had happened to Big Red. She put the baby in his crib and sat down on a bench in the kitchen and cried and cried, wiping her eyes on her blue cotton apron.

"We will never see him again," she sobbed. "He is such a big strong man, he is so good, he is such a fine worker, they will never let him go. And now he is a prisoner! Oh, if I had only made him go to the mountains yesterday!"

"What is in the mountains, Mother?" Little Red asked.

Then his mother told him, "In the mountains there are men from many villages gathering together in an army to fight the enemy. They wanted your father to come yesterday and lead them, and he promised to go as soon as the enemy drew near. This morning, even, he might have gone, and been safe, if he had not stayed to plant those wretched cabbages. How can I eat them now? They would choke me, for it is because of them he is taken prisoner."

Little Red listened to all of this and said nothing.

He was at this time twelve years old and he knew that there are times when it is better for a boy to listen and say nothing, especially when he is planning something very big. He let his mother cry until she was tired, and he held the baby when that small one began to fret, and he burned the grass under the caldron in the stove when his mother stopped crying after a long time and sighed and said, "Well, I suppose we must eat, even if he is gone. But you eat—I can't eat a thing."

She was rather astonished when he ate an unusually big supper, and she was inclined to be a little cross with him for it. "I am glad you have a big appetite," she said, "but I am surprised, when you know how your poor father is suffering."

He still said nothing. He went to bed very early and so did she, and they had not opened the door since he barred it shut at noon. The mother had cried so much that she went to sleep although she had not thought she could. But Little Red did not sleep. In his bed he had put a bit of broken brick, and he lay with it in the middle of his back. He lay a long time thus, purposely to keep awake, and when at last he began to hear his mother breathe as though she were sound asleep, he rose and made ready to carry out his plan. In his belt he thrust the kitchen chopping knife. In his red kerchief he tied some bread, rolls, and salted cabbage, and two hard-boiled salted duck eggs, which his mother always kept on hand. Then he felt in the broken teapot and took out half of the family money which they kept there. It was never very much, but he thought half would be enough for him, in case he did not get home for a long time.

He wished that he could tell his mother where he was going, but she could not read, and there was no use in writing her a note. So he had to go without a word.

He opened the back door and slipped through. The moon was bright and better than any lamp, but he walked softly just the same. He had a long way to go and he set out swiftly and steadily southward. He knew exactly what he was going to do. He was going to find out where his father was and, with the knife, he would cut the ropes that bound him and help him to get away.

He thought exactly how it would go. They would have to stop for the night somewhere. Probably the prisoners would all be lying on the ground. Of course they would be guarded by the soldiers. But he would creep forward carefully, making use of every shadow. Perhaps there might be a shadow over the moon by then to help him. Often enough clouds came out of the mountains in the night and spread up over the sky. But the sky was clear now.

He had never been out in the night alone before and he did not like it very well. The frogs were croaking loudly in the ponds, and a bird wailed out of a bamboo grove. But he went on. Two hours passed, and he came at last to a village, where he hoped to find his father. It was empty. On the silent street every door was barred. His dream of finding Big Red there was only a dream.

He was so tired that for a moment he was discouraged. Where now should he turn?

"But if they were going south," his reason told him, "they would still be going south."

He got down on his knees and looked at the road in the bright moonlight. Like all the roads of that province, it had a stone path down the middle, made of flat stones from the mountains and polished smooth by people's feet. If many people had walked down the road today, the dust would be tramped away, and it would be a sign of which way his father had gone. Sure enough, the polished stone was smooth and clean of dust. He got up again and followed it. When the road forked he fol-

73

lowed the one which was clean of dust upon its stone path. It led steadily south.

Now Little Red knew that if you keep going south far enough you reach the great river, and if the prisoners and his father reached the river they would be put on boats, and then there would be no way of following them, for the water could give him no hint and no clue. He began to run instead of walk, dog-trotting along on his tired feet.

"I must take the nearest way to the river port!" he thought.

He had been to the river port twice with his father, because that is where the fair is held every year, and he knew the way. But of course the gates of the city would be locked at such an hour, and a country boy with a red kerchief full of bread and cabbage and two duck eggs would certainly not be let in or even listened to, if he knocked.

"There's nothing to do but go around the city," Little Red now told himself.

So he went around the city to the river's edge and crawled along in the mud for a long way. The city wall came right down to the river, and he had to step into the water to get past, but he did that easily enough, and was indeed quite ready to swim if the water were deep. But at this season the river was low, and he was able to walk around the wall.

Now, he knew that the boats were all tethered to iron rings, fastened in the stones of the river wall on either side of steep stone steps that went to the river, and so to the steps he went. There was not a sign of anyone. The moonlight shone down on the wet steps, and the quiet boats bobbed up and down on the slight swell of the river, and the whole city slept.

He had a dreadful moment of dismay. Suppose they had not come here at all! Perhaps he had guessed entirely wrong! Then he remembered that he had come around the city, and they perhaps would come another way. And he had come quickly, being alone, and they would come slowly. He sat down on a corner of the step and made himself very small, and waited. He was so hungry that although he tried not to, he felt compelled to eat a piece of the bread he had brought for his father,

74

but he would not allow himself to eat one of the duck eggs.

Scarcely had he done this when he heard a loud noise in the city. Shots rang out in the night, men yelled and cursed, and he heard the heavy squeak of the city gates.

"I am right," he thought wildly. "I shall see my father!" and he squeezed himself very small against the wet wall, into a shadow, indeed, which the parapet just above his head cast down on the steps. The red kerchief of food he hid between his knees.

Sure enough, in a few minutes of heartbeats so loud that they sounded in his ears like drums, he saw the weary line of men drag themselves around the corner. His father was still at the head of them. He knew his father, for he held up his head, and besides there was the red kerchief about his neck, clearly to be seen in the white moonlight. It was all Little Red could do not to call out, not to press forward. But he knew this would never do. So he sat small and close in the shadow.

It was well he did, for now the soldiers rushed after the prisoners and herded them down the steps together, and Little Red lost sight of his father entirely. A soldier brushed past him as he hurried down to the boats, and for a moment he was terrified. The soldier looked down at him, saw him, and gave him a kick and then went on. Little Red sat motionless while the prisoners were pushed on the boats.

Now he was glad that his father was Big Red. For he watched the spot of red on the tall man who got into the boats with all the others. Then Little Red put down his kerchief but he kept the knife in his belt, and silently as the boats left the shore, he crept down the steps. Into the water he went as cleanly and deeply as one of the river animals that live along the shores of rivers. He paddled softly after the boats and after the big man who sat on the edge of one of them, his red kerchief fluttering in the night wind.

The boats were rowboats, sampans, and small cargo boats, and the men to whom they belonged rowed slowly and unwillingly, knowing that they would get no pay for what they did. It was not too hard for Little Red to paddle along like a small dog and reach the side of the boat where Big Red sat, his head in his hands, tied to the other prisoners by the rope around his waist. Little Red dared not call. He hung on to the boat by one hand and with the other he reached for the knife and slipped it to his father's foot. Then he pounded lightly on that foot.

Big Red looked down from under his hands. He saw a kitchen knife, nothing else. Then he saw something bob up out of the water, a dark wet little face. He could not see who it was, and before he looked again, the head was bobbing away toward the shore again.

For Little Red had very sensibly reasoned that he would go back and wait on the steps, so that his father would have only himself to save. Purposely he did not let his father see who he was.

"If he knows it is me," he thought, "he will stay to see that I am all right and then maybe we'll both be caught."

So he took care of himself and dragged himself out of the river and sat on the steps very wet and a little cold. The red kerchief was still there, to his joy, for he had been afraid a dog might find it. The food smelled delicious, and he had to be very stern with himself and not even open the kerchief lest he eat more of it. He simply sat and waited.

Now Big Red, when he saw the knife, could not imagine how it had got there. If he had believed in strange things as some people did, he would have said a river god had come to his help. He was so astonished that he was almost ready to believe it. But he knew that he must not waste time wondering. He took the knife, which was very sharp, and softly cut his ropes. Then quietly he laid it on the foot of the next man and slipped into the water without a ripple. It was easy enough, for the boat was so laden with prisoners that its side was almost level with the river. He sank under the water and began to swim, holding his breath as long as he could. And then one of those clouds came out of the mountains, as they so often did just before dawn, and covered the face of the setting moon. When he came up again he was quite safe. No one could have seen his dark head against the muddy water of the river.

Little Red sat in the darkness on the step and shivered. Now he could not see his father and he must listen carefully. Yes, in a few moments he heard a man breathing heavily and trying not to breathe. He called out softly, "My father!"

There was no answer. The breathing stopped suddenly. His father was afraid. Little Red understood at once.

"Big Red!" he whispered loudly. "It is Little Red!"

"Little Red?" his father whispered. "Then where are you?"

Feeling for each other along the step, they found one another, and each gave the other a big hug.

"Why, you Little Red," his father gasped in a whisper. "How did you come here?"

"I brought the kitchen knife," Little Red whispered back.

But Big Red did not stop while he listened. With his arm about his son's shoulder, they went around the city wall and struck over a narrow path to the hills. And all the time Little Red told his father exactly what had happened, and Big Red laughed and hugged Little Red and said over and over again, "You see why the enemy can never conquer our country—no country can be conquered whose boys are like you!"

When they had reached the mountains, they went into a little cave and now they felt safe.

"Here is the food," Little Red said proudly. Then he felt he must tell the worst. "I did eat one piece of bread because I was so hungry," he confessed, "but I would not allow myself to have a duck egg."

His father took the kerchief and opened it and divided the food exactly into half. "You are a brave man," he said, "and brave men must eat. Moreover, they must share equally all that they have."

So they ate, and Little Red ate the duck egg, and it tasted even better than he had imagined.

"Now," his father said when they had eaten, "I must go up higher into the mountains and stay there."

"Oh," cried Little Red. "Let me come with you, Father!"

At this Big Red looked grave. "Who will look after the family?" he asked.

It was now Little Red who looked grave. "I should so much like to live in the mountains," he begged, "with you, Father! Because the baby keeps me awake at night when he cries!"

His father laughed and clapped him on the shoulder. "Now," he said, "here's a compromise. You shall be the messenger between home and mountains. One night at home, one night in the mountains—how is that? Messengers we must have."

And that is how Little Red became what he is today, a messenger between the men on the plains and the men in the mountains. He stops often to see how his mother and the baby are, but he never stays more than one night. But sometimes by coaxing his father he stays a couple of nights and more in the mountains in an old ruined temple, where the villagers have made a fort. From there they go down into the valley and fight the enemy, and, as often as he can, Little Red tells them where the enemy is. He is too young to enlist, but how can Big Red do without him?

This is a story that takes place on a ranch in Hungary. Kate and her father live in the big city of Budapest. He sends her to visit her aunt, uncle, and cousin Jancsi in the country because she has been ill. Kate misses her father very much and hopes he'll come to see her. Now it is spring—Kate's first spring on the ranch.

Kate Seredy

THE ROUND UP

ILLUSTRATED BY THE AUTHOR

THE apple tree was in full bloom. White strawberry blossoms covered the edge of the pastures. The farmyard was teeming with new life. Baby chicks swarmed in the grass, pink piglets squealed in an inclosure. Máli, the cow, had a brown and white calf, marked like a chestnut. It was tottering and tumbling after Máli, getting in everybody's way. Mother's vegetable garden was coming along splendidly. The fresh green plants were standing in even rows, like so many pert little green soldiers. Swallows darted between the squatty white pillars of the porch, repairing their nest. Early one morning the stork couple came home from the south. Soon mother stork was spending all her time sitting in their nest on top of the chimney.

"The old lady is sitting on her eggs," said Mother. "It's time to start my flower garden."

Kate remembered when Mother had planted the vegetable garden. She remembered the flat wooden boxes full of tiny seedlings. She knew that the seedlings had been transplanted into the soil. Now Mother said she was planting a flower garden, but she didn't have any seedlings.

Kate watched her make furrows with a little stick and scatter

80

something like sand into them. She looked up at Kate. "These will be rosemaries. Now I'll put snapdragons in the next bed."

"How can you tell, Auntie?"

"Good gracious, child," exclaimed Mother, "I saved the seeds myself from last year."

Kate watched her in silence. Plant life was a mystery to her.

"Auntie! If I put some of that sand into the ground, would flowers grow for me?"

"Seeds, you mean. Of course they would. You can have a garden of your own if you want to."

Kate wanted to. Mother gave her a spade and a rake and showed her how to dig up the soil and rake it smooth. Kate worked hard. After a while she paused.

"I know, Auntie. The seeds are the eggs of the flowers, aren't they?"

Mother laughed. "I never thought of it that way, but they are."

She gave Kate little bags of seeds. Each bag had the name of the flower written on it—hollyhocks, sunflowers, bluebonnets, marigolds, carnations.

"Don't plant them deep—just so the seeds are covered."

"What next?" asked Kate when all her seeds were planted.

"We'll water them now, very carefully, so the water doesn't wash away the seeds."

"And then what?" was the next question.

"Well, we'll have to water the soil twice a day, and just wait until they grow."

When Father and Jancsi came home, Kate ran to meet them. "Uncle Márton, you know what? I laid some flower eggs today. I am going to have a garden!"

She was a very busy little person from then on. Jancsi let her take care of the whole poultry yard; then there was Milky to feed and clean and exercise. She was very conscientious about watering her garden. Every morning before sunrise, every evening after the sun went down, Mother often found her flat on her stomach, "waiting for the flowers to come up."

Days passed, sunny days, rainy days. Then one morning

Kate roused the household, crying at the top of her voice: "Auntie-e-e! Uncle! Jancsi! Come quick!"

They came running from all directions, Mother from the kitchen, Father from the stables, Jancsi from the cow-barn. "Where is she? What happened?"

Kate was kneeling in her garden, waving her hands, yelling for all she was worth: "Look! Look what happened!" They looked.

The black soil she had tended so carefully showed the first promise of a future garden. Tiny seedlings, hardly visible, were pushing up bravely.

"Phoo!" cried Jancsi when he understood that he had been brought here just to look at seedlings. "A person would think that something wonderful had happened. And here you raise all this fuss for a few seedlings. Seedlings!"

"You know, Jancsi, I think something wonderful has happened," said Father thoughtfully. "It's such an everyday story to us. We know that seeds will grow into plants. But how? Why? What makes them? To Kate it's a miracle—and so it is. Look at those tiny seedlings. See how they struggle up through heavy clumps of earth to reach the light and sun. We are so used to it that we take it for granted, instead of getting on our knees to thank the Lord for another gift!"

He smiled at Kate. "Little monkey, you are teaching me a lesson, too."

"And now," he went on, "I have a surprise for all of you. I met the judge yesterday, and he told me that the big county fair will be held near our village this year—one week from today."

"Oh! And can we all go?" asked Jancsi eagerly.

"Of course we will go, but I have to get some horses for the animal show. I'm riding out to the herds across the river to round up about twenty. I want to sell some at the fair. Jancsi, you're coming with me. And if Kate wants to leave her garden for a day, she may come along."

Kate looked at Mother. "Will the baby flowers be safe if I leave them?" she asked.

"Don't you worry, child, I'll take good care of them," said Mother, smiling.

They rode out of the yard while the morning dew was still sparkling on the grass. The north road they took today wasn't at all like the one leading to the sheep herds. There were large wheat and rye fields on both sides. Narrow paths forked out of the main road, leading to white cottages nestling under shade trees. From the distance they looked like small white mushrooms under their heavy thatched roofs. The scenery was changing gradually. There were more and more trees. They crossed many small wooden bridges, spanning brooks. Soon they could see the river Tisza, like a wide blue ribbon on the green velvet of the fields. Jancsi rode ahead. Suddenly he waved and cried: "The 'Komp' is in. Hurry, Father, they're waiting for us." They spurred their horses and clattered on to the floating ferry, the Komp. It was attached to stout ropes on both sides. The ropes stretched across the river and were wound on large wooden pulleys. There were several wagons and riders on the wide platform of the Komp.

Kate, following the example of Father and Jancsi, got off her horse and tied him to a hitching-post. "How will we get across? Row?" she asked.

"Watch these men, Kate. They'll pull the Komp across by the ropes. We can help, too," said Jancsi. A bell sounded. Another answered from across the river. Everybody walked to the ropes. "Here, Kate. Grab this rope! Pull when they say 'Hooo-ruck!' "

"Hooo-ruck!" Kate pulled for all she was worth. "Hooo-ruck!" they cried with every pull. The Komp began to move. "Hooo-ruck! Hooo-ruck!" chanted everybody, pulling and slacking. The far bank seemed to come nearer and nearer. They could see other wagons and riders waiting. There was a scraping sound when the Komp touched bottom and came to a stop. A man on the bank fastened it to a high post.

"Coming back tonight, Mister Nagy?" he asked Father when they rode past him.

"Yes, Géza, we'll bring about twenty horses. Wait for us."

83

The road led through a small forest of acacia trees. Their
branches were heavy with clusters of white flowers. The air was
drenched with their sweet, heady perfume. White petals drifted
in the breeze, covering the ground like snow.

As soon as they left the forest, they saw the first corrals. They
were huge grassy squares, surrounded by tall fences. Long, low
stables and a few white cottages were scattered among them.
Corrals and buildings formed an immense triangle. In the distance hundreds of horses were grazing placidly. Here and there
a horse herder sat his horse, motionless as a statue against the
blue sky. One of them saw Father and rode to him. He was an
old man, but straight-shouldered and strong, with snow-white
hair and a clearly modeled, sunburned face. Under bushy white
eyebrows his black eyes were sharp as an eagle's.

"Welcome, Mister Nagy. We got your message. The boys are
ready for the round up." He looked at Kate and Jancsi. "The
young ones could stay with my wife, out of harm's way."

Father shook his head. "Jancsi is working with us this year;
he is old enough to know what it's all about. But—Kate, I think
you'd better stay with Árpád's wife."

"Oh, Uncle Márton, please let me go too. Please!" cried Kate.

Father looked at the old herder. Árpád shook his head. "If
those horses stampede, Mister Nagy, you know what it means!
A round up is no place for a girl child."

84

"She isn't a girl child. She's almost as good as a boy," said Jancsi stoutly. "Father, let Kate ride with me. I can take care of her."

Father hesitated for a second. Then he said: "Kate, you kept your word to me once. Will you promise me now to keep close to Jancsi and not to scream or yell no matter what happens?" He was very serious. "If these wild horses hear one of your famous screams, they'll run right off the face of the earth."

"I promise!" said Kate, looking straight into his eyes.

"Very well, you may go with Jancsi. Árpád! You take two men and start the drive from the north. Send four men to me. Two will go with Jancsi and Kate and drive from the east. I'll take two men to the west."

Even Árpád's straight back expressed his disapproval as he rode away. They saw him stop and speak to the men.

"Jancsi." Father's voice rang sharp—he was giving orders now. "You are one of the men today. Do you know what to do?"

"Yes, Father. I ride slowly to the east fields, about two miles from here. When I pass the last herds, I turn and start the drive back to the corrals. If they stampede, I ride with them and try to take the lead to turn the herd."

"If they stampede, you take Kate out of the way and let the herders turn them. Understand?"

Then Father gave his orders to the waiting herders, and they rode off.

Kate and Jancsi followed the two young herders in silence. They rode slowly, keeping well away from the grazing horses. Kate watched the men. She wondered if they ever got off their horses or were grown to them. Straight, yet supple, their bodies followed the swinging movement of the horses in perfect, smooth rhythm.

Jancsi touched her arm and whispered: "You won't scream, Kate? Promise?" He looked worried.

"I won't make a sound, no matter what happens. Thank you for sticking up for me."

A tall split-rail fence showed in the distance. "Here's where we spread out," said one of the herders.

Kate was terribly excited. They were riding along the fence now, about fifty feet from each other. "Stampede, stampede," kept ringing in her ears. What if they stampede? But everything went well. They turned back toward the corrals. At their approach there was a ripple of movement in the herd. They stopped grazing, neighed uneasily, but weren't frightened. Slowly they began to move in the direction of the corrals. Jancsi and Kate were directly behind them, the herders slightly to the sides.

Jancsi took off his hat and wiped his forehead. His first round up was going off well and he felt very proud. The herd was moving peacefully—surely there wouldn't be any trouble. But —what was the sudden stir in front there? He stood up in the stirrups, saw a flock of partridges fly up, heard the sharp, frightened neighing of the leaders, saw the whole herd sway and swerve . . .

"They're turning! Get out of the way, Kate! Follow me!" he yelled. It was too late. The frightened herd was thundering down on them. He couldn't stop to help Kate. His own horse was caught in the panic and raced at break-neck speed. Looking around he saw Milky go like a white flash in the other direction, with Kate bent close to his neck. He yelled: "To the left, Kate!" It was useless. He could hardly hear his own voice in the deafening tumult. His own words flashed in his memory: "If they stampede, I take the lead to turn the herd!"

With a desperate struggle he pulled at the reins, his horse swerved to the right. The herd followed! "Now back to the corrals, if I can only keep ahead of them! Come on, Bársony!" He dug his heels into the horse's sides. Almost flying over the pasture, he turned his head to look for Milky. Why, the herd must have split in half! There was Kate to his far right, racing ahead of more horses than he had behind him! She was leading them to the corrals!

"What a girl!" shouted Jancsi. "Hurray!"

He was almost at the first corral gate. He checked his horse, pulling him sharply to one side. The wild horses thundered past him and raced around into the inclosure. He closed the gate

quickly, just as the rest of the herd rushed into the adjoining corral. Milky, shivering and snorting, pressed close to Bársony. Kate grinned at Jancsi as she closed the gates. "Look at the herders," she said with a wink; "we beat them to it."

The two men looked rather sheepish and bewildered. There was no time for conversation, though. Father's herd came in, closely followed by old Árpád from the north. When all the horses were safely closed behind the gates, a cottage door opened, and Árpád's wife came out ringing a bell. "Dinner's ready," she cried.

Father turned to the silent herders. "How did my youngsters behave?"

The herders grinned sheepishly. "Behave, Mister Nagy? Behave? Why, the two of them turned the worst stampede we ever saw and brought the herd in, before we knew what happened."

"What?" cried Árpád and Father together.

"I didn't scream, Uncle Márton, did I, Jancsi?" cried Kate.

"She didn't, Father. A flock of partridges started them off. But can she ride! She rides 'most as good as you!"

"That's saying a lot, Sonny," smiled old Árpád. "Your father is the best horseman in seven counties. But tell us all about it while we eat."

They dismounted and walked to the cottage. In the doorway Árpád took off his hat. "Welcome to my house and table," he said.

"Welcome, and thank the Lord you are all here," cried his wife. "When I saw this girl child ahead of the horses, I thought we'd be picking her up in little pieces instead of sitting down to dinner! My, my, what is this world coming to! When I was her age, and a stout husky girl I was, I had to sit by the window and sew all day, and here she is, no bigger than a flea, racing with the best of you. Oh, oh, forgive my chatter, sit down and eat hearty, you must be starved!"

"Womenfolks talk more than magpies—sit down and welcome," said Árpád.

He said a prayer and a huge pot of steaming stew was set on the table.

"Now, let's hear the story," said Father when everybody was served. Jancsi laughed. "The story of a flea on horseback. She has a new name, Father. We can't call her screaming monkey any more!"

Little by little the story was pieced together. "But how did you know what to do, Kate?" asked Father.

"There was nothing else to do," she said calmly. "I remembered what Jancsi said about taking the lead if they stampeded. I didn't have to take it—they chased me!" She grinned. "Then we came to the horseyards—"

"Corrals, Kate," interrupted Jancsi.

"Corrals, then. Anyway, I saw you pull Bársony to one side. So I did the same thing. It was easy!"

Old Árpád shook his head. "A guardian angel watched over you, child. You were in great danger."

"Maybe—maybe it was my mother," whispered Kate with sudden tears in her eyes.

There was a long silence. Father spoke then in a husky voice: "I shouldn't have let you go, Kate, but now that everything is over, I am very proud of both of you." He turned to the herders: "Ready, boys? Get your ropes. I want twenty horses, two-year-olds, the best we have."

Selecting the best of the big herd was no child's play. Jancsi and Kate watched them as they lassoed horse after horse. Their ropes swung and looped around the singled-out animals with uncanny precision. Not once did they miss the horse they wanted. It was almost dark when twenty sleek, silky horses stood haltered in the stable. Father looked them over once more.

"Faultless beasts," he said. "You are the master horse-herder, old Árpád. May you live long!"

Árpád lifted his proud old head. "Should know something about horses; all my ancestors were born to the saddle."

"How about a nice story while we rest? The youngsters would enjoy one of your tales," asked Father.

Árpád smiled. "Jancsi here knows most of them. Which one shall it be, Son?"

Kate whispered in Jancsi's ear. "Does he know the story of the Milky Way?"

"That's right. Pista told us to ask you for the story of the Milky Way. Will you please tell it?" said Jancsi.

Árpád looked at the sky. "The stars are coming out. Let's walk to the open fields; there's fresh cut hay near the well. There we can see the Milky Way from end to end."

"Don't make it too long, Árpád," said Father when they were settled in the sweet-smelling hay. "We have to ride home tonight."

"The stars will guide you home, Mister Nagy. It's a long

89

story, the story of all Hungarians. The Milky Way is a good enough name for other people but we call it the 'Skyway of the Warriors.'"

On the vast plains—he began—and in the mountains of far-away Asia, lived two wild, brave tribes. Huns and Magyars they were called. When their people grew so numerous that they needed more land, the Huns set out to look for a place where they could settle. After many hardships, many years, they came to a land which was green with pastures, blue with swift-flowing rivers, rich with wooded mountains. But it wasn't free land, it belonged to the Romans who called it Pannonia. The Huns were strong and bold, they wanted this beautiful land. After many cruel, terrible battles they took it from the Romans. The bravest of the Huns was a young prince, Attila, so they chose him for their king. Attila grew into a mighty monarch. He and his vast army of warriors were so feared that people called him the "Scourge of God." Attila took more and more land and ruled over his people with an iron hand. When his wife died, leaving him with two sons, Csaba and Aladár, he boldly demanded the daughter of the Roman Emperor for his wife. And not only the daughter, but half of the Roman Empire for a dowry. The Emperor refused. Attila, hurt in his immense pride, called his army and set out to conquer the Romans. But the Franks, Goths, and Burgundians came to the aid of the Roman Emperor. Huge masses of hostile warriors gathered against Attila. The two opposing armies advanced like two thundering storm clouds. The earth shook and trembled under the hoofs of millions of horses. Forests disappeared in their wake as they built rafts and floats to cross the rivers. Finally they clashed at Katalaun. The battle was terrific and merciless. The light cavalry of the Huns swept down on the Roman army like a furious whirlwind, just to be battered to pieces on their iron-clad, massive ranks. The screams of wounded men and horses could be heard for miles. Placid rivers turned into rivers of blood, green fields were covered with thousands—no, millions —of corpses. The battle went on far into the night. Both armies

were exhausted, and at the break of dawn there was mutiny on both sides. For weeks parleys went on. Terrible diseases swept through the ranks, weakening both armies. Franks, Goths, and Burgundians deserted, leaving the Romans to Attila's mercy. But the Scourge of God was broken. He ordered a retreat and led his remaining army home. Old and broken in spirit, he died shortly, leaving his army to his sons, Csaba and Aladár.

When the neighbors heard about Attila's death, they came with their armies to take revenge on the Huns. Without their powerful leader the Huns had to surrender more and more land. They lost many warriors and finally took refuge in the high mountains of Erdély. Here Csaba decided that he would take the bravest, strongest men and return to far Asia, where the Huns had left their brother tribe, the Magyars. He would bring the Magyars to help them. When he was ready to go, he called all his people together. "Dead or alive, we will return to you if you are in danger. From faraway lands we shall come to your aid if we are alive, from the starry sky we shall swoop down if we are dead," he said.

A few months passed. The Huns were attacked again by their bitter enemies. When the danger was greatest, when all hope was lost, came the thundering army of Csaba. He returned from faraway lands and saved them. Three times he returned, always when they needed him sorely. Then he was gone again. Years went by. Nobody knew where he was, whether he would ever return. A vaster army than ever marched against the Huns. Endless columns of ruthless warriors swept into their stronghold, burning their houses, killing their wives and children, threatening to destroy the whole tribe. Aladár was killed in the battle. Among the Huns there was complete disorder and great despair. Forced back to their last stronghold, they heard the mocking chant of the advancing foe. "Where is Csaba now? Why doesn't he come? Where is your brave rescuer? Where is your great leader?"

The Huns fell on their knees and prayed. Prayed for Csaba, for help, for courage to face this last battle.

Thunder, long, deep, ever-increasing thunder answered them. It grumbled and roared, deafening all with its mighty voice. There wasn't a cloud in the starry sky, but the thundering grew louder and louder. A sparkling white streak appeared among the stars, forming a great arch like a rainbow. It widened and grew so brilliant that the night became brighter than the day. With flashing swords, the battlecry of thousands of men, the clattering hoofbeats of thousands of horses, Csaba and his warriors swept down from the sky, scattering the terror-struck enemy. Before the sky army disappeared, the Huns heard a cry: "From the starry sky we shall swoop down to save you if we are dead!"

Nobody dared to attack the Huns after this. They prospered, living peacefully and industriously. Then Csaba and his spirit army came back once more. They were leading the Magyars, to join their brothers in this beautiful land of ours. After that Csaba never came back, but the sparkling skyway, the "Skyway of the Warriors," remained there forever. If we are in great danger, if we need him, from the starry sky he shall swoop down again to help us.

When old Árpád finished the story, nobody broke the silence for a long time. They were gazing at the shimmering skyway, almost hearing the clatter of swords, the hoofbeats of horses.

"This wasn't just a story, it is history. I read about Attila and Csaba in school—they really lived," said Kate.

"They lived again tonight for all of us," said Father.

They said good night to old Árpád. Two herders were driving the horses; they were to stay with Father until after the fair. Father rode with Kate and Jancsi.

"I'll write your father, Kate," he said, "and tell him how proud I am of you."

Kate was gazing at the sky. "Can he see the Skyway of the Warriors, as we see it now?" she asked.

"I'm sure he can, Kate—why?"

"I wish—Prince Csaba would bring him home . . ." whispered Kate.

Father patted her hand. "I think he will, Kate my dear. Good wishes always come true if you say them with your face turned up—toward the sky."

PIPPI LONGSTOCKING is a nine-year-old girl who lives alone in an old house in the town of Villa Villekula. She has a monkey, Mr. Nilsson, and a horse, too. Her two best friends are Tommy and Annika, who live next door. She is always surprising them with her great strength. This story tells how her strength and daring made her a heroine in the town.

Astrid Lindgren

PIPPI ACTS AS A LIFESAVER

ILLUSTRATED BY *Louis Glanzman*

ONE Sunday afternoon Pippi sat wondering what to do. Tommy and Annika had gone to a tea party with their mother and father, so she knew she couldn't expect a visit from them.

The day had been filled with pleasant tasks. She had gotten up early and served Mr. Nilsson fruit juice and buns in bed. He looked so cute sitting there in his light blue nightshirt, holding the glass in both hands. Then she had fed and groomed the horse and told him a long story of her adventures at sea. Next she had gone into the parlor and painted a large picture on the wallpaper. The picture represented a fat lady in a red dress and a black hat. In one hand she held a yellow flower and in the other a dead rat. Pippi thought it a very beautiful picture; it dressed up the whole room. Then she had sat down in front of her chest and looked at all her birds' eggs and shells, and thought about the wonderful places where she and her father had collected them and about all the pleasant little shops all over the world where they had bought the beautiful things that were now in the drawers of her chest. Then she had tried to teach Mr. Nilsson to dance the schottische, but he didn't want

94

to learn. For a while she had thought of trying to teach the horse, but instead she had crept down into the woodbox and pulled the cover down. She had pretended she was a sardine in a sardine box, and it was a shame Tommy and Annika weren't there so they could have been sardines too.

Now it had begun to grow dark. She pressed her little pug nose against the windowpane and looked out into the autumn dusk. She remembered that she hadn't been riding for a couple of days and decided to go at once. That would be a nice ending to a pleasant Sunday.

Accordingly, she put on her big hat, fetched Mr. Nilsson from a corner where he sat playing marbles, saddled the horse, and lifted Mr. Nilsson down from the porch. And off they went, Mr. Nilsson on Pippi and Pippi on the horse.

It was quite cold and the roads were frozen, so there was a good crunchy sound as they rode along. Mr. Nilsson sat on Pippi's shoulder and tried to catch hold of some of the branches of the trees as they went by, but Pippi rode so fast that it was no use. Instead, the branches kept boxing him on the ears, and he had a hard time keeping his straw hat on his head.

Pippi rode through the little town, and people pressed anxiously up against the walls when she came storming by.

The town had a market square, of course. There were several charming old one-story buildings and a little yellow-painted town hall. And there was also an ugly wretch of a building, newly built and three stories high. It was called "The Skyscraper" because it was taller than any of the other houses in town.

On a Sunday afternon the little town was always quiet and peaceful, but suddenly the quiet was broken by loud cries. "The Skyscraper's burning! Fire! Fire!"

People came running excitedly from all directions. The fire engine came clanging down the street, and the little children who usually thought fire engines were such fun now cried from fright because they were sure their own houses would catch fire too. The police had to hold back the crowds of people gathering in the square so that the fire engine could get through.

The flames came leaping out of the windows of the Skyscraper, and smoke and sparks enveloped the firemen who were courageously trying to put out the fire. The fire had started on the first floor but was quickly spreading to the upper stories.

Suddenly the crowd saw a sight that made them gasp with horror. At the top of the house was a gable, and in the gable window, which a little child's hand had just opened, stood two little boys calling for help. "We can't get out because somebody has built a fire on the stairs," cried the older boy.

He was five and his brother a year younger. Their mother had gone out on an errand, and there they stood, all alone. Many of the people in the square began to cry, and the fire chief looked worried. There was, of course, a ladder on the fire truck, but it wouldn't reach anywhere near to the little boys. To get into the house to save the children was impossible. A wave of despair swept over the crowd in the square when they realized there was no way to help the children. And the poor little things just stood up there and cried. It wouldn't be long now before the fire reached the attic.

In the midst of the crowd in the square sat Pippi on her horse. She looked with great interest at the fire engine and wondered if she should buy one like it. She liked it because it was red and because it made such a fearful noise as it went through the streets. Then she looked at the fire and she thought it was fun when a few sparks fell on her.

Presently she noticed the little boys up in the attic. To her astonishment they looked as if they weren't enjoying the fire at all. That was more than she could understand, and she had to ask the crowd around her, "Why are the children crying?"

First she got only sobs in answer, but finally a stout gentleman said, "Well, what do you think? Don't you suppose you'd cry yourself if you were up there and couldn't get down?"

"I never cry," said Pippi, "but if they want to get down, why doesn't somebody help them?"

"Because it isn't possible, of course," said the stout gentleman.

Pippi thought for a while. Then she asked, "Can anybody bring me a long rope?"

"What good would that do?" asked the stout gentleman. "The children are too small to get down the rope, and, for that matter, how would you ever get the rope up to them?"

"Oh, I've been around a bit," said Pippi calmly. "I want a rope."

There was not a single person who thought it would do any good, but somehow or other Pippi got her rope.

Not far from the gable of the Skyscraper grew a tall tree. The top of it was almost level with the attic window, but between the tree and the window was a distance of almost three yards. And the trunk of the tree was smooth and had no branches for climbing on. Even Pippi wouldn't be able to climb it.

The fire burned. The children in the window screamed. The people in the square cried.

Pippi jumped off the horse and went up to the tree. Then she took the rope and tied it tightly to Mr. Nilsson's tail.

"Now you be Pippi's good boy," she said. She put him on the tree trunk and gave him a little push. He understood perfectly what he was supposed to do. And he climbed obediently up the tree trunk. Of course it was no trouble at all for a little monkey to do that.

The people in the square held their breath and watched Mr. Nilsson. Soon he had reached the top of the tree. There he sat on a branch and looked down at Pippi. She beckoned to him to come down again. He did so at once, climbing down on the other side of the branch, so that when he reached the ground the rope was looped over the branch and hung down double with both ends on the ground.

"Good for you, Mr. Nilsson," said Pippi. "You're so smart you can be a professor any time you wish." She untied the knot that had fastened the rope to Mr. Nilsson's tail.

Nearby, a house was being repaired, and Pippi ran over and got a long board. She took the board in one hand, ran to the tree, grasped the rope in her free hand, and braced her feet against the trunk of the tree. Quickly and nimbly she climbed up the trunk, and the people stopped crying in astonishment. When she reached the top of the tree she placed the board over a stout branch and then carefully pushed it over to the window sill. And there lay the board like a bridge between the top of the tree and the window.

The people down in the square stood absolutely silent. They were so tense they couldn't say a word. Pippi stepped out on the board. She smiled pleasantly at the two boys in the gabled window. "Why do you look so sad?" she asked. "Have you got a stomach-ache?"

She ran across the board and hopped in at the window. "My, it seems warm in here," she said. "You don't need to make any more fire in here today, that I can guarantee. And at the most four sticks in the stove tomorrow, I should think."

Then she took one boy under each arm and stepped out on the board again.

"Now you're really going to have some fun," she said. "It's almost like walking the tight rope."

When she got to the middle of the board she lifted one leg in the air just as she had done at the circus. The crowd below gasped, and when a little later Pippi lost one of her shoes several old ladies fainted. However, Pippi reached the tree safely with the little boys. Then the crowd cheered so loudly that the dark night was filled with noise and the sound drowned out the crackling of the fire.

Pippi hauled up the rope, fastened one end securely to a

branch, and tied the other around one of the boys. Then she let him down slowly and carefully into the arms of his waiting mother, who was beside herself with joy when she had him safe. She held him close and hugged him, with tears in her eyes.

But Pippi yelled, "Untie the rope, for goodness' sake! There's another kid up here, and he can't fly either."

So the people helped to untie the rope and free the little boy. Pippi could tie good knots, she could indeed. She had learned that at sea. She pulled up the rope again, and now it was the second boy's turn to be let down.

Pippi was alone in the tree. She sprang out on the board, and all the people looked at her and wondered what she was going to do. She danced back and forth on the narrow board. She raised and lowered her arms gracefully and sang in a hoarse voice that could barely be heard down in the square:

> "The fire is burning,
> It's burning so bright,
> The flames are leaping and prancing.
>
> It's burning for you,
> It's burning for me,
> It's burning for all who are dancing!"

As she sang she danced more and more wildly until many people covered their eyes in horror for they were sure she would fall down and kill herself. Flames came leaping out of the gable window, and in the firelight people could see Pippi plainly. She raised her arms to the night sky, and while a shower of sparks fell over her she cried loudly, "Such a jolly, jolly fire!"

She took one leap and caught the rope. "Look out!" she cried and came sliding down the rope like greased lightning.

"Three cheers for Pippi Longstocking! Long may she live!" cried the fire chief.

"Hip, hip, hurray! Hip, hip, hurray! Hip, hip, hurray!" cried all the people—three times. But there was one person there who cheered four times.

It was Pippi Longstocking.

In 1940 the Nazis invaded Norway. Although their names have been changed, this is a true story of how some Norwegian children helped to save $9,000,000 worth of gold bullion, which is gold before it is made into money. Peter Lundstrom's father was a banker who had the bullion. When Mr. Lundstrom was called to the army, he and his brother, Peter's Uncle Victor, tried to think of a plan to save the gold. Peter volunteered to form a Defense Club, and he and his friends, including Helga Thomsen, Michael Berg, his own sister Lovisa, and brother Bunny, hid the gold bricks under them on their sleds. They coasted past the German sentries down to a hidden part of the valley called the Snake, where they hid the gold under snowmen. Uncle Victor planned later to take it aboard his fishing boat, the *Cleng Peerson,* which was now camouflaged in the Snake as a tree. Then he would sail with it to America and safety! The children began to recognize the different Germans, and called one Lieutenant Sit-Down because he couldn't stay on his feet with skis on. At the *konditeri,* or pastry shop, they were often spoken to by a private, but they didn't answer, for they had taken a vow never to speak to the Germans. Peter began to fear that he was being watched by this private, and he noticed him at the Holms' barn where the boys often slept. One day, as Peter was unloading his gold, he heard a noise— and looked up into the eyes of the German private!

Marie McSwigan

SECRET IN THE SNOW

ILLUSTRATED BY *Hardie Gramatky*

SO IT was all over. They'd been discovered. The Nazis knew what they were doing and had come to stop them.

Peter knelt in the snow, trembling. The blue eyes under the fringe of fair hair were familiar. Even in his fright Peter knew he had seen this private before. He'd seen him the very first day they'd passed the Nazi sentries. He had been helping un-

Taken from *Snow Treasure* by Marie McSwigan, published and copyright, 1942, by E. P. Dutton & Co., Inc., New York.

load the supplies. He was the one who had seemed to want to go sled-riding too. More. He was the soldier who came to the *konditeri* for the *smorsbord.*

Then Peter had another surprise. The brush behind the soldier parted, and Uncle Victor sprang out. He grabbed the soldier's arms and pinned them behind him, and before he could make an outcry he had a gag over his mouth.

Behind Uncle Victor came Rolls, the mate. His revolver was pointed at the captive. When the latter made no effort to free himself, it was lowered. Then the men turned back into the brush towards the *Cleng Peerson.*

It all happened so fast that none but Peter saw. Not even Helga, a few feet away, knew what took place. She was hard at work on her snowman.

"Helga, take my team back with yours," Peter asked. "I want to see Uncle Victor."

Helga wanted to see Uncle Victor, too, and to go aboard the *Cleng,* now that Peter knew where to find it. But Peter was president of the Defense Club. All of them had to obey him. When he refused to let her come with him, she had to do as he asked.

Peter had no idea whether or not his uncle would allow him aboard the boat. But he was going to find out. What was happening on the smack was something no boy of twelve was going to miss if he could help it. So he hurried through the brush to the side of the water.

From below the deck came strange sounds. Not to lose any of the excitement, Peter almost fell down the companionway in his haste.

Uncle Victor and Rolls had untied the prisoner's arms and had taken the gag from his mouth.

Then the captive soldier drew off his round army cap and threw it on the floor and tramped on it. He beat it with his feet, up and down. Then he tore at the insignia on his collar and tried to rip it off. All the while he was making hideous faces.

"What is it, man? Speak. Your mouth is no longer tied," Uncle Victor commanded sharply.

Then came a torrent of words, Norwegian and some other tongue Peter did not recognize.

"I'm no German even if I do wear the uniform. I'm a Pole. They took me and made me serve them, and the deceit is theirs, not mine."

"But what are you doing with a German army of occupation?" Uncle Victor asked.

"I tell you it is not my fault. It's theirs. I'm no more to blame than, than,—than that boy there."

He pointed at Peter and now Uncle Victor and Rolls saw him, too. But Uncle Victor made no move toward Peter. He gave him a glance that seemed to say, "It's all right. At your age I wouldn't have missed it, either."

"I want to go to the United States," the Pole went on. "If you'll take me on this boat, I'll cook and I'll scrub the decks. I'll sew the sails and carpenter. I'll stand watch. I'll do anything you ask. Only don't leave me here with those merciless machines, those Germans."

"What's he talking like that for?" Uncle Victor turned to

Rolls. "What makes him think I'd take a man in a German uniform anywhere? How do I know he's a Pole and hates the Germans? Does he think I'm a baby to take him on his own word?"

Then he turned on the Pole and spoke severely.

"Come, now tell us what you know? How long have you been following these children?"

"If I follow the children, it's only because I'm lonely. It's because I want to be with someone I can like and trust. I will not make friends with the Germans. They don't even speak to me unless I can do them a service." Tears came into his blue eyes.

"Come, now, that's absurd. You have been following these children because you are spying on them. You want to find out what brings them here on their sleds. Then you go tell the Commandant and win a promotion. I know your sly German tricks."

"No! No! No! I have no sly German tricks. I'm a Pole. I have no love for the Germans. To me, they have done every wrong short of putting me to death. If I follow the children, it's not to do them harm."

He spoke convincingly. Peter believed he told the truth. Even Uncle Victor seemed inclined to believe him, for his next question was put in milder tones.

"But if you wanted to be with the children, why did you not make yourself known when you were here last week?"

"I was on the other side of the fiord. I could not cross over."

"But what were you doing in Holms' barn?" Peter asked. "For it was you, of course."

"If one is lonesome, even cows can be companions."

Uncle Victor turned away.

Peter spoke again. He was sorry for the captive, believed his story. But with so much at stake they couldn't afford to take chances.

"But it was you who were in the *konditeri* the day you posted the notices about going back to school. Why is it you can have so much liberty and the others have to go back to the barracks?"

"They don't have to go. It's by choice. When they found the Norwegians were ignoring them they decided they would stay

104

He began kicking . . .

together entirely. And then when the epidemic came they were frightened."

"Weren't you frightened, too?"

"Not I, because death, it is nothing. I live only that some day I can help my country. Poland is my country."

Uncle Victor cleared his throat. If he was going to say something, the Polish boy didn't give him a chance.

"But won't you take me with you to America, for surely that is where you are going?" He looked about the cabin. "From the other side of the fiord, I saw the boat in its clever disguise and I knew you'd be sailing soon for that country. I'll be no trouble if you take me. And when I get there I've a place to go. I have a married sister in Pittsburgh."

"But that's utter nonsense," Uncle Victor protested. And his voice was again loud and angry. "Even if I didn't think this some sly Nazi trick, how could I land you there? They wouldn't let you in without a passport. . . ."

"Well, what are we going to do with him?" Uncle Victor asked when they had put him in the hold while they discussed the problem.

"We daren't turn him loose, that's certain," Rolls replied. "We can't take the risk that he won't tell the Commandant."

"He'd never do that," Peter spoke quickly.

"His story sounds true enough," Uncle Victor decided. "I can well believe what he's told us. We know about the disguises ourselves, about men who came to Norway dressed as sports lovers but who turned out to be secret police. But I think it's dangerous to let him go. Whether he meant to or not, he could accidentally say something that would put the Germans on our trail."

"But what shall we do with him?"

"He'll have to be kept in the hold. We can't stand guard over him. I've a crew coming on tomorrow, but even so, I cannot spare a man just to watch him."

Rolls was laying the table for supper. Since it was so late, Peter was to spend the night aboard the *Cleng,* and there was no place on earth he would rather be. His mother would not

105

miss him that night for he was supposed to be at the Holms' farm.

"Couldn't you take him with you to America, Uncle Victor?" Peter pleaded. "It seems a shame he can't go."

"But I *can't* take him without a passport. That's all there is to that," his uncle said shortly.

"It would be a terrible thing to go that distance and be turned back at the end," Rolls explained.

"I could sign him on as a sailor," Uncle Victor answered. "But he'd be interned because I'm not planning to return. I'm afraid that would be pretty hard on him after all he's gone through."

"You could land him somewhere along the coast where the fighting is going on," Rolls suggested. "There are Poles with the British army."

"Too dangerous," his captain replied. "Once I get out of this fiord, I'm going to stay out to sea. Overnight the Germans have been capturing our towns. I might run into an enemy occupation. Once I get past, I'm going to stay past."

The Polish boy had been frightened when they told him they would have to lock him up for the night.

"Nothing will harm you," Uncle Victor said. "You won't have to go back to the barracks. We're hiding, and you can hide with us."

They had to wait for the long twilight to fade to bring in the gold that the children had buried that day. They didn't dare carry a light.

"You see now why I had you build the snowmen?" Uncle Victor asked Peter. "We just have to feel our way. So all we do is to feel for a snowman, and under him is the gold."

With three of them at work it wasn't long before they had the bullion aboard the *Cleng*.

"Fifty-one bricks," Rolls grunted in satisfaction.

"And each brick is worth five thousand United States dollars," Uncle Victor spoke cheerfully. "That's two hundred and fifty-five thousand dollars we collected from these snowmen. And quite a lot of money."

106

"Uncle Victor, that's just about all the gold in the cave. One day more'll bring it all out. This morning I asked Per Garson how much was left and he said a hundred bricks. Well, here are fifty-one of them right here."

"That's what I've been hoping. As soon as this Polish boy is missed, the Germans will start searching for him. They may come here. Even with the camouflage, it's dangerous if they get too close. If I had my crew, I think I would sail tonight. Although I'd have to leave the rest of the gold, I'd do it to be safe."

Before he turned in that night Rolls quizzed Jan Lasek about when he would be missed at the camp.

Jan said he *might* be missed that night, but they couldn't help noting his absence at roll call in the morning.

When Rolls told his chief, Peter thought his uncle looked solemn.

"Then the search may start tonight." He went to the porthole to look through a slit in the fir branches.

"You don't expect them here already?" Peter asked.

"No, I want to see if there's any sign of my sailors. They'll come at night."

"But the curfew, Uncle Victor?"

"It'd be a lot safer for them at night. But don't worry. Hans Torp and Sten and Dino are resourceful fellows. They'll manage. I told them to be here no later than tomorrow, and they'll be here."

There were voices out of the night beyond the portholes. From the direction of the beach came calls. Crowded at the peepholes in the fir branches, the three in the cabin waited. The voices grew louder. Outside in the snow were several squads of Germans.

"So the search has started," Victor spoke softly. "And they're even looking here. Whew! What a narrow squeak! If they'd come an hour earlier, they would have found us out there with the gold!"

It had taken the Germans until taps to miss the Polish recruit. Then the hunt for him had started.

107

Nearer and nearer to the *Cleng Peerson* came the searching party. But Uncle Victor was calm.

"If you couldn't find the boat in the daytime, knowing it was here, they're not going to find it at night," he comforted Peter. "So let's not worry about their finding us. I'm only hoping that Torp and the other two don't pick this time to come aboard."

The Germans trailed up the valley well beyond the two fallen trees. But here the snow was clear of footprints, as the three in the cabin knew. So their trip only served to churn the snow and widen the hunt. For with many footprints on the ground, later search parties would have more territory to cover.

Uncle Victor, Rolls, and Peter continued to crowd at the peepholes in the fir branches over the ports. After a time they saw the Germans turn back towards the cliff and the beach.

"If they search the woods, they can't help coming on the ski trail of our friend here." Uncle Victor meant Jan Lasek. "That'll lead them here by the back way, and you can be sure they'll do some close searching."

The next morning the Snake was quiet as always. The Germans evidently had not yet found the ski trail, and Uncle Victor hoped to be at sea before they did. Just before dawn, Hans Torp and the two other sailors came aboard. They took turns watching for the enemy's approach, but the morning wore away, and they neither saw nor heard anything. The last of the gold would be brought down that afternoon. When it was dark the *Cleng* could sail.

It was going to rain, Peter noted with satisfaction. It wouldn't matter now. The gold had been saved.

Lovisa's and Michael's teams came to the Snake that day. Peter went out to join them, for he would be going back to town with them. He longed to remain in the Snake to see Uncle Victor set sail. But for the safety of them all and for the accomplishment of all they had set out to do, he made no protest when Uncle Victor said he must go back to town.

"Oh, Peter! We did it! We did it!" Lovisa threw her arms around him. "Every last brick's out of the cave. It's all down here. We fooled them! We fooled those old goose-steppers!"

108

"What about the soldier that's missing?" Peter wanted to know at once. "Was there a search for him in town last night?"

"Was there? Well, you should have been at home! In the middle of the night they pounded on the door. Per Garson went to open it. They almost knocked him down pushing past him. They started searching the house. They looked in closets, even with Mother's dresses. They woke up Bunny, and he started hollering. Mother told them she didn't know what they were looking for but if they'd tell her she'd know how to help them. But they just went on poking behind curtains. Do they think we'd hide one of their men? Why are they making this fuss?"

"I guess on account of his being a Pole. And forced against his will to join their army."

"Was he? How do you know that? How do you know he's a Pole? Nobody in town said he was a Pole."

But Peter wouldn't tell. Lovisa went on:

"There's a notice on the school door. It said that anyone with information about this missing soldier must report at once to the Commandant, and if anyone is found to know something and *hasn't* told, he'll be punished with death. Ugh, these Germans!"

"Whew!" Peter whistled.

"Mother's afraid for the Holms," Lovisa went on. "She thinks the missing man might be hiding around their barn, and she's going down this afternoon to warn them to get him out. For she said if they did find anyone there it'd be pretty hard to make the Nazis understand the Holms didn't want him. She'll be there when we get back."

Peter nodded. "Let's get these bricks down and get out."

Lovisa turned back to her sled and Peter, watching her, saw her stiffen in fright.

"Look, Peter," she whispered.

Into the Snake filed a company of German soldiers and an officer.

"They've come to search," Lovisa said.

"They did that last night. I guess they've come to look again."

"Peter, what'll we do?" They'll see us with the gold."

"Right," he snapped into action. "The kids'll have to hurry. Get your bricks in the snow. Quick, team," he lowered his voice. "Here come the Germans."

Like squirrels burying nuts, the children burrowed in the snow. It flew in all directions.

"Not so deep," Peter directed. "Just lay the bricks down and start the snowmen. Faster. They're coming."

Mittened hands had unloaded the sleds. Now the snow was being patted into hard lumps. The children were well practiced after so many months of winter. Soon was standing a fine army of snowmen.

Michael's team was farther up the valley by the farthest of the two fallen trees. Peter gave the whistle they used at school when Mr. Anders was coming.

Michael whistled back. Then he must understand. He'd know that someone was coming, that danger was near.

"All right, Lovisa, let them come," Peter dropped on his knees in the snow and began another figure. It was easier to do that than to stand waiting for the Germans. In all the weeks they'd been coming to the Snake, this would be the first time the Germans had come there at the same time. Lovisa thought something of this, too.

"They had to wait for the very last day," she grumbled.

110

"They let us bring every last bit of gold out. Then they come and find it."

"Shhh," Peter cautioned. "Don't let them know you think anything is out of the ordinary in their coming here. They're only looking for the runaway soldier, you know."

It was Lieutenant Sit-Down who led the company into the Snake. They came plodding through the snow to the level space between the two trees, and here the ground was dotted with children and snowmen.

"There's no one here but these youngsters," he told the sergeant. "There's no use to ask them if they saw anyone for they won't answer. I think we might as well go back."

The sergeant drew up stiffly. "Pardon, Herr Lieutenant," he said, "the Commandant comes."

Near the cliff Peter could see the bulky figure of the Commandant, the head of the German forces at Riswyk. He was picking his way up the valley.

Peter and Lovisa continued playing in the snow. Peter had begun a snowman, and Lovisa was making hers a fancy hat.

They wanted to get up and start for home but they didn't dare move. They felt they would be less noticed if they stayed where they were.

The Commandant came puffing along. He seemed to have trouble lifting his feet in the deep snow. In his hand he carried a light little cane, a swagger stick.

He plodded along until he came to the children. When he got there he stopped in his tracks.

"If he'd only go on," Peter growled to himself. But he didn't dare look up to see. His hands were busy with the snow. His head was hot and his mouth dry and there was a buzzing in his ears.

What would happen now? What if the Commandant found the bricks buried under the snowmen. Why there were more than a million kroner right here at their feet!

"We're searching for a German infantryman," the Commandant announced to the children. "Have any of you seen a man in these woods?"

111

Of course there was no answer. He turned aside to whisper a few words to Lieutenant Sit-Down. Then he spoke to the children in a loud voice,—

"I said we are looking for a German infantryman. It's very important for you children to tell if you've seen one on this part of the coast. There's a severe penalty attached if anyone has seen him and has not reported it."

Still the children said nothing.

"I've a good mind to give you children a lesson in manners," his voice was angry. "When you're spoken to, it's only right that you should answer. Has no one taught you that? Now then. Yes or No? Have you seen a German infantry soldier in this fiord?"

The children acted as if they had not heard him. Lovisa sat back on her heels to admire her handiwork. But Peter, for all he tried to be cool, felt a terrible thumping in his chest. His cheeks must be red as rowan berries. For if any snowman were to be knocked down—.

The Commandant strode across the snow and stood above Lovisa.

"Little girl, tell me, did you or did you not see a German infantryman?" he screamed in anger. "Answer me."

Lovisa only turned her big blue eyes up at him. Not so much as a nod did she give him.

"Don't you know I can make you talk? Don't you realize that we Germans can make anyone do our will? We've only to command to be obeyed."

Peter remembered the pact they had made the day they had started their undertaking. They had sworn on the sword they wouldn't give information about what they were doing. Of course, this wasn't the same. But even so, they weren't to talk to the Germans for fear they would say something to make them suspicious. But no need to worry about Lovisa. Pledge or not, she wouldn't talk.

The Commandant's eye fell. There was something he didn't like about Lovisa's snowman.

"Bah, you Norwegians!" With his stick he slashed off the

112

snowman's head. It was as if he would do the same to Lovisa's. Then he raised the stick and cut the snowman neatly in two. The upper part rolled beside the head. Only the haunches remained.

"Down you go," he shouted in his rage. "Just the way all people go who stand in our Fuehrer's way. The way Norway goes. And Holland and Belgium and France and England and all countries that oppose the German will."

Lovisa was near to tears, Peter could tell. But she winked them back.

"Now, little girl," the Commandant went on, "you see what will happen to all your people if you do not help the good Germans who have come to save you from the hardships your country makes you endure."

"Hardships!" Peter had to bite his tongue to keep from saying. "It's you who bring the hardships, you with your talk of 'the good Germans.'"

"So, little girl, let this be a lesson," the high officer was still in a rage. "Unless you want yourself and all who belong to you to go rolling over like that—and that—and that—."

He began kicking the stump of Lovisa's snowman. The snow flew out in a shower. With each kick, Peter winced. For the Commandant's foot could only be a few inches from her two bricks. In their haste that day they had not been able to bury deep but had to count on the snowmen to hide the gold.

The high officer had evidently decided to give Lovisa a thorough lesson for he lifted his foot for another kick. Like a football player he stood back to swing at what was left of the snow figure.

"In another minute he'll stub his toe against the bricks," Peter thought.

Then he gathered up a handful of snow. He rolled it into a hard ball. Then he stood back and took aim.

It landed exactly on the Commandant's right ear as Peter meant it should.

Then Peter took to his heels and ran for the woods.

"There he goes! After him!"

Peter had little chance to escape. Lieutenant Sit-Down and almost his whole company were chasing him.

But Peter knew these woods, and the foreigners did not. He hoped to cross the Snake above where it was narrower and take the ski trail up the mountain. In the forest above he had a good chance to hide.

But he was cut off before he could get upstream far enough to cross. The Germans spread out in a circle and blocked all points. Peter felt like a rabbit facing a pack of hounds.

Rough arms were around him and he fell to the ground. There was a tussle, and Peter all but succeeded in throwing off his captor. But the others came up and he was one against many, a boy surrounded by men.

There was nothing to do but submit. They dragged him to his feet. He fell in step with them. They were marching him off to their barracks.

But the snowball trick had worked!

He had succeeded in distracting the Commandant. The outrage of being snowballed by a Norwegian boy was enough to make him forget the lesson he was giving Lovisa,—showing her how the Norse would be treated by the German conquerors. And so, he had not uncovered the gold she had buried beneath the very snowman he was kicking.

Yes, the snowball trick had worked! When Peter was led back to the place between the two fallen trees, he saw the Commandant was leaving. The snowmen were still standing and the children were filing out of the Snake.

Peter did not mind being a German prisoner if he had saved the gold.

How much of this had Uncle Victor seen? he wondered. No doubt every bit of it.

But could he do anything to help him?

Frightened as he was, not knowing what was going to happen, he still didn't want any aid from Uncle Victor. His uncle's only concern was to get the gold out of Norway. If he did that, it was all that anyone could expect of him.

But Uncle Victor wasn't the one to let a fellow down, Peter

knew. He had always been ready to help before. But in a case like this, with so much—the money, involved, may be their very lives, Peter didn't think his uncle could do much.

A soldier marched on his right, and one on his left. Ahead and behind were others. When they reached the sentries, these sprang up, their rifles on their shoulders. So they were quite a little company when they turned into the barracks they had built before the fishing wharf.

The heavy boots of the Nazis clumped in rhythm over the wooden boards of the barracks floor. Thump, thump, thump, thump, down a long hallway they pounded. Then they stopped. Peter was shoved into a box of a room no bigger than a clothes closet. A key was turned in the door. Then the thump, thump, thump, of the soldiers as they left him alone in the twilight.

He stumbled against something like a low shelf. It was supposed to be his bed, he guessed. There was a window at one end of the tiny room. It was barred. Through it he could see the beach, snow-covered to the very edge of the black lapping water. Through the snow the sentry stepped, up and down, up

and down, his legs swinging straight out from his hips like those of a toy soldier wound with a key.

What were they going to do with him, Peter wondered. Would he be tried at a court martial?

Up past the window stepped the sentry. Then he turned and followed his own footprints back in the direction he had come.

Was it a serious offense to snowball a high German officer? Peter believed it was. It had something to do with order and respect for authority. Well, he didn't care how serious it was. They could shoot him if they liked. He was glad he had thrown that snowball.

But still, he was horribly afraid.

Would even the Germans put a boy to death? He couldn't be sure. From the stories of what they did in Poland, he could believe almost anything. Still, these Germans in Norway didn't seem so bad. The captain who had gone away had moved his troops out of their sled track, and they had all been very decent and had kept to themselves and had not even raided the food supplies as they had done in other countries. They had all been very friendly except this Commandant. But even he had offered to have an orderly help Mrs. Lundstrom pull the sled on which Bunny and the others sat on thousands of kroner of gold.

But Jan's story of Poland kept coming back,—of how they had turned the people out of their houses and had taken the priest off the altar at mass.

When he thought of Jan his mouth was hot and dry again. For whether or not he was in serious trouble for having snow-balled the Commandant, he knew he would be if it were known he'd seen the escaped Pole. Lovisa said there was a notice on the school door saying that anyone who was found to know something about him and not telling would be punished by death.

By death.

How cold it was in this barracks! Even in his windbreaker and heavy outdoor clothes he felt cold. His teeth were coming together and apart like hammers.

The sun had gone down and there was only a dim gray light

116

coming from the outside. It seemed to be raining. Maybe that was why it got dark so early. Anyway, the northern afternoon was over. Outside it all seemed so wet and sad, down here by the fishing pier.

After a time a soldier came to the door. He brought Peter a deep dish of stew and some dark bread.

The soldier spoke to him. "I come back to get your dish. Then I will take you to the Commandant," he said in German.

Peter couldn't eat. He tried to but it was no use.

Later there were footsteps in the hall. A key turned in the lock. The time was up. The soldier had come to take him to the Commandant. He stepped into the cell. Even in the dim light Peter could tell it was not the same soldier.

The soldier came inside and shut the door and leaned against it.

Peter looked hard at him. He could see so little from the streak of light from the window. But there was something familiar.

The soldier was Jan Lasek, the Pole. But, no. That couldn't be. Jan was on Uncle Victor's boat in the Snake. Peter had seen him there that day.

"Shhhh," Jan put his finger to his lips. From his tunic pocket he dug a scrap of paper. It was so dark Peter had to go over and over it before he could make it out. It was a note from Uncle Victor. Peter read:

"Jan Lasek is risking his liberty and perhaps his life for you. Follow him at all costs, wherever he goes. On that depends your safety and his."

There was so signature but Peter knew well his uncle's bold handwriting. He nodded to show he understood.

Jan kept listening for a sound. What was he waiting for, Peter dared not ask. From afar Peter could make out a kind of din, a rattle like knives and forks, pans and mugs. When the rattle became much louder Jan seemed satisfied. He looked out of the door. He stepped outside and closed it.

When he came back into the cell there was high excitement in his whisper.

117

"Come now," he said, "quickly!"

They were out in the hall. Jan stopped to turn the key in the lock outside the door where Peter had been kept prisoner. Into his pocket went the key.

And now Peter could hear the tramp, tramp, tramp, of boots. It came from a distant end of the barracks but it grew noisier with each step.

"We'll have to run," Jan whispered.

All the time the sound of the marching soldiers came closer.

They seemed to be coming down a hall that would meet the corridor at right angles. And now Peter could hear nothing because of sound in his own ears. He wanted to run in the opposite direction. Why go this way? he wondered. We'll only run into them.

The marching men must be nearing the corner. But Jan only kept going faster towards them. Uncle Victor said he was to follow Jan at all costs. So behind him ran the breathless frightened Peter.

And now, on the right, Peter saw a door. Through it Jan pulled him. There was just time to close it softly. The Germans were turning the corner as Peter could tell by the sound of their steps on the other side of the door.

Peter fell into the wet snow of the beach. They were outside the barracks and, for the moment, safe.

Jan flattened himself against the wall of the building and Peter stood up beside him. The shadow of the barracks hid them. The rain was loud on the crusted snow.

"We're lucky the sentry was going up the beach, not down," Jan whispered. "Otherwise he'd have seen the light when we opened the door."

Peter felt a throbbing in his ears. He tried not to pant, but his breath was loud. Now there was another soft pod, pod, pod, —more marching. Against the snow they could see a dark figure. It was the sentry returning. He walked up to a point on a line with the door, the very door over which he stood guard. He was not ten feet away from where Jan and Peter were flattened against the wall.

Slap, slap, slap, his heavy leather mittens thumped his shoulders. He changed his rifle from one side to the other, and changed it back again. Then he turned and began goose-stepping back in the direction he had come.

Jan tugged at Peter's sleeve. It was now or never, he seemed to say.

Peter was not prepared for what happened next. Jan led him down the beach to the very edge of the fiord and then right into the water itself.

The cold water bit his body. The breath left him. He didn't think he could stand another minute of it. He wanted to run back to the beach, but Jan kept wading out, and Peter, remembering the warning in the note, found himself following him.

It seemed forever, these few minutes they waded in the water. And now Jan was swimming and Peter found himself doing the same. But you couldn't swim in that close-to-frozen water. You had no strength. Peter felt the breath going out of him. But somehow or other it seemed better to freeze to death out here than to stay in those barracks and wait for no one knew what. Then there was a numbness over him. He closed his eyes.

He must be dreaming for nothing like this could happen in real life. A hand reached out and grabbed his arm and he was pulled into a boat. Someone put a flask to his mouth and told him to drink. But the fiery stuff made him sputter, and it ran down over his chin. A heavy coat was put over him and a pair of arms were cradling him. Rolls, Uncle Victor's mate, was holding him. There was another sodden mass on the bottom of the boat. It was Jan Lasek, Peter heard them say his name.

But now he found he was beyond caring about anything. The boat, he knew, was the *Cleng Peerson's* life boat. Strong arms were pulling it towards the fishing smack.

Peter was dry and warm in Uncle Victor's cabin.

The coast of Norway was somewhere out in the blackness. The Atlantic rolled, and the *Cleng Peerson* pitched, and Peter was jounced up and down with the wash of the waves.

Ahead lay America.

So Peter was going to America!

He was going to see New York and go to Pittsburgh with Jan Lasek and then travel to Minnesota where his uncle was a professor in St. Olaf's College in Northfield.

Uncle Victor could arrange it, he said.

"You can be admitted as a minor in my custody. Our minister in Washington will do that much for us. He'll be only too glad to do something in return for all this gold."

"But what about Jan Lasek?" Peter asked. "How can he go without a passport?"

"But he *has* a passport,—he told us it was stolen. There'll be a record of it in Washington and they'll be grateful for the information about the one who is masquerading in his name. They won't be long finding him."

Peter was overjoyed with this good news for Jan. Since he had risked his life for him, there was no reward too high. Uncle Victor said something like this.

"It wasn't as easy for Jan as it looks, Peter. He ran a grave risk. He did it simply because I didn't feel right about sailing and leaving you there. Of course he knew the routine of the camp. He knew that at supper hour the barracks would be deserted, except for the mess hall. And he knew about the side door and the sentry. But he was still in danger of being caught himself. If one little thing had gone wrong, he would have been caught."

"He had his uniform, too," Peter mused. "One German uniform looks pretty much like another."

Then a thought struck him. "But how did he get the key to open the cell door?" he wanted to know.

"The keys are kept on a panel in the guardroom. The room was empty while the guard was at mess. All Jan had to do was to slip in and take the key marked *"das Gefängnis."*

His uncle went on. "All that part was easy. The only hard part was getting him to the barracks without his being seen on the way there. For he was being looked for everywhere. So we didn't dare have him go by foot from the Snake to the beach and barracks."

"It was Rolls who solved it for us," his uncle went on. "He suggested that, since the roads were being watched, we make a landing by water. The *Cleng* was pretty well covered by camouflage so she could be moved to the mouth of the Snake where it meets the big fiord. We were lucky it was a bad night. The rain and mist shortens the day. When it got dark Rolls and Hans Torp and Sten lowered the lifeboat and rowed him right up to the fishing pier. But they couldn't wait for him because it was too dangerous. They had to get back to the cover of the *Cleng*. That's why you had to swim so far."

121

"But how did Jan get past the sentries into the barracks?"

"Just the way you got out. He waited for one to come up, turn and start back. The minute his back was turned, he stepped inside the door. It isn't bolted till taps and Jan knew that. The sentry was there to guard that very door, but there are ways to get past sentries if you can think of those ways."

"Wasn't Jan afraid he'd be caught when he got inside the barracks?"

"Of course. Terribly. But he had to risk it."

"He did it for me?"

"For you, and because I said I'd take him to America if he got you out."

"We heard the soldiers marching in the hallway. Were they coming to get me?"

"Whether they were or not, you and Jan would have been in a pretty tight place if you'd run into them."

Peter fell back in the bunk. "So I'm to go to America. But what about Mother and Lovisa and Bunny?"

"Peter, I know you think it high-handed of me to be taking you this long distance without so much as asking if you wanted to go. But there was nothing else to do with you. I couldn't go all the way across the Atlantic Ocean without knowing what would become of you. And when I got you on board, there was nothing to do with you but to take you along. We daren't turn back with all this gold."

"Oh, Uncle Victor, it isn't that. Only—only—."

"Only what?"

"Well, when Father left, he said I was the man of the family and was to look after the others."

"Peter, don't worry about your mother's not being able to look out for herself and for her children. And although I'm sorry to have to tell you this, your father may soon be home. The British have withdrawn their forces from much of the coast. Our army is putting up a magnificent defense but it's only a question of time until it can no longer hold out. Then the order will come to cease firing."

Peter thought about the night his father had gone away, the

122

123

night of the first blackout. And of all the things that had happened since.

"It's a shame, Peter, for you to be leaving without so much as saying good-bye to your family and Helga and Michael and Per Garson and the others. But your mother was glad when I told her what we were going to try to do. You know she had gone to the Holms to warn them that the missing Nazi might be in their barn. When Lovisa got to the farm with the news of what happened to you she strapped on her skis and took the back trail through the woods to the Snake.

" 'Take him to America by all means,' she said. 'I want him to grow up in a country where people are free.' She asked to have you promise that you will always remember you come of liberty-loving people who think freedom is a greater heritage than gold."

There was a clatter of steps in the companionway. Rolls came into the cabin.

"Submarine off sta'board," he said.

Uncle Victor jumped to his feet in alarm. Then he saw the sheepish grin on Rolls' face.

"But it's a British sub," he spoke lamely. "The *Cleng's* doing five knots in this sea," he added.

"She ought to ride well," Uncle Victor answered. "She's got a cargo of gold for ballast."

The flag of Norway was draped above the map on the bulkhead.

Into the cabin came the notes of a cornet.

"It's my old horn. I lent it to the Polish boy," Rolls explained.

In the galley Jan Lasek was practicing "The Star Spangled Banner."

Part II: FOR OLDER READERS

Hubert Evans

A TRUST FULFILLED

ILLUSTRATED BY *Dorothy Bayley Morse*

PROSPECTORS often visited the Olsen cabin at the Moose River ferry, but to Dell and Jimmy Olsen, old Scotty was the most exciting. Seldom did the talkative old fellow come out of the unmapped wilderness to the northward without some thrilling new story for them. It might be of hair-raising danger in wilderness or rapids, or of some dramatic meeting with bear or wolf or caribou. But this bright spring morning, after the bearded old timer had hurried into the cabin nestling among its spruce beside the ferry landing, the secret he wanted to entrust to them nearly took their breath away.

"Dad and Mother paddled down to the trading post less than an hour ago," Jimmy explained. "But we can take you in our canoe as far as the rapids. Maybe you'd catch up with them on the portage trail."

"And another thing," Dell put in excitedly, "the trader has a safe, and Dad could ask him to keep your ore samples in it while you're away recording your claim."

"Na, na, lassie," Scotty objected, "I've no time to go to the post. If you'll take care of this ore sack and put me across the river, I'm for heading overland. That way I can get to the mining recorder's office a full day sooner. But I do wish your dad was here," he went on anxiously. "Y'see, I may be wrong. This may not be pitchblende after all."

"Is pitchblende very valuable?" twelve-year-old Dell asked. Her merry gray eyes had become very serious.

"Valuable?" Jimmy almost snorted. Being two years ahead of his sister in the correspondence courses the Government broadcast to school children beyond the fringe of settlement, Jimmy had learned from his lessons in commercial geography the pricelessness of the green-gray rock, the sack of which Scotty wanted to leave hidden in their cabin. "I guess it's the most precious ore on earth. Why, they get radium from it!"

"Aye," Scotty broke in. "An' if I've really found the stuff, it'll mean health for thousands of sick folk." The faded old eyes were shining now. "Think o' me, plain old Scotty, doing good like that!"

"And you'll be ever so rich," Dell exclaimed. "Oh! I'm so glad."

"Me nor nobody else'll get rich out of this find. That's why I'm in such an almighty hurry," the excited prospector declared.

When Dell was puzzled her nice eyebrows had a habit of lowering so that tiny crinkles showed in the corners of her eyes. "I don't understand," she said. It was hard to explain. Scotty was the very soul of honesty, but suddenly she had the feeling that he was keeping something unpleasant from them.

"What don't you understand?" Jimmy demanded with brotherly frankness. "Anybody knows that when you've found a claim you've got to be the first one to the Government office to record it. If you're not you may be cheated out of it—claim jumpers and all that."

Scotty gave the fourteen-year-old an understanding glance. "Sure. And I reckon the Creator put radium in the world to heal the sick, not to make a few slickers rich."

Then, standing in the cabin doorway, with the sunlight sparkling on the swift river and, high in air, the glad bugles of migrating wild geese heralding the defeat of the long winter, old Scotty quickly outlined radium's gripping story. It was a splendid story, and a sordid one. It was the story of the Curies, like true scientists, enduring hardship and poverty to give their discovery to a suffering world, only to have a scheming European monopoly buy up all the known supply and cruelly exploit the sick who needed it. It was the story of how poor hospitals could not afford to give radium treatment to their patients. But it was also the story of the discovery, elsewhere here in the Canadian North, of more pitchblende which, in the hands of honest men, had

126

freed radium from the clutches of those Old World schemers.

"But even yet the fight's not won," Scotty pointed out. "The more pitchblende that's found, the cheaper radium becomes, and the more sick people can get well again. That's why I daren't lose an hour in getting my discovery to the Government. It's the only safe way." He looked anxiously from one young face to the other. "Well—how about it?"

Jimmy, who sometimes had the name of being reckless, found himself hesitating. This was a terrific secret for him and Dell to be trusted with. "Couldn't you just wait till Dad gets home?"

"They said they'd be back early this afternoon," Dell put in.

"And lose a day's traveling?" Abruptly Scotty laid a gnarled hand on the shoulder of each as he scanned their faces. "You two are in on this now. You wouldn't let old Scotty and all those sick folk down?" His voice was pleading.

And now Jimmy, like his more observant sister, sensed that all of Scotty's story had not yet been told. "You know we wouldn't, but—"

"All right, I'll tell you. Out alone so much in the bush, a fellow gets to imagining all sorts of things. But these last two days I had the feeling I was being followed."

Dell gasped. "You saw someone?"

Scotty shook his head. "Like I say it may all be in my imagination. But suppose some claim jumpers did find out what's in this ore sack? The whole secret would be out." Dell felt the hand on her shoulder tremble. "We want our find to belong to those who need it most, not just a gang of speculators, don't we?"

Even as Dell nodded, Jimmy was taking the paddles from the rack beside the door. "We'll take you across the river to the overland trail," he agreed. "Then we'll come straight back here and watch the cabin till Dad and Mum get home."

As soon as they had concealed the ore sack in the storeroom leading from the kitchen, the cabin door was padlocked and the canoe launched. From the eddy just below the ferry landing Felix, the crippled Canada goose Dell had been mothering all winter, swam out to meet them.

"C-r-o-nk!" the old fellow greeted. An hour ago Dell had scattered his breakfast of wild rice for him, but now, made restless by the distant voices of his kind who were winging northward to the tundras where he could not follow, Felix followed them in the wake of the canoe.

In the bow, Dell's lithe young body swung to her paddle strokes. With her fair hair held in the folds of a red kerchief and the fringes of her buckskin jacket tossing to the rhythm of every skillful flash and fall of her paddle blade, she made a lovely picture. Kneeling in the stern with Scotty seated amidships, Jimmy set an angling course across the broad, swift river. A mile downstream, beyond the trees on Cottonwood Island, the cliffs walling in the rapids stood warm and friendly in the sunlight.

Even with what he knew of the struggle to free radium for the use of all, the boy found it hard to believe that here, in his splendid North, he and his sister were being called upon to play a part in the long fight. Was it not that Scotty, agitated and overwrought by his great discovery, had merely imagined that he was being shadowed? Plots and violence had little part in the free, openhanded life of this vast and unspoiled land. But half an hour later, after they had seen old Scotty vanish up the overland trail abreast of Cottonwood Island, Jim was given sudden proof that he was wrong.

He and Dell were working the canoe upriver through the shoreline backwaters, and as they slipped past a narrow slough

128

where the budding willows formed a lattice across the entrance, Dell shot a look over her shoulder at him. Following her glance, he noted the sudden change that had come over the big gray goose, now swimming between them and the shore.

Felix's long neck had stiffened. Every line of his feathered body seemed taut with wariness. Then abruptly he sounded his warning call. It was the same call—vibrant, challenging—he had often given when as a wise old leader he had stood guard above his feeding flock. And the out-of-door boy and girl were quick to heed.

Only those well schooled in wilderness lore would have noted that willow twig broken in such a way that its lighter underside showed silver against the darker branches. Then, just behind, they could make out the low, unpainted shape of a dugout canoe.

But it was Felix who had first seen the stealthy movement of those two crouching forms, and as his primitive trumpet blared defiance, the paddles of the two Olsens bit the water in unison and shot the canoe ahead. Minute after minute in the short-clipped racing stroke they sped upriver, while Felix, paddling with both wings and feet, splashed in their wake.

Midway across the swirling river, Jimmy looked back. The strange canoe had not showed itself. Suddenly doubt smote him.

"Maybe I should go back and try to warn Scotty," he panted between strokes. "If they follow him on the overland trail—"

"No," Dell answered instantly. "They must have seen him start."

"You mean—"

"That it's the samples, not Scotty, they're after," Dell broke in.

Even after they were back in the cabin, Jimmy could see no other reason for the pair remaining at the river. Sliding back the window, he brought his father's binoculars and crouching with his head level with the sill, scanned the stretch of water between Cottonwood Island and the rapids.

"It may be hours before Dad and Mum get back," Dell reminded him.

It was very quiet in the cabin. Outside, in the spruces, a flock

129

of evening crossbeaks, gaudy and talkative as tiny parrots, chattered with disarming gaiety. Below, on the sunny side of their drawn-up canoe, old Felix stood and preened himself.

"If those two come here to get the ore samples, we couldn't stop them, could we?" Jimmy said at last.

Slowly Dell shook her head. "What's more, I think they will come."

Jimmy put away the binoculars and came to join her at the window. "If we went down this side and kept Cottonwood Island between us and the slough mouth, there's just a chance we could get to the portage before they saw us," he suggested.

"And take the ore samples to the post?"

"That's it. Our canoe's a lot faster than that old dugout. Even if they did see us leave, with the current helping us, we could beat them."

Dell considered. "Then I think we should try it," she decided.

A moment later, with the ore sack across his sturdy shoulders, Jimmy slid down the bank. Dell was launching the canoe and as they pushed off, Felix, with a sociable "Cr-onk," slipped into the water after them. Cutting the eddies, Jimmy steered into the full sweep of the current.

On their way downriver, neither spoke of the hazard ahead. But as Dell saw how trustfully Felix kept abreast of them, she found something fortifying in the loyalty of this wild creature they had befriended. Swept along by the current, it was only a matter of minutes before the upstream tip of Cottonwood Island came abreast of them. The slough mouth was out of sight behind it now. Half a mile ahead they could see the familiar portage trail and, just beyond, the black mouth of the canyon leading to the rapids.

Felix swam with his head well up, so close now that Dell could see his small, bright eyes. It gave her confidence to find him so alert. But as they were passing the island's lower end the two Olsens saw that even the wise old bird had been tricked. For as they came abreast of the last of the cottonwoods they saw the dugout canoe angling out to try to head them off.

"Hold on there, you two!" the man in the bow yelled at them.

Dorothy Bayley Morse

"Faster!" Jimmy whispered. "Head straight for the portage."

The light canoe leaped ahead and not until they were in full flight did Jimmy risk a backward look. What he saw steeled him to desperation. For, clumsy though the dugout looked, it was overtaking them and already had cut off any chance of their beating it to the portage.

Just ahead, with outstretched neck and striving wings, Felix too showed he knew it was too late to turn back. But instead of stopping, the great bird honked defiantly and headed boldly for the entrance to the rapids.

The dugout was closing now, but as Dell glimpsed the exultant face of the man in the bow she knew that, sooner than surrender Scotty's great secret, there was but one thing to do.

Sullen swirls, with here and there a vortex to give a hint of the whirlpools lurking between those high rock walls, broke the surface of the river. But though Jimmy and Dell Olsen knew that all but experienced canoemen portaged these rapids, they had no thought of turning back.

"We'll follow Felix!" Jimmy shouted as the blurring canyon walls loomed close ahead. Whatever happened, they would not betray their prospector friend's discovery to these schemers. Sufferers in years to come might never know it, but health would be theirs again because a Northland boy and girl had been loyal to their trust.

Then just ahead, Dell saw the wild goose lifted on the first tongue of white water marking the spouting V-wave from the canyon walls. Felix disappeared for a second, but when they themselves were into the smother they saw the bird again. His instinct seemed to tell him where the only safe channel lay, and, though the boom of water against the sheer walls seemed deafening, Jimmy fancied he could still hear that valiant old trumpet call. Drenching spray all but blinded them, the torn water seemed to want to wrench their paddles from their hands. The stout canoe bucked and sideslipped like a living thing, but with knees braced against its sides, they still rode the rapids. Then, abruptly as it had begun, the race ended, and they found themselves riding safely in the foamy pool below.

132

"Good old Felix," Dell was beginning, when a shout made them look up, and there was their father bounding down the rocks.

Behind him, on the portage trail, their mother stood pointing at something across the pool. Jimmy looked. There, behind him, their pursuers were clinging desperately to their battered and overturned dugout. Then it grounded in the shallows, and the two beaten men waded ashore and made off through the brush.

When their father had beckoned them down the pool to the foot of the portage trail where his own canoe was beached, the two young Olsens explained to their astounded parents the reason for Scotty's haste in reaching the mining recorder's office.

"He had good reasons to be in a hurry, too," their father declared when he stood up after closely examining the samples in the ore bag. "It's pitchblende all right." Even he seemed excited. "No wonder those two rascals wanted to get in on the secret. Why, this is the biggest discovery in years. And you two, because you weren't afraid and used your heads—"

A reassuring "C-r-onk," interrupted him as Felix, his long neck proudly arched, came swimming down the pool to join them.

Mrs. Olsen held her children close. "I think he's trying to say 'well done' to you two," she said.

Dell and Jimmy looked at each other soberly. Suppose, when the choice had come between facing the dangers they had encountered or of surrendering the secret which would bring radium's blessing to thousands, they had not lived up to Scotty's faith in them? But they had, and the wild creature they had befriended had helped them more than it could ever know.

"It's us who should be saying 'well done' to Felix, isn't it, Jimmy?" Dell suggested.

And Jimmy, the light of victory in his eyes, nodded happily.

133

L. R. Davis

WHY BOTHER
WITH LADDERS?

ILLUSTRATED BY *Bob Fink*

WHEN the bright towers of the Triborough
Bridge began to climb skyward, wiry Jim Burroughs signed up
for work. The first columns were tall and bare. They stood out
grimly against the black rock of the riverbank. Jim stood back,
and his black eyes looked up at the columns as they faced each
other across the whirling river. Erecting the towers would be
a real job. But after a year in the steel trade Jim wasn't looking
for crip jobs.

He got a break at once. The foreman said, "You're totin'
rivets for the Rivers Gang."

The Rivers Gang! Best gang in the city—and nerviest. Maybe
after they got to know him, they'd even make him one of the
gang. That would be *something*.

The first morning at work Chad Rivers sent Jim down for
some special pound-and-a-quarter bridge rivets. When Jim
came back, they began to drive them, and Jim had a chance to
watch in admiration. The rivets were long and heavy. But the
men handled them like carpet tacks. Chad strained at the
hammer, the muscles of his back taut as an alder bow. Chad's
left leg was stiff from an accident years ago; he kept himself
in position with his right. He looked awkward, but there was
nothing awkward about the way he handled the gun.

Jim's rapt gaze was passed on to the heater, a small Irishman
called Flaherty, who was so short that his shoulders hardly came
even with the forge. Chad's brother, Bill Rivers, was the

134

bucker-up; a thin, dry-looking Swede named Olafsen was the catcher.

The men kept the red-hot rivets flying between them. They worked as though one brain guided them all. As Chad turned on his gun, Bill silently leaned on the dolly bar. Olafsen and Flaherty passed their rivets without speaking. Words weren't necessary in the perfect organization of the Rivers Gang.

Steel rang, and the big shaking hammer beat out a war dance. Jim grinned at the noise and the heat. There was excitement and fire and skill in the work of these men. More than he had ever wanted anything in his life, Jim wanted to be one of them.

At the end of three months' work it looked as though Jim were going to have his chance. The winter was warm and wet and unhealthy. One day Chad came to work with a long face. Olafsen was in bed with pneumonia.

"Can you catch?" Chad asked Jim.

"You bet!" Jim answered. He hadn't practiced during all those lunch hours for nothing.

"Okay. Hop to it," Chad said. "But when Olafsen gets well you go back to totin' rivets."

Jim picked up the battered can with big, eager fingers. He'd show them he could catch.

Flaherty turned his blower handle and fanned his coals. When the rivets gleamed with heat, he grabbed one with his tongs. "Ready?" he shouted to Jim.

"Let 'er go!" Ready? Jim had never been readier in his life. Catching hot steel was what he was made for. Catching with the Rivers Gang.

The first rivet plunked in his can. He lifted it out for Chad to drive. Confidence swept over Jim. He was as good at catching as he was at climbing, and he knew it.

The first day ended successfully. So did the second. On the third Chad came to work with his mouth set like a double steel brace. "Olafsen's washed up," he said. "He's through. The doctor says he'll live, but there's no more riveting for him. Foreman says he'll give him a job as a timekeeper."

Jim's heart pounded. Poor Olafsen was through. But Jim

135

couldn't help thinking about the job. Whom would they take on as a permanent catcher of their gang? He looked up to ask, and the words died on his lips. The other men had forgotten that Jim existed. Little Flaherty was crying openly. Chad's steely mouth was harder than ever, and Bill's gray eyes traveled out over the river for comfort he couldn't find.

Jim put his hands in his pockets and moved off. In time they would make him a member of the gang.

But February eased in March and nobody mentioned Jim's becoming a member of the gang. Once Jim spoke of it to Chad. Chad cut him short. "When we want a new member in this gang," he said, "we ask him. This is a racket where you can't make mistakes." He nodded at the gun and forge and dolly bar. "You can't just guess about the man who's going to handle these trinkets day in and day out."

Jim had nothing more to say. Anybody could see that one slip in riveting might be fatal. If the catcher missed the rivet, it would strike the gunman. If the gunman were careless, he would blow the bucker-up to kingdom come. Their lives were interwoven like the strands of a basket.

Each day Jim went to work feeling more discouraged. He was doing riveter's work, and he wasn't being paid for it. He wasn't even laying any foundation for another job. Men were hired and fired by gangs. Unless Chad and the others recognized him as one of themselves by time to sign up on a new structure, he'd have to begin all over again as a rivet boy.

But it wasn't just the pay. The men apparently still considered him a rivet boy. They were the kings of their trade, and they didn't know he was on earth.

Jim felt a lump in his throat as he hadn't felt one since he was about six. He didn't want them to make a fuss over him; he just wanted to be one of the crowd. To shove his clothes in the same locker box in the morning, to walk home with them at night, to work with the proud knowledge that they trusted him as they trusted one another. But they ignored him.

Then Jim got his idea. What they wanted was a demonstration. They knew he could catch rivets and climb around a bit,

136

but how'd they know he had more than ordinary nerve? Nonchalance in high places wasn't enough—that was just the job.

Between rivets, Jim hitched up his trousers, and for the first time in days a broad grin settled down between his ears. He'd show them. Danger was his meat. Didn't he want to belong to the Rivers Gang mainly because it was known all over that they took jobs other gangs were afraid to tackle?

He waited until they were ready to go home. At five o'clock the three men crowded around the ladder on Flaherty's platform to go down.

Jim flapped one of the platform ropes over a beam and down the outside of the building. He would beat them to the next floor by sliding down the rope. It was a trick to make anyone take notice.

Jim looked down at the rocks and the river far below. If his hands slipped—if he lost his balance for just a fraction of a second— But Jim didn't hesitate. He'd show them something new. They couldn't ignore him forever.

"Coming down?" Chad Rivers asked.

Jim's heart thumped. Now was his moment. "That way's too slow," Jim said. "Why bother with ladders?"

He let himself over the side!

He heard Chad call out, and the high Irish voice of Flaherty. But he went on, letting himself down hand over hand. Confidence returned. He'd show them!

Finally the red beams of the floor below came up. Gingerly he reached for the welcome steel with his toes and swung free of the rope.

Jim turned and walked the narrow beam to the center of the building where the men were coming down the ladder. One false footstep and he'd be gone, but he wasn't thinking about false footsteps. He was thinking about the other men and what they'd say to him. Jim swaggered down toward the center of the building to meet them.

He went quite close to them, waiting for someone to speak. Then slowly it dawned on him that none of them thought it was nearly as bright as he did himself.

"What's the point?" Bill Rivers asked disgustedly. "You're supposed to be a riveter—not a gorilla."

Jim looked at Chad. Surely *he* would recognize a good show. But Chad said, "That kind of nerve's not worth a hang. Kid stuff. You got some growing up to do before we'll trust you with our necks, fellow."

"I'm safe as any of you lugs!" Jim flared.

"Sure," Chad answered, "when the going's soft. But when trouble comes, the show-offs are usually the first to dog it."

The men walked down the stairs, and Jim fell in silently behind them. The future, which had been so bright, now spread out bleakly before him. He was just a substitute holding down the position 'til a varsity man came along.

The next day was cold and raw, with a taste of rain in the air. Jim turned up his collar and went up the stairs and ladders to the top of the building. All the hope and enthusiasm that had kept him going these past months was no longer with him. Work was work now, and nothing more.

The morning was gusty, and the wettish wind made the steel beams treacherous. Jim looked up. The derrick hands were not

138

working. He shrugged his shoulders. But he didn't blame anyone for not working when the steel was slippery as black ice.

By eleven o'clock all the other riveting gangs on the tower had quit work. By twelve it was drizzling steadily, and the beams and girders were wicked. Jim looked at Chad. Any steel worker knew that you couldn't drive rivets in the rain. Rain wasn't just dangerous on the top of a skyscraper. It was suicidal.

But their part of the building was behind, and this was a good chance to catch up. Chad kept them at it.

Once they stopped to gulp down coffee and eat their soggy sandwiches while huddled around Flaherty's forge. "You going on working?" Jim asked.

"How about it?" Chad came back. "Does the trick rope climber want to quit?"

Jim's neck and face got an angry red. He started back to his platform. Suddenly he felt his left heel slipping, but he caught himself and plunged to safety on the wooden platform.

Jim's heart pumped in his throat. For the first time he knew what it was like to be petrified with fear.

"Don't cross," he yelled hoarsely at the others. "It's terrible!"

The others looked at one another, then crossed without speaking. Jim fumbled for his catcher's can. He had lost his nerve. And the rest of the gang knew it. There was nothing to do but finish the day and quit for good.

The afternoon darkened, but they stayed at work. The drizzle turned to rain, and the wind stiffened. Nobody tried to speak against the volleying of the gun. When Flaherty was ready to throw a rivet, he beat on the side of his stove with the tongs.

Once they stopped for a moment, and Jim realized for the first time that he was shaking. Drenched with sweat, his head reeling, Jim gripped his can and tried not to look at rocks and the river far down there below him.

As they worked, the wind grew stronger, until it seemed to blow directly on Jim's raw nerves. His cap blew off and whirled down sickeningly, until it disappeared in the river.

Jim caught a rivet mechanically and lifted it out with shaking tongs. He hardly knew what he was doing.

139

Suddenly there was a shriek of pain. Bill Rivers began to swear! "You blasted fool!" he shouted. "Look where you're working!"

Jim understood, then, what had happened—he had burned Bill with the rivet! There was a searing line deep through Bill's thick leather glove. He knew Bill was thinking that he wasn't to be trusted, and that when he lost his nerve he went to pieces.

Before they had time to speak, a tornado-like gust of wind shook the very columns. A sudden clap echoed through the skeleton building. The ladder! The long wooden ladder had blown backwards to the floor below.

"The ladder!" Flaherty shrieked.

Chad dropped on all fours and started across to Flaherty's platform. It was still possible to crawl where you couldn't walk. He inched himself forward with hands and thighs. When he got to the platform, he looked for Bill, ignoring Jim. "All right?" he bellowed.

Bill nodded and moved himself along the beam, wincing when he had to touch the steel with his pain-seared hand.

Jim followed behind him. The dread ring of fear was around his heart, and with it a deep hopelessness. He'd lost his nerve in a pinch and he'd hurt one of the gang. He was through.

By the time they were on the platform Flaherty was wild. He moved around the boards like a banshee. "We're licked! I tell you, we're licked! With this wind growing we'll be blown to kingdom come before morning."

Jim said nothing. Slowly in the back of his mind he realized what he had to do. Somehow he had to get down to the floor below *without* a ladder. Chad, with his stiff leg, couldn't. Flaherty was too short to grip the steel. Bill had a burned hand.

"I'll get down," he told the others. He felt the tastelessness of rain against his lips. He hardly heard what they said. Inside he was frozen with fear.

"You'll never make it!" Chad said.

Jim shook his head. "Tie the rope around my waist. I'm going down the column."

Chad hesitated, looking toward the river. In another hour

the platform would be impossible. If they didn't get off soon they might all die.

"Hurry up!" Jim said. Chad hurried.

Jim kicked off his heavy shoes and moved to the edge of the building. He knew better than to look down.

He twisted his legs around the column and began to lower himself. Inch by inch he moved down the column. His toes fought for footholds on the rivet heads, and his arms hugged the column in a frozen grip.

He felt the skin of his water-soaked hands tear painfully. The wind battered his stocking feet against the steel. The inside of his arms and legs scraped against the rough column.

The wind bore down against his back and pinned him to the column. If it shifted for as much as one second he'd be flipped off into space.

Down, down, down. Perilous inch by inch. He could see the upward sweep of the other tower. "Keep looking up!" he told himself. But it was unnecessary, now. He wasn't afraid any more. Just tired. Like a drowning man who wants nothing but to let go.

Suddenly his toe stubbed against the crossbeam, and Jim knew that he was down. He heard the men shout, but their voices were dulled by the wind. He lowered himself so that he straddled the crossbar. Jerking himself free of the rope, he began to move inch by inch toward the platform.

Slowly, carefully, he fought against the wind and the slippery steel. Finally the platform was just ahead. He pulled himself up on it.

Reeling as the full impact of the wind blew against him, he stood up. He plunged forward and managed to reach the ladder.

He tugged and lifted it, still fighting the enemy wind. The ladder wavered, then was upright. He let it drop against the side of Flaherty's platform. The men lashed it with rope. Then they began to come down.

By the time they reached the platform, Jim was sitting dumbly, holding his bleeding hands.

"Boy, you're all right!" Flaherty's voice pierced the wind.

"Ain't he got nerve?" Bill said.

Chad agreed. "He's the genuine article," he said. "To lose his nerve and then pull a stunt like that!"

"You didn't have to go after that ladder, you know. I've never asked a member of my gang to do anything I wouldn't do myself."

Jim came to life. "A member of your gang, did you say?"

Chad nodded. "Sure," he said. "Once we find a guy like you, you don't suppose we'd let him go, do you? You've got to try a man, and try him again, and see him get scared, and see him get unscared. And if he still clicks, you know he's your man."

The blood thumped into Jim's head.

"Then I'm on the gang—for good?"

"You bet you're on!" Bill broke in, with his burned hand thrust deep into his wet jacket. "You're on as long as any one of us can throw a rivet."

A POWER–PLANT

Harriet Monroe

The invisible wheels go softly round and round—
Light is the tread of brazen-footed Power.
Spirits of air, caged in the iron tower,
Sing as they labor with a purring sound.
The abysmal fires, grated and chained and bound,
Burn white and still, in swift obedience cower;
While far and wide the myriad lamps, aflower,
Glow like star-gardens and the night confound.
This we have done for thee, almighty Lord;
Yea, even as they who built at thy command
The pillared temple, or in marble made
Thine image, or who sang thy deathless word.
We take the weapons of thy dread right hand,
And wield them in thy service, unafraid.

William Heyliger

STEELMAN'S NERVE

ILLUSTRATED BY *John Merryweather*

URNING pressure had been put on the twelve-story, steel-construction apartment that the All-Continental Contractors were erecting in the Bronx, in New York City. There was a penalty clause in the contract, and the job was days behind. Snow and ice, forty-mile winds and delayed deliveries from the fabricating plant had helped to hamper operations. And now Mike Peace, the erecting foreman, and Bill Dykes, his young timekeeper, seven months out of engineering school, were fighting to regain that time.

"Fourteen days late," Mike Peace said bitterly.

Bill Dykes wrote figures on a report sheet. "What's the penalty?"

"Three hundred a day. Forty-two hundred so far."

"But it's not your fault," Bill protested. "The breaks have gone against you. The railroads lost one shipment and took a week to find it; another shipment—ten gondolas of steel—got stalled in a blizzard."

"Breaks go with the job," said Mike. "A foreman isn't supposed to throw away $4200 of the company's money." He glowered at the January sky, and his thin, brown jaws clamped wickedly on a quid of tobacco. A rivet-jack at sixteen, carrying drinking water, coke, and rivets to the riveting gangs, the man had practically cut his eyeteeth on steel. At sixty he was still as tough, as leathery, as indomitable a tiger as the day, twenty years earlier, a brawling ironworker had smashed at his face with a spud wrench. They had carted Mike Peace to the hos-

144

pital. And ten years later he had caught up with that iron-worker on a Mississippi river bridge job.

"Any chance for a heater?" a voice had asked.

Mike Peace, recognizing that voice, had spun around. "I can always use a good heater, but not until I've handed you what's coming." The scar on his right cheekbone would always be ghastly, livid. But that day on the Mississippi he washed the memory of it from his mind with his fists.

"We've gained a day on the lost time," said Bill.

The foreman grunted. "There's plenty of winter left. Tell Larsen to see me at noon."

"Right," said Bill. His voice had subtly changed.

Mike Peace walked to the office shanty door. He had been watching Bill for weeks and he knew. One of those men who grew giddy and sick when you took them off the ground. Mike had seen them before. Sometimes it was a young river jack on his first job, shaking with a palsy of dread. Sometimes a sure-footed, oldtimer who fell, and lived, and could never again force himself to go up. Sometimes—Well, sometimes a man beat it.

A chair scraped slowly on the shanty floor. Mike knew what he would see if he looked back—a mouth with pinched lines and a face bleak with tell-tale pallor. His voice was harsh when he spoke.

"You're an engineer."

"Yes," said Bill.

"How's an engineer going to stay in steel? You whip it or it whips you. Tell Larsen."

Larsen was a pusher with the riveting gangs. He had come to steel construction from a sailing ship as has so many another man; and these ex-sailors, at home among the spars and ratlines of a heaving ship, are the surest-footed of all. A big-boned man, Larsen, lean and sinewy, with a careless contempt for height. Twice Bill, as part of his work of keeping peace on the job, had had to arbitrate heated rows between Larsen and the riveting gangs he drove hard. One of his decisions had gone against Larsen. Larsen didn't like him.

145

He crossed the yard. The compressor thundered; he stepped over the airline and began to climb. At first there were stairs with a temporary strip of guard-rail, then open stairs without a rail. Carpenters had not yet carried stairs beyond the third tier—the sixth floor. He climbed a steep, perpendicular ladder. All that was solid in the world fell away, and he climbed higher through a gaunt, open skeleton of floorless columns, beams, trusses, and stringers. One false step— Why did he always have to keep thinking of that?

Loose planks had been thrown across beams at the ladder head. He stepped upon the planks, and all around him was a yawning void spaced thinly by threads of steel. There was nothing over him but the sky, and a hundred-foot drop if he fell. "Larsen!" he shouted.

Larsen and a rivet gang were at a sheer end of the building driving rivets into a column. The heater, his forge on a platform, took a red rivet from the coals and swung his tongs. The smoking rivet curved through the air and clanged into the can of the catcher. The catcher lifted it out with his pickup and held it down to a hole. The rivet hammer broke into a deafening *rat-tat-tat*.

The din died and Bill shouted again: "Larsen!"

The pusher looked up.

"See Mike at noon."

"What?"

"See Mike at noon."

"Can't hear you."

Bill thought: "He's lying. He's going to make me walk out."

Walking out meant he'd have to walk an *I*-beam. His armpits were all at once cold and clammy with sweat. He'd done it before, he told himself desperately. Mike had said: "Whip it or be whipped." Why, as a boy he'd tightrope walked the thin tops of crooked, back-yard fences. An *I*-beam was wider than his shoe—perhaps ten times as wide as a fence top. He swallowed a lump in his throat and stepped out upon the beam.

Don't look down, don't look down! But a frightful fascination made him steal a look. The high compressor had flattened

146

out to the size of a stub of pencil, and a man crossing the yard seemed a small, squat dot. He fought a swimming giddiness. The planks on which the catcher stood appeared to come toward him in harsh jerks. Larsen gave him a sidelong glance. The pusher, scorning the platform, was a cool, unconcerned figure against the sky as he watched the riveters from the narrow edge of an outside beam.

"A little faster with those rivets," he snapped.

The man at the forge shrugged and pumped the bellows. You can't hurry a rivet. It must be lifted out of the fire at the exact moment when it is the exact shade of cherry-red. A rivet not hot enough won't hammer home and a rivet overheated turns brittle. A pusher with the riveting gangs must know just how hard he dare drive.

Larsen came half a dozen light steps along the beam. Bill envied him. "Spit it," the pusher said.

"Mike wants to see you at noon," explained Bill.

"O.K. Nice view from here. Wait until we get up to the sixth tier. You'll like that." His eyes were bland.

Bill came away. Funny, the going back never bothered him —much. It was the first stepping out, with open space on either side and appalling depth below. The rivet hammer was momentarily silent, and voices followed him. "Did you see his face?" Larsen laughed. "No guts."

"I don't know," said the man with the rivet hammer. "It takes guts for a guy to walk a beam when he's scared."

"He won't stay in this game," said Larsen.

Bill's face was hot. When the gangs began to say that of a man— Not that they'd say it in malice as Larsen said it, for your ironworker holds a sort of rough pity for the man who can't go up. He knows what it is. But when the gangs began to talk about a man, that man was marked.

He was back on the platform at the head of the ladder. Larsen was probably watching him. Deliberately, with his heart in his throat, he forced himself to walk another beam toward an angle edge of the building and the bell ringer's platform. The bell ringer was the man who, watching from the edge

where he could see the ground, the hooker-on, and every perpendicular foot of the skeleton structure, rang the bells that
controlled all derrick movements. A set of push buttons was
strapped around the man's waist and wires trailed from him.
He had to have a platform. It would be suicide to walk a beam
with wires dangling from the waist. Even on the platform a
man might be tripped—and—Bill swallowed another lump. This
thing was getting him.

"Larsen's pushing them," said the bell ringer.

Bill nodded and walked to the edge. Strangely, looking down
now didn't freeze and pinch his stomach. It wasn't height; it
was the nothingness all around him when his feet were on that
thread of beam. If he couldn't beat that— He walked back to
the ladder.

Mike Peace had watched through a shanty window. He could
have told you unerringly the why of everything that happened
on the job. He could have told why Bill had walked out across
that first beam.

"Larsen going deaf?" he asked.

"It's hard to hear with a rivet hammer going," said Bill
casually.

A thought ran through old Mike's mind. Game! His face was
expressionless, and his thin jaws worked on their cargo of tobacco. If Bill had been his son he'd have sent him up just the
same. Not through callousness or indifference, but because of
the hard necessity of the job. That's steel. A man can take it or
he can't. If he can't take it, he's through.

Larsen came into the shanty at noon. "Did you want me,
Mike?"

"We've picked up a day," said Mike. "Lots more to pick."

"I'm a pusher," Larsen told him. "You just give me the word."

"They're being pushed hard now. Can they stand more?
We're getting rigid inspection on this job."

"I've been on rigid-inspection jobs before," Larsen said con-
fidently. He sat out in the sun, on a pile of re-enforcement rods
for the arches, and ate out of a dinner pail.

Bill had no appetite. Whip it or be whipped! He didn't want

148

to be whipped. Steel was his game. Was he always going to be like this, trembling with reaction even after he came off a beam? If he were, he thought bitterly, he might just as well— He threw coal in the stove, went back to his chair and stared out at the yard through the window above his desk.

Danger? Sure; he'd known that while still in college. There was always danger on a steel job. Painters took a one-hand hold, leaned out into blood-chilling space, and daubed the under side of a beam. Connectors balanced themselves on the dizzy end of a column and guided a girder being boomed into position. A hooker-on could pick up a light stringer in his arms and walk with it eight hundred feet in the air. Steelmen did these things all over the world every day. It wasn't a trick—it was the job. What had happened to him? Why was he air-shy? What was wrong with him, anyway?

"I'm thinking about it too much," he decided.

But he hadn't been thinking fear at all the first day fear had made him weak and flabby. The whole world turned bleak.

149

Compressors and rivet hammers made a din through the afternoon. The derrick lifted steel from the ground and, with a tag-line man guiding the load away from the two walls that formed an angle of the building, boomed up its cargo.

In one of the rare moments of quiet a little, gray man came from the building. He was one of those little, gray men who, seemingly, never grow old—slim, active, agile. Here was the person who make this a tough-inspection job. His name was Frank Hall, and he came from the offices of the architect who had drawn the plans for the building. He stopped at the shanty.

"Mike," he said crisply, "Larsen's pushing the riveting gangs a little too hard to suit me."

Mike Peace looked at him sharply. "You haven't found much to condemn, have you?"

"Not yet."

"Larsen knows his job."

"I hope so. I'd hate to rub it up your back."

Old Mike was worried. He had demanded of Larsen "Can they stand it?" and now the inspector was expressing a doubt. Condemned rivets meant rivets to be burned out and new rivets to be driven home. Condemned work meant lost time.

"Better give Larsen a hint, Bill," the foreman said in an undertone, and followed Hall toward the gate. Hall was a man whom it was wise to placate. Sometimes an inspector had to make hairline decisions that could go either way, and if you hadn't rubbed him the wrong way you might get a break.

Again Bill climbed stairs and ladder and felt his lips twitching. This time the pusher was with a gang so near the ladder platform that there was no need to walk a beam. "Hall thinks those rivets are going in too fast," Bill said.

"So what?" Larsen jeered.

"You know what that means?"

"Sure. He'll strain his eyes to make inspection a little tougher. So what?" The rivet hammer, with Bill's appearance, had become silent. Larsen swung around. "What's the matter with you guys, going to sleep?" The hammer volleyed its strident, metallic *rat-tat-tat*.

150

The yard cleared at quitting time, and Bill worked on, completing the timekeeping records. The skeleton structure leered at him in the fading light of the January day. "Whip me!" it challenged. His throat was dry.

Next day before noon Frank Hall appeared from the building and came toward the shanty. There was something decisive in the little gray man's stride. All at once Bill was apprehensive.

"Where's Mike?" the inspector demanded.

"Just stepped out," said Bill.

"I warned him about Larsen. I've put the mark on one hundred and ten bad rivets. God knows how many more I'll find this afternoon. Tell Mike."

Bill was staggered. "That's impossible. We don't average one hundred and ten in—"

"You did this time," Hall snapped with finality, and was gone. The noon whistle blew.

Ironworkers came down out of the building like flies. A woman pushed a hand-wagon in through the gate and began to sell fruit, sandwiches, bottled milk, and pie. Bill caught Larsen and some of his riveters on the ground.

"What about those rivets?"

"Where does this Hall think he gets off?" Larsen snarled.

"Where are we going to get off? He said he's X-ed one hundred and ten so far."

"Is it my fault I have gangs that handle rivets as though they were cripples and let them cool in the pickup?"

"Don't try to pin this on us," a riveter cried angrily. "I told you those rivets were too cold. You can't push a rivet in the forge. You've got to give it time."

Bill looked at Larsen.

"What are you trying to do?" the pusher shouted. "Give me the bird? I don't take guff from no white-livered punk whose knees knock together every time he walks a beam. Where do you get off to tell me anything? Go get some guts first. I'll talk to Mike."

Bill's face was white. What answer, he thought miserably, could he give to the truth? Eyes avoided his. Whatever the

151

riveters might be thinking, they gave no sign. This wasn't their affair—this was something between a pusher and a timekeeper. Somebody pulled the top off a dinner pail and the sound seemed explosive.

Bill walked toward the building. He was cold as he climbed the ladder—cold with despair. And he wanted so much to stay with steel! From the platform he looked around the job. Chalk-marked white X's were on rivets everywhere. He shook his head and came down, and went back to the shanty and waited for Mike Peace.

The foreman returned from the restaurant. Suddenly, in the yard, his steps quickened. "I can smell trouble," he said harshly. "It's in the air. What's happened?"

Bill told him.

Mike went into a rage. Bill had heard him swear before, but never like this. He was a man whipped by fury, and in a fury he catapulted from the shanty. He lashed out at Larsen and the riveters, and they appeared to shrink. Fury carried him up through the building and down. He stood before Larsen again, and before his wrath the pusher quailed. The riveters edged away. This was Tiger Mike Peace on a rampage. He stamped into the shanty and passed Bill without a word and went around the partition to the blueprint room. A rolled print stood on a high desk. Mike poured forth a sulphuric stream of profanity and hurled the print to the floor.

Bill kept out of his way—this was a Mike Peace it was wise to sidestep. Frank Hall came back through the gate, old Mike joined him, talking vehemently, and together they went up through the building. This afternoon no riveter was being pushed against time. The mad *rat-tat-tat* of the hammers was not quite so mad. Sparks began to shoot from points on the fourth tier as the burners torched out the condemned rivets.

Mike and Hall were in the yard again, and now the inspector was doing the talking, stabbing an emphatic forefinger against the foreman's chest. Bill passed them on his way up to the working-floor to check steel. The derrick cable hung still at the moment. The weight-ball was above him, the cable almost in

152

front of his nose, the hook almost at his feet. He saw Mike Peace and Hall walk toward the street.

"She's popping today," the bell ringer said. "Mike's tearing the job apart."

Bill nodded absently. Why was it height here brought no nausea, no sick giddiness? Below him a rivet gang had a planked platform at the sheer edge, and Larsen was with them. The burners had finished, and new rivets were going in. The cement men were preparing to pour goulash for the eight floor arches; the supporting joists the carpenters had set in place—joists of thin, broad pine, regularly spaced—stuck out from the building like close, ragged teeth. The riveter was talking to Larsen; the hammer was across his arm, silent. The compressor, having built up necessary pressure, was silent, too. Peace had a brooding moment, and it was hard to believe that this could be a job splashed thickly with danger.

The heater tossed a glowing rivet. Bill marveled. Here was a control that made a baseball pitcher's control laughable. A heater might throw five hundred rivets and not throw two of them wild. The catcher held the hot rivet to the hole, and the hammer began to pound.

And then, suddenly, peace was gone.

With a roaring hiss the airline came away from the hammer. Bill heard an inarticulate yell, and the rivet gang was leaping from the platform for safety. Like a destroying demon the free hose slashed right and left, leaping and sweeping around. It struck Larsen a glancing blow. The foreman made a frantic, clutching effort to save himself, tottered toward the edge, fell— Bill cried out and closed his eyes.

When he opened them the airline hung between two beams writhing madly and hissing. Larsen had rolled off the building, but not to death. Not yet. There he hung, five feet out from the wall, one hundred feet above the ground, his clothing miraculously caught on the end of a joist.

Bill sweated with horror. The man dared not move, lest movement tear his clothing away. As it was, the thin joist, never intended to hold 170 pounds at its end, might break at any

153

moment. Riveters were back on the floor, but they could not go out to him. The joist would snap at once under the weight of two. And it was only a question of minutes, at most, before wood broke under the strain or clothing tore loose.

Larsen looked up, and his face was something Bill would remember all his life. The eyes protruded, and the lips were drawn back in a ghastly grimace. This was terror, stark and stripped.

What Bill did then was done instinctively. There was no time to think. The derrick-cable was close. He reached out, caught it, got a hand grip. His foot found the hook and the cable swung away from the floor.

"Down!" he cried.

The bell ringer was a veteran who had touched steel at many points. Constant danger sharpens men to danger. His hand, steady, went to a button at his waist.

Bill swung there, an atom in space. Nothing above him and death below. Larsen's eyes rolled up to him and stayed there. The pusher's lips moved. Bill heard only the awful silence that had fallen over the job, but he read Larsen's lips. "Hurry!"

The boom swung out at a crawl and the cable began to go down. Bill prayed. Hurry! If he started to swing at the cable's end, if he knocked Larsen off— But the weight-ball held him almost steady. Down and down. He slid a little past the joist

154

and signalled with his free hand. Boom in. He found himself moved closer. A little more. Now to the right. Dimly he was conscious of white faces staring up from the ground.

"Can you hear me, Larsen?"

The pusher whispered. "Yes."

"Go easy or we'll both go down. Get a grip on the cable."

Larsen, sailor-bred, called upon an iron nerve. Slowly a hand came out. Any movement might tear him loose. The hand found the cable. The cable trembled almost imperceptibly.

"I've got to get a grip on you," Bill panted. "I'll take you under the arms. As soon as I get you, you get a grip on me. Slowly." Was it imagination, or had he heard the joist cracking? "We've got to stay on balance."

His arm stole around the pusher. Slowly, oh, so cruelly slow, his arm tightened. They'd have to hug together with all the strength they had.

"Now—Larsen."

Again that slow, that agonizingly slow movement of an arm. This time Larsen's arm. His face was a mask of white. If the cable swung out a little, as little as four or five inches—Bill dared not think of that. Larsen had to think of it.

"Now!" the pusher whispered.

Bill, with no hand free to signal, shouted. After long years of waiting the boom took them out. Slowly. The joist bent and, with a *ziiiip*, clothing tore loose. And now two human atoms clung together in space.

In that moment crushing weight dragged at Bill. Larsen could not put a foot in the hook; Larsen could not, dared not, try to move. Cling and strain. The man was all weight. Dead weight. Torture tore through Bill's tendons and muscles. His grip on the cable slipped an inch and Larsen's grip on him became a grip on life.

"Don't let go," the pusher gasped. "It's only a minute. If one goes, we both go."

A minute? It was centuries. Weren't they ever going to go down? But they were slipping down. The third tier was gone. The hook became a torturing knife pushing its way up through

155

Bill's foot to his knee. Larsen had him gripped where it caught his chest. His breath began to whistle through his nostrils and for one black moment his senses reeled. He opened his mouth and sucked in air. The dead weight was tearing him loose. He couldn't hold on much longer. His grip crushed the harsh cable into his palm.

How much longer *could* he stand it? His hand slipped again, and unheeded blood trickled down his wrist. Voices were reaching him, confused voices like the voices of madmen. It was no use. He was slipping, slipping— Arms were around him, arms held him, the world was a sea of faces. Why, they were on the ground! He saw Larsen slide forward and lie still. He staggered against a trailer truck, leaned against it weakly, and was sick.

Mike Peace burst through the crowd and had him by the shoulders. "Bill!" At that moment Tiger Mike Peace owned a voice that shook. "Are you all right, boy?"

Bill couldn't answer. The wave of sickness passed and he looked up in a sort of awe at the building. The bell ringer was leaning out from the working-floor of the derrick, a pigmy shape against the sky. So he had come all the way down from there with one hand gripped to a cable, and one foot in a hook, and a man in his arm. He stared up steadily at the height.

"Are you all right, Bill?" Old Mike bent close.

"Swell," said Bill. That's how he meant it—swell. He'd never be afraid again.

Larsen had come out of his faint and was on his feet. He wobbled and was steady. Iron-nerved. A steelman. "That was close," he said thickly.

Somebody laughed loudly. "No guts."

It wasn't a taunt. It was the reaction of strong men who had seen death cheated. But Larsen stiffened.

"Who said that about Bill Dykes? I'll make him eat it."

The same voice answered. "You said it yourself, Swede."

There was a moment of silence.

"I'm eating it," said Larsen. He looked across at Bill, a time-keeper who wanted to stay with steel, and his soul was in his eyes. "Kid, you're a man."

157

Mary Hastings Bradley

GORILLAS AND LIONS!

ILLUSTRATED BY *Rod Ruth*

OUR objective was a tiny triangle in the heart of Africa. It was bounded by three volcanic mountains and was a high plateau of bamboo forest, eternally cold, eternally clouded, eternally rainy.

It was there that Mr. Akeley was going to find gorillas for a group for the American Museum of Natural History of New York, and we were going with Mr. Akeley because we wanted to see Africa, as well as gorillas, and the way to this triangle was through one of the loveliest and least known parts of the continent, the Eastern Congo. No Americans had yet been in the country to which we were going. . . .

I know that Africa first touched my imagination when my great-grandfather read aloud to me his favorite book, Stanley's *In Darkest Africa.* I received then a vivid intimation of Africa's mysterious spell, stirring pictures of a vast continent peopled with savages, of feverish jungles and mighty rivers, of treacherous beauty and swift death, of a primitive barbarism that had been going on from the beginning of time, unchanged and unchanging, living its own life through the centuries unknown and untouched by trade or civilization. . . .

Mr. Bradley and I were taking our five-year-old daughter,

Alice, with us. But it wasn't as mad as it sounded. Mr. Akeley's experience would not burden the expedition with a child unless it were both safe and feasible. We were going into a healthy region, up from the Cape through the Belgian Congo to Lake Kivu, along the mountainous backbone of Africa, where, although almost under the equator, the altitude would insure cool nights and pleasant days. . . .

Once the decision was made, the matter of outfit was upon us. Tents, camp equipment, and "chop" boxes of food were ordered by Mr. Akeley from London firms to be ready for shipment when we arrived; the various cameras—motion picture, plate and film—and the developing apparatus were all collected here by Mr. Akeley, and the guns were arranged for here. My husband and I each had rebuilt Springfield rifles, 30-30, with hard and soft nose ammunition, and in addition my husband had a .475 Jeffery. . . .

We outfitted in Chicago during a spell of July weather that made us wonder weakly why on earth we were trying to get any nearer the equator anyway; we packed, with the valiant assistance of friends, complicated trunks for hold and baggage room and stateroom—with the inevitable after-panic lest the gold slippers be in the hold and hunting trousers appear in the stateroom!—we bade farewells that savored almost of the eternal and turned our backs upon home and family and friends and the familiar perils of civilization. . . .

[ONCE IN AFRICA Mrs. Bradley with her husband, Herbert, and several friends started on the trail of the gorillas. For several days they were unable to find any sign of them.]

We had intended starting again on Monday, but a runner from Mr. Akeley caused us to change our plans. He wrote that he was ill, that he had "broken something." So, on Monday, Herbert, and Martha Miller, and I and sixty porters started up the mountain to his camp, leaving Alice and Priscilla Hall in the White Sisters' house. It was a great comfort to have them there, where the untiring, kind Fathers did everything possible for them.

159

Mr. Akeley had written that we had better take two days to the trip as only veterans might make it in one, but we felt decidedly veteranish by now, and, as his letter made us anxious, determined to get through at all cost. We had not gone more than three hours before we came up with the porters opening their loads with unusual alacrity; the cook was busy spreading out his magnificent red mattress which constituted an entire porter's load.

This was in a damp glade on the mountainside, and the march we had made was not a day's work, so I—being ahead—told them to go on with all the vehemence and Swahili I possessed. *"Pana mazuri hapa"* (not good here) was repeated vigorously until they got up and hoisted their loads upon their heads. They didn't really hope to put it over, the headmen had been told at the Mission they were to go all the way, but they considered it decidedly worth trying.

Later I was to hear that *Pana mazuri* flung back at me by a half a hundred of them as they slipped and sloshed and scrambled up that mountain's sides.

We had thought we could go up in six hours. It took us nine. The last six hours were a steady, interminable climb, up through the forest, into the bamboos, through the bamboos into a higher forest again. The path was the same sort of mud chute that Herbert and I had climbed before, and we had to cling to the trees at the side for leverage.

I understood then why soldiers at the Front had thrown away rations, water, ammunition. Sometimes every step seemed literally the last possible effort. The altitude had its effect, of course, in conjunction with the continual struggle.

There were times, about the sixth hour, when we found cheer in song, peculiarly suitable songs such as "There's a long, long trail a-winding," and "Smile, smile, smile," but after that our breath gave out and we saved it for such valuable speech as "Rest here—we can take the day to it."

But our spirits did not flag. When Herbert, following our steps and watching us, chuckled at the load of mud that went up and down with each foot and announced that we wouldn't

160

do for fairy-footed partners at a dance, we looked at his own weighted feet and assured him of his complete unsuitability.

At intervals he cheered us on by telling us we were going to be the only women in the world who had seen wild gorillas. We retorted that we hoped they'd appreciate the trouble we were taking, and if a wild gorilla would only appear and perform that much advertised act of carrying women off we wouldn't offer any resistance.

The end of the ninth hour we reached the camp, and found Mr. Akeley looking as if years instead of days had intervened. . . . We felt troubled when we first saw him, but a good dinner, an incentive toward appetite, began to make him feel better.

The camp was high on Mikeno, the mountain's citadel-like crags above, a world of forest and valleys and mountains at its feet, with clouds floating up the chasms and stealing among the trees. There was only a tiny clearing for the tents with the porter's huts of grass tucked in behind; the gorilla skeletons were hanging from poles in grisly sociability, while from the tent of Mr. Akeley hung a small, mummified figure, a skinned and dried two-year-old gorilla whom we christened "Clarence."

Besides securing his specimens, Mr. Akeley had fulfilled the hope which had been only a dream of the expedition: he had taken motion pictures of wild gorillas—a mother and two little ones—something that had never before been done. . . .

Friday opened with glorious sunshine and an ultimatum from the guides. They were going. The cold nights prevailed over the passion for francs. They had enough now anyway for several wives and a long lifetime of ease. However, they were prevailed upon to wait one more day and we started forth in haste before they changed their minds.

This time we took another trail up the Karisimbi heights, with ever more and more glorious views as we climbed. At last Mr. Akeley halted. "This is the most beautiful place in the world and I am going to photograph it," he announced with a certain defiance, knowing the guides viewed any dallying with the cameras with distaste. They understood a gun; the camera was, to them, resultless.

161

But he did not; as he poised his machine, the men pointed. On the slopes to the left the bushes were waving, giving a glimpse of something like a black bear.

Hurriedly we marshaled in line and scrambled up the trail, then in and out the trees and bushes, Herbert and Mr. Akeley first, then Martha and I, our gun boys, though relieved of our guns, hurrying excitedly after us. We went under a hollow tree feet first and emerged on the other side with a clear view of the slopes before us. There, on the steep mountainside stood a gigantic creature, black and shaggy. My first impression was of shoulders—incredible shoulders—huge, uncouth, slouching shoulders. His side was toward us and his back was silver gray. We were seeing at last the great beast we had come so far to see—a male gorilla in his savage haunts.

It seemed an eternity before my husband fired. I suppose it was only an instant or two. The roar of the gun sounded as unreal in the silence as the sight of the gorilla. Immediately the gorilla went crashing down into the welter of vegetation. We thought him dead and raced down towards him after Herbert, but we then found he had made off, leaving a trail of crushed greenery and blood. For a few moments the waving bushes gave us the only clue, then he emerged on the slopes above and looked back over his shaggy shoulder as the gun crashed again, as if trying to comprehend this sudden assault upon his solitudes. I shall never forget the humanness of that black, upturned face.

Then he went plunging down the slope, passing near Herbert, who put in a finishing shot. The great body struck against a tree and lay still. There had been no sound from him, no bark or roar. He had shown no instinct of fight, nothing but the rush of a wounded beast to escape.

We found him dead against the tree, face down, a huge, shaggy, primeval thing, like something summoned out of the vanished ages. And the scene in which he lay had a beauty that was like nothing earthly.

From that high place, whose forested slopes swept down, down, like a green flood to the distant valleys and the blue sheen of Kivu, we looked out across to the purple heights of Chaninagongo and Nyamlagira, crested with clouds that were golden with sun and rose with volcanic fires. To our right, sharply silhouetted against the distant azure and amethyst, stretched the superb slope of Mikeno edged with delicate little trees, exquisite miniatures relieving that long line, that went up, up, to the citadel crag of the top, glowing with umbers and emerald moss.

The gorilla proved a huge gray-backed male. When he was tugged and propped upright I shall never forget the impression he made. The great girth, the thickness and length of arm, the astounding shoulders made him a giant.

His face was ferocious only when the mouth was open. The normal expression was of a curiously mild and patriarchal dignity. Without being sentimental you could see in that face a gleam of patient and tragic surmise, as if the old fellow had a prescience that something was happening in the world against which his strength was of no avail—as if he knew the security of his high place was gone.

For generations he had lived without fear. He preyed upon no one for his food; he ate the wild carrot and fresh greens, disturbing no one and disturbed by none of his world. He could have crushed a lion or strangled it, and an elephant, if gripped by the trunk, would have no thought but of escape. He had been indeed the King of the African forests.

We took measurements and found his height to be five feet seven and a half inches; the reach from his upraised hand to the ground eight feet and two inches, and from hand to hand seven feet eight and a half inches. His chest was between sixty-two and sixty-three inches. He was, we felt sure, the big bull of Karisimbi, of which we had heard. This bull had been shot at before and we found an old wound in the hip, which had given a decided curvature of the spine, shortening the height.

Looking at his great arm and curving fingers, the fist as big as a man's head, I could understand how unwary hunters in the old days had been scooped out like soft-shell crabs.

All that day the men worked on the gorilla, for Mr. Akeley preserved everything for museum and medical records. They paused often to photograph the changing clouds and mountains.

It was a marvelous day! The sheer beauty of it was a spell, and the presence of this great gorilla made it seem like a page from the very beginning of time. . . .

Once the gorilla hunt was over we had planned to turn our attention to some of the smaller fry of the African fauna which usually lure the adventurous overseas—the elephants, the buffalo, and the lion.

We were not at all bloodthirsty, and we hadn't the slightest desire for indiscriminate slaughtering, but we did feel the lure of big game hunting, and I was convinced that I was offering any of the animals I mentioned a more than sporting chance in the present state of my shooting. I had shot at one elephant, two targets, and three crocodiles in the three months in Africa.

Mr. Bradley particularly wanted a buffalo, Miss Miller and I were eager for lions. Miss Miller already had one elephant to her credit, and I was hoping for similar luck. We had very little time, for, although Mr. Bradley and I were unhurried, Mr. Akeley had lecture engagements in America, and the constant delays of safari had reduced our hunting plans. . . .

There is a distinct difference of opinion among hunters as to which is the most dangerous, the lion, the elephant, the buffalo, or the rhinoceros. Drummond puts the rhino first, the lion second; but Mr. Akeley has discredited the dangers of the rhino, believing most of his so-called charges are simply blundering rushes, not actuated by any sight of the enemy.

Mr. Akeley puts the buffalo first, with the elephant a close second, yet he said he would rather hunt elephant than lion; he knew he could stop an elephant, but that Leslie Tarlton's experience had shown that a charging lion could come fifty yards with a bullet in his heart.

Stigand puts the lion first, the buffalo last. Frederick Selous, mightiest of big game hunters, puts the lion first and the buffalo and the elephant on a par. Colonel Roosevelt stated that the weight of opinion among those best fitted to judge was that the lion was the most formidable opponent of the hunter under ordinary conditions.

In the Congo we had not been in game country to any extent, so we accumulated few stories until we reached Kivu, and most of these were about leopards. We were warned to close our tents and never stir without a light at night for fear of prowlers, and the native runners were never sent alone, but always in pairs.

If half the native stories were true, the leopards exacted an amazing toll. Even allowing for exaggeration, their terror was so real that it must have a good basis of fact. The Belgian officials and missionaries had many instances. At Lulenga the Father Superior pointed to a banana grove that we were passing one day and remarked casually that there a leopard had eaten a young native woman about two months before. The beast had entered the hut at night, seized her, and dragged her into the banana grove. The natives had not attempted a rescue,

but at daybreak had gone for the White Father, who came down with his gun, but the leopard was gone.

At the Mission was a child with fresh leopard marks on its forehead. The leopard had entered the hut, not for the child, but for something else, a dog, I believe—a leopard delicacy— and had wounded the child in its spring.

It is rarely one sees a leopard. They are too wily and cat-like. Men have lived in Africa for years without a glimpse of one. Most of those leopards are killed by gun traps at night. On the other hand, Monsieur Flamand, of Ruindi, ran into three one afternoon and shot two.

For months we had heard of the Ruindi plains as one of the richest game fields left in Africa, where we could find antelopes by the thousand, and buffalo, elephants, and lions everywhere. There were no rhinos, but we were not after rhino. It seemed the very place for our needs and we planned to move out there with all speed.

Moving with all speed in the Congo means going into camp and waiting for porters. Porters from Lulenga would go no further than Ruchuru, two days away, and at Ruchuru we would have to get fresh porters to take us out on the Ruindi plains, a three days' march. There we would have to get porters from Luofu, two days farther on, because the Ruchuru porters would not remain on the plains.

With real regret we bade farewell to our good friends at the Mission, and on December 4 started north through the Rift Valley to Ruchuru.

As usual, we had sent a runner ahead to notify the chiefs, and at noon of the first day we found a chief out to greet us, with the grass cut for a camping place and eggs and delicious bananas for a present. I spent that afternoon writing on the Corona with the usual crowd of natives sitting curiously about; they believed the typewriter some sort of musical instrument, and must have marveled at the monotony of the air.

Next morning we made a leisurely departure at seven-thirty, and about noon we crossed the wild-rushing Ruchuru River on a picturesque bridge and wound up the slopes into Ruchuru, one of the most important stations on the Eastern frontier of the Congo. It is on high ground, at an elevation of about five thousand feet, with Lake Edward on the north and the M'fumbiro volcanoes to the south. From the elevation the climate ought to be very healthy, but it is not considered as excellent as Kivu. Its wide, spacious, flower-bordered avenues gave it the air of being quite a place. Like Kissenyi and Albertville, it seemed a stage setting waiting to be filled with the actors.

There were several officials at Ruchuru, the Commissioner, the *chef de poste,* the *agent territorial,* a banker, and there had been a doctor, but he had left to escort Madame Deriddar home, leaving the infirmary in charge of native orderlies. . . . A domestic touch was given to the streets by seeing two Belgian babies being wheeled about in improvised perambulators, one by a black boy nurse, one by a black girl. It was the first time since entering the Congo that we had seen a native woman employed by "Europeans"—the term for all whites. Always it is the men, who are called "boys" to their last days, who are employed for cooking, baby tending, sewing, and washing. Alice was enchanted with the babies; the little blue-eyed Elizabeth Piquard was her especial delight.

Here we camped in a grassy square, a former marketplace, that became a muddy square through the rains, waiting for our porters and making arrangements to leave Alice, for we heard that Ruindi was too hot for her. Commissioner Van de Ghinste and his bride offered to care for her, but we borrowed the little two-room house that belonged to the Mission Church, hospitably vacated by our very kind Père Van Hoef, who had come up from Lulenga for special services here, and installed her there with Priscilla. They had the devoted and untiring Mablanga for cook and caretaker, Jim for assistant, and all the resources of Ruchuru. Attached to every Belgian post is a herd of cattle, so fresh milk was obtained often from an official's private supply. Filtered water was also provided, and the Mission at Lulenga sent in fruit and vegetables. The thoughtfulness and kindness of the Belgians were unvarying in all these things, which mean so much—especially to the happiness of

167

a child. We went over our supplies here and stored the super-fluous things in the warehouse, for we were to return that way, and with seventy porters set out the morning of December 9, northeast toward Lake Albert, with a penciled map from Père Van Hoef to mark the marches and the haunts of game.

Down a long hill we coasted gloriously on our bicycles out onto the plains where a blue rim of mountains seemed pushed back against the horizon. But the bicycling did not last long. The elephant grass was high and the path through it a wind-ing tunnel. Elephant grass is so called because you never find elephants in it; it is an inedible, giant grass, in its earlier stages a flat, sharp-edged, green blade and when matured and dry it is like young bamboo.

At the foot of a long climb we abandoned our bicycles for the following bicycle boys to carry—that is, we believed there were following bicycling boys. But they had abdicated. We never saw them more. They had melted away to their villages, and probably figured among those taken by leopards. It took time for us to be convinced of their departure, and no amount of time reconciled us to it, for we were forced to retrace our steps and push those wheels the rest of the day.

That morning we passed a group of natives in great excite-ment. They said one of their number had been seized by a leopard in broad daylight, not an hour before our arrival. In the story which reached Ruchuru, the leopard had taken one of our men.

That night, and again the next night, we camped on the banks of the Ruchuru River, a swiftly rushing stream, whose banks were so netted with tropic luxuriance of palm and vine that we had great difficulty in forcing our way through to see the hippos who were snorting and blowing all about.

Our only way was to follow the hippo trails, which were wide enough, but very low, like tunnels through the thick green, and raked by every imaginable thorn. Possibly the thorn pro-duced an agreeable tickling in the hippo's hide. It did some-thing else to mine.

The hippo comes out at night to feed, and the ground was

We whirled about . . . a little distance away, were a lion and a lioness

crisscrossed by these trails. I shall never forget the first hippo I saw climbing out of the water. His back was towards me and I thought that it must be an elephant. They are huge beyond belief.

They were not at all shy, and one old lady who came snorting and blowing down the river with the current, whirled about at sight of us, her eyes rounded, her small ears cocked, her wide mouth set with astonishment. She faced us while the current bore her away, then she sank and either swam back to us under water or galloped on the bottom, and came up nearer than before. She did that half a dozen times, then appeared with a comical replica beside her—her baby—as big as a young bull. She had probably been keeping the baby on her back all the time. They kept coming back delightedly until we wearied of their entertainment and remarking, *"kwa heri"* (good-bye), strolled away.

The porters wanted one killed for meat, but fortunately for the hippos and our feelings, the animals did not show themselves on land where we could get them. A hippo shot in water sinks and is carried off by the current.

On the second day's march we came to Maji ja Moto, or Hot Water, streams of really scalding water smelling of sulphuretted hydrogen, gushing from a rock. It was here the Duke of Mecklenburg experienced his most stirring lion hunts, and here a leopard had sprung like a flash at him from a bush, even as he aimed at the gleam of her. His shot had pierced her neck and she rolled dead at his feet. . . .

We, however, saw no leopards and heard no lions that night; we saw only antelope and heard nothing but the incessant snorting of the hippos as they splashed in the river or stumbled in the darkness against our tent ropes.

The third day's march brought us into the territory of the Ruindi. Here Monsieur Flamand, the administrator of the territory and until the last month the only white man within its borders, came striding towards us, having walked a day and a night and half another day from Luofu, his residence beyond the mountains, to greet us.

169

Our camp on the Ruindi was on a high plateau, cleared like a parade ground for fear of lion and encircled by a moatlike ravine through whose jungles rushed the Ruindi River. Across the ravine we looked out on a wide sweep of plains, with a range of mountains against the sky. It reminded me of some Colorado highland, and we began to wish that we had brought Alice.

Our tents were strung in a military line with the grass rest houses, one of which we used for a dining room. Across from us, on the edge of the plateau, was a mound weighted with stones and embellished with antelopes' horns, the grave of a young Englishman, R. C. Foster, killed by a lion two years before. He and his brother, both experienced hunters from British East Africa, had gone in long grass after a lion, shoulder to shoulder. The lion had charged, and the older brother's gun missed fire, and the lion seized the young brother by the neck, bit him savagely, then sprang away. The young man lived for two hours.

It was a melancholy reminder with a strong personal interest to those about to seek the lion in its lair. It was here, too, at Ruindi, that Mme. Deriddar had been so savagely mauled. It was this same Monsieur Flamand who had cared for Foster's grave, nursed Mme. Deriddar, and tried to save her husband who had died of the fever.

It was December 12, the day after our arrival, that Monsieur Flamand took us out to tempt Providence and the lions.

Now in British East Africa lion hunting is a ceremony. Half a hundred beaters cover the brush for you, driving the game your way, and you have gun boys who can be relied on in critical moments, and you have horses whose four legs can be used to run the lions down. In the Congo you have no horses, no beaters, and no boys who can do more than carry your guns until you need them. Your only hope is to run on a lion in the daytime, lying up after the night's gorge, or to stay out in the bush all night with a bait to attract lions.

This morning at dawn we struck across the plains, with Monsieur Flamand for guide. The trail ran like a ribbon over the

level land to the mountains. Against the dry browns of the burnt grass the green of the scattered thickets stood out darkly.

The plains were simply alive with antelope. There was the graceful Thomas cob, a lovely dun creature, with conspicuous white markings and horns like a big gazelle, moving off at our approach, then pausing to regard us; there was the little reed buck, green-gray, springing away with a sharp whistle of alarm; there were droll, dark topis, slant-backed, turning to stare, then with a comical plunge breaking into a gallop and making off in a line like race horses. The topi is a rare antelope, and it was extraordinary to see it in such numbers; it is from four to five feet high, with deeply grooved, backward curving horns. The skin is marvelous, fine and brilliant as watered silk—a dark, warm-toned brown on top, brightening to cinnamon below, with splashes of black on shoulder and thigh, all overlaid with a sheen of bluish gray.

For a few miles we went along the path, then struck out across the plains where the tree clumps and thickets were frequent and might house a lion lying up after the night's hunting. It was necessary to have meat for the men, and Monsieur

171

Flamand brought down a cob buck at about three hundred yards, a perfect shot, but it was sad to see the lovely creature sink down with a swanlike lift of its head. I knew then I should never be able to kill one—and I never did. It was sheer shirking on my part, though, for someone had to kill them for meat and for the skins which we wanted.

At Monsieur Flamand's suggestion we strung out, the better to cover the ground. Mr. Akeley, seeing no signs of lion, went off with Miss Miller to photograph the antelope, but Herbert, Monsieur Flamand, and I walked on, some distance apart, scrutinizing the tangles and little hollows.

"Be careful," Monsieur Flamand had warned me. "Remember Mme. Deriddar."

I wondered, as I strolled along, clasping my gun and eyeing the innocent looking thickets, how I was to be careful and get my lion. It was a lovely morning. The freshness of dawn was in the air, the dew sparkling on the grass. Golden-crested crane preened themselves in a little marsh. There was a pastoral sweetness to the scene, with its grazing herds of antelopes, that was unrelated to anything like lion. I felt a self-conscious humor in my scrutiny of the bushes for the waving tail and pricked ears I had been told to look for.

Lions were unreal—fantastic. But here and there a pile of bleached bones told of their nocturnal suppers. Certainly lions had been here. I had no idea how old the kills were, for the vultures pick the bones in a day.

It was eight o'clock. We had walked a little over two hours. I was just speaking to Monsieur Flamand, whose path had neared mine, when a call came from Herbert: "Here's your lion, Mary—look!"

We whirled about and at our left, a little distance away, were a lion and lioness going through the grass. We raced towards them, and they went up a little slope and paused on the crest to look back at us. They were the most marvelous picture of wild life that Africa can give.

For the moment they stood unmoving—green-gray statues, cast in verdigris. The lion seemed tremendous, his ruffled mane

172

crisp against the sky. Then they made off, with a supple rippling of muscles, heading for a long reach of brush at our right. We ran as hard as we could to cut them off, but they were out of sight among the thickets when we reached the edge of the depression in which the thickets were scattered, surrounded by fairly long grass. The grass was tawny and the thickets rusty-leaved, and as we peered and watched we felt the matter of protective coloring was decidedly overdone.

As we stood on one edge, Herbert watched the other side, sure the lions had not escaped that way. The wind was blowing from that direction, so we went around and started a fire to try to drive them out. But the grass burned only a little way, then died at the first green creeper.

We circled the rim, and a native who had joined us told us he had just seen the lions, and in another moment we had a glimpse of the big fellow, slouching across a little opening, his tail waving. We saw the lioness a little farther away, gliding from one thicket to another. They were getting farther off, and we were afraid we might lose them, so we went down into the brush, our guns ready, scrutinizing every tangle and tree clump. It was a popular covert. Generous piles of antelope bones told of cob and topi that had been dragged there to conclude an evening of small joy to them.

Monsieur Flamand, advising extreme caution, would seize one of these bones and hurl it nonchalantly into a thicket, observing hopefully, "Now he may be there!" When I did the same, trying to keep my gun pointed at the bombarded thicket, "I have such fear for you—you are so imprudent," he told me. "Remember Mme. Deriddar!"

We went on through the grass, trying to be as sharp-sighted as possible. There is a real thrill to life when you know that at any moment the rusty leaves and the tawny grass may part before a hurtling form. We glimpsed the lioness some distance ahead and started hurrying along on a little trail, Monsieur Flamand ahead and Herbert and I following.

"Keep midway between bushes," Herbert advised. "That lion might be anywhere," and just that moment, eyeing the thicket

173

at my left, I saw the lion. He was about twenty feet away. It was a green thicket, for a wonder, and through a hole I saw the ruddy mane, the ears pricked forward. His right side was towards me, as he was facing the place where the little trail ran towards the thicket.

I did not have time for any fear except the ignoble one that I might not get the lion before the men did. It was to be my lion—they had made me a present of the first one met—but it was so near, so ready to spring, that their guns went up with mine.

I fired as fast as I could, sighting by that ear and neck. Monsieur Flamand fired immediately after, but the lion had gone down at the first shot with a roar that reverberated with the crashing of the guns.

We waited. There was absolute silence. Not a snarl. Holding our guns in readiness we made our way where we faced the opening in the thicket which the lion had been facing, waiting for us to pass.

A deep growl greeted us and I fired again. There was a gurgling roar that died away to silence, a silence unbroken, even when we tossed in experimental stones.

We tried to wait a decently cautious interval, but we didn't overdo the matter of caution. We went in, guns ready, and there in the cavelike interior a large lion was stretched on his side, motionless, apparently having just breathed his last.

If ever a lion looked dead that one did. He wasn't stirring, he wasn't breathing. We examined the wounds; my bullet had gone in the neck at the base of the skull. The frontal one had gone between the eyes. He had a beautiful skin and mane, and his appearance was majesty itself. I had to remind myself that his death was salvation for three hundred gentle antelope each year.

It was just eight-thirty, and Monsieur Flamand triumphantly reminded me that he had promised me a lion by half-past eight. He was certainly a man of his word. Hastily we cut down the overhanging branches, and I propped the lion's head in my lap, and Herbert took my picture.

Now that lion had his eyes screwed up. If I had known as much about dead lions then as I did a little later I should have known that when they die the eyes are open—not with the lids drawn in a paralyzed sort of wink. The shade was too thick for a good picture, and we had the boys, who had now come up, drag him a little bit more into the light. Then I knelt by him for a second picture. In that picture the eyes are wide open—a change I did not happen to notice. I made ready for a third picture by kneeling behind him and trying to hold up the heavy head.

It was a magnificent head. It had a dignity so impressive that somehow it forbade sympathy. A wounded antelope sinking down is poignant, but a lion's life is swift and violent, and a sudden death is no unfit conclusion—it is better than the hyenas.

I was thinking all this and trying to keep the head up when suddenly that lion growled. It was a low gurgling growl, and for a moment I was sympathetic as I held him.

"Is it the death rattle?" I asked. Monsieur Flamand assured me the lion was certainly finished, he wasn't moving, so we went on to get the picture, the lion growling a little more and more. And then—just as that picture was taken—the lion roared! The roar isn't audible in the picture, but it is visible in my expression. It was the most astonished moment of my life. I left the lion, left him abruptly. I joined the man, and we stared at him. We saw that his eyes were open, and he was breathing with a regularity and vigor that would have been reassuring to an anxious nurse.

Just then Mr. Akeley, who had heard the shots, came hurrying up with Miss Miller, and I shall never forget the astoundedness of his expression nor the vigorous disapproval of his remarks. Fortunately for the *entente cordiale,* he spoke no French. He was conveying that the lion was very much alive and would recover from his temporary paralysis at any moment and kill us all.

Anthony, as I had christened him—quoting, "I am dying, Egypt, dying"—had ceased growling; he was breathing naturally and his eyes, full of intelligence, followed us watchfully. His expression was positively benign, but I did not know how far one could trust to it. So far he had not stirred, and recklessness inspired me, and while Mr. Akeley kept the gun on him, we took one last photograph, and then I shot him through the heart. His convulsive bound before he fell back on his side was proof of astonishing vitality, and then the swift glassy change told me how death really looked.

He was a young male, with a fine skin and mane, the only mane of any lion we got that was not alive with ticks.

The lioness had gone out of sight and, after the grim business of skinning, we went on after her and later walked unending hours across the dry stubble of the plain or through longer

176

tangling grass trying for a lion for Martha or Herbert. We saw three others in the early part of the morning, but they got into wood so dense there was no hope in following.

Later, after a conservative estimate had placed our walk at twenty miles, we felt a positive indifference to finding anything more—unless we found it right in front of us and in a recumbent attitude! We came back to camp after nine hours of exercise and found a herd of elephants squealing and racketing in the woods by the river. They had chosen their time well!

We matabeeshed (rewarded) the gun boys and porters, and bathed and changed, and found a black runner had brought in a packet of mail from home. With devouring eagerness we read our three-months-old letters, then dined outdoors in a lovely sunset, while the elephants trumpeted about and the baboons came out on the ravine slopes for food. Then, as night came on, a fire in the brush spread out in ebony silhouette. The cracklings came across to us like firecrackers. Then the flame died to an amber glow. The moon swung suddenly out from the clouds overhead and turned the world to silver. Out of the stillness came the hunting grunt of lions on the plains.

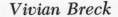

Vivian Breck

A TOUCH OF ARAB

ILLUSTRATED BY *Helen Prickett*

USUALLY the day we rode into the canyon to open the ranger cabin was the happiest of the whole year. On that day my father stopped being Professor Mallory of the Geology Department and changed into Ranger Mallory of Merced Canyon, and I had Cirque to ride. After a little time in the Sierra Nevada you get used to the light, but on the day you ride in, the sun seems so near and shines so gold-and-silver bright that it stirs you up inside. The mountains sparkle.

Always before—and that's eleven summers, because we have been going to the Merced cabin ever since my mother died when I was three—Ranger Mallory's eyes would get sort of big behind his glasses, and the tip of his nose would quiver at the smell of wild azaleas in Little Yosemite. He'd crack silly jokes as we rode and call himself *Old Sourdough*. But this year he looked as if he had just flunked one of his favorite students.

"Look at Cirque, Daddy," I said. "Isn't he beautiful? He's so glad to be out of pasture he wants to dance uphill." Cirque is Western stock horse with just a touch of Arab. That makes him strong and dependable and brave, but a little flashy, too. He likes to prance.

But Daddy didn't seem to appreciate Cirque's polished granite coat and lovely legs. Surely, I thought, after we climb the zigzags and get to foaming water, or to where we can see the Clark Range, he will get his mountain face.

It was when we stopped for lunch that Daddy told me. We had built a cooking fire and were waiting for the water to boil for tea when he said: "I wish you'd stop trying to balance yourself on that branch, Meggie. I really don't want an acrobat for

178

a daughter. Besides, I need to talk to you." He kept digging at the damp crust of pine needles on the ground as he spoke. "I'm sorry, Meg, but this is going to be a mighty short summer."

"What on earth do you mean?" I asked him. "It's not even July yet."

"But this year I'm having just a two-weeks' businessman's vacation." He put his hand on my arm. "Meg, my dear," he said almost pleadingly, "I do hope you'll understand." Then he told me that he had resigned from the Forest Service to accept a job teaching at summer session, and that he wanted me to go to a girls' camp.

"I don't want you growing up one-sided," he said, "with no interests outside of your riding. You must cultivate other enthusiasms. You need friendship with boys and girls your own age. That's why I want you to go to this camp and make an honest effort to get along with the other girls and join in all their different activities."

"But Cirque!" I cried. "Darling Cirque! What will we do—"

"A professor's salary is not designed to include boarding a horse in town," Daddy answered slowly. "I'm sorry, but I think the time has come when we'll have to sell Cirque. Surely you wouldn't want to keep an educated young gentleman at pasture indefinitely. Would you, Meggie?"

I shook my head, but deep inside I knew there was more behind this selling Cirque than just money. Several times that spring I had cut school to practice for the gymkhana, and when Daddy found out about it he'd looked pretty grim.

"Education," he had said to me, his jaw particularly square, "is the bones of life. Without it you may grow up bright and pretty, but sometime life will crumble on you because you haven't the right bones underneath."

"Why do you have to be a professor all over your private life?" I'd railed. "You know I'm going to live on a ranch and raise stock horses. What's analyzing *The Merchant of Venice* got to do with that?"

"Quite a lot," Daddy had said, and I knew there was no use arguing with him.

After that miserable lunch on the trail we rode the rest of the fourteen miles to our cabin trying to talk about things that wouldn't hurt too much. But as we passed the granite slide where the Merced tumbles down in foaming sheets of water, I couldn't help remembering old Mr. Scripps.

"Did they ever find him?" I had to ask.

"Yes, they did," Daddy answered, as if rushing water were no longer beautiful. "At the bottom of Nevada Falls. There will be one advantage to our short summer, anyhow."

"How could there be?"

"I probably won't have to hunt for any lost fishermen or campers."

Usually when we arrive at the Ranger Station I want to squeal for joy. Our brown log cabin looks so welcoming, under the Jeffrey pines! This year I could only wonder whose name would be tacked up on the bulletin board where the little metal sign, *Ranger Arthur B. Mallory*, had hung for so long. Cirque was all for dashing upstream to see if the big bridge, where the Lyell Fork joins the Merced, had lasted out the winter. Since the trail gang put a concrete pier under the bridge it has never washed out, but before that, every time we had a heavy storm the melted snow, swirling down in torrents from the upper falls, had carried the bridge with it. I unsaddled Cirque and turned him into the corral beside the cabin, then went inside to unpack. What I really wanted to do was bury my face in a pillow, or run across the river on my log and crawl into the underbrush, where the does hide their new fawns.

It was silly for Daddy to think that getting rid of Cirque would make me spend more time with what he calls "comrades of my own age." Those dopes! Last year he practically drove me to join a sort of dancing club. The dancing part wasn't bad. Dancing is pretty good exercise. But the girls were so silly and the boys so juvenile in their conversation, I only went once. But it had never occurred to me that my not going to dances, and being bored by my schoolmates, would get mixed up in Daddy's mind with my loving Cirque so much. How could I make him understand the way I felt about my darling? My

180

father wouldn't sell me, no matter how much I cost to keep!

Suddenly an idea hit me. Cirque looks especially beautiful standing on his hind legs or jumping. If, every day for two weeks, Daddy had to watch my horse doing extra-special, prancy tricks, perhaps—

I raced into the cabin for my lucky T-shirt, the green-and-white striped one I wore when I won the bareback hackamore race at the gymkhana. Then I jerked the top bars off the corral gate and made Cirque jump so that every muscle showed under his glossy coat. Finally, to rest him, we practiced a kind of circus trick I have been wanting to learn. That was when Wake came along.

Right next to our cabin is a mammoth Jeffrey pine with one branch overhanging the corral. I stood on Cirque's back—that isn't hard if you have grippy toes and are used to climbing over logs—and swung myself to the overhanging branch. The hard part was dropping down again on Cirque's back while he was loping by. I was riding around standing up when I spotted something that looked like a great big heron—all legs, with a hump on top—leaning against the corral, one of his legs wound around the other. When I rode over, the hump turned out to be a knapsack, and the heron asked: "Can I take a picture of you doing that stunt? You're a wonderful color. Like the ocean, extremely clean green-and-white."

"I don't mind," I said, wondering if he meant that my shirt looked like the ocean. My eyes of course are blue, and my eyebrows and hair looked mighty pale against my sun-browned skin.

While he set up a tripod Cirque and I did our trick again.

"What's your horse's name?" he asked.

"Cirque."

"Circ, for circus?"

"Circus nothing! He's a mountain horse. His name is C-i-r-q-u-e. Don't you know any geology? A cirque is the round place hollowed out of the granite at the head of a stream by a glacier. You ought to study geology," I told him. "It makes the mountains much more interesting."

181

He said he doubted if he'd ever have time.

That was Wake. His whole name was Wakefield Bender. He was seventeen, and this was his first trip into the Sierra Nevada. He had heard that the Merced, just below the Ranger cabin, was full of cascades running between granite cliffs, and he thought they would make interesting pictures.

Daddy suggested I help him choose a place to camp. It was lucky I did. Wake didn't know any more about the woods than I know about photography.

"This looks like a fine place to hang my hat," he announced at the place where the trail crossed Rafferty Creek, two minutes from our cabin. "I'd like to wake up in the morning looking at those big black rocks sticking out through the bubbles."

"You'll wake up in a puddle, if it rains," I told him. "Rafferty catches a tremendous runoff. It spreads out all over the place after a shower."

As he was looking back at the foam of water he stumbled and nearly went flat. If I had known how easy it was for Wake to stumble I never would have cut through the woods on a deer trail! He laughed about his clumsiness, though, even when a rock sent him sprawling. I couldn't help laughing, too. He looked so silly with his heron legs waving in the air.

"Your legs remind me of Alice and her neck," I said. "They've grown so fast you don't know how to manage them."

"Quick!" he shouted. "Find me a mushroom to nibble!"

After that we were easy together. Somehow, when people too old for fairy tales both like *Alice in Wonderland* it gives them the feeling of being old friends.

The place I had in mind for Wake's camp didn't suit him at all. "This has no character," he objected.

"But look at the firewood! And it has perfect screening from the wind."

He still shook his head. "It's just shrubbery. I want to camp where the outlook has form, composition of some kind. A picture to live with."

Finally he made camp on a granite shelf, where the little crooked pines grow out of the cracks in the rock. As I watched him unpack I hoped he had food in his knapsack as well as camera stuff, because he was awfully thin. You could see his shoulder blades right through his shirt. I couldn't help liking him. He had nice brown eyes that looked straight at you, that is, when one of them wasn't covered up with a piece of rumply hair. I asked him why he didn't get a haircut before he came away.

"There wasn't time," he said. "And anyhow, I'd spent all my allowance on film."

Wake walked over to our cabin quite often to watch me jumping Cirque, and sometimes I rode past his camp to tell him about something I thought he might like to photograph. I never picked the things he wanted, though. It was the cascades that fascinated him. They were difficult to photograph because the canyon walls are so steep, and he was anxious to explore the other side of the river for a better angle, so one day I

183

showed him where my log crosses. My log—I call it mine because I've used it so many years—is the only way over the
Merced between our cabin and the big junction bridge five
miles upstream. Wake said he wished he could skitter about
fallen trees the way I do. His legs reminded me of a colt's, they
wouldn't quite obey him.

We had several conversations before I asked him about
dancing. I wanted to know if he thought dancing was important
for a girl, the way Daddy seemed to think it was.

"I certainly don't think it's important," he told me. "Most
girls at dances are so silly I can't find anything to talk to them
about. I only go to parties myself because I don't wish to become a recluse."

If Wake felt tongue-tied at dances I decided I needn't bother
with them, either. Because certainly Wake had more ideas to
the minute than anyone I'd ever known, except my father.

Half our businessman's vacation was gone when the first
storm broke. It had been building for two days, but I couldn't
make Wake believe that those cloudy afternoons meant the
sky would pour down buckets of water some day soon. First
the clouds grew gray, then black. Daddy looked at the barom-
eter and put the fattest chunk of pine he could find into our
stove. Big drops began to spatter against the glass, hitting slowly
at first, in little spurts between the gusts of wind. Then the
wind came roaring down off the Clark Range, and whole sheets
of water pounded the windows.

We could almost see the river rising as every crack and gully
on the canyon walls filled with rain and melted snow. I knew
my log would soon be under water, might even be swept away.
After a little the rain changed to hail, big, mountain hail, like
moth balls. I thought the windowpanes would shatter.

But if the rain comes fast, it never lasts long. The minute
the storm was over I went out to see how Cirque was. He
looked pretty shivery, huddled against Daddy's horse in one
corner of the corral. Even his beautiful tail was droopy.

"How about a good run to warm up?" I asked him.

His ears said "Let's go!"

I was wondering about Wake, too, remembering the casual way he'd anchored his pup tent to a couple of twiggy bushes. If his bedding was wet I thought it would be friendly to invite him into the cabin to dry off. I was sure Daddy wouldn't mind, though he always says we can't take in all the campers in the Sierra to dry off every time it rains.

I jumped on Cirque bareback, and we galloped down the trail to where I could see Wake's tent. The granite sand was still full of puddles that splashed as we tore along, and Cirque skidded to a quick stop with his forefeet in the air. He's glorious when he does that. I wished Daddy could see him.

"Hi, Wake!" I shouted. "Did you get all your stuff under cover?"

When nobody answered I crashed Cirque right across the dead timber to Wake's camp. He wasn't there. All his things were spread around outside the tent, soaking wet, so I knew he must have been off taking pictures when it began to rain.

Suddenly I was frightened. I don't think I ever felt really frightened in the mountains before. Daddy never lets us get into jams, because he knows ahead of time where danger lies, but Wake was such a baby in the woods, slipping and stumbling, never paying any attention to where he was going because he was so busy thinking about his lovely pictures. I was sure he had gone to photograph the cascades, for he'd been talking about them so much, never satisfied with the shots he had already made.

My heels dug into Cirque, and he bounded straight ahead, like a deer through underbrush. I headed for my log because I was positive that was where Wake had crossed the river. The Merced had risen at least ten inches, and the current was so strong that even a champion swimmer would have been dashed over the falls. It was sweeping across the top of the log now, and I dared not try to cross on it.

Then I saw his head—the rest of him was under water. I'm never going to forget the way his eyes looked. They were wide open and glinty, like a wild animal's facing a light at night. With one hand he was clinging to a branch of driftwood that

185

had wedged against my log; with the other, he was trying to hold his camera out of the water. He saw me, too, but I knew he couldn't hear my voice. The water was so loud it drowned the sound.

There was no time to go for Daddy. Wake was on the upstream side of the log, but the driftwood he was clinging to might come loose any minute. Then the water would sweep him right under the log. If that happened he wouldn't have a chance. Not against the Cascades. I thought of old Mr. Scripps swept the whole way down to Nevada Falls. Cirque and I were going to have to get Wake out! There wasn't any other way.

"Please God," I prayed, "make the driftwood stick together until we get there."

Cirque understood too, I think. He began quivering all over as I urged him right to the edge of the river. "Come on, Cirque," I whispered, wishing my bare heels were spurs. In a moment the current was swirling around his knees. He planted his forefeet on the bottom and refused to budge.

"Cirque!" I cried. "We've got to get Wake out of there quickly!"

He lowered his head, sniffling the roily brown water, then looked around at me as if he were saying: "Meg, old girl, it's too much for us. The old Merced is too strong for you and me."

A terrible gust of wind whipped the branches of a tree against my face. I realized then exactly what I would have to do. Without my weight Cirque stood a chance of crossing the river. But he would have to be driven forcibly into the water. I leaned as far forward as I could and screamed at Wake, "Catch Cirque's tail!"

Then I stood up on Cirque's back and grabbed the tree branch with one hand. With one foot I whacked him across the rump with all my might and bellowed, "Go on, Cirque!" Startled, he lunged into the stream, while I swung over the water. It was hard getting my legs up on the branch, because it wasn't steady like the pine over the corral. But finally I made it.

Blessed Cirque. He understood. He waded out as far as he could toward Wake, and all I could do was to sit there, biting blood out of my lips. When the current took him he began to swim, struggling with all his brave stock-horse heart against the flood water. Wake had to let his camera go, but he caught Cirque's tail and the horse dragged him, slowly but surely, up on the other side.

I thought, of course, that Wake would jump on Cirque, ride to the junction bridge and back to the Ranger cabin for Daddy. But I could see that he was too exhausted to move.

Cirque stood over him, sniffing with his velvet nose. Then he pawed the ground as if he were saying, "Come on! My mistress can't hang on that branch forever." But Wake just lay there, shivering. Cirque tossed his head and whinnied, then crashed off into the underbrush alone. It's five miles to the junction bridge and five miles back on our side of the river, so I knew I'd have to hang on a good long time. But I never supposed any time would *feel* so long. I tried to settle myself more comfortably in the crotch of the tree, and watched the mad waters swirling around the trunk.

Daddy came at last. He lassoed me with a rope, then threw another rope over the branch for me to shinny down. When I felt the ground under my feet again and Daddy's arms around me, I got silly and cried. He tossed me up in back of his saddle, and all the way back to the cabin I hugged him around the waist, tight, the way I used to ride when I was a little girl. Daddy said Cirque must have galloped every inch of the way. He'd come to the corral fence lathered with sweat, in spite of the icy wind, and Daddy had known right away, when he saw him, riderless, that something had happened to me.

"Get yourself warm, Meg. Then put plenty of water on to heat and fill every bottle you can lay your hands on. Make a hot drink," he called back as he dashed out the door, "and warm some blankets in front of the fire."

I was so busy carrying out his instructions that it didn't seem any time before he was back with the still dripping Wake. Daddy took off Wake's clothes, bundled him into a pair of flannel pajamas, and wrapped him in the warm blankets lined with bottles of hot water. In a little while he was able to sit up and take the hot drink, and by evening he was enjoying the huge meal we brought to him on a tray.

The next morning I was getting breakfast in the kitchen when Daddy came in with a load of wood.

"I can't wait any longer to ask you, Dad," I said, putting down the coffee I'd been measuring. "I've got to know about it now. Are we still going to sell Cirque?"

Daddy stood stock-still. "Sell him!" he exclaimed. "What an idea! Cirque can have a golden stall and feed on star dust mixed with diamonds as far as I'm concerned. Perhaps I rushed into things a bit too fast. You seem to be working matters out pretty well in your own way. I'm sorry about the camp, but all the arrangements are made, so I'm afraid you'll have to be a good sport about it this summer."

"Oh, I will, Dad," I vowed. "And I'll promise to enjoy it, if only we don't have to sell Cirque."

He dropped the armful of wood by the stove and went back for another. Then I did the silliest thing. I was so glad inside, too glad for words, I guess. I just cried and cried.

Wake doesn't know I cried, though. He has often told me since that he thinks I was very brave about everything. I'd rather not let him know I cried, because I'd like him to go on thinking that.

Kenneth M. King

THE MYSTERY
OF THE BAY

ILLUSTRATED BY *Robert Sinnott*

SAN FRANCISCO!" Gerald looked at his mother unbelievingly. "A holiday in San Francisco?"

"Why not?" asked Mrs. Cain calmly. "Uncle Edward seems happy to have you."

But Gerald's mother had been born and brought up in San Francisco. To her it was the old home town. To Gerald, born and brought up in an English village, it was a world, a war and several financial crises away.

Mrs. Cain's brother, Edward, had only recently gone back to San Francisco himself after leading a somewhat wandering existence since just before the war. When his father, Gerald's grandfather, had died leaving him the big house overlooking the Bay, Edward had gone back and fallen in love all over again with the Pacific Coast, the Golden State in general, and San Francisco in particular. Selling the family house because it was too big for his needs, he had bought a bungalow and settled down. Now he was ready to entertain the nephew he had never seen. He even offered to pay for Gerald to fly over so as not to waste time on the journey.

Gerald needed no pressing. San Francisco was more than just a beautiful city to him; it was the home of his pioneer ancestors; the young men who had "gone West" and stayed there, successful and respected.

When at last he stood with his uncle on the veranda of the bungalow and looked over the hills of Mill Valley towards the steep, irregular shores of San Francisco Bay, he felt that he belonged every bit as much as his great-great-grandfather, the Sheriff, had belonged.

"Big, isn't it?" remarked Uncle Edward.

"It must be the biggest in the world," said Gerald, and Uncle Edward laughed.

"Spoken like a good American."

"Half American."

"Well, O.K. But San Francisco Bay belongs to the American half of you."

Gerald, who was always fiercely pro-American in England, found himself rushing to the defence of his father's nation.

"An Englishman discovered it."

"Did he?"

"Sure. Sir Francis Drake. Even I know that."

"He never mentioned it."

Gerald turned to his uncle in surprise. "Oh, but he must have. When he sailed round the world he stopped and refitted here along this coast. . . ."

"Oh, that's certain enough. After capturing the Manila galleon *Cacafuego* off Panama he had to lay up his ship, and he sailed up the coast of California to find a suitable harbor. We know that in June, 1579, he found a little bay near Point Reyes, which is called "Drake's Bay" even now. We know that he named the area New Albion because the chalky cliffs reminded him of England, and he claimed it in the name of Queen Elizabeth. People have found the very brass plate he left here. We also know that he careened the *Golden Hind*, refitted and re-victualled her in this little bay. And he stayed there two months —only thirty miles from here, and yet there isn't a shred of evidence that he or any of his company ever saw it."

Gerald was silent for a moment, staring out into the sun-shine and adjusting his ideas about his favorite historical character. Then he said, "Well, I always thought he was a pretty good explorer. Now I'm not sure. If he didn't explore far enough to spot a huge bay like this he can't have been so clever."

Uncle Edward grinned. "Maybe the Indians hid it from him. Maybe they put up a smoke screen. Pretty smart, our Indians."

Gerald gave him a sharp look. "Not *that* smart."

His uncle laughed. "Perhaps not. But there you are—there's your famous explorer, an adventurous man, an experienced sailor only thirty miles up the coast, and yet in the narrative of his voyage the bay isn't even mentioned. So perhaps you're right—he wasn't so smart. Now, how would you like to go fishing?"

The subject was dropped, but a day or two later, while Uncle Edward drove him in his huge car round the hills beyond the Bay, Gerald brought it up again.

"You know, I can't understand it. Surely Drake must have done some exploring after he discovered New Albion. And if he'd done any, he'd have seen the Bay from the distance, even if he didn't get this far."

"Yes, I know. That's the oddest part of the story. He *would* have explored, if only as an elementary military precaution. And if he'd seen it he certainly would have told Queen Elizabeth about it, because the immense possibilities of such a fine landlocked, easily defended harbor would surely have interested that ambitious lady. But he didn't tell her—or anybody else—so we must assume he didn't see it."

"Yet if he or any of his men had climbed this hill they couldn't have missed it."

"If it was there."

Gerald laughed. "Sure. If the Indians hadn't taken it away for safety."

Uncle Edward smiled rather thoughtfully and then shrugged. "As a matter of fact no one seems to have found the Bay until 1769, nearly 200 years later when some Spaniards came overland from San Diego and discovered it."

"Wouldn't *that* have made Queen Elizabeth furious?" said Gerald. "Spaniards, of all people, finding what Drake missed. I should think it was a good thing for Sir Francis that nobody found it while the old Queen was alive."

"Um." Uncle Edward smoked thoughtfully for a moment and then started the car again. "Well, I guess we'll just never know. Ready to go home now?"

192

That evening, while Gerald was reading on the veranda, Uncle Edward opened a cupboard and took out an armful of documents, several bulging old briefcases and some box files.

"Stuff from the old house," he said. "My father kept every letter and document he ever laid hands on, I think. I've promised his lawyer I'd go through them to see if there's anything important. But most of it seems to be mementoes."

Gerald wandered in, book in hand, and looked over his uncle's shoulder.

". . . have endeavored for some years to convince him that the Indians of the territory . . ." he read, and he shut his book and put it down.

"Can I help? I think I'd like to," he said.

"Sure, if you like, but it's not all interesting. This thing happens to be because it's a letter from a great-uncle of mine who worked, more or less as a missionary, among the Indians. But a lot of it is just dull stuff."

Nevertheless, Gerald helped and found that among the dull stuff there were enough interesting documents to make the job an enjoyable one. Every evening that they spent at home was devoted to their job, and the worth-while papers were put in one pile, the rubbish in another ready to be destroyed.

One day they were walking through the streets of San Francisco when Gerald remarked, "It's all so new-looking and sort of clean. Our towns are so different."

"Well, this is comparatively new, especially this part. But it used to be very different. This was one of the parts of San Francisco that were completely destroyed in the earthquake of 1906. Before that, I guess this was a pretty poor area."

"Tell me about the earthquake. It was the worst California ever had, wasn't it?"

"It was pretty bad. It caused fires, you see, so that what wasn't destroyed in the 'quake itself, went up in flames afterwards. But whether it was the worst ever, I'm not sure."

"There were others?"

"The whole area gets earthquakes, you know, some small, some bigger. There's a sort of legend about one that was far,

193

far bigger than the one in 1906, but I'm not sure; it probably is just a legend. How about some Chinese food in that restaurant over there?"

Chinese food being one of the things Gerald had "discovered" with great enthusiasm since he came to San Francisco, they wasted no further time on earthquakes and went to lunch.

That evening Gerald was going through one of the oldest of all grandfather's boxes when he came upon an ancient, yellowed document, which he had to unfold with great care in case it fell to pieces. The ink was brown, the characters sloped queerly and were difficult to read, but the first few words made Gerald leap to his feet with a yell that sent his uncle's pencil flying out of his hand: "I, Thomas Watkyn, son of Alfred Watkyn, yeoman of Barnstaple, once of the crew of Master Francis Drake and now stranded here upon this foreign shore . . ."

Uncle Edward retrieved his pencil while Gerald excitedly but with great care smoothed out the paper.

"Look at this. Just look!"

Uncle Edward looked and slipped slowly on to Gerald's chair, never taking his eyes off the document.

"Well, I'll be darned! This is really *some*thing!"

Gerald pulled up another chair, and with the papers spread in front of them they read:

"I, Thomas Watkyn, son of Alfred Watkyn, yeoman of Barnstaple, once of the crew of Master Francis Drake and now stranded here upon this foreign shore, must hereby write of the strange events which have happened to me since I left the ship which brought me from England. One day, while the good ship *Golden Hind* was being refitted, I was sent out upon a hunting expedition by our gallant captain; for he knew me to be an excellent bowman and a hunter, having gone with my father on divers occasions to hunt the red deer. And so one day I found myself amongst some hills in pursuit of a herd of deer here in what Master Francis has named New Albion.

"So intent was I upon the chase, that, before I knew it, night had descended and I had to sleep in the forest. Next morning I spied a fine buck and tried to stalk close enough to shoot it.

194

"Intent upon the game I was pursuing along a hillside track made by the animals, I slipped upon a stone and hurtled down a steep precipice, falling into the rocky brook which rushed through a narrow gully below. A sharp stab of pain told me that I had broken my ankle in the fall.

"Now it is strange for a healthy young man, as I was then, to find himself suddenly as helpless as a baby, unable to walk. Yet such was my plight then. There was, in my hapless condition, no way for me to climb out of this steep-walled canyon. Painfully, I dragged myself a few feet to a little shelf of rock, where some bushes offered a slight shelter and where I at least was on dry land. Even that small effort exhausted me, and I lay where I was, groaning with pain.

"I know not how long I remained there. I seemed to contract a fever, which came and left me. As hunger, too, made its inroads upon my strength I had strange visions. Fortunately, with the stream at my side, I had enough water so that I might expect to live for a few weeks even without food.

"There is no telling how much time passed. At length I saw what I believed to be another vision. I seemed to see a brown Indian maiden bending over me, speaking in strange clucking sounds. Then I lapsed again into unconsciousness. But later I awoke to find myself in a rude hut, filled with acrid smoke from a fire mingled with a divine smell of roasting meat.

"I ate a little food, but soon the fever returned, and I knew no more. In waking moments, I learned that the Indian maid had found me and had her tribesmen bring me to the little village. As soon as I could make myself understood to Ahkoonah, my young preserver, I tried to ask her to get news back to the ship. But when she comprehended my signs she made me understand, to my horror, that the ship had departed.

"At length I mended and, being treated as a member of Ahkoonah's family, little by little I became accustomed to life in the Indian village. In fact, due to my knowledge of farming and other useful skills, I became one of the honored young men of the tribe.

"One day I went out on a hunting expedition to the south,

taking with me two young Indians. After a day and a half we arrived in a beautiful forest made up of trees whose bark is soft and of a dark red color, and we camped there that night.

"The next morning I climbed, alone, to the top of a near-by hill to see what was beyond. So beautiful was the countryside that I believed I should see something wonderful beyond the hills.

"What I saw when I reached the hilltop was indeed marvelous. A great valley stretched before me, as far as the eye could reach. Away off to the east two rivers debouched from the rolling hills, converging and meandering westward. The valley was surrounded by high hills and in the midst of it were several small peaks, rising steeply out of the valley. I was lost in admiration, thinking of Moses seeing for the first time the Promised Land.

"At that moment I was startled by a crashing sound. Some heavy body was breaking through the underbrush. I could not see what it was but I had only too strong a suspicion. Nothing smaller than a bear would make that kind of crashing sound. My bow and arrows were slender protection against the great bears that roam this country.

"The bear came weaving into sight and stopped, his little red-shot eyes glaring wickedly at me. I took careful aim and let fly, but as ill-luck would have it my arrow just missed his throat and only gave him a painful wound which served but to madden him.

"With an angry roar he came at me. My escape was almost cut off by the thick brush. Frantically I tried to get another arrow into place, but the bear was almost upon me. I could see his great yellow claws waving closer and closer . . .

"Then a strange thing happened. I heard a distant sound like thunder afar off. Yet the day was clear, and there was no lightning to be seen. Still the sound reverberated, a strange subterranean rumbling which seemed to come from the center of the earth.

"Nameless fear overtook the giant grizzled monster before me. He stopped dead in his tracks, and into his bloodshot eyes

197

came a look of abject terror. His fright communicated itself to me. Then a strange thing happened—a thing which few men can have seen since the creation of the earth.

"That whole great valley that I had been admiring was sinking, to the accompaniment of stupendous rumblings. I even seemed to hear shrieks as great rocks tore apart and huge cracks opened into yawning crevasses. For the whole valley was sinking, sinking, leaving great scars and rents in the red earth, as whole hills plummeted into the abyss.

"Then the most awe-inspiring moment came. On the westward side a great rent in the hills opened, and the valley was cleft in twain.

"As this gorge opened, so, with a mighty roar, a spate of sea water gushed through the opening carved between the great brown hills. Terrible was the thunder of waters as the inrushing sea plunged fields and forests below the surface of the swirling flood, until only a few of the peaks I had at first seen still projected above the surface as islands.

"The bear, by this time, had taken to his heels. Many animals were now stampeding madly from the valley to higher ground.

"I cannot tell how long all this took for I was so afraid that I lost all count of time.

"How I got back to the Indian camp I do not now remember. That terrible, magnificent sight numbed my senses for days.

"Now, having lost hope of seeing ships from Europe on this distant coast, I have settled among Ah-koonah's family. Because, in age, my memory of it may grow dim, I write this story as best I can to preserve, if some man from England should ever chance this way, a record of this strange and wonderful event. Yet I cannot but wonder whether such a man would believe my story. Sometimes I cannot believe it myself, and this is why I go on a journey each year to the high, quiet hills overlooking the bay which I saw created by a miracle in the year of the Great Earthquake."

For a moment when they finished reading there was silence. Then Gerald said, "So that's why Drake didn't mention the Bay. It wasn't there."

198

Uncle Edward said nothing for a moment. He got up and filled his pipe, and as he did so he said, almost casually, although Gerald felt he was inwardly excited, "You know, that isn't a genuine document."

"Oh, but—" began Gerald, almost angrily.

"I don't necessarily mean it's a fake. It may be a copy of an earlier document. Let's see what other papers there are with it."

They searched through the rest of the box and found a small piece of paper on which was scrawled, "This document was given to me by an old man. He'd got it from his father, a settler, who said he had seen the original document but that it was so faded and torn that he had copied it and left the original with the Indian tribe who owned it. I don't know if this is all true, but it is interesting."

"Great Uncle George, the missionary, again," said Uncle Edward with a grin. "And he's certainly right; it's interesting."

"Do you think it's true?" asked Gerald.

"Could be. I've heard the legend before, you know, but I never believed it. Now, I'm not so sure."

"I am," said Gerald firmly.

"O.K." Uncle Edward laughed. "So your bowls-playing Englishman didn't slip up. Even Sir Francis couldn't have seen a bay that wasn't there."

Noel Streatfeild

UNDERSTUDY

ILLUSTRATED BY *Hilda Frommholz*

THE Allison School of Stage Training for Children was in North London. Four houses joined together to make one big house. The children who attended the school were mostly of school age, so the classes were arranged in such a way that it did not interfere with lessons. Every evening from five to seven there were classes, and there were classes all Saturday mornings. Of course no child who was still at school went to a class every day, that would be too much work. The stage training lessons were graduated according to age. The youngest pupils usually came to classes on Saturday mornings only. As they grew older they attended one evening class as well. Later, two evening classes, then a class every other evening. Margaret Allison, the head of the school, had once been a well-known actress, but illness had kept her off the stage for some years. When she got better she decided that she would not return to the stage, but instead use her talents to train future actresses, so she started her school of stage training for children.

She had strong views on child actors. She wanted the children to have a first-class all-round training in ordinary lessons as well as stage work, but she was sure it should not stop at that. Too many children showed a certain amount of talent, and even played good parts, but either the talent did not last or their shape and looks were wrong when they grew up, and there was no future for them on the stage. So, as well as preparing her pupils for the stage, she insisted on a high school standard. Any pupils who were not educationally up to scholarship standard by the time they were sixteen were asked to leave. All pupils over sixteen had to be trained for some other career, as well as the stage, typing, shorthand, bookkeeping or something of the sort. "You never know," Mrs. Allison would say. "The stage is a chancy career. You must have something else to turn to if things go wrong."

It was a spring morning just before the end of term. Jane Jameson walked slowly up the steps to the pupils' entrance of the Allison School for Stage Training. Jane's shoulders were sagging, in fact she drooped all over with depression. "How awful," she thought. "Here is Jane Jameson coming up the pupils' steps for the last time. I shall never again feel the gorgeousness of being at a proper training school. I will just go back to the ordinary world outside." She opened the door. She stood on the mat and sniffed. Classes were held in the art of make-up. There was a faint smell of grease paint and powder in the air. To Jane it was the most perfect smell in the world. She gulped back a sob and walked slowly down the stairs to the changing-room. "This is the last time. I must remember every foot of this. The jagged bit sticking out from this step. The shiny piece of carpet at the bottom because we all jump the last three steps. The letter B on the changing-room door. The feel of the door handle in my hand. The voices that rush to meet me as I open the door."

Outside the changing-room door Jane paused to straighten her shoulders. She was not pretty, but she had an unusual, attractive face. Pale and thin, with large gray-green eyes. Her heavy dark hair, which fell into the nape of her neck, suited her perfectly. Just at the moment her face lacked animation, but at other times, when she was happy and interested, she had a vividness of expression that was quite outstanding.

Fourteen girls shared B dressing-room. They were in various stages of changing. Few of Mrs. Allison's girls had much money to spare, so there were no regulations about uniform. For the acting classes they wore anything they liked and when, as now,

201

they changed for dancing, they put on something which gave free movement and allowed the teacher to see what their legs were up to. Jane had a skimpy silk tunic she had made out of a worn-out summer frock. She opened her locker and took it off its hanger. From the back of the locker she pulled out her much-darned ballet shoes. Jane's ambition was to be a straight actress, but the sight of her ballet shoes brought a lump into her throat. She enjoyed dancing and she knew it was good training for an actress. She would never forget the thrill the day she was promoted to block shoes. When would she wear them again? Never, most likely.

"What's up? You do look miserable."

Jane swallowed the lump and smiled. It was difficult to be gloomy with Sally about. Sally was the school's star pupil. She showed real promise as an actress. She had a pretty speaking voice. She could sing, and she was one of the best dancers in the school. As well she was lovely to look at. Flaming copper-colored hair. Huge blue eyes with black lashes. The perfect complexion that sometimes goes with red hair. Jane sat on the floor to put on her ballet shoes.

"I'm feeling end-of-termish."

Sally sat beside her. She pushed the ribbons of her ballet shoes through the supporting loop at the back of the heel.

"The Easter holidays aren't long. You'll be back in three weeks. Old Sergius will look at us at our first ballet class and say, 'Young ladies, you haf not practice. Miss Sally, to me you do not lie. Your leg is so stiff it might be carve of wood.'"

Jane tried to laugh, but a very dismal sound came out of her. You can't laugh properly at a joke about next term when you know you won't be there next term.

Sally was quick at feeling things about anybody, and particularly about people she was fond of. She was very fond of Jane. She put an arm round her shoulders.

"What's up?"

Jane was afraid she was going to cry. She whispered in a fierce sort of way.

"Can't explain." To prevent any further questioning she got

202

up and began dragging her frock over her head.

Sally, too, got up. She glanced round to see if the other girls were listening, while she buttoned the shoulder of the green bathing dress she wore for dancing. Nobody but herself had noticed that anything was wrong with Jane. Most of the girls had changed and were filling up the time before their class limbering up. Sally pulled Jane out of her frock and hung it up for her.

"I won't ask you just now, but you've simply got to tell me what's wrong. We'll sit in the corner next to each other while Sergius takes Celia through her variations. Come on, get into your tunic. It's almost ten. And you don't want a row with Sergius on the last day of the term."

The ballet classes were held in the main hall. Down each side were practice bars. At the end was a small stage on which was a piano. Sergius had not yet arrived. The girls went straight to their places and limbered up.

Jane was next to Celia. Celia was small and fair. She held the bar in both hands and stood on her points.

"Oh, goodness, I wish I needn't do my variations today. I'm

sure Sergius will think I haven't practiced, but I have, only it's so difficult at home. The people underneath make the most awful row if I bump."

There was a murmur of sympathy. Many of the class lived in flats and knew from bitter experience what the people underneath thought about dancing practice. Jane was busy with her *pliés*.

"Thank goodness it's you that have got to do them and not me."

Celia set her feet wide apart in the first position. She bent her knees.

"You thank your stars you're going to be an actress and not a dancer. No underneath flat, however nasty the people in it, mind a person practicing to be an actress over their heads."

Sally, who was in the middle of a *plié*, straightened up.

"That's all you know. I was rehearsing Beatrice in a scene with Benedict. The man below us beat on the door and said if I couldn't argue more quietly he'd call the police."

Jane raised her head; her eyes were shining.

"I wouldn't care how much anybody beat on the door or what anybody said. If I wanted to work at a part I'd work anywhere, in the road, in a train, even in the middle of Piccadilly Circus."

Some of the other girls had gathered round during the discussion. One of them said,—

"Listen to her! We know where you got that from, Jane."

The girls looked up at the wall above Jane's head. All round the hall were photographs of great actors and actresses of the past and the present. One family was especially represented, the Billingtons. There had been Billington stars for four generations. Over Jane's head was a photograph taken in 1930. It was of a young girl in the part of Nell Gwyn.

Sally looked up at the photograph adoringly.

"Judy Billington. She must have been simply gorgeous. I wish, oh, how I wish I'd seen her."

Celia changed the position of her feet and once more bent her knees.

204

"Gosh, I'm stiff!" She glanced up at the photograph. "I'd like to have seen her when she rehearsed in the street. Mrs. Allison says she forgot everything when she thought about a part. Once she saw her being Nell Gwyn on Holborn Underground station. Such a place to choose!"

Jane spoke quickly.

"She wasn't showing off. She just thought of something for the part, and then, of course, she had to try it out. She just didn't notice where she was."

A girl said,—

"Don't you be encouraged to do that, Jane. You aren't Judy Billington. You'd probably get taken for a lunatic."

Sally lifted her left leg over her head.

"Quite likely Jane will be a Judy Billington. You don't know."

Celia was back at her *pliés*.

"If she is, she'd better not waste any more time here. She'll give up acting the moment she's famous, just like Judy Billington did."

Sally stood on her points staring at the photograph.

"She must have been terribly in love. Of course I haven't been in love yet, but if I was I'm quite sure I wouldn't give up my career to be married. Would you, Jane? I bet she's sorry now that she did."

Jane too was gazing at the picture.

"Of course she's sorry sometimes, but the man she married hates the theater. She promised to give it up. Of course we aren't grown-up, it's difficult for us to understand. I just hope and hope I'll never fall in love like that. She stopped being Judy Billington the day she married. I think she tries to forget Judy Billington. It's the only way."

Sally had taken her eyes from the photograph and was staring at Jane. She opened her mouth to say something. At that moment Celia gave both her and Jane a nudge.

"Ssh! Sergius."

Half an hour later Sergius signed to the pianist to stop playing.

"Rest, young ladies." The fourteen girls thankfully relaxed. They leaned against the practice bars and moved their toes up

206

and down in their shoes to ease their insteps. Sergius nodded to the pianist. "We will now take the leetle variations." He turned to Celia. "Mees Celia," he waved a hand. "Young ladies, you may sit."

The girls ran to a bench at the bottom of the room. They picked up their cardigans as they ran and either put them on or hung them round their shoulders. Sally put her arm through Jane's.

"Come on. Right up in that corner, and then the others won't hear."

Jane had not meant to tell anybody about herself, but it was difficult to keep Sally at arm's length. Besides, it would be nice to confide in somebody. Not everything, of course; she could never tell anybody everything. The big secret she must keep to herself, but she could explain about it being her last term. That would be a help; it was so hateful being miserable alone.

"I'm not coming back next term."

Sally was so surprised that she felt as if the wind had been knocked out of her.

"Not coming back! Why on earth not? You were doing so well at the acting classes. You aren't fourteen yet. You've years of training to do."

"It's the money. There isn't any more."

Sally was puzzled, and not for the first time. Jane was obviously not poor. Her clothes were better than most girls' in the school. There seemed to be something queer about Jane's home. She hated talking about it. Sally did not want to seem inquisitive, but as Jane was obviously unhappy she simply had to probe.

"Has your father lost his job?"

Jane fidgeted with the hem of her tunic.

"No. You won't understand, Sally, because I can't explain about me. There's a good reason—my father and mother don't know I'm training here. As a matter of fact, I pay for myself."

"Pay for yourself! Your family don't know?" Suddenly the corners of Sally's eyes crinkled and she began to laugh. "You, of all people, looking so quiet and so yes-sir-no-sir-three-bags-

207

fullish. How do you manage to fool them?"

Jane flushed.

"I haven't fooled them exactly. I'd hate to fool them because I adore them, but—I simply had to do it. It was desperate to think I was growing up without any proper stage training. My school doesn't work on Saturdays, so Saturday mornings are all right. When I come here on Mondays, Wednesdays, and Fridays I'm supposed to be at my piano lessons."

Sally giggled.

"What happens about those? I should like to be around when your family ask you to play the 'Moonlight Sonata' and you can't strike a note."

"Oh, but I can play." Jane hesitated, choosing her words carefully. "The person who teaches me is a relation; he knows why I have to wangle to come here. He gives me a quick music lesson before school twice a week, and two hours on Saturday afternoons."

"Gosh! Every Saturday? How simply awful. I couldn't give up every Saturday afternoon. I'd never get to a matinée."

Jane lifted one leg on to the bench and hugged it to her.

"No. That is awful. But I want so terribly to be a good actress, I simply had to have some coaching. I've known about Mrs. Allison ever since I was born. She's got an international reputation as a teacher, you know. I simply had to learn from her."

Sally's attention was caught by the lesson.

"Celia's *fouettés* are shocking. I shouldn't think they'd take her in that ballet if she does them like that at her audition." She turned back to Jane. "How did you get the money?"

"Presents. It was in the Post Office."

Sally let out a big breath.

"Jane Jameson, you surprise me more every minute. Do you mean to say you drew all your money out of the Post Office without asking your dad if you might? And having got it out you spent the whole lot on lessons here?"

"Yes."

"And now you've nothing in the Post Office?"

"Only five shillings. I left that so that I could keep my book."

Sally was really distressed.

"But you can't leave. You're awfully promising. You were perfect in that scene from *St. Joan* last term."

Jane let go of her knee. Both legs sprawled in front of her in a hopeless sort of way.

"I've thought of everything. Even selling something, but the only jewelry I've got my mother looks after."

Sally swung round on the bench. She spoke in a whisper.

"If I tell you something will you absolutely swear not to tell anyone else?"

"Of course."

"Cross your heart." Jane crossed her heart. "Well, I may be

209

going to play in a revival. It's Margaret in *Dear Brutus*. The Glay Management may put it on."

"Margaret!"

Sally nodded.

"Mrs. Allison said to say nothing until they're sure because it's unlucky."

Jane managed to sound tremendously pleased. Some people had all the good fortune.

"How gorgeous for you. I am glad."

Sally brushed aside Jane's interruption.

"I have an idea that might help you. If the Glay Management does revive *Dear Brutus* I don't suppose they've got an understudy. They're only going to make up their mind this week end, so they won't have got far about engaging understudies. Why don't you go to Mrs. Allison? Tell her what you've just told me. You can tell her that I told you about *Dear Brutus*. Ask her if she would recommend you for the understudy. She thinks an awful lot of your work; you know she does."

Jane stared at Sally, her eyes bigger than usual with excitement.

"An understudy! I never thought of that. I never thought I could earn money on the stage until I was twenty-one and could do what I liked. But being an understudy I could earn money, and nobobdy would see me." Then her eyes clouded. "But I don't expect the Glay Management would have me. They probably want somebody pretty, like you."

Sally surveyed Jane dispassionately.

"You wouldn't look bad made up." Celia's lesson was coming to an end. She got up. "You know, Jane Jameson, you don't deserve to get on. How you ever had the guts to come here at all I don't know." She made her face look scared and imitated, "I don't expect the Glay Management would have me. They probably want somebody pretty, like you."

Jane longed to answer back, but she knew Sally could not understand. An understudy! It was a wonderful idea if only it could come true. Nobody would know she was being an understudy. If she could get the job! If only she could! It would not

210

only be the money, it would mean being in a theater. Acting on a real stage at understudy rehearsals. Enough money for the fees for next term. Perhaps, if the revival ran long enough, for lots of terms. She jumped to her feet and caught hold of Sally's arm.

"Come with me after class and talk to Mrs. Allison."

Sergius was calling.

"Come, young ladies. Come to the center."

Sally looked consideringly at Jane.

"You'd probably better do it on your own. Still, it might be a good idea if I told Mrs. Allison that I'd told you about *Dear Brutus.*" She gave a quick nod. "All right, directly after class is over, just as soon as we have changed."

.　　.　　.　　.　　.　　.　　.　　.　　.

Mrs. Allison was at her office desk when Sally tapped on her door. She smiled at the two girls.

"Well?"

Sally was shy of nobody. She drew a chair up by the desk and in a minute was pouring out Jane's troubles. Mrs. Allison held out a hand to Jane, who was standing awkwardly, listening.

"I think you might have told me all this before."

Jane looked at the carpet and rubbed it up the wrong way with the toe of her ballet shoe.

"There's reasons."

Mrs. Allison turned over her ledger. Her mouth had a half smile.

"Your fees are paid by a Mr. Jameson. Who's he?"

Jane was crimson.

"He teaches me the piano."

"A relation?"

"Yes. My brother."

Mrs. Allison tapped her ledger with a pencil.

"A parent has to sign a contract, you know, if you were engaged."

Jane swallowed nervously.

"I sometimes think my mother guesses."

Mrs. Allison leaned forward to say something more, but before

211

she could speak her secretary knocked and came in. The secretary was a flustered little woman, and now she looked scared.

"It's Mr. Glay."

Mrs. Allison was quite unmoved.

"Ask him to come in." Sally's hand was lying on her desk. She patted it. "Now we shall know your fate." Jane was turning to leave the room; she stopped her. "No, stay. We'll see what we can do about this understudy."

Mr. Glay was an important-looking man. His clothes probably did not cost any more than anybody else's but somehow they looked expensive. He wore horn-rimmed spectacles. He shook Mrs. Allison's hand, but his eyes were on Sally. He began to speak almost before he was in the room.

"This is a wonderful opportunity for you, young lady, a wonderful opportunity. Margaret is a peach of a part. One of the most moving scenes in any play."

Sally was trembling. Mrs. Allison held out her hand and drew her to her.

"Congratulations, my child. Now Mr. Glay and I have got to talk business. You run along home and tell your parents. I know they'll be proud."

Sally was breathing in little short, excited breaths. She was going to play Margaret! How wizard! How thrilled mum and dad would be. Mum would run out and try and get some ice cream to celebrate, and dad would take them all to the pictures tonight. Suddenly she remembered Jane. She turned impulsively to Mr. Glay.

"Do you want an understudy for Margaret?"

Mr. Glay thought he had a real find in Sally. He was prepared to please her if he could.

"I haven't engaged one yet."

Sally ran to Jane and pulled her towards Mr. Glay.

"She doesn't look very interesting, but she's very clever. Her name's Jane Jameson."

Mr. Glay studied Jane. She was not his idea of the part. He wanted a strikingly pretty child. He wanted Sally's curls for the moment when she knelt by the pool and said: "Daddy, now

I'm putting up my hair." He could not imagine Jane's hair looking childishly grown up, held in place by a wreath of flowers. Still, there was no reason why Sally should ever be off. It was not a bad idea, having a friend as her understudy. The girl could sit in Sally's dressing-room. It was true, too, she did look clever. He settled himself in a chair and turned to Jane.

"Would you like to recite something?"

Jane moved to the middle of the room. She closed her eyes for a moment to get rid of them all, to feel away from herself. Mrs. Allison watched her with a half smile. She glanced at Mr. Glay to see if he saw what she saw, but Mr. Glay was looking at Sally.

Jane had left Mrs. Allison's room, she was St. Joan speaking to the King of France. Centuries fell away, she grew older and taller, her voice took on a country burr.

For a moment there was complete silence when Jane finished acting. Then Mr. Glay turned to Mrs. Allison.

"She'll do."

Mrs. Allison dismissed the girls. The business arrangements had nothing to do with them. She held out a box of cigarettes.

"Won't you smoke?"

Mr. Glay got up and took a cigarette as if he did not know he was taking it.

"Jane Jameson!" He shook his head. "Curious, while that child was acting she reminded me of somebody. I can't think who. . . ."

Mrs. Allison smiled.

"Can't you? I guessed long ago."

.   .   .   .

The rehearsals went fairly well. Sally found that playing a part at a stage school and playing a part in a real production were two different things. Every line, every inflection important, every bit of business and step taken marked in the prompt book. *Dear Brutus* was a play which had been first acted early in the nineteen twenties. It had been acted very often since and, as happens when plays are revived, moves and inflections put in by previous actors had become part of the production, and it was difficult to get away from them. In the play the part of Margaret was a dream daughter of an artist called Dearth. He had never had a daughter, and his dream child was the daughter he ought to have had. Sir J. M. Barrie, in the stage directions, said of Margaret, "She is as lovely as you think she is, and she is aged the moment when you like your daughter best."

The man who was playing Dearth in the Glay Management's revival, a Mr. Kingston, was a very distinguished actor indeed. It had been his idea that a real child ought to play Margaret, and that she ought not to look more than twelve or thirteen. In previous productions a grown-up actress had played Margaret, and she had looked as if she was fifteen or sixteen. The actor who played Dearth knew exactly what he wanted Margaret to be like. Rather hoydenish, very unsophisticated, and with abso-

214

lute understanding between herself and her father. He thought that physically Sally was perfect, but he was not entirely pleased with her acting. He kept saying to her, "Don't do so much. Just be a simple little girl."

Sometimes Sally would lose her temper with him and say, "How can I be simple when everything I do is fixed and arranged and I can't make one spontaneous movement?"

After rehearsals Mr. Kingston would talk to Sally exactly as if she were his daughter. He would ask her how much pocket money she had, and if she was getting short to tell him, and he would give her the sort of presents a father would give a daughter, and he teased her. He sometimes gave her an affectionate slap on her tail, just like a father might do. He liked Sally, but treating her as his daughter was for the good of the play. He knew that if Sally could feel easy with him and he with her they would act much better together.

In the half-dark theater Jane sat with the understudies, marking in her copy every direction given to Sally. Cross left. Stand on one leg. Lean against the tree and while you speak play with the bark. Jane loved the theater during rehearsals. It was not a bit like the theater when a performance was on. There were no lights in the auditorium, the seats were covered with sheets. On their hands and knees, paying no attention to what was happening on the stage, were the theater charladies. They started cleaning in the stalls, often under the understudies' feet. " 'Scuse me, dearie." They moved to the pit, then the dress circle, then the upper circle and, finally, you could hear their dustpans clattering in the gallery.

The stage itself looked mysterious at rehearsals. When Sally and Jane arrived each morning Sally went on to the stage and sat about chatting to the other actresses and actors. There was only very dim lighting. Jane, sitting in the stalls, thought that a stage before rehearsal looked rather like a badly-lit railway carriage, with the actors talking to each other to pass the time. Then suddenly everything would change. The actors stopped talking. The stage manager would call to the electricians and the stage be flooded with light. Mr. Kingston, who was produc-

215

ing as well as acting, had arrived. At this moment at every rehearsal Jane felt excited. The theater suddenly coming alive.
The scenery was not up; it was going to be a wood, so chairs
stood about for the trees and there were chalk marks showing
the exits and entrances. To Jane scenery was not needed, for the
stage was thrilling in itself. As soon as the scene started, for her
the chairs disappeared and she was seeing a real wood.

As well she liked the stage for itself. The bits of scenery standing about belonging to past plays. The gallery up above the
stage known as "the flies," to which, at the end of each act,
some of the scenery would be pulled up so as to make room for
the scenery for the next act. There was a drop-curtain at the
back of the stage which hid, Jane knew because she had looked,
a lot of space behind it. They called this the scene dock. It was
a glorious place full of scenery, properties, theater baskets and
pieces of furniture. It was all looked after by a property master,
who did not like his things touched, but all the same Jane and
Sally managed to peep. They had seen banqueting sets made of
what, from a distance, would look like gold. A royal throne.
Yards of lawn neatly rolled up like a carpet. A sedan chair. Just
staring at the things made their imaginations whirl. What actor
had sat on the royal throne? What garden did the lawn belong

to? Could it have been the one that Alice saw in Wonderland? Who had ridden in the sedan chair?

Directly the rehearsal was over Jane went to Sally's dressing-room. There, or while they had lunch, or tea, they discussed the rehearsal.

"They aren't pleased with me. Mr. Kingston isn't pleased, I can feel he isn't." Or, on days when things went well, "It was a super rehearsal today."

Jane managed to let Sally think that she agreed with her when she was pleased, and disagreed with her when she was depressed. It was no good fussing Sally, who was sufficiently worked up already, but loyal as Jane was to Sally she did not always agree with the way she played Margaret. Especially she did not agree with her way of acting the end of the act.

Dearth and his daughter had been having a lovely time in the wood, Dearth painting and Margaret talking, as a daughter would, to her father about what she was going to be like when she was grown up, and about what she was like when she was little. As well they talked to a gypsy who passed through the wood, and Margaret, rather to her father's embarrassment, told the gypsy all about their financial affairs. Then they began talking about losing each other, an idea put into Margaret's head by the gypsy, who was Dearth's childless wife in real life, and from that moment the wood began to fade. Dearth, the father, became more real and Margaret more of a dream. Just as the curtain fell Margaret tried to call her father back. She ran from tree to tree, and the stage direction said, "We begin to lose her among the shadows." She had to say, "Daddy, come back; I don't want to be a might-have-been." To Jane, Margaret's fate was almost unbearable. How terrible to be only a dream. To see your father walk towards a house and people and know that you only lived in his imagination.

Up to a point Sally felt as Jane did, but only up to a point. To her, Margaret at the end was saying, "I don't want to be a might-have-been," because she knew that she was interesting and vital, and it was a pity that she should remain a dream and nobody know about her. She did not feel, as Jane did, the

217

appalling horror of the darkening wood and the child lost and forgotten.

A teacher from the school looked after the two girls. She took them to the County Hall for their licenses, took Sally to the dressmaker to have her dress fitted, and to the shoemaker for sandals, and to various restaurants for lunch. It was still the Easter holidays, so they had all day free from lessons, and except for a brief appearance at the end of the play, Sally was only concerned with the second act, and so she did not have a rehearsal every day. All the same, it seemed to her queer that Jane could be away so much and nobody notice.

"Don't your family wonder where you are all day?"

Jane was evasive.

"Mother's had to know. She had to sign my contract. Dad thinks I'm with my brother."

Sally was exasperated.

"If I wasn't so thrilled about me I'd be nearly mad with curiosity about you."

A week before the production day Sally arrived at rehearsal looking ill. The mistress from the school said,—

"You do look white, child; what's the matter?"

Sally answered rudely.

"Nothing. Why should there be?"

To Jane she told the truth.

"I can't think what's up. I keep getting an awful pain and I was sick three times during the night."

"Does your mother know?"

"Of course not. She wouldn't have let me get up. Oh, Jane, I can't be going to be ill. My lovely, lovely part!"

The rehearsal went badly. Sally was slow and stupid. Mr. Kingston would not scold her because he thought she might get frightened of him, and they would lose their easy father-and-daughter atmosphere on the stage, but you could see he was a little exasperated. Margaret's first entrance was to race her father on to the stage. They were looking for the place where Dearth had put his painting easel the night before. Margaret's first line was, "Daddy, daddy. I have won. Here is the place.

Crack-in-my-eye Tommy!" "Crack-in-my-eye Tommy" was Margaret's nickname for her father. The whole line needed saying with great gaiety but complete naturalness. As a rule Sally was charming in that entrance, but today she simply could not do it; she sounded lifeless and, because she was trying to put in life where she did not feel it, affected. After three attempts at the line Mr. Kingston let it pass and they went on with the scene. It was a sad, dreary performance. They came to a bit where Margaret pretended to be grown up and put up her hair. They had to say,—

MARGARET: "Shut your eyes, please."

DEARTH: "No, Margaret."

MARGARET: "Please, daddy."

DEARTH: "Oh, all right. They are shut."

MARGARET: "Don't open them till I tell you. What finger is that?"

DEARTH: "The dirty one."

MARGARET (*on her knees among the leaves*): "Daddy, now I'm putting up my hair. I have got such a darling of a mirror. It is such a darling mirror I've got, dad. Dad, don't look. I shall tell you about it. It is a little pool of water. I wish we could take it home and hang it up. Of course the moment my hair is up there will be other changes also; for instance, I shall talk quite differently."

While Sally was saying this speech she had to pull her curls to the top of her head and fasten them up there with a little piece of bracken. When she got up from the pool she was something like what the grown-up Margaret might have looked. That morning she fumbled with her curls, her voice seemed to tail away, she tried to get up but she only succeeded in raising her head, her face was green. She opened her mouth to say the next words, but before a sound came out she crumpled up on the floor.

Sally was carried to her dressing-room and the faint seemed nothing at first, but when she recovered from the faint she still seemed so ill a doctor was sent for. A few minutes after he arrived the bad news was all over the theater. Sally had an inflamed appendix. She was to be operated on immediately.

Jane, sitting in the stalls clutching her script, felt her inside turning over and over. "How awful. Poor Sally!" Then she thought of herself. "Oh, goodness, I shall have to play at this rehearsal." She shut her eyes and whispered. "Let me act well. Let me act really well."

The stage manager, Mr. Kingston and Mr. Glay were having a conversation on the stage. Suddenly the stage manager came to the footlights. With one hand he shaded his eyes from the glare and peered into the stalls.

"Is Jane Jameson there? Come up here, my dear, we want you."

Jane hardly heard the muttered "Good luck, Jane," of the other understudies. Her heart was beating too fast; she stumbled out of her seat and through the pass door on to the stage.

The principals had not seen Jane before; they looked at her with interest and kind smiles. Jane tried to smile back but her mouth felt stiff. "However nicely they smile," she thought, "they can't help thinking I look pretty drab after Sally."

The wood scene was up. Queer, thin trees, which under the proper lighting would have the enchantment of moonlight. The wood had appeared magically at the end of act one. When the act started there had been a garden outside the window, but when it finished there was a wood of trees pressed close to the pane. Everybody in the play, except the child Margaret, was a guest in the house of a queer old man called Lob, and each of the guests thought they could have been much happier if they had a second chance in life. In act two, in the wood, they get the second chance that they wanted and, of course, find out that human nature doesn't change even with second chances.

Because of Sally's illness and the upset it had caused, Mr. Kingston decided they would take act two all over again. Margaret did not come on until halfway through the act. The other characters, wandering about two-and-two, were in the wood first. Jane stood in the wings. She knew her cue. She knew her lines. But could she make her voice speak? She was panting as if she had been running. Take deep breaths when you're nervous, Mrs. Allison had taught her. She took a deep breath, and then another. Then she felt a hand on her shoulder. Mr. Kingston smiled down at her. He did not seem to notice that she was nervous. He did not even seem to know that he had never spoken to her before. He said,—

"A nice night for a stroll in the woods, daughter, but you ought to be in bed, you know."

Jane hardly knew what to answer. She murmured rather feebly,—

"I suppose it is late if the moon's out."

He rearranged her hair on her shoulders.

"Silly daughter. Of course it's late when there is a moon. Why, I haven't had you out in moonlight for years. Not since that time we went bathing by moonlight."

Suddenly Jane stopped being frightened and entered into the spirit of the game. If he was her pretense father, she could make up stories for a pretense daughter.

"And then we sat on the beach and ate strawberries and cream."

He laughed.

"Highly indigestible at that time of night, especially when accompanied by lobster. It was lobster we ate, wasn't it?"

She nodded.

"And then we had ice cream."

He gave her shoulder an affectionate pat.

"Off we go then. The nightingale is singing, and the wood is all ours. Which of us is going to find my painting easel first?"

It was almost easy after that. When you had played at being father and daughter off-stage it was only natural to go on being father and daughter on the stage. After a very few minutes Jane was enjoying herself. It was such sensible conversation that she and Mr. Kingston had to have. Just like the conversation they had both been making up.

MARGARET: "The moon is rather pale tonight, isn't she?"

DEARTH: "Comes of keeping late hours."

MARGARET (*showing off*): "Daddy, watch me, look at me. Please, sweet moon, a pleasant expression. No, no, not as if you

221

were sitting for it; that is too professional. That is better; thank you. Now keep it. That is the sort of thing you say to them, dad."

DEARTH: "I oughtn't to have brought you out so late; you should be tucked up in your cosy bed at home."

It was not difficult to feel the end of the play. Jane was not being Jane. She was Margaret, and when she saw Mr. Kingston walking off towards Lob's lighted house, a sort of panic came over her. Once inside there, with all the other real people, he would forget that alone in the middle of a darkening wood was a daughter who was only a dream. Terrified she ran from tree to tree, her voice rang through the theater.

"Daddy, come back; I don't want to be a might-have-been."

Mr. Glay, Mr. Kingston, and, surprisingly, Mrs. Allison, whom Jane had not supposed was in the theater, were whispering on the stage. Jane stood watching them with a queer feeling of slowly coming out of being Margaret and back into being Jane. Then Mr. Glay beckoned to her. He held out his hand and drew her into the group.

"We're very pleased with you, young lady. If you work hard in the next few days you should give a very touching performance."

Mrs. Allison stooped and kissed Jane.

"Well done, my child. This is a wonderful chance for you."

Mr. Kingston put his arm round her. He raised her chin.

"I'm looking forward to knowing more of my new daughter."

It was the first night. Jane's dresser gave the green skirt Jane was wearing a last nervous tweak. The teacher from the Academy and the girl who had become her understudy wished her luck. Jane took a quick look at herself in the glass. She looked very ordinary, she thought, in a jersey and skirt, bare legs and sandals, but she was improved by make-up. It was a pity she had not Sally's red hair. Sally looked so glorious in green. There was a knock on her dressing-room door. It was the call boy.

"Miss Jameson, your entrance, please."

She took a deep breath and, followed by the teacher, went up on to the side of the stage, passing the canvas scenery backs,

and mysterious silver-blue lighting from arcs and battens; she could hear the voices of "Mabel" and "Purdie," two characters in the scene before her entrance. Stepping quietly, she moved into the wings.

It was lovely to find Mr. Kingston waiting. He was quite unflustered. He was just as he had been at her first rehearsal. He said,—

"My word! The wood looks nice. Doesn't the bracken smell good?"

Jane peered on to the stage. It was bathed in moonlight and the trees were queer and ghostly. There was no bracken to smell, but the moment Mr. Kingston mentioned it, Jane knew it was there and could smell it too. She knew too of the other things that were there. The rabbits, the birds, and the squirrels.

The nightingale, whose song was the cue for their entrance, began to trill. Jane caught a quick, frightened breath. Mr. Kingston put an arm round her shoulders.

"Look up, daughter. Nightingales are in the trees, not on the ground. It's a lovely night to go painting in a wood. We'll have such fun."

He was quite right. It was fun. It seemed to Jane that she really was in a magic wood. Not once did she remember that Mr. Kingston was an actor and she was an actress. He was her father and she was his daughter. Because she felt like that the end was terrible. He was going away, he would never come back, she was never going to live, the wood would go, and she would fade away with it. Mr. Kingston had to hum a song as he went off, and she was supposed to count a hundred, by which time he said he would come back. But the wood was growing darker, and the humming voice was out of earshot. She could no longer count because she was too afraid. She was so afraid that she could hardly get out her words. Even the trees seemed to be fading. Everything was going. It was with a despairing gasp that she said her last line.

There was complete silence for a moment after the curtain had come down, then there was a roar like the sea on a stormy night. Mr. Kingston caught hold of Jane's hand.

"Come along, daughter. We've got to go and bow."

When the curtain had been up and down several times Jane came off the stage, feeling rather flat. She wished Margaret had a part in the third act. It was dull to wait in her dressing-room all through the act just to dance across the stage silently at the end. Mr. Glay was waiting by the door from the stage to the dressing-room.

"Well done, young lady."

She looked at him anxiously.

"Was I all right?"

"Fine, Miss Jameson, fine." He gave her a funny smile. "I saw Sally today."

"Did you? How is she?"

"Getting on well. Mad as a hornet, of course. Still, as I told her, it would take more than an appendicitis to hold Sally down."

"I didn't know she might see anyone yet."

"She sent for me."

Jane was shocked. Even if you were ill Mr. Glay was not the sort of man you sent for.

"Did she?"

He laughed.

"Yes, Miss Jane Jameson, she did." He saw the stage manager wanted to speak to him, so he moved away. "Run along to your dressing-room. I'll see you at the end of the play."

Jane had made a success. It was very difficult to make a success in a part like Margaret, which everybody knew so well, but the part fitted her as it could never have fitted Sally. With her rather coltish movements, her brown hair and charming, but not pretty, face, she was what Sir J. M. Barrie had intended Margaret to be. Everybody's dream-daughter. When the curtain had been up and down several times Mr. Kingston said,—

"This time we'll bow just by ourselves, and we'll see which of us can bow best."

There was such a lot of applause for that curtain that they took another one all alone before they took the final curtain with the whole company. At the end of that curtain Mr. Kingston made a nice little speech thanking everybody, and at the

225

end of the speech he stopped the applause by holding up his hand. He said,—

"I'm now going to introduce you to Mr. Glay, who has something he wants to say to you."

Mr. Glay strolled on to the stage. He looked even better dressed than usual. He had such grand evening clothes that he looked more like an advertisement than a man.

"Ladies and gentlemen, I want to tell you a story. This child, Jane, was the understudy. The child I had engaged, Sally, is ill. Many of you, I think, watching the play tonight, have guessed a secret. I saw the likeness but I could not place it." He stepped back and took Jane by the hand and led her forward. "This is the fifth generation of the Billingtons. Judy Billington's daughter."

. . . .

Jane sat by Sally's bed.

"How did you know, Sally? Mr. Glay told me you told him."

"Mrs. Allison. She came to see me while I was waiting for the operation. I said I was afraid you were too scared to act, and she laughed. She said, 'Not with that blood in her veins.' Then she told me."

Jane leaned back in her chair.

"All the Billingtons have been actors, as you know, but when my mother, Judy Billington, gave up acting to marry dad, she promised she wouldn't encourage her children to act. She didn't. My brother Lawrence, luckily, wanted to be a pianist. I think she had always guessed about me. She signed my contract without a word. She cried when she heard I was to play Margaret, she was so pleased."

"What did your father say when he found out?"

"He came to see me act the second night. All the family were there. Grandfather Billington, and grandmother, and Uncle Andrew. Mum and Lawrence were at the first night, of course."

"Your uncle, the film star?"

"Yes. And my aunts. They're all actresses, you know. Dad wouldn't sit with them. He sat alone in the dress circle. I was awfully nervous."

"What did he say afterwards?"

"He waited till mum brought me home. Then he said, 'All right. I lose. You can't stop a Billington.'"

Sally gave her bedclothes a tug.

"And if I hadn't had my appendicitis none of this would ever have happened."

Jane sniffed at some roses she had brought Sally.

"You'll be all right. I showed Uncle Andrew a photograph of you. You are to have a film test directly you are well."

Sally forgot her appendix and bounced in the bed with excitement.

"Oh, Jane! You are an angel!"

Jane shook her head.

"No, it just happened."

Sally's eyes shone.

"How heavenly!" She looked at Jane and her eyes crinkled with laughter. "You are queer. You make a big success, everybody's pleased, and you look not a bit different. You still look yes-sir-no-sir-three-bags-fullish."

Jane got up. She crossed to the window. She stared down into the street below. How could she make Sally see? The family tradition. The eyes that were watching. It was so easy to fail. She said,—

"You'd feel like me if you had so much to try to live up to."

227

Clay Perry

GUIDES WITH WINGS

ILLUSTRATED BY *Kay Lovelace*

PIKE GARDNER in his jalopy galloped over Mill Hill in a hurry, clutching a telegram, which he waved at Button Burnside and Lefty Brown, fellow members of the Explorers' Patrol.

"Listen to this, from Doc Nasmith, Button," he cried as he brought his roadster to a lurching halt in the cottage yard, where his friends were working on an iceboat for the coming winter's scudding about the beautiful Berkshire lake.

> "Sailing for Bermuda to hunt migrants. Will you
> try to band bats in the Alps Cave, Berlin, N. Y.
> Shipped cages, bands, marked map, express yesterday.
> Take strong rope, be careful. If time try Cave of
> Winds, Mt. Aeolus, too. Watch for Eptisicus f. fuscus."

"Sounds sort of shuddery to me," remarked Button, a sturdy, button-nosed lad with a freckled grin, "but when do we start?"

"What in Tophet is a—an eptic fuscus?" demanded Lefty, in the slow drawl which went with his lanky, wiry frame and long Yankee face.

"We start soon as I can get the traps from the express office," Spike answered Button, and to Lefty, "An *Eptisicus f. fuscus* is a Big Brown bat, with wingspread up to twelve inches, largest cave bat in this part of the country, and rather rare."

"Gosh, I'd hate to get one of them fussy-cusses in my hair!" exclaimed Lefty.

"They don't go for your hair unless you've got something in it for 'em to eat," snickered Button. "Bats eat bugs, you know."

"Then you're in danger," snorted Lefty. "But this is all Greek to me."

"It's Latin," Spike corrected, seriously. "Doc Nasmith is now with the United States Biological Survey, banding bats to learn all about 'em. He took Button and me, once, to the Chester Emery Mines where lots of 'em hibernate, and now he has assigned me to collect some at the big Berlin Cave, while he's chasing to Bermuda to see if tree bats migrate there for winter. Are you game, mates?"

"I caught an owl once with a wingspread of eight feet," remarked Lefty. "No bat can batter me down, I'm all set."

"Is the cave anything like the Chester Mines?" inquired Button. "My folks didn't like the idea of my going in an old mine."

"This is a big limestone cave, safe as a church, Doc Nasmith told me last spring. We can drive almost to its entrance. It has never been completely explored."

That was enough, and soon the three scattered to pack duffle, rations for three days, and Spike to pick up the express shipment.

It was early November, the time when colonies of bats, which haunt attics and other hot shelters in summer, retreat to cool but unfreezing caverns to hang upside down in a dormant state for the winter, seldom stirring unless unseasonable warmth brings them out for a last meal of insects.

Half an hour later the trio met and were off over the winding concrete Highway U.S. 7, northerly, then via Broadie Mountain road, across the state line, and into the Alps range, a wild section of the Taconics in western New York state. They planned to be gone at least three days and to extend their trip to Dorset, Vermont, to explore and capture bats in the lofty, windy Mt. Aeolus cavern.

The jalopy behaved like a pacer, as Spike bragged, and shortly before noon they swerved onto a sandy wood-road that climbed through a forest reserve and brought them out in a small clearing facing a dark, lofty ledge of limestone. They had not seen a house nor a person since leaving the highway. The pine grove offered excellent shelter for the roadster when they left it to enter the cave, but the surroundings were strangely sinister. Beneath the cliffs a deep hollow lay, filled with black water covered with a thin film of ice. Stark, dead stubs of trees rose above it, and cawing crows flapped from them, shouting hoarse warnings. The air was raw and biting.

Button shivered despite thick layers of warm clothing, as he looked about, frowning.

"Into the valley of death rode the three bat-banders," he chattered.

"It'll be warmer in the cave," Spike promised, lifting out two cages made of five-gallon milk cans with sides of fine wire mesh.

In one was a flat aluminum case with hundreds of tiny aluminum bands strung in numbered series on wires, and several pairs of duck gloves, with the thumbs and forefingers of each left one cut off.

"D'you have to catch 'em with gloves?" inquired Lefty, suspiciously.

"No, these are to keep 'em from biting you when you band 'em," Spike explained. "They can't even puncture your skin, but after two or three hundred have tried, you get sore."

"I ain't afraid. Look what a big, horned owl did to my arm."

He exhibited a long, white welt on his cordy forearm.

"Well, now for the rope," suggested Spike, all business. "It's a jackknife entrance, rather deep. Can you see it from here?"

Neither could spot it, but Spike showed them the carefully made map drawn by Dr. Nasmith, and they found the old stump overhanging a slot in the ledge and were soon at the opening.

They had brought some sandwiches from the car, a thermos bottle of coffee, flashlights, cages, rope.

"It'll be more comfortable eating inside," Spike suggested.

"And I'll be more comfortable with eats inside of me," Button declared.

"We'll have our main meal when we come out, and maybe

230

we will be glad we didn't fill up too much before crawling in.
There are some tight places that Doc calls 'lemon squeezers'
where you have to wriggle through."

He knotted one end of the half-inch rope about a tough, live
root that arched over the hole.

The very first drop was a tight squeeze. Spike went down
first, leaving it to Lefty to hand down the cages, with Button
as rearguard.

"Better peel off a coat or two," he advised the burly Button.
"You'll get stuck, for sure."

"I'm a bigger cave man than you are, Jug-o-jin," grunted
Button, as he removed a thick leather jacket and one of two
sweaters. "But now I'm a regular Mahatma Ghander."

Button's voice was high and excited as he stared into the
narrow, deep shaft and then looked up at what seemed danger-

ously loose strata of stone above. But he chucked his spare clothing in with the cages, after Spike had gone down the rope to a ledge.

"Typical slot entrance to a big cave," Spike was grunting. "Seems as if—they build—these caves too close—Ouch!"

"A bat bite you?" drawled Lefty.

Only a mumble reached them, then a faint, seemingly smothered voice announced, "I'm down to the second level. Come on in!"

Lefty took a deep breath and looked up at the sky while Button regarded him, narrowly.

"Got a case of claustrophobia?" he inquired, giggling nervously.

"Santy Claustrophobia, I guess," grinned Lefty. "It looks like snow. Well, here goes nothin' down the chimney!"

Button took more than one look about, and his legs were shaky as he descended. He had penetrated for a thousand feet underground at the emery mines, but that had been a walk into a horizontal shaft carved from the hardest kind of rock, and this shaft was like a well, and bits of earth and soft limestone dropped on and about them as they crouched on a rubble of rock and debris in a narrow chamber of dark, damp stone which was beaded along every crack with tiny drops of yellowish fluid. Spike explained that it was water, charged with dissolved lime, the first evidence of a "live cave," one in which the chemical processes of nature were still at work making formations.

From the first level they dropped the rope end into another well-like shaft, and Spike slid down to the bottom, poking his flashlight beam into corners for a few moments.

"I found it!" he called up, at length. "It's a horizontal passage, at the left. Pass the stuff down. Watch Button with that lunch!"

"I could down it all," Button declared, "I feel like a half-starved cave man, right now."

The entrance to the adit was a "lemon squeezer," indeed, and Button lost some buttons off his sweater getting through, remarking that he was glad he had not put on any lumps with lunch. But within a few minutes they sat at ease in a high-roofed tunnel that seemed to extend ahead endlessly. Every inch of the walls and roof gleamed and sparkled as if from diamonds. Spike settled back into a shell of pure white flowstone, large enough to hold him, shaped like a huge helmet of ancient Grecian design, a formation built up through unknown ages by the slow chemistry of water working on the limestone.

As they became quiet, strange, faint sounds came to them. "I hear somethin' ahead like a bear growlin'," said Lefty, fingering his holster-axe.

Spike burst into a laugh. "It does sound like a growl but it's running water, far ahead—as you'll soon find out. It'd be a pretty starved, slim bear that'd get in here."

"Like me," chuckled Button, whose nerve was somewhat restored by food, and to it was added the curious elation which comes to a group of cave-crawlers, poking into underground mysteries.

They walked upright along the lofty passage which was plastered with yellowish-white alabaster, decorated with every possible shape of stalactite, stalagmite, flowstone, and drip. Fragments littered the floor, and slabs of rock lay buried in "cave mud," the dross of dissolved limestone, as slippery as wet soap, but at the depth of a half-inch, solid as adamant.

Their voices rang hollowly in the chamber, but soon mingled with the babble and increasing roar of water, as if a sizeable waterfall were ahead. Then, suddenly, the roof sloped down, and the passage ended abruptly at a low tunnel into which they had to creep on hands and knees.

It proved to be the megaphone that magnified the voice of a shallow brook running the way they traveled. The floor was roughly littered with flat rocks, old boards, and poles, covered with slime, evidently dragged in from outside, years ago, by some cave-crawlers to help keep knees and elbows out of water.

"If that first one was a lemon-squeezer, this must be a lime-squeezer," panted Button. "Wow! That water is wet! Is it good to drink?"

"Pure as driven snow," said Spike, who was pushing and rolling the bat cages ahead of him, "except where I'm paddling in it."

"Glad I'm upstream from you, though I always did (gulp) like flavor (gulp) to my drink. Say, it's as sweet as—"

"As lime water," Spike supplied. "Careful, don't drink too much and turn into a human stalagmite. Did you fetch the thermos along?"

"No, I left it back in the Greek diner. It and me couldn't have got through here—together—Wow!"

In some places there was no way of avoiding a wetting; in fact, in the last few yards of the thirty or so of this low tunnel they had to lie flat and make motions like a caterpillar or a

worm; but then the tunnel turned sharply, the brook vanished in a crevice at one side, and the floor became mud, then sandy, but greasy and easier on their "four-point landings," as Lefty put it.

In the last bend they had to run on one side, extend one arm in front, one back, and inch through into a low-roofed room whose upper portion was completely filled with strange, pendant "wings" of limestone, like the flies of a theater stage, tapering to sharp edges at the bottom, glittering with liquid beads of golden hue. The room was roughly circular, a sort of maze, with huge rounded boulders here and there, and mounds of mud-glued rock.

As Button threshed through, kicking and scratching, something moved behind him, but made no sound in the soft, earth floor, and went unnoticed by any of them; for they were eagerly crawling toward a great empty space, and Lefty gave an awed cry as his flashlight beams shot upward to a lofty blackness studded with sparkling dots.

"Looks like gold stars in a black sky," he announced. "I wouldn't a'believed it if I didn't see it."

"Those gold stars are bats, hanging upside down, with their claws hooked in crevices and onto little ridges in the roof and walls. They are covered with tiny grains of silicate that shines in the light," Spike explained.

For moments the three surveyed the vast auditorium of brownish rock and earth, a chamber large enough to hold a battalion, and with a steep slope of rocks and mud rising against the farther wall, almost to the ceiling, like stadium seats. Its vast size affected them all, and the strange shadows cast from their lights increased the somber mystery of the silent, hidden recesses of the underearth.

Lefty, who was perspiring, doffed his mackinaw and sat on it on a rock. He gazed upward, open-mouthed, spellbound.

Button broke the spell with a high-pitched exclamation, "Well, let's climb dem golden stairs and pick us some stars."

He started off, recklessly, across the damp floor toward the hill.

235

"Hold everything!" Spike warned. "Don't rush about like that in a cave. We don't know what we'll strike next. We could get badly hurt or even lost in such a cavern as this."

Button faced about, quickly, his eyes round, his face rather white, but he piped up cheerfully enough.

"On my honor, I will do my best to be a good *spelunker*," he chanted, his hand raised in the scout salute. "From the Latin, *speluncca*, a cave! But, gosh, that looks easy to climb."

"I bet it's tricky," ventured Lefty, the neophyte cave man. "Not as easy as it looks."

His guess proved correct. The slope was of moist, slippery mud on the surface, and it took clawing, toe-digging work to get up along one wall, toward the group of bats that hung lowest. It was like a greased slide or a ski-run in a thaw, and only by projecting rocks could they make any progress.

Lefty watched as Spike began detaching the tiny, brownish bats from their hang-up.

"It's like pickin' live grapes, ain't it?" he observed, and soon joined his companions in the work of removing the gilded little mouselike creatures and putting them carefully into the cages.

The luster of their fur vanished as hands touched them, and they became more like mice with wings—and they squeaked like mice, too.

The funnel-shaped mouths of the cans prevented them climbing or flying out, and they scratched and squeaked about constantly, as they wakened from their first slumber.

For a long time the boys were absorbed in the collecting. Time passed, for there was nothing to suggest its passage in this buried world, no sun or wind, no sound save that which they created and the silly symphony of the piping bats.

They were counting, too, and Button crowed, at last, "I bet I've got the first hundred."

"Hundred and ten," was Lefty's laconic comment.

"Hundred and forty-three," Spike said. "Anybody get a Big Brown?"

"I think I got two of 'em," Lefty said. "They had a wide wingspread."

"We'll make sure when we fish 'em out to band 'em," Spike remarked, then glanced at his watch and exclaimed, "Say, it's after four o'clock, already! We'll call it quits because it'll take —well, I think we'd better not try to band 'em in 'here. We ought to get out before dark. We can band 'em faster outside. They'll fly back in again."

They descended to the floor level, sliding and slipping, but guarding the cages carefully. Button, now that his preoccupation with bats was over, made immediately for the circular chamber through which they had entered the large room, while Spike halted to inspect the cages, and to tie cheesecloth over the tops in case in the scramble one fell on its side. Lefty watched and helped, said something about wishing they had time to explore more of the cave—and then they heard that shrill, muffled cry from Button.

"Say, I can't get back."

"Aw, you're all swelled up about something," chuckled Spike. "Pull in your stomach. You been eating some more?"

But the joke died on his lips as Button came scrambling back and faced them, his face as white as a sheet, his eyes glaring oddly in the light.

"I tell you," he gasped. "The—the passage is too small. It's closed up—or something. I tried. It looks like some slab of rock had dropped down from the top and choked it up. How'll we get outa here?"

He licked dry lips and tried to grin, but his expression was ghastly.

"Lemme try it," drawled Lefty, calmly, and with a significant glance at Spike. "I'm built more like a worm. You sure you got the right hole?"

"I—I dunno. Why, yes, it's the *only one*," stammered Button. "There isn't another—but there's two slabs—"

Spike went with Lefty, leaving the bat cages in the big room, and Button crawled after them, breathing hard.

Lefty found the hole and thrust head and shoulders in. He withdrew very soon.

"Looks like he's right," he announced. "Some sharp-edged

237

stones hanging down close to the floor—now. *I* can't get through, either."

"That—that tunnel was as solid as a concrete culvert," muttered Button in a strained voice. "I pushed out of it on my back and—and I saw it was smooth and solid—the roof of it. It—that can't be the right hole. Let's look—"

He began to range about the room, but his movements were more aimless than effective. Spike whispered to Lefty.

"Keep your head, old man; he'll be O.K. if we—"

"Why, say, we can pry those rocks out of there," declared Lefty. "I think they're only a couple of loose pieces that slipped down."

As he spoke his flashlight winked out. It proved to be a burned-out bulb, and he had no spares. Spike fumbled in his breast pocket, and his hand came out with blood on it.

"Busted my bulbs to smithereens, wedging through lemon-squeezers," he muttered. "Well, we've got two, and spare cells, anyhow."

His own voice was a bit grim, but he thrust his head in the tiny tunnel—which proved to be blocked a distance of about four feet from the wall.

"If we had a strong stick or something," he mused, backing out, "we might break one or both of those slabs."

Button huddled close to them, now, saying nothing, waiting. Spike said, calmly, "It's time we went back into the big room and sat down and did a little thinking."

"I—I've been doing a lot," gulped Button. "Nobody knows we are in here except the folks at home—and they think we're heading for Dorset, to be gone three days. Lunch is outside. Coffee, too. All we've got is—water if we can get to it. I think—"

"Let's go find some water. I heard some running under rocks in one side of the big room, I think," cut in Lefty, practically.

They returned to the huge chamber, and Lefty made his way to where the floor sloped off and there was a jagged hole in the wall, half-filled with loose stones, rounded by the wash of water. By pulling out an armful of them, with Spike's help, he got his leather helmet into a pool and brought it out, half-

238

full. They drank greedily, then dug further among the loose stones.

"Maybe—we can get out that way," suggested Button.

"There's some wood under these rocks," Lefty reported. "Looks like an old rail. Probably washed through, somehow. No way out here at all."

By some more digging and lifting they managed to drag out a section of an old, water-soaked fence-rail and, armed with this, they went back to the opening with its two sharp-edged stones hanging within six inches of the hard floor.

Prying at them, they discovered that they were "frozen" solidly with flowstone, and that they must have been there for a long, long time.

A chill swept over Spike as their solidity became evident and their efforts to pry them loose proved useless.

"You're right, Button," he declared, as cheerfully as he could. "We certainly didn't come in this way."

They spent a quarter of an hour searching all around the walls of the circular room, then Spike called for another council in the big chamber, and this time they sat down and devoted themselves to concentrated consideration of their situation and sought a possible solution.

"You said—we could get lost—in here," mumbled Button.

"We're not lost!" declared Spike, sharply. "We're just temporarily cave-blind."

The bats rustled feebly in their cages.

"D'you suppose we could eat roasted bats?" Lefty mused. "They're animals. Say, there goes a couple or three flying around, up above!"

Spike spotted them, tiny, flitting forms, seeming to be flying aimlessly; but he knew that bats do not fly aimlessly. They have the homing instinct of a carrier pigeon. It set him thinking along another line.

But his meditations were interrupted by Button, who got suddenly to his feet and announced:

"I'm going—to climb that hill and see what's over in that far corner where we didn't get to."

"Take it easy," warned Spike, but nodded to Lefty to let him go.

Action, he believed, would be better for Button's shaky morale than anything else.

As Button clambered up and across the rocky incline, Lefty began hacking away at the fence-rail with his hatchet.

"What you doing?" called Button, nervously, from above.

"Oh, jest thought I'd build a fire and see if we can roast a bat when you catch one up there. Get a—an epic fuscus, it's bigger."

"A good idea," said Spike, "to build a fire if we can start one. It'll save our flashlights and we can keep warm—anyway."

Button had vanished over an upthrust of rough, jagged rock as Lefty cut into the center of the rail and found pitchwood, which, in slender splinters, caught fire from a match.

Spike was preparing to band bats. Taking the flat case from his pocket he drew one of the tiny strips of aluminum off its wire, jotting down the number in a notebook.

"Lefty," he said, "I want you to take all the bats out of one cage and put them in the other. I want to keep the banded bats together until they're all done and try an experiment."

His voice was a bit shaky with excitement, and so were his fingers. But he worked fast and Lefty, after transferring the catch from one cage to the other, donned gloves and began to help.

"They're so lively—some of 'em flying around up there," Spike said, "it gave me an idea. Doc Nasmith says bats have the most perfect sense of direction—"

"Which we ain't got, now," put in Lefty, "or else this cave growed shut on us. I can't figger it out. D'you suppose there's any other way out? Maybe Button will find—"

He was interrupted by a sound that startled both of them. It was a wild, eerie scream that came from far up in the dark corner where Button had vanished. They jumped to their feet as another cry sounded, louder and more terror-stricken, the voice of Button; and just as Spike lunged toward the slippery hill to start climbing, the beams of Button's flashlight showed

out of the corner, then his form, scrambling recklessly out of the gloom, rose on the pinnacle of the steep mound.

He was half-sobbing out, *The thing! The thing! It's a human—*

He began to descend, and even as Spike yelled, "Watch out!" he slipped as if his feet had been knocked from under him and careened down the soapy slide, his flashlight flying from his hand and crashing against a rock, dead out.

His fall was checked, abruptly, as he struck a protruding slab of rock. When Spike and Lefty reached him he was moaning, but he went entirely unconscious as they lifted him. One leg was bent under him, awkwardly.

They half-slid, half-carried him to the floor level where Spike made quick advantage of his insensibility to remove boot and sock and examine the bent leg.

"No bones busted," he announced, after a careful examination, "but he's got bad bruises from ankle to knee. Get some more water, Lefty. I'll get my first aid kit undone."

He fished his kit from his bulging pocket, a towel from another, and when Lefty returned with a dripping helmet of water, made a cold compress for the knee, bound the ankle and dashed some water in Button's face.

"What d'you suppose he saw up there?" husked Lefty, with a quick look up toward the stygian corner.

"*—skull. A human skull, I tell you!*"

Button came to consciousness, completing what he had been saying before his fall, and struggling to get on his feet and run.

"Well, well, well!" chided Spike, holding him down. "Come out of that, Button, old mate!"

His chum's voice checked Button's violent fright, and he fell back, groaning, "My leg—is it broken?"

"No, but you've got a twisted ankle, I guess, and some bad bumps. Now, what in heck—?"

"I tell you I saw a skull—a human skull—grinning at me, on a sort of shelf, right at the mouth of that big hole up there."

"Didn't bite you, did it?" demanded Lefty sharply, a bit too sharply to sound funny. "Did you find a way out?"

242

Button shook his head, gritting his teeth.

"How do you feel, old man?" inquired Spike.

"Sort of—ch—chilly."

"Stir up that fire, Lefty. I'm going up there and see that chamber of horrors myself."

"Don't!" gasped Button. "That thing—is—maybe someone else got lost in here and—"

"We are going to get out of here, Button. Hear me? I've thought of a way. Here, let me prop you up against this rock. You get busy, now and *band bats.*"

Wrapping his own coat about Button's shoulders they got him in a fairly comfortable position, gave him a drink and then Spike thrust the band case in his hands, the notebook, and the gloves. His face set and grim, he began the ascent of the slope.

With trembling fingers Button began to clamp the tiny bands on the bat's hind legs, bands that weighed less than one-hundredth of an ounce each and were less than three-sixteenths of an inch long, yet before the legible legend, "Notify Biol. Surv. Wash. D.C.," a serial number, and letter of identification for species.

"Th—that's what we come in for—to band bats," he mumbled to Lefty as the latter built the tiny fire into a blaze.

He let his first fly away, but Lefty cautioned him.

"Spike wants to keep 'em all together in one cage. He's got some idea they'll help us."

"Your flash is a dead one, anyway," Spike called down. "Smashed to smithereens. Keep that fire going, Lefty."

He vanished, his bright light with him, and the two were left squatted by the splinter fire, their shadows dancing grotesquely on the walls.

"I tell you I saw—" began Button, through his teeth, but he was interrupted by a burst of laughter, booming down from the hillock, and Spike's voice.

"Say, I got your blasted skull! Someone was a darned good, grisly *skull*ptor. It's made outa cave mud."

He came down carrying the "thing" in the crook of his arm, chuckling.

It was a rather good imitation, its empty eye-sockets and toothless jaws well modeled. Spike propped it up on a stone pedestal.

"You didn't stop to read what the sign under it said, did you, Button?" he asked. "It said 'NO PASSAGE.'"

"No—no, but I found that out, for myself," stuttered Button, sheepishly. "I went down to the end before I saw that thing. Good gosh, what a fright it gave me! I felt my skin coming off."

"It looks like a relic from the time when this cave was used by a gang of gamblers or a band of cloth thieves, as the stories go."

"It made me shrink up so that I think maybe I could crawl out through between those slabs in the tunnel," Button said, beginning to laugh a little.

"We got most of the bats banded, now," said Lefty, quietly.

"Good! Now, we are going to see if they are any good at finding their way out."

He tipped one cage on its side. "I'll let 'em all out at once. Lefty, you take my flash and go into the circular room and lie down—and listen for wings passing over you. Follow them. Watch close!"

The tiny creatures, *Myotis l. Lucifugus* or Common Little Brown Bat, *Pippistrelle,* with frosty looking fur, and a pair of the *Eptosicus f. fuscus,* which Lefty had found, began to flop out of the cage, fell to the floor, fluttered up, circled, vanishing from sight in the dim firelight.

"Suppose they're going—out the roof?" whispered Button, chokingly.

"Come a-runnin'!" burst out a resounding command from Lefty, in the near-by chamber. "Some of 'em came in here, by gosh. And here's some more. Spike! Button! They's going—"

Spike did not run but he crawled almost as fast as a bear walks, and Button, forgetting his injuries, crept after him. Soon the three lay flat on the sand beneath the hanging rocks, as tiny wings beat the air and flitting forms flashed through the misty beams of the flash, which Lefty was directing upon the wall near the tiny tunnel they had failed to get through.

244

"See, they're not going in there!" gasped Button. "It isn't the right way!"

"By gum, they must be borin' a hole in the wall close to it," husked Lefty. "All I can see is solid rock and that big, round boulder up against it."

Spike lunged suddenly toward the boulder, taking the flashlight from Lefty and focussing it on a crack between the rock and the wall.

"There's a hole back here!" he cried. "And the bats are going through it."

He got his feet against a "wing" and his back against the boulder and pushed. It rolled over into a shallow depression in the mud and revealed the opening of a tunnel.

Button burst into a giggle. "Say—say, I think I remember hearing something move behind me when I came out of there! Look! There's been water running half under it sometime and left just balanced so it would roll over."

The tiny fliers were now streaming into the tunnel in a steady file.

"Who said 'blind as a bat'?" demanded Lefty, gleefully. "Spike, how'd you know they could find a way out?"

"I didn't *know*," Spike replied. "But Doc Nasmith told me bats have an inner ear so delicate they can catch the 'echo' from

245

any object they fly near, and avoid it." He thrust his head in the opening beside the flashlight. "Yes, sir, this is our way out. Ain't we the Pied Pipers in reverse English?"

They collected the cages, smothered the fire with wet mud, and Spike inspected Button's leg again. He used Lefty's padded helmet as a kneecap for Button's bad knee. Button refused to consider Lefty's suggestion of making a travois from poles in the passage and dragging him.

"Drag nothin', I can crawl on one knee, as long as I'm on the way out," declared Button, whose spirits had risen high. "I feel like a cave man called to breakfast, but I'd feel like a cannibal eating one of those blessed bats," he added.

It took them a solid hour to get to the outer room where the thermos with hot coffee helped to refresh them.

"Say!" demanded Button, suddenly, after a hot drink. "What made you think the bats would fly out of the cave?"

"I was just hoping that they'd know it was warming up outside and go out after a meal."

"Me and the bats, both. Let's go!"

It was raining and strangely warm and quite dark outside, but not as dark as in the cave, and it was good to feel the open air and stand erect and hear the wind and rain singing in the pines.

Spike banded the rest of the bats and let them go. To the gray-bearded country doctor whom they found at Berlin the three related their weird and what might well have been worse experience.

"Yes, three days would have been pretty tough on you," said the doctor. "Good thing you had guides. Somethin' like the miracle in the Bible, when the ravens fed Elisha, wa'nt it? That leg will bother you for a few days. Rest it."

"It and me need a bed," yawned Button.

But the first question he asked as they headed for home was this: "When do we start for Mt. Aeolus?"

"Don't tell me you want to get into another cave right away!" exclaimed Spike.

"Yeah. On top of a mountain where we can *fall out*."

Howard Pyle

TOM CHIST AND
THE TREASURE BOX

ILLUSTRATED BY *DeWitt Whistler Jayne*

To TELL about Tom Chist, and how he got his name, and how he came to be living at the little settlement of Henlopen, just inside the mouth of the Delaware Bay, the story must begin as far back as 1686, when a great storm swept the Atlantic coast from end to end. During the heaviest part of the hurricane a bark went ashore on the Hen-and-Chicken Shoals, just below Cape Henlopen and at the mouth of the Delaware Bay, and Tom Chist was the only soul of all those on board the ill-fated vessel who escaped alive.

This story must first be told, because it was on account of the strange and miraculous escape that happened to him at that time that he gained the name that was given to him.

Even as late as that time of the American colonies, the little scattered settlement at Henlopen, made up of English, with a few Dutch and Swedish people, was still only a spot upon the face of the great American wilderness that spread away, with swamp and forest, no man knew how far to the westward. That wilderness was not only full of wild beasts, but of Indian savages, who every fall would come in wandering tribes to spend the winter along the shores of the fresh-water lakes below Henlopen. There for four or five months they would live upon fish and clams and wild ducks and geese, chipping their arrowheads, and making their earthenware pots and pans under the lee of the sand hills and pine woods below the Capes.

Sometimes on Sundays when the Rev. Hilary Jones would be preaching in the little log church back in the woods, these half-clad red savages would come in from the cold, and sit squatting in the back part of the church, listening stolidly to the words that had no meaning for them.

247

But about the wreck of the bark in 1686. Such a wreck as that which then went ashore on the Hen-and-Chicken Shoals was a godsend to the poor and needy settlers in the wilderness where so few good things ever came. For the vessel went to pieces during the night, and the next morning the beach was strewn with wreckage—boxes and barrels, chests and spars, timbers and planks, a plentiful and bountiful harvest to be gathered up by the settlers as they chose, with no one to forbid or prevent them.

The name of the bark, as found painted on some of the water barrels and sea chests, was the *Bristol Merchant,* and she no doubt hailed from England.

As was said, the only soul who escaped alive off the wreck was Tom Chist.

A settler, a fisherman named Matt Abrahamson, and his daughter Molly, found Tom. He was washed up on the beach among the wreckage, in a great wooden box which had been securely tied around with a rope and lashed between two spars —apparently for better protection in beating through the surf. Matt Abrahamson thought he had found something of more than usual value when he came upon this chest; but when he cut the cords and broke open the box with his broadax, he could not have been more astonished had he beheld a salamander instead of a baby of nine or ten months old lying half smothered in the blankets that covered the bottom of the chest.

Matt Abrahamson's daughter Molly had had a baby who had died a month or so before. So when she saw the little one lying there in the bottom of the chest, she cried out in a great loud voice that the Good Man had sent her another baby in place of her own.

The rain was driving before the hurricane storm in dim, slanting sheets, and so she wrapped up the baby in the man's coat she wore and ran off home without waiting to gather up any more of the wreckage.

It was Parson Jones who gave the foundling his name. When the news came to his ears of what Matt Abrahamson had found he went over to the fisherman's cabin to see the child. He examined the clothes in which the baby was dressed. They were of fine linen and handsomely stitched, and the reverend gentleman opined that the foundling's parents must have been of quality. A kerchief had been wrapped around the baby's neck and under its arms and tied behind, and in the corner, marked with very fine needlework, were the initials T.C.

"What d'ye call him, Molly?" said Parson Jones. He was standing, as he spoke, with his back to the fire, warming his palms before the blaze. The pocket of the greatcoat he wore bulged out with a big case bottle of spirits which he had gathered up out of the wreck that afternoon. "What d'ye call him, Molly?"

"I'll call him Tom, after my own baby."

"That goes very well with the initial on the kerchief," said Parson Jones. "But what other name d'ye give him? Let it be something to go with the C."

"I don't know," said Molly.

"Why not call him 'Chist,' since he was born in a chist out of the sea? 'Tom Chist'—the name goes off like a flash in the pan." And so "Tom Chist" he was called and "Tom Chist" he was christened.

So much for the beginning of the history of Tom Chist. The story of Captain Kidd's treasure box does not begin until the late spring of 1699.

That was the year that the famous pirate captain, coming up from the West Indies, sailed his sloop into the Delaware Bay, where he lay for over a month waiting for news from his friends in New York.

For he had sent word to that town asking if the coast was clear for him to return home with the rich prize he had brought from the Indian seas and the coast of Africa, and meantime he lay there in the Delaware Bay waiting for a reply. Before he left he turned the whole of Tom Chist's life topsy-turvy with something that he brought ashore.

By that time Tom Chist had grown into a strong-limbed, thick-jointed boy of fourteen or fifteen years of age. It was a miserable dog's life he lived with old Matt Abrahamson, for

249

the old fisherman was in his cups more than half the time, and when he was so there was hardly a day passed that he did not give Tom a curse or a buffet, or, as like as not, an actual beating. One would have thought that such treatment would have broken the spirit of the poor little foundling, but it had just the opposite effect upon Tom Chist, who was one of your stubborn, sturdy, stiff-willed fellows who only grow harder and more tough the more they are ill-treated. It had been a long time now since he had made any outcry or complaint at the hard usage he suffered from old Matt. At such times he would shut his teeth and bear whatever came to him, until sometimes the half-drunken old man would be driven almost mad by his stubborn silence. Maybe he would stop in the midst of the beating he was administering, and, grinding his teeth, would cry out: "Won't ye say naught? Won't ye say naught? Well, then, I'll see if I can't make ye say naught." When things had reached such a pass as this Molly would generally interfere to protect her foster son, and then she and Tom would together fight the old man until they had wrenched the stick or the strap out of his hand. Then old Matt would chase them out of doors and around and around the house for maybe half an hour, until his anger was cool, when he would go back again, and for a time the storm would be over.

Besides his foster mother, Tom Chist had a very good friend in Parson Jones, who used to come over every now and then to Abrahamson's hut upon the chance of getting a half dozen fish for breakfast. He always had a kind word or two for Tom, who during the winter evenings would go over to the good man's house to learn his letters, and to read and write and cipher a little, so that by now he was able to spell the words out of the Bible and the almanac, and knew enough to change tuppence into four ha'pennies.

This is the sort of boy Tom Chist was, and this is the sort of life he led.

In the late spring or early summer of 1699 Captain Kidd's sloop sailed into the mouth of the Delaware Bay and changed the whole fortune of his life.

And this is how you come to the story of Captain Kidd's treasure box.

Old Matt Abrahamson kept the flat-bottomed boat in which he went fishing some distance down the shore, and in the neighborhood of the old wreck that had been sunk on the Shoals. This was the usual fishing ground of the settlers, and here old Matt's boat generally lay drawn up on the sand.

There had been a thunderstorm that afternoon, and Tom had gone down the beach to bale out the boat in readiness for the morning's fishing.

It was full moonlight now, as he was returning, and the night sky was full of floating clouds. Now and then there was a dull flash to the westward, and once a muttering growl of thunder, promising another storm to come.

All that day the pirate sloop had been lying just off the shore back of the Capes, and now Tom Chist could see the sails glimmering pallidly in the moonlight, spread for drying after the storm. He was walking up the shore homeward when he be-

251

came aware that at some distance ahead of him there was a ship's boat drawn up on the little narrow beach, and a group of men clustered about it. He hurried forward with a good deal of curiosity to see who had landed, but it was not until he had come close to them that he could distinguish who and what

they were. Then he knew that it must be a party who had come off the pirate sloop. They had evidently just landed, and two men were lifting out a chest from the boat. One of them was a negro, naked to the waist, and the other was a white man in his shirt sleeves, wearing petticoat breeches, a Monterey cap upon his head, a red bandana handkerchief around his neck, and gold earrings in his ears. He had a long, plaited queue hanging down his back, and a great sheath knife dangling from his side. Another man, evidently the captain of the party, stood at a little distance as they lifted the chest out of the boat. He had a cane in one hand and a lighted lantern in the other, although the moon was shining as bright as day. He wore jack boots and a handsome laced coat, and he had a long, drooping mustache that curled down below his chin. He wore a fine, feathered hat, and his long black hair hung down upon his shoulders.

All this Tom Chist could see in the moonlight that glinted and twinkled upon the gilt buttons of his coat.

They were so busy lifting the chest from the boat that at first they did not observe that Tom Chist had come up and was standing there. It was the white man with the long, plaited queue and the gold earrings that spoke to him. "Boy, what do you want here, boy?" he said, in a rough, hoarse voice. "Where d'ye come from?" And then dropping his end of the chest, and without giving Tom time to answer, he pointed off down the beach, and said, "You'd better be going about your own business, if you know what's good for you; and don't you come back, or you'll find what you don't want waiting for you."

Tom saw in a glance that the pirates were all looking at him, and then, without saying a word, he turned and walked away. The man who had spoken to him followed him threateningly for some little distance, as though to see that he had gone away as he was bidden to do. But presently he stopped, and Tom hurried on alone, until the boat and the crew and all were dropped away behind and lost in the moonlight night. Then he himself stopped also, turned, and looked back whence he had come.

There had been something very strange in the appearance of the men he had just seen, something very mysterious in their actions, and he wondered what it all meant, and what they were going to do. He stood for a little while thus looking and listening. He could see nothing, and could hear only the sound of distant talking. What were they doing on the lonely shore thus at night? Then, following a sudden impulse, he turned and cut off across the sand hummocks, skirting around inland, but keeping pretty close to the shore, his object being to spy upon them, and to watch what they were about from the back of the low sand hills that fronted the beach.

He had gone along some distance in his circuitous return when he became aware of the sound of voices that seemed to be drawing closer to him as he came toward the speakers. He stopped and stood listening, and instantly, as he stopped, the voices stopped also. He crouched there silently in the bright, glimmering moonlight, surrounded by the silent stretches of sand, and the stillness seemed to press upon him like a heavy hand. Then suddenly the sound of a man's voice began again, and as Tom listened he could hear some one slowly counting. "Ninety-one," the voice began, "ninety-two, ninety-three, ninety-four, ninety-five, ninety-six, ninety-seven, ninety-eight, ninety-nine, one hundred, one hundred and one"—the slow, monotonous count coming nearer and nearer—"one hundred and two, one hundred and three, one hundred and four," and so on in its monotonous reckoning.

Suddenly he saw three heads appear above the sand hill, so close to him that he crouched down quickly with a keen thrill, close beside the hummock near which he stood. His first fear was that they might have seen him in the moonlight; but they had not, and his heart rose again as the counting voice went steadily on. "One hundred and twenty," it was saying—"and twenty-one, and twenty-two, and twenty-three, and twenty-four," and then he who was counting came out from behind the little sandy rise into the white and open level of shimmering brightness.

It was the man with the cane whom Tom had seen some time before—the captain of the party who had landed. He carried his cane under his arm now, and was holding his lantern close to something that he held in his hand, and upon which he looked narrowly as he walked with a slow and measured tread in a perfectly straight line across the sand, counting each step as he took it. "And twenty-five, and twenty-six, and twenty-seven, and twenty-eight, and twenty-nine, and thirty."

Behind him walked two other figures; one was the half-naked negro, the other the man with the plaited queue and the earrings, whom Tom had seen lifting the chest out of the boat. Now they were carrying the heavy box between them, laboring through the sand with shuffling tread as they bore it onward. As he who was counting pronounced the word "thirty," the two men set the chest down on the sand with a grunt, the white

254

DeWitt Whistler Jayne

man panting and blowing and wiping his sleeve across his forehead. And immediately he who counted took out a slip of paper and marked something down upon it. They stood there for a long time, during which Tom lay behind the sand hummock watching them, and for a while the silence was uninterrupted. In the stillness Tom could hear the washing of the waves beating upon the distant beach, and once the far-away sound of a laugh from one of those who stood by the ship's boat.

One, two, three minutes passed, and then the men picked up the chest and started on again; and then again the other man began his counting. "Thirty and one, and thirty and two, and thirty and three, and thirty and four"—he walked straight across the level open, still looking intently at that which he held in his hand—"and thirty and five, and thirty and six, and thirty and seven," and so on, until the three figures disappeared in the little hollow between the two sand hills on the opposite side of the open, and still Tom could hear the sound of the counting voice in the distance.

Just as they disappeared behind the hill there was a sudden faint flash of light; and by and by, as Tom lay still listening to the counting, he heard, after a long interval, a far-away muffled rumble of distant thunder. He waited for a while, and then arose and stepped to the top of the sand hummock behind which he had been lying. He looked all about him, but there was no one else to be seen. Then he stepped down from the hummock and followed in the direction in which the pirate captain and the two men carrying the chest had gone. He crept along cautiously, stopping now and then to make sure that he still heard the counting voice, and when it ceased he lay down upon the sand and waited until it began again.

Presently, so following the pirates, he saw the three figures again in the distance, and, skirting around back of a hill of sand covered with coarse sedge grass, he came to where he overlooked a little open level space gleaming white in the moonlight.

The three had been crossing the level of sand, and were now not more than twenty-five paces from him. They had again set down the chest, upon which the white man with the long queue

256

and the gold earrings had seated to rest himself, the negro standing close beside him. The moon shone as bright as day and full upon his face. It was looking directly at Tom Chist, every line as keen cut with white lights and black shadows as though it had been carved in ivory and jet. He sat perfectly motionless, and Tom drew back with a start, almost thinking he had been discovered. He lay silent, his heart beating heavily in his throat; but there was no alarm, and presently he heard the counting begin again, and when he looked once more he saw they were going away straight across the little open. A soft, sliding hillock of sand lay directly in front of them. They did not turn aside, but went straight over it, the leader helping himself up the sandy slope with his cane, still counting and still keeping his eyes fixed upon that which he held in his hand. Then they disappeared again behind the white crest on the other side.

So Tom followed them cautiously until they had gone almost half a mile inland. When next he saw them clearly it was from a little sandy rise which looked down like the crest of a bowl upon the floor of sand below. Upon this smooth, white floor the moon beat with almost dazzling brightness.

The white man who had helped to carry the chest was now kneeling, busied at some work, though what it was Tom at first could not see. He was whittling the point of a stick into a long wooden peg, and when, by and by, he had finished what he was about, he arose and stepped to where he who seemed to be the captain had stuck his cane upright into the ground as though to mark some particular spot. He drew the cane out of the sand, thrusting the stick down in its stead. Then he drove the long peg down with a wooden mallet which the negro handed to him. The sharp rapping of the mallet upon the top of the peg sounded loud in the perfect stillness, and Tom lay watching and wondering what it all meant. The man, with quick-repeated blows, drove the peg farther and farther down into the sand until it showed only two or three inches above the surface. As he finished his work there was another faint flash of light, and by and by another smothered rumble of thunder, and Tom, as he looked out toward the westward, saw

257

the silver rim of the round and sharply outlined thundercloud rising slowly up into the sky.

The two white men were now stooping over the peg, the negro man watching them. Then presently the man with the cane started straight away from the peg, carrying the end of a measuring line with him, the other end of which the man with the plaited queue held against the top of the peg. When the pirate captain had reached the end of the measuring line he marked a cross upon the sand, and then again they measured out another stretch of space.

So they measured a distance five times over, and then, from where Tom lay, he could see the man with the queue drive another peg just at the foot of a sloping rise of sand that swept up beyond into a tall white dune marked sharp and clear against the night sky behind. As soon as the man with the plaited queue had driven the second peg into the ground they began measuring again, and so, still measuring, disappeared in another direction which took them in behind the sand dune where Tom no longer could see what they were doing.

The negro still sat by the chest where the two had left him, and so bright was the moonlight that from where he lay Tom could see the glint of it twinkling in the whites of his eyeballs.

Presently from behind the hill there came, for the third time, the sharp rapping sound of the mallet driving still another peg, and then after a while the two pirates emerged from behind the sloping whiteness into the space of moonlight again.

They came direct to where the chest lay, and the white man and the black man lifting it once more, they walked away across the level of open sand, and so on behind the edge of the hill and out of Tom's sight.

Tom Chist could no longer see what the pirates were doing, neither did he dare to cross over the open space of sand that now lay between them and him. He lay there speculating as to what they were about, and meantime the storm cloud was rising higher and higher above the horizon, with louder and louder mutterings of thunder following each dull flash from out the cloudy, cavernous depths. In the silence he could hear an

258

occasional click as of some iron implement, and he opined that the pirates were burying the chest, though just where they were at work he could neither see nor tell.

Still he lay there watching and listening, and by and by a puff of warm air blew across the sand, and a thumping tumble of louder thunder leaped from out the belly of the storm cloud, which every minute was coming nearer and nearer. Still Tom Chist lay watching.

Suddenly, almost unexpectedly, the three figures reappeared from behind the sand hill, the pirate captain leading the way, and the negro and white man following close behind him. They had gone about halfway across the white, sandy level between the hill and the hummock behind which Tom Chist lay, when the white man stopped and bent over as though to tie his shoe.

This brought the negro a few steps in front of his companion.

That which then followed happened so suddenly, so unexpectedly, so swiftly that Tom Chist had hardly time to realize what it all meant before it was over. As the negro passed him the white man arose suddenly and silently erect, and Tom Chist saw the white moonlight glint upon the blade of a great dirk knife which he now held in his hand. He took one, two silent, catlike steps behind the unsuspecting negro. Then there was a sweeping flash of the blade in the pallid light, and a blow, the thump of which Tom could distinctly hear even from where he lay stretched out upon the sand. There was an instant echoing yell from the black man, who ran stumbling forward, who stopped, who regained his footing, and then stood for an instant as though rooted to the spot.

Tom had distinctly seen the knife enter his back, and even thought that he had seen the glint of the point as it came out from the breast.

Meantime the pirate captain had stopped, and now stood with his hand resting upon his cane looking impassively on.

Then the black man started to run. The white man stood for a while glaring after him; then he, too, started after his victim upon the run. The black man was not very far from Tom when he staggered and fell. He tried to rise, then fell forward again, and lay at length. At that instant the first edge of the cloud cut across the moon, and there was a sudden darkness; but in the silence Tom heard the sound of another blow and a groan, and then presently a voice calling to the pirate captain that it was all over.

He saw the dim form of the captain crossing the level sand, and then, as the moon sailed out from behind the cloud, he saw the white man standing over a black figure that lay motionless upon the sand.

Then Tom Chist scrambled up and ran away, plunging down into the hollow of sand that lay in the shadows below. Over the next rise he ran, and down again into the next black hollow, and so on over the sliding, shifting ground, panting and gasping. It seemed to him that he could hear footsteps following, and in the terror that possessed him he almost expected every instant to feel the cold knife blade slide between his own ribs in such a thrust from behind as he had seen given to the poor black man.

So he ran on like one in a nightmare. His feet grew heavy like lead, he panted and gasped, his breath came hot and dry in his throat. But still he ran and ran until at last he found himself in front of old Matt Abrahamson's cabin, gasping, panting, and sobbing for breath, his knees relaxed and his thighs trembling with weakness.

As he opened the door and dashed into the darkened cabin (for both Matt and Molly were long ago asleep in bed) there was a flash of light, and even as he slammed the door behind him there was an instant peal of thunder, heavy as though a great weight had been dropped upon the roof of the sky, so that the doors and windows of the cabin rattled.

Then Tom Chist crept to bed, trembling, shuddering, bathed in sweat, his heart beating like a trip hammer, and his brain dizzy from that long, terror-inspired race through the soft sand in which he had striven to outstrip he knew not what pursuing horror.

For a long, long time he lay awake, trembling and chattering with nervous chills, and when he did fall asleep it was only to

260

drop into monstrous dreams in which he once again saw ever enacted, with various grotesque variations, the tragic drama which his waking eyes had beheld the night before.

Then came the dawning of the broad, wet daylight, and before the rising of the sun Tom was up and out of doors to find the young day dripping with the rain of overnight.

His first act was to climb the nearest sand hill and to gaze out toward the offing where the pirate ship had been the day before.

It was no longer there.

Soon afterward Matt Abrahamson came out of the cabin and he called to Tom to go get a bite to eat, for it was time for them to be away fishing.

All that morning the recollection of the night before hung over Tom Chist like a great cloud of boding trouble. It filled the confined area of the little boat and spread over the entire wide spaces of sky and sea that surrounded them. Not for a moment was it lifted. Even when he was hauling in his wet and dripping line with a struggling fish at the end of it a re-current memory of what he had seen would suddenly come upon him, and he would groan in spirit at the recollection. He looked at Matt Abrahamson's leathery face, at his lantern jaws cavernously and stolidly chewing at a tobacco leaf, and it seemed monstrous to him that the old man should be so un-conscious of the black cloud that wrapped them all about.

When the boat reached the shore again he leaped scrambling to the beach, and as soon as his dinner was eaten he hurried away to find the Dominie Jones.

He ran all the way from Abrahamson's hut to the parson's house, hardly stopping once, and when he knocked at the door he was panting and sobbing for breath.

The good man was sitting on the back-kitchen doorstep smok-ing his long pipe of tobacco out into the sunlight, while his wife within was rattling about among the pans and dishes in preparation of their supper, of which a strong, porky smell already filled the air.

Then Tom Chist told his story, panting, hurrying, tumbling one word over another in his haste, and Parson Jones listened, breaking every now and then into an ejaculation of wonder. The light in his pipe went out and the bowl turned cold.

"And I don't see why they should have killed the poor black man," said Tom, as he finished his narrative.

"Why, that is very easy enough to understand," said the good reverend man. "'Twas a treasure box they buried!"

In his agitation Mr. Jones had risen from his seat and was now stumping up and down, puffing at his empty tobacco pipe as though it were still alight.

"A treasure box!" cried out Tom.

"Aye, a treasure box! And that was why they killed the poor black man. He was the only one, d'ye see, besides they two who knew the place where 'twas hid, and now that they've killed him out of the way, there's nobody but themselves knows. The villains—Tut, tut, look at that now!" In his excitement the dominie had snapped the stem of his tobacco pipe in two.

"Why, then," said Tom, " 'tis indeed a wicked, bloody treasure, and fit to bring a curse upon anybody who finds it!"

" 'Tis more like to bring a curse upon the soul who buried it," said Parson Jones, "and it may be a blessing to him who finds it. But tell me, Tom, do you think you could find the place again where 'twas hid?"

"I can't tell that," said Tom, " 'twas all in among the sand humps, d'ye see, and it was at night into the bargain. Maybe we could find the marks of their feet in the sand," he added.

" 'Tis not likely," said the reverend gentleman, "for the storm last night would have washed all that away."

"I could find the place," said Tom, "where the boat was drawn up on the beach."

"Why, then, that's something to start from, Tom," said his friend. "If we can find that, then maybe we can find whither they went from there."

"If I was certain it was a treasure box," cried out Tom Chist, "I would rake over every foot of sand betwixt here and Henlopen to find it."

" 'Twould be like hunting for a pin in a haystack," said the Rev. Hilary Jones.

As Tom walked away home, it seemed as though a ton's weight of gloom had been rolled away from his soul. The next day he and Parson Jones were to go treasure-hunting together; it seemed to Tom as though he could hardly wait for the time to come.

The next afternoon Parson Jones and Tom Chist started off together upon the expedition that made Tom's fortune forever. Tom carried a spade over his shoulder and the reverend gentleman walked along beside him with his cane.

As they jogged along up the beach they talked together about the only thing they could talk about—the treasure box. "And how big did you say 'twas?" quoth the good gentleman.

263

"About so long," said Tom Chist, measuring off upon the spade, "and about so wide, and this deep."

"And what if it should be full of money, Tom?" said the reverend gentleman, swinging his cane around and around in wide circles in the excitement of the thought, as he strode along briskly. "Suppose it should be full of money, what then?"

"By Moses!" said Tom Chist, hurrying to keep up with his friend, "I'd buy a ship for myself, I would, and I'd trade to Injy and to Chiny in my own boat, I would. Suppose the chist was all full of money, sir, and suppose we should find it; would there be enough in it, d'ye suppose, to buy a ship?"

"To be sure there would be enough, Tom; enough and to spare, and a good big lump over."

"And if I find it 'tis mine to keep, is it, and no mistake?"

"Why, to be sure it would be yours!" cried out the parson, in a loud voice. "To be sure it would be yours!" He knew nothing of the law, but the doubt of the question began at once to ferment in his brain, and he strode along in silence for a while. "Whose else would it be but yours if you find it?" he burst out. "Can you tell me that?"

"If ever I have a ship of my own," said Tom Chist, "and if ever I sail to Injy in her, I'll fetch ye back the best chist of tea, sir, that ever was fetched from Cochin Chiny."

Parson Jones burst out laughing. "Thankee, Tom," he said, "and I'll thankee again when I get my chist of tea. But tell me, Tom, didst thou ever hear of the farmer girl who counted her chickens before they were hatched?"

It was thus they talked as they hurried along up the beach together, and so came to a place at last where Tom stopped short and stood looking about him. " 'Twas just here," he said, "I saw the boat last night. I know 'twas here, for I mind me of that bit of wreck yonder, and that there was a tall stake drove in the sand just where yon stake stands."

Parson Jones put on his barnacles and went over to the stake toward which Tom pointed. As soon as he had looked at it carefully he called out: "Why, Tom, this hath been just drove down into the sand. 'Tis a brand-new stake of wood, and the

Why had Captain Kidd kept these bloody records?

pirates must have set it here themselves as a mark, just as they drove the pegs you spoke about down into the sand."

Tom came over and looked at the stake. It was a stout piece of oak nearly two inches thick; it had been shaped with some care, and the top of it had been painted red. He shook the stake and tried to move it, but it had been driven or planted so deeply into the sand that he could not stir it. "Aye, sir," he said, "it must have been set here for a mark, for I'm sure 'twas not here yesterday or the day before." He stood looking about him to see if there were other signs of the pirates' presence. At some little distance there was the corner of something white sticking up out of the sand. He could see that it was a scrap of paper, and he pointed to it, calling out: "Yonder is a piece of paper, sir. I wonder if they left that behind them?"

It was a miraculous chance that placed that paper there. There was only an inch of it showing, and if it had not been for Tom's sharp eyes, it would certainly have been overlooked and passed by. The next windstorm would have covered it up, and all that afterward happened never would have occurred. "Look, sir," he said, "it hath writing on it."

"Let me see it," said Parson Jones. He adjusted the spectacles a little more firmly astride of his nose as he took the paper in his hand and began conning it. "What's all this?" he said; "a whole lot of figures and nothing else." And then he read aloud, " 'Mark—S. S. W. S. by S.' What d'ye suppose that means, Tom?"

"I don't know, sir," said Tom. "But maybe we can understand it better if you read on."

" 'Tis all a great lot of figures," said Parson Jones, "without a grain of meaning in them so far as I can see, unless they be sailing directions." And then he began reading again: " 'Mark—S.S.W. by S. 40, 72, 91, 130, 151, 177, 202, 232, 256, 271'—d'ye see, it must be sailing directions—'299, 335, 362, 386, 415, 446, 469, 491, 522, 544, 571, 598'—what a lot of them there be—'626, 652, 676, 695, 724, 851, 876, 905, 940, 967. Peg. S.E. by E. 269 foot. Peg. S.S.W. by S. 427 foot. Peg. Dig to the west of this six foot.' "

"What's that about a peg?" exclaimed Tom. "What's that

about a peg? And then there's something about digging, too!"
It was as though a sudden light began shining into his brain.
He felt himself growing quickly very excited. "Read that over
again, sir," he cried. "Why, sir, you remember I told you they
drove a peg into the sand. And don't they say to dig close to
it? Read it over again, sir—read it over again!"

"Peg?" said the good gentleman. "To be sure it was about a
peg. Let's look again. Yes, here it is. 'Peg, S.E. by E. 269 foot.' "

"Aye!" cried out Tom Chist again, in great excitement. "Don't
you remember what I told you, sir, 269 foot? Sure that must
be what I saw 'em measuring with the line."

Parson Jones had now caught the flame of excitement that
was blazing up so strongly in Tom's breast. He felt as though
some wonderful thing was about to happen to them. "To be
sure, to be sure!" he called out, in a great big voice. "And then
they measured out 427 foot south-southwest by south, and they
then drove another peg, and then they buried the box six foot to
the west of it. Why, Tom—why, Tom Chist! if we've read this
aright, thy fortune is made."

Tom Chist stood staring straight at the old gentleman's excited face, and seeing nothing but it in all the bright infinity
of sunshine. Were they, indeed, about to find the treasure chest?
He felt the sun very hot upon his shoulders, and he heard the
harsh, insistent jarring of a tern that hovered and circled with
forked tail and sharp white wings in the sunlight just above
their heads; but all the time he stood staring into the good old
gentleman's face.

It was Parson Jones who first spoke. "But what do all these
figures mean?" And Tom observed how the paper shook and
rustled in the tremor of excitement that shook his hand. He
raised the paper to the focus of his spectacles and began to
read again. " 'Mark 40, 72, 91—' "

"Mark?" cried out Tom, almost screaming. "Why, that must
mean the stake yonder; that must be the mark." And he pointed
to the oaken stick with its red tip blazing against the white
shimmer of sand behind it.

"And the 40 and 72 and 91," cried the old gentleman, in a

voice equally shrill—"why, that must mean the number of steps the pirate was counting when you heard him."

"To be sure that's what they mean!" cried Tom Chist. "That is it, and it can be nothing else. Oh, come, sir—come, sir; let us make haste and find it!"

"Stay! stay!" said the good gentleman, holding up his hand; and again Tom Chist noticed how it trembled and shook. His voice was steady enough, though very hoarse, but his hand shook and trembled as though with a palsy. "Stay! stay! First of all, we must follow these measurements. And 'tis a marvelous thing," he croaked after a little pause, "how this paper ever came to be here."

"Maybe it was blown here by the storm," suggested Tom.

"Like enough; like enough," said Parson Jones. "Like enough, after the wretches had buried the chest and killed the poor black man, they were so buffeted and bowsed about by the storm that it was shook out of the man's pocket, and thus blew away from him without his knowing aught of it."

"But let us find the box!" cried out Tom Chist, flaming with his excitement.

"Aye, aye," said the good man; "only stay a little, my boy, until we make sure what we're about. I've got my pocket compass here, but we must have something to measure off the feet when we have found the peg. You run across to Tom Brooke's house and fetch that measuring rod he used to lay out his new byre. While you're gone I'll pace off the distance marked on the paper with my pocket compass here."

Tom Chist was gone for almost an hour, though he ran nearly all the way and back, upborne as on the wings of the wind. When he returned, panting, Parson Jones was nowhere to be seen, but Tom saw his footsteps leading away inland, and he followed the scuffling marks in the smooth surface across the sand humps and down into the hollows, and by and by found the good gentleman in a spot he at once knew as soon as he laid his eyes upon it.

It was the open space where the pirates had driven their first peg, and where Tom Chist had afterward seen them kill the poor

DeWitt Whistler Jayne

black man. Tom Chist gazed around as though expecting to see some sign of the tragedy, but the space was as smooth and as undisturbed as a floor, excepting where, midway across it, Parson Jones, who was now stooping over something on the ground, had trampled it all around about.

When Tom Chist saw him he was still bending over, scraping sand away from something he had found.

It was the first peg!

Inside of half an hour they had found the second and third pegs, and Tom Chist stripped off his coat, and began digging like mad down into the sand, Parson Jones standing over him watching him. The sun was sloping well toward the west when the blade of Tom Chist's spade struck upon something hard.

If it had been his own heart that he had hit in the sand his breast could hardly have thrilled more sharply.

It was the treasure box!

Parson Jones himself leaped down into the hole, and began scraping away the sand with his hands as though he had gone crazy. At last, with some difficulty, they tugged and hauled the chest up out of the sand to the surface, where it lay covered all over with the grit that clung to it. It was securely locked and fastened with a padlock, and it took a good many blows with the blade of the spade to burst the bolt. Parson Jones himself lifted the lid. Tom Chist leaned forward and gazed down into the open box. He would not have been surprised to have seen it filled full of yellow gold and bright jewels. It was filled half full of books and papers, and half full of canvas bags tied safely and securely around and around with cords of string.

Parson Jones lifted out one of the bags, and it jingled as he did so. It was full of money.

He cut the string, and with trembling, shaking hands handed the bag to Tom, who, in an ecstasy of wonder, and dizzy with delight, poured out, with swimming sight upon the coat spread on the ground, a cataract of shining silver money that rang and twinkled and jingled as it fell in a shining heap upon the coarse cloth.

Parson Jones held up both hands into the air, and Tom stared at what he saw, wondering whether it was all so, and whether he was really awake. It seemed to him as though he was in a dream.

There were two-and-twenty bags in all in the chest: ten of them full of silver money, eight of them full of gold money, three of them full of gold dust, and one small bag with jewels wrapped up in wad cotton and paper.

" 'Tis enough," cried out Parson Jones, "to make us both rich men as long as we live."

The burning summer sun, though sloping in the sky, beat down upon them as hot as fire; but neither of them noticed it. Neither did they notice hunger nor thirst nor fatigue, but sat there as though in a trance, with the bags of money scattered on the sand around them, a great pile of money heaped upon the coat, and the open chest beside them. It was the hour of sundown before Parson Jones had begun fairly to examine the books and papers in the chest.

Of the three books, two were evidently log books of the pirates who had been lying off the mouth of the Delaware Bay all this time. The other book was written in Spanish, and was evidently the log book of some captured prize.

It was then, sitting there upon the sand, the good old gentleman reading in his high, crackling voice, that they first learned from the bloody records in those two books who it was who had been lying inside the Cape all this time, and that it was the famous Captain Kidd. Every now and then the reverend gentleman would stop to exclaim, "Oh, the bloody wretch!" or, "Oh, the desperate, cruel, villains!" and then would go on reading again a scrap here and a scrap there.

And all the while Tom Chist sat and listened, every now and then reaching out furtively and touching the heap of money still lying upon the coat.

One might be inclined to wonder why Captain Kidd had kept those bloody records. He had probably laid them away because they so incriminated many of the great people of the colony of New York that, with the books in evidence, it would have been impossible to bring the pirate to justice without dragging a

270

dozen or more fine gentlemen into the dock along with him. If he could have kept them in his own possession they would doubtless have been a great weapon of defense to protect him from the gallows. Indeed, when Captain Kidd was finally brought to conviction and hung, he was not accused of his piracies, but of striking a mutinous seaman upon the head with a bucket and accidentally killing him. The authorities did not dare try him for piracy. He was really hung because he was a pirate, and we know that it was the log books that Tom Chist brought to New York that did the business for him; he was accused and convicted of manslaughter for killing his own ship carpenter with a bucket.

So Parson Jones, sitting there in the slanting light, read

through these terrible records of piracy, and Tom, with the pile of gold and silver money beside him, sat and listened to him.

What a spectacle, if anyone had come upon them! But they were alone, with the vast arch of sky empty above them and the wide white stretch of sand a desert around them. The sun sank lower and lower, until there was only time to glance through the other papers in the chest.

They were nearly all goldsmiths' bills of exchange drawn in favor of certain of the most prominent merchants of New York. Parson Jones, as he read over the names, knew of nearly all the gentlemen by hearsay. Aye, here was this gentleman; he thought that name would be among 'em. What? Here is Mr. So-and-so. Well, if all they say is true, the villain has robbed one of his own best friends. "I wonder," he said, "why the wretch should have hidden these papers so carefully away with the other treasures, for they could do him no good?" Then, answering his own question: "Like enough because these will give him a hold over the gentlemen to whom they are drawn so that he can make a good bargain for his own neck before he gives the bills back to their owners. I tell you what it is, Tom," he continued, "it is you who shall go to New York and bargain for the return of these papers. 'Twill be as good as another fortune to you."

The majority of the bills were drawn in favor of one Richard Chillingsworth, Esquire. "And he is," said Parson Jones, "one of the richest men in the province of New York. You shall go to him with the news of what we have found."

"When shall I go?" said Tom Chist.

"You shall go upon the very first boat we can catch," said the parson. He had turned, still holding the bills in his hand, and was now fingering over the pile of money that yet lay tumbled out upon the coat. "I wonder, Tom," said he, "if you could spare me a score or so of these doubloons?"

"You shall have fifty score, if you choose," said Tom, bursting with gratitude and with generosity in his newly found treasure.

"You are as fine a lad as ever I saw, Tom," said the parson, "and I'll thank you to the last day of my life."

Tom scooped up a double handful of silver money. "Take it, sir," he said, "and you may have as much more as you want of it."

He poured it into the dish that the good man made of his hands, and the parson made a motion as though to empty it into his pocket. Then he stopped, as though a sudden doubt had occurred to him. "I don't know that 'tis fit for me to take this pirate money, after all," he said.

"But you are welcome to it," said Tom.

Still the parson hesitated. "Nay," he burst out, "I'll not take it; 'tis blood money." And as he spoke he chucked the whole double handful into the now empty chest, then arose and dusted the sand from his breeches. Then, with a great deal of bustling energy, he helped to tie the bags again and put them all back into the chest.

They reburied the chest in the place whence they had taken it, and then the parson folded the precious paper of directions, placed it carefully in his wallet, and his wallet in his pocket. "Tom," he said, for the twentieth time, "your fortune has been made this day."

And Tom Chist, as he rattled in his breeches pocket the half dozen doubloons he had kept out of his treasure, felt that what his friend had said was true.

As the two went back homeward across the level space of sand Tom Chist suddenly stopped stock-still and stood looking about him. "'Twas just here," he said, digging his heel down into the sand, "that they killed the poor black man."

"And here he lies buried for all time," said Parson Jones; and as he spoke he dug his cane down into the sand. Tom Chist shuddered. He would not have been surprised if the ferrule of the cane had struck something soft beneath that level surface. But it did not, nor was any sign of that tragedy ever seen again. For, whether the pirates had carried away what they had done and buried it elsewhere, or whether the storm in blowing the sand had completely leveled off and hidden all sign of that tragedy where it was enacted, certain it is that it never came to sight again—at least so far as Tom Chist and the Rev. Hilary Jones ever knew.

This is the story of the treasure box. All that remains now is to conclude the story of Tom Chist, and to tell of what came of him in the end.

He did not go back again to live with old Matt Abrahamson. Parson Jones had now taken charge of him and his fortunes, and Tom did not have to go back to the fisherman's hut.

Old Abrahamson talked a great deal about it, and would come in his cups and harangue good Parson Jones, making a vast protestation of what he would do to Tom—if he ever caught him—for running away. But Tom on all these occasions kept carefully out of his way, and nothing came of the old man's threatenings.

Tom used to go over to see his foster mother now and then, but always when the old man was away from home. And Molly Abrahamson used to warn him to keep out of her father's way. "He's in as vile a humor as ever I see, Tom," she said; "he sits sulking all day long, and 'tis my belief he'd kill ye if he caught ye."

Of course Tom said nothing, even to her, about the treasure, and he and the reverend gentleman kept the knowledge thereof to themselves. About three weeks later Parson Jones managed to get him shipped aboard of a vessel bound for New York town, and a few days later Tom Chist landed at that place. He had never been in such a town before, and he could not sufficiently wonder and marvel at the number of brick houses, at the multitude of people coming and going along the fine, hard, earthen sidewalk, at the shops and the stores where goods hung in the windows and, most of all, the fortifications and the battery at the point, at the rows of threatening cannon, and at the scarlet-coated sentries pacing up and down the ramparts. All this was very wonderful, and so were the clustered boats riding at anchor in the harbor. It was like a new world, so different was it from the sand hills and the sedgy levels of Henlopen.

Tom Chist took up his lodgings at a coffee house near to the town hall, and thence he sent by the postboy, a letter written by Parson Jones to Master Chillingsworth. In a little while the boy returned with a message, asking Tom to come up to Mr. Chillingsworth's house that afternoon at two o'clock.

Tom went thither with a great deal of trepidation, and his heart fell away altogether when he found it a fine, grand brick house, three stories high, and with wrought-iron letters across the front.

The counting house was in the same building; but Tom, because of Mr. Jones's letter, was conducted directly into the parlor, where the great rich man was awaiting his coming. He was sitting in a leather-covered armchair, smoking a pipe of tobacco, and with a bottle of fine old Madeira close to his elbow.

Tom had not had a chance to buy a new suit of clothes yet, and so he cut no very fine figure in the rough dress he had brought with him from Henlopen. Nor did Mr. Chillingsworth seem to think very highly of his appearance, for he sat looking sideways at Tom as he smoked.

"Well, my lad," he said, "and what is this great thing you have to tell me that is so mightily wonderful? I got what's-his-name—Mr. Jones's—letter, and now I am ready to hear what you have to say."

But if he thought but little of his visitor's appearance at first, he soon changed his sentiments toward him, for Tom had not spoken twenty words when Mr. Chillingsworth's whole aspect changed. He straightened himself up in his seat, laid aside his pipe, pushed away his glass of Madeira, and bade Tom take a chair.

He listened without a word as Tom Chist told of the buried treasure, of how he had seen the poor negro murdered, and of how he and Parson Jones had recovered the chest again. Only once did Mr. Chillingsworth interrupt the narrative. "And to think," he cried, "that the villain this very day walks about New York town as though he were an honest man, ruffling it with the best of us! But if we can only get hold of these log books you speak of. Go on; tell me more of this."

When Tom Chist's narrative was ended, Mr. Chillingsworth's bearing was as different as daylight is from dark. He asked a

Chillingsworth

thousand questions, all in the most polite and gracious tone imaginable, and not only urged a glass of his fine old Madeira upon Tom, but asked him to stay to supper. There was nobody to be there, he said, but his wife and daughter.

Tom, all in a panic at the very thought of the two ladies, sturdily refused to stay even for the dish of tea Mr. Chillingsworth offered him.

He did not know that he was destined to stay there as long as he should live.

"And now," said Mr. Chillingsworth, "tell me about yourself."

"I have nothing to tell, Your Honor," said Tom, "except that I was washed up out of the sea."

"Washed up out of the sea!" exclaimed Mr. Chillingsworth. "Why, how was that? Come, begin at the beginning, and tell me all."

Thereupon Tom Chist did as he was bidden, beginning at the very beginning and telling everything just as Molly Abrahamson had often told it to him. As he continued, Mr. Chillingsworth's interest changed into an appearance of stronger and stronger excitement. Suddenly he jumped up out of his chair and began to walk up and down the room.

"Stop! Stop!" he cried out at last, in the midst of something

Tom was saying. "Stop! Stop! Tell me; do you know the name of the vessel that was wrecked, and from which you were washed ashore?"

"I've heard it said," said Tom Chist, "'twas the *Bristol Merchant.*"

"I knew it! I knew it!" exclaimed the great man, in a loud voice, flinging his hands up into the air. "I felt it was so the moment you began the story. But tell me this, was there nothing found with you with a mark or a name upon it?"

"There was a kerchief," said Tom, "marked with a T. and a C."

"Theodosia Chillingsworth!" cried out the merchant. "I knew it! I knew it! Heavens! To think of anything so wonderful happening as this! Boy! Boy! Dost thou know who thou art? Thou art my own brother's son. His name was Oliver Chillingsworth, and he was my partner in business, and thou art his son." Then he ran out into the entryway, shouting and calling for his wife and daughter to come. So Tom Chist—or Thomas Chillingsworth, as he now was to be called—did stay to supper, after all.

This is the story, and I hope you may like it. For Tom Chist became rich and great, as was to be supposed, and he married his pretty cousin Theodosia (who had been named for his own mother, drowned in the *Bristol Merchant*).

He did not forget his friends, but had Parson Jones brought to New York to live.

As to Molly and Matt Abrahamson, they both enjoyed a pension of ten pounds a year for as long as they lived; for now that all was well with him, Tom bore no grudge against the old fisherman for all the drubbings he had suffered.

The treasure box was brought on to New York, and if Tom Chist did not get all the money there was in it (as Parson Jones had opined he would) he got at least a good big lump of it.

And it is my belief that those log books did more to get Captain Kidd arrested in Boston town and hanged in London than anything else that was brought up against him.

In THE dangerous days of Henry IV, when Myles Falworth was still a young boy, his father was blinded in an attack by a mysterious enemy. Later, when Myles grew older and had become a knight, his father was unjustly accused of being a traitor by this same enemy, who, Myles finally discovered was the powerful Earl of Alban. He challenged him at the Court of Chivalry to a battle to avenge his father's honor. Our story begins on the day of the battle: a matter of life or death to Myles.

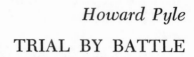

Howard Pyle

TRIAL BY BATTLE

ILLUSTRATED BY *Henry C. Pitz*

IN THE days of King Edward III a code of laws relating to trial by battle had been compiled for one of his sons, Thomas of Woodstock. In this work each and every detail had been arranged and fixed, and from that time judicial combats had been regulated in accordance with its mandates.

It was in obedience to this code that Myles Falworth appeared at the east gate of the lists (the east gate being assigned by law to the challenger), clad in full armor of proof, attended by Gascoyne, and accompanied by two of the young knights who had acted as his escort from Scotland Yard.

At the barriers he was met by the attorney Willingwood, the chief lawyer who had conducted the Falworth case before the High Court of Chivalry, and who was to attend him during the administration of the oaths before the King.

As Myles presented himself at the gate he was met by the Constable, the Marshal, and their immediate attendants. The Constable, laying his hand upon the bridle-rein, said, in a loud voice: "Stand, Sir Knight, and tell me why thou art come thus armed to the gates of the lists. What is thy name?"

Myles answered, "I am Myles Falworth, a Knight of the Bath

by grace of his Majesty King Henry IV and by his creation, and do come hither to defend my challenge upon the body of William Bushy Brookhurst, Earl of Alban, proclaiming him an unknightly knight and a false and perjured liar, in that he hath accused Gilbert Reginald, Lord Falworth, of treason against our beloved Lord, his Majesty the King, and may God defend the right!"

As he ended speaking, the Constable advanced close to his side, and raising the umbril of the helmet, looked him in the face. Having approved his identity, he ordered the gates to be opened, and bade Myles enter with his squire and his friends.

At the south side of the lists a raised scaffolding had been built for the King and those who looked on. It was not unlike that which had been erected at Devlen Castle when Myles had first jousted as belted knight—here were the same raised seat for the King, the tapestries, the hangings, the fluttering pennons, and the royal standard floating above; only here were no fair-faced ladies looking down upon him, but instead, stern-browed Lords and knights in armor and squires, and here were no merry laughing and buzz of talk and flutter of fans and kerchiefs, but all was very quiet and serious.

Myles riding upon his horse, with Gascoyne holding the bridle-rein, and his attorney walking beside him with his hand upon the stirrups, followed the Constable across the lists to an open space in front of the seat where the King sat. Then, having reached his appointed station, he stopped, and the Constable, advancing to the foot of the stairway that led to the dais above, announced that the challenger had entered the lists.

"Then call the defendant straightway," said the King, "for noon draweth nigh."

The day was very warm, and the sun, bright and unclouded, shone fiercely down upon the open lists. Perhaps few men now-adays could bear the scorching heat of iron plates such as Myles wore, from which the body was only protected by a leathern jacket and hose. But men's bodies in those days were tougher and more seasoned to hardships of weather than they are in these our times. Myles thought no more of the burning iron

279

plates that incased him than a modern soldier thinks of his dress uniform in warm weather. Nevertheless, he raised the umbril of his helmet to cool his face as he waited the coming of his opponent. He turned his eyes upward to the row of seats on the scaffolding above, and even in the restless, bewildering multitude of strange faces turned towards him recognized those that he knew: the Prince of Wales, his companions of the Scotland Yard household, the Duke of Clarence, the Bishop of Winchester, and some of the noblemen of the Earl of Mackworth's party, who had been buzzing about the Prince for the past month or so. But his glance swept over all these, rather perceiving than seeing them, and then rested upon a square box-like compartment not unlike a prisoner's dock in the courtroom of our day, for in the box sat his father, with the Earl of Mackworth upon one side and Sir James Lee upon the other. The blind man's face was very pale, but still wore its usual expression of calm serenity—the calm serenity of a blind face. The Earl was also very pale, and he kept his eyes fixed steadfastly upon Myles with a keen and searching look, as though to pierce to the very bottom of the young man's heart, and discover if indeed not one little fragment of dry rot of fear or uncertainty tainted the solid courage of his knighthood.

Then he heard the criers calling the defendant at the four corners of the list: "*Oyez! Oyez! Oyez!* William Bushy Brookhurst, Earl of Alban, come to this combat, in which you be enterprised this day to discharge your sureties before the King, the Constable, and the Marshal, and to encounter in your defence Myles Falworth, knight, the accepted champion upon behalf of Gilbert Reginald Falworth, the challenger! *Oyez! Oyez! Oyez!*"

So they continued calling, until, by the sudden turning of all faces, Myles knew that his enemy was at hand.

Then presently he saw the Earl and his attendants enter the outer gate at the west end of the barrier; he saw the Constable and Marshal meet him; he saw the formal words of greeting pass; he saw the Constable raise the umbril of the helmet. Then the gate opened, and the Earl of Alban entered, clad *cap-a-pie* in a full suit of magnificent Milan armor without juppon or

adornment of any kind. As he approached across the lists, Myles closed the umbril of his helmet, and then sat quite still and motionless, for the time was come.

So he sat, erect and motionless as a statue of iron, half hearing the reading of the long intricately-worded bills, absorbed in many thoughts of past and present things. At last the reading ended, and then he calmly and composedly obeyed, under the direction of his attorney, the several forms and ceremonies that followed; answered the various official questions, took the various oaths. Then Gascoyne, leading the horse by the bridle-rein, conducted him back to his station at the east end of the lists.

As the faithful friend and squire made one last and searching examination of arms and armor, the Marshal and the clerk came to the young champion and administered the final oath by which he swore that he carried no concealed weapons.

The weapons allowed by the High Court were then measured and attested. They consisted of the long sword, the short sword, the dagger, the mace, and a weapon known as the hand-gisarm, or glavelot—a heavy swordlike blade eight palms long, a palm in breadth, and riveted to a stout handle of wood three feet long.

The usual lance had not been included in the list of arms, the hand-gisarm being substituted in its place. It was a fearful and murderous weapon, though cumbersome, unhandy, and ill-adapted for quick or dexterous stroke; nevertheless, the Earl of Alban had petitioned the King to have it included in the list, and in answer to the King's expressed desire the Court had adopted it in the stead of the lance, yielding thus much to the royal wishes. Nor was it a small concession. The hand-gisarm had been a weapon very much in vogue in King Richard's day, and was now nearly, if not entirely, out of fashion with the younger generation of warriors. The Earl of Alban was, of course, well used to the blade; with Myles it was strange and new, either for attack or in defence.

With the administration of the final oath and the examination of the weapons, the preliminary ceremonies came to an end, and presently Myles heard the criers calling to clear the lists. As those around him moved to withdraw, the young knight drew off his mailed gauntlet, and gave Gascoyne's hand one last final clasp, strong, earnest, and intense with the close friendship of young manhood, and poor Gascoyne looked up at him with a face ghastly white.

Then all were gone; the gates of the principal list and that of the false list were closed clashing, and Myles was alone, face to face, with his mortal enemy.

There was a little while of restless, rustling silence, during which the Constable took his place in the seat appointed for him directly in front of and below the King's throne. A moment or two when even the restlessness and the rustling were quieted, and then the King leaned forward and spoke to the Constable, who immediately called out, in a loud, clear voice, "Let them go!" Then again, "Let them go!" Then, for the third and last time, "Let them go and do their endeavor, in God's name!"

At this third command the combatants, each of whom had till that moment been sitting as motionless as a statue of iron, tightened rein, and rode slowly and deliberately forward without haste, yet without hesitation, until they met in the very middle of the lists.

In the battle which followed, Myles fought with the long sword, the Earl with the hand-gisarm for which he had asked. The moment they met, the combat was opened, and for a time nothing was heard but the thunderous clashing and clamor of blows, now and then rising with a ceaseless uproar and din, now and then beating intermittently, now and then pausing. Occasionally, as the combatants spurred together, checked, wheeled, and recovered, they would be hidden for a moment in a misty veil of dust, which, again drifting down the wind, perhaps revealed them drawn a little apart, resting their panting horses. Then, again, they would spur together, striking as they passed, wheeling and striking again.

Upon the scaffolding all was still, only now and then for the buzz of muffled exclamations or applause of those who looked on. Mostly the applause was from Myles's friends, for from the very first he showed and steadily maintained his advantage over the older man. "Hah! well struck! well recovered!" "Look ye! the sword bit that time!" "Nay, look, saw ye him pass the point of the gisarm?" Then, "Falworth! Falworth!" as some more than usually skilful stroke or parry occurred.

Meantime Myles's father sat straining his sightless eyeballs, as though to pierce his body's darkness with one ray of light that would show him how his boy held his own in the fight, and Lord Mackworth, leaning with his lips close to the blind man's ear, told him point by point how the battle stood.

"Fear not, Gilbert," said he at each pause in the fight. "He holdeth his own right well." Then, after a while: "God is with us, Gilbert. Alban is twice wounded, and his horse faileth. One little while longer and the victory is ours!"

A longer and more continuous interval of combat followed this last assurance, during which Myles drove the assault fiercely and unrelentingly as though to overbear his enemy by the very power and violence of the blows he delivered. The Earl defended himself desperately, but was borne back, back, back, farther and farther. Every nerve of those who looked on was stretched to breathless tensity, when, almost as his enemy was against the barriers, Myles paused and rested.

283

"Out upon it!" exclaimed the Earl of Mackworth, almost shrilly in his excitement, as the sudden lull followed the crashing of blows. "Why doth the boy spare him? That is thrice he hath given him grace to recover; an he had pushed the battle that time he had driven him back against the barriers."

It was as the Earl had said; Myles had three times given his enemy grace when victory was almost in his very grasp. He had three times spared him, in spite of all he and those dear to him must suffer should his cruel and merciless enemy gain the victory. It was a false and foolish generosity, partly the fault of his impulsive youth—more largely of his romantic training in the artificial code of French chivalry. He felt that the battle was his, and so he gave his enemy these three chances to recover, as some chevalier or knight-errant of romance might have done, instead of pushing the combat to a mercifully speedy end—and his foolish generosity cost him dear.

In the momentary pause that had thus stirred the Earl of Mackworth to a sudden outbreak, the Earl of Alban sat upon his panting, sweating war horse, facing his powerful young enemy at about twelve paces distant. He sat as still as a rock, holding his gisarm poised in front of him. He had, as the Earl of Mackworth had said, been wounded twice, and each time with the point of the sword, so much more dangerous than a direct cut with the weapon. One wound was beneath his armor, and no one but he knew how serious it might be; the other was under the overlapping of the *épaulière*, and from it a finger's-breadth of blood ran straight down his side and over the housings of his horse. From without, the still motionless iron figure appeared calm and expressionless; within, who knows what consuming blasts of hate, rage, and despair swept his heart as with a fiery whirlwind.

As Myles looked at the motionless, bleeding figure, his breast swelled with pity. "My Lord," said he, "thou art sore wounded and the fight is against thee; wilt thou not yield thee?"

No one but that other heard the speech, and no one but Myles heard the answer that came back, hollow, cavernous, "Never, thou dog! Never!"

Then in an instant, as quick as a flash, his enemy spurred straight upon Myles, and as he spurred he struck a last desperate, swinging blow, in which he threw in one final effort all the strength of hate, of fury, and of despair. Myles whirled his horse backward, warding the blow with his shield as he did so. The blade glanced from the smooth face of the shield, and, whether by mistake or not, fell straight and true, and with almost undiminished force, upon the neck of Myles's war horse, and just behind the ears. The animal staggered forward, and then fell upon its knees, and at the same instant the other, as though by the impetus of the rush, dashed full upon it with all the momentum lent by the weight of iron it carried. The shock was irresistible, and the stunned and wounded horse was flung upon the ground, rolling over and over. As his horse fell, Myles wrenched one of his feet out of the stirrup; the other caught for an instant, and he was flung headlong with stunning violence, his armor crashing as he fell. In the cloud of dust that arose no one could see just what happened, but that what was done was done deliberately no one doubted. The Earl, at once checking and spurring his foaming charger, drove the iron-shod

285

war horse directly over Myles's prostrate body. Then, checking him fiercely with the curb, reined him back, the hoofs clashing and crashing, over the figure beneath. So he had ridden over the father at York, and so he rode over the son at Smithfield.

Myles, as he lay prostrate and half stunned by his fall, had seen his enemy thus driving his rearing horse down upon him, but was not able to defend himself. A fallen knight in full armor was utterly powerless to rise without assistance; Myles lay helpless in the clutch of the very iron that was his defence. He closed his eyes involuntarily, and then horse and rider were upon him. There was a deafening, sparkling crash, a glimmering faintness, then another crash as the horse was reined furiously back again, and then a humming stillness.

In a moment, upon the scaffolding all was a tumult of uproar and confusion, shouting and gesticulation; only the King sat calm, sullen, impassive. The Earl wheeled his horse and sat for a moment or two as though to make quite sure that he knew the King's mind. The blow that had been given was foul, unknightly, but the King gave no sign either of acquiescence or rebuke; he had willed that Myles was to die.

Then the Earl turned again and rode deliberately up to his prostrate enemy.

When Myles opened his eyes after that moment of stunning silence, it was to see the other looming above him on his war horse, swinging his gisarm for one last mortal blow—pitiless, merciless.

The sight of that looming peril brought back Myles's wandering senses like a flash of lightning. He flung up his shield and met the blow even as it descended, turning it aside. It only protracted the end.

Once more the Earl of Alban raised the gisarm, swinging it twice around his head before he struck. This time, though the shield glanced it, the blow fell upon the shoulder-piece, biting through the steel plate and leathern jack beneath even to the bone. Then Myles covered his head with his shield as a last protecting chance for life.

For the third time the Earl swung the blade flashing, and then

286

it fell, straight and true, upon the defenceless body, just below the left arm, biting deep through the armor plates. For an instant the blade stuck fast, and that instant was Myles's salvation. Under the agony of the blow he gave a muffled cry, and almost instinctively grasped the shaft of the weapon with both hands. Had the Earl let go his end of the weapon, he would have won the battle at his leisure and most easily; as it was, he struggled violently to wrench the gisarm away from Myles. In that short, fierce struggle Myles was dragged to his knees, and then, still holding the weapon with one hand, he clutched the trappings of the Earl's horse with the other. The next moment he was upon his feet. The other struggled to thrust him away, but Myles, letting go the gisarm, which he held with his left hand, clutched him tightly by the sword-belt in the intense, vise-like grip of despair. In vain the Earl strove to beat him loose with the shaft of the gisarm, in vain he spurred and reared his horse to shake him off; Myles held him tight, in spite of all his struggles.

He felt neither the streaming blood nor the throbbing agony of his wounds; every faculty of soul, mind, body, every power of life, was centered in one intense, burning effort. He neither felt, thought, nor reasoned, but clutching, with the blindness of instinct, the heavy, spiked, iron-headed mace that hung at the Earl's saddlebow, he gave it one tremendous wrench that snapped the plaited leathern thongs that held it as though they were skeins of thread. Then, grinding his teeth as with a spasm, he struck as he had never struck before—once, twice, thrice full upon the front of the helmet. Crash! crash! And then, even as the Earl toppled sidelong, crash! And the iron plates split and crackled under the third blow. Myles had one flashing glimpse of an awful face, and then the saddle was empty.

Then, as he held tight to the horse, panting, dizzy, sick to death, he felt the hot blood gushing from his side, filling his body armor, and staining the ground upon which he stood. Still he held tightly to the saddlebow of the fallen man's horse until, through his glimmering sight, he saw the Marshal, the Lieutenant, and the attendants gather around him. He heard the Marshal ask him, in a voice that sounded faint and distant, if he was dangerously wounded. He did not answer, and one of the attendants, leaping from his horse, opened the umbril of his helmet, disclosing the dull, hollow eyes, the ashy, colorless lips, and the waxy forehead, upon which stood great beads of sweat.

"Water! water!" he cried, hoarsely; "give me to drink!" Then, quitting his hold upon the horse, he started blindly across the lists towards the gate of the barrier. A shadow that chilled his heart seemed to fall upon him. "It is death," he muttered; then he stopped, then swayed for an instant, and then toppled headlong, crashing as he fell.

But Myles was not dead. Those who had seen his face when the umbril of the helmet was raised, and then saw him fall as he tottered across the lists, had at first thought so. But his faintness was more from loss of blood and the sudden unstringing of nerve and sense from the intense furious strain of the last few moments of battle than from the vital nature of the wound. Indeed, after Myles had been carried out of the lists and laid upon the ground in the shade between the barriers, Master Thomas, the Prince's barber-surgeon, having examined the wounds, declared that he might be even carried on a covered litter to Scotland Yard without serious danger. The Prince was extremely desirous of having him under his care, and so the venture was tried. Myles was carried to Scotland Yard, and perhaps was none the worse therefore.

The Prince, the Earl of Mackworth, and two or three others stood silently watching as the worthy shaver and leecher, assisted by his apprentice and Gascoyne, washed and bathed the great gaping wound in the side and bound it with linen bandages. Myles lay with closed eyelids, still, pallid, weak as a little child. Presently he opened his eyes and turned them, dull and languid, to the Prince.

"What hath happed my father, my Lord?" said he, in a faint, whispering voice.

"Thou hath saved his life and honor, Myles," the Prince answered. "He is here now, and thy mother hath been sent for, and cometh anon with the priest who was with them this morn."

Myles dropped his eyelids again; his lips moved, but he made

no sound, and then two tears trickled across his white cheek.

"He maketh a woman of me," the Prince muttered through his teeth, and then, swinging on his heel, he stood for a long time looking out of the window into the garden beneath.

"May I see my father?" said Myles, presently, without opening his eyes.

The Prince turned around and looked inquiringly at the surgeon.

The good man shook his head. "Not today," said he; "haply tomorrow he may see him and his mother. The bleeding is but new stanched, and such matters as seeing his father and mother may make the heart to swell, and so maybe the wound burst afresh and he die. An he would hope to live, he must rest quiet until tomorrow day."

But though Myles's wound was not mortal, it was very serious. The fever which followed lingered longer than common—perhaps because of the hot weather—and the days stretched to weeks, and the weeks to months, and still he lay there, nursed by his mother and Gascoyne and Prior Edward, and now and again by Sir James Lee.

One day, a little before the good priest returned to Saint Mary's Priory, as he sat by Myles's bedside, his hands folded, and his sight turned inward, the young man suddenly said, "Tell me, holy father, is it always wrong for man to slay man?"

The good priest sat silent for so long a time that Myles began to think he had not heard the question. But by-and-by he answered, almost with a sigh, "It is a hard question, my son, but I must in truth say, meseems it is not always wrong."

"Sir," said Myles," I have been in battle when men were slain, but never did I think thereon as I have upon this matter. Did I sin in so slaying my father's enemy?"

"Nay," said Prior Edwards, quietly, "thou didst not sin. It was for others thou didst fight, my son, and for others it is pardonable to do battle. Had it been thine own quarrel, it might haply have been more hard to have answered thee."

Who can gainsay, even in these days of light, the truth of this that the good priest said to the sick lad so far away in the past?

In the days of Louis XVIII of France many men were unjustly imprisoned or killed if they were suspected of plotting to restore Napoleon to the throne. Edmond Dantès was falsely accused of being a spy. He was convicted without a fair trial and imprisoned in the Château D'If. There he dug a secret passage to the cell of another prisoner, the old Abbé Faria. He was grief-stricken when, after many years, his only friend died, but he suddenly sees how he now has a chance to solve his problem.

Alexander Dumas

DANTÈS' ESCAPE FROM THE CHÂTEAU D'IF

ILLUSTRATED BY *DeWitt Whistler Jayne*

ON THE bed, at full length, faintly lighted by a dim ray that entered through the window, Dantès saw a sack of coarse cloth, under the ample folds of which he could distinctly discern a long, stiff form: it was Faria's shroud. All was over then. Dantès was separated from his old friend. Faria, the helpful, kind companion, to whom he had become so attached, to whom he owed so much, existed now but in his memory. He sat on the edge of the bed and became a prey to deep and bitter melancholy.

Alone! He was quite alone once more! Alone! No longer to see, to hear the voice of, the only human being that attached him to life! Would it not be better to seek his Maker, as Faria had done, to learn the mystery of life even at the risk of passing through the dismal gates of suffering?

The idea of suicide, which had been dispelled by his friend

291

and which he himself had forgotten in his presence, rose again before him like a phantom beside Faria's corpse.

"If I could only die," he said, "I should go where he has gone. But how am I to die? It is quite simple," said he with a smile. "I will stay here, throw myself on the first one who enters, strangle him, and then I shall be guillotined."

Dantès, however, recoiled from such an infamous death, and swiftly passed from despair to an ardent desire for life and liberty. "Die? Oh, no!" he cried out, "it would hardly have been worth-while to live, to suffer so much, and then to die now. No, I desire to live, to fight to the end. I wish to reconquer the happiness that has been taken from me. Before I die, I have my executioners to punish, and possibly also some friends to recompense. Yet they will forget me here, and I shall only leave this dungeon in the same way that Faria has done."

As he uttered these words, Edmond stood stock-still, with eyes fixed like a man struck by a sudden and terrifying idea.

"Oh, who has given me this thought?" he murmured. "My God, comes this from Thee? Since it is only the dead who go free from here, I must take the place of the dead!"

Without giving himself time to reconsider his decision, and as though he would not give reflection time to destroy his desperate resolution, he leaned over the hideous sack, slit it open with the knife Faria had made, took the dead body out, carried it to his own cell, and placed it on his bed, put round the head the piece of rag he always wore, covered it with the bedclothes, kissed for the last time the ice-cold forehead, endeavored to shut the rebellious eyes, which were still open, and stared so horribly, and turned the head to the wall so that, when the jailer brought his evening meal, he would think he had gone to bed as he often did. Then he returned to the other cell, took the needle and thread from the cupboard, flung off his rags that the men might feel naked flesh under the sacking, slipped into the sack, placed himself in the same position as the corpse, and sewed the sack up again from the inside. If the jailers had entered then, they would have heard the beating of his heart.

Now this is what Dantès intended doing. If the grave-diggers

discovered that they were carrying a live body instead of a
dead one, he would give them no time for thought. He would
slit the sack open with his knife from top to bottom, jump out,
and, taking advantage of their terror, escape; if they tried to
stop him, he would use his knife. If they took him to the cemetery and placed him in a grave, he would allow himself to be
covered with earth; then, as it was night, as soon as the grave-
diggers had turned their backs, he would cut his way through
the soft earth and escape; he hoped the weight would not be
too heavy for him to raise.

He had eaten nothing since the previous evening, but he
had not thought of his hunger in the morning, neither did he
think of it now. His position was much too precarious to allow
him time for any thought but that of flight.

At last, toward the time appointed by the governor, he heard
footsteps on the staircase. He realized that the moment had
come, he summoned all his courage and held his breath.

The door was opened, a subdued light reached his eyes.
Through the sacking that covered him he saw two shadows
approach the bed. There was a third one at the door holding a
lantern in his hand. Each of the two men who had approached
the bed took the sack by one of its two extremities.

"He is very heavy for such a thin old man," said one of them
as he raised the head.

"They say that each year adds half a pound to the weight of
one's bones," said the other, taking the feet.

They carried away the sham corpse on the bier. Edmond made himself rigid. The procession, lighted by the man with the lantern, descended the stairs. All at once Dantès felt the cold fresh night air and the sharp northwest wind, and the sensation filled him at once with joy and with anguish.

The men went about twenty yards, then stopped and dropped the bier onto the ground. One of them went away, and Dantès heard his footsteps on the stones.

"Where am I?" he asked himself.

"He is by no means a light load, you know," said the man who remained behind, seating himself on the edge of the bier.

Dantès impulse was to make his escape, but, fortunately, he did not attempt it. He heard one of the men draw near and drop a heavy object on the ground; at the same moment a cord was tied round his feet, cutting into his flesh.

"Well, have you made the knot?" one of the men asked.

"Yes, and it is well made. I can answer for that."

"Let's on, then."

The bier was lifted once more, and the procession proceeded. The noise of the waves breaking against the rocks on which the Château is built sounded more distinctly to Dantès with each step they took.

"Wretched weather!" said one of the men, "the sea will not be very inviting tonight."

"Yes, the abbé runs a great risk of getting wet," said the other, and they burst out laughing.

Dantès could not understand the jest, nevertheless his hair began to stand on end.

"Here we are at last!"

"No, farther on, farther on! You know the last one was dashed on the rocks, and the next day the governor called us a couple of lazy rascals."

They went another five yards, and then Dantès felt them take him by the head and feet and swing him to and fro.

"One! Two! Three!"

With the last word, Dantès felt himself flung into space. He passed through the air like a wounded bird falling, falling, ever

294

falling with a rapidity which turned his heart to ice. At last—though it seemed to him like an eternity of time—there came a terrific splash; and as he dropped like an arrow into the icy cold water he uttered a scream which was immediately choked by his immersion.

Dantès had been flung into the sea, into whose depths he was being dragged down by a cannon ball tied to his feet.

The sea is the cemetery of the Château d'If.

Though stunned and almost suffocated, Dantès had yet the presence of mind to hold his breath and, as he grasped the open knife in his right hand ready for any emergency, he rapidly ripped open the sack, extricated his arm and then his head; but in spite of his efforts to raise the cannon ball, he still felt himself being dragged down and down. He bent his back into an arch in his endeavor to reach the cord that bound his legs, and, after a desperate struggle, he severed it at the very moment when he felt that suffocation was getting the upper hand of him. He kicked out vigorously and rose unhampered to the surface, while the cannon ball dragged to the unknown depths the sacking which had so nearly become his shroud.

Dantès merely paused to take a deep breath and then he dived again to avoid being seen. When he rose the second time, he was already fifty yards from the spot where he had been thrown into the sea. He saw above him a black and tempestuous sky; before him was the vast expanse of dark, surging waters; while behind him, more gloomy than the sea and more somber than the sky, rose the granite giant like some menacing phantom, whose dark summit appeared to Dantès like an arm stretched out to seize its prey. He had always been reckoned the best swimmer in Marseilles, and he was now anxious to rise to the surface to try his strength against the waves. To his joy he found that his enforced inaction had not in any way impaired his strength and agility, and he felt he could still master the element in which he had so often sported when a boy.

An hour passed. Exalted by the feeling of liberty, Dantès continued to cleave the waves in what he reckoned should be a direct line for the Isle of Tiboulen. Suddenly it seemed to him that the sky, which was already black, was becoming blacker than ever, and that a thick, heavy cloud was rolling down on him. At the same time he felt a violent pain in his knee. With the incalculable rapidity of imagination, he thought it was a shot that had struck him, and he expected every moment to hear the report. But there was no sound. He stretched out his hand and encountered an obstacle; he drew his leg up and felt land; he then saw what it was he had mistaken for a cloud. Twenty yards from him rose a mass of strangely formed rocks looking like an immense fire petrified at the moment of its most violent combustion: it was the Isle of Tiboulen.

Dantès rose, advanced a few steps, and, with a prayer of gratitude on his lips, stretched himself out on the jagged rocks which seemed to him more restful and comfortable than the softest bed he had ever slept on. Then, in spite of the wind and storm, in spite of the rain that began to fall, worn out with fatigue as he was, he fell into the delicious sleep of a man whose body becomes torpid but whose mind remains alert in the consciousness of unexpected happiness.

For an hour he slept thus, and was awakened by the roar of a tremendous clap of thunder. A flash of lightning that seemed to open the heavens to the very throne of God, illuminated all around, and by its light he saw about a quarter of a mile away, between the Isle of Lemaire and Cap Croisille, a small fishing boat borne along by the wind, and riding like a phantom on the top of a wave only to disappear in the abyss below. A second later it appeared on the crest of another wave advancing with terrifying rapidity. By the light of another flash, he saw four men clinging to the masts and rigging; a fifth was clinging to the broken rudder. Then he heard a terrific crash followed by agonizing cries. As he clung to his rock like a limpet, another flash revealed to him the little boat smashed to pieces, and, amongst the wreckage, heads with despairing faces, and arms stretched heavenward. Then all was dark again. There was nothing left but tempest.

By degrees the wind abated; the huge gray clouds rolled toward the west. Shortly afterward a long, reddish streak was

He summoned all his strength to swim toward it

seen along the horizon; the waves leaped and frolicked, and a sudden light played on their foamy crests, turning them into golden plumes. Daylight had come.

It must have been five o'clock in the morning; the sea continued to grow calm. "In two or three hours," Dantès said to himself, "the turnkeys will enter my cell, find the dead body of my poor friend, recognize him, seek me in vain, and give the alarm. Then they will find the aperture and the passage; they will question the men who flung me into the sea and who must have heard the cry I uttered. Boats filled with armed soldiers will immediately give chase to the wretched fugitive who, they know, cannot be far off. The cannon will warn the whole coast that no one shall give shelter to a naked, famished wanderer. The spies and police of Marseilles will be notified, and they will beat the coast while the Governor of the Château d'If beats the sea. And what will become of me pursued by land and by sea? I am hungry and cold and have even lost my knife. I am at the mercy of the first peasant who cares to hand me over to the police for the reward of twenty francs. Oh God! my God! Thou knowest I have suffered to excess; help me now that I cannot help myself!"

As Dantès finished this fervent prayer that was torn from his exhausted and anguished heart, he saw appearing on the horizon what he recognized as a Genoese *tartan* coming from Marseilles.

"To think that I could join this vessel in half an hour if it were not for the fear of being questioned, recognized as a fugitive, and taken back to Marseilles," said Dantès, to himself. "What am I to do? What can I say? What story can I invent which might sound credible? I might pass as one of the sailors wrecked last night." So saying he turned his gaze toward the wreck and gave a sudden start. There, caught on a point of rock, he perceived the cap of one of the shipwrecked sailors, and close by still floated some of the planks of the unfortunate vessel.

Dantès soon thought out a plan and as quickly put it into action. He dived into the sea, swam to the cap, placed it on his head, seized one of the timbers, and turning back, struck out in a direction which would cut the course the vessel must take.

297

The boat changed her course, steering toward him, and Dantès saw that they made ready to lower a boat. He summoned all his strength to swim toward it, but his arms began to stiffen, his legs lost their flexibility, and his movements became heavy and difficult. Breath was failing him. A wave that he had not the strength to surmount passed over his head, covering him with foam. Then he saw and heard nothing more.

When he opened his eyes again, Dantès found himself on the deck of the *tartan*; a sailor was rubbing his limbs with a woolen cloth, another was holding a gourd to his mouth, and a third, who was the master of the vessel, was looking at him with that feeling of pity which is uppermost in the hearts of most people when face to face with a misfortune which they escaped yesterday, and of which they may be the victim tomorrow.

"Who are you?" the skipper asked in bad French.

"I am a Maltese sailor," replied Dantès in equally bad Italian. "We were coming from Syracuse laden with wine and grain. We were caught in a storm last night off Cape Morgion, and we were wrecked on the rocks you see yonder."

"Where have you come from?"

"From those rocks over there. Fortunately for me I was able to cling to them, but our poor captain and my three companions were drowned. I believe I am the sole survivor. I saw your ship, and I risked swimming towards you. Thank you," he continued, "you have saved my life. I was lost when one of your sailors caught hold of my hair."

"It was I," said a sailor with a frank and open face, encircled by long black whiskers. "It was time, too, for you were sinking."

"Yes," said Dantès, holding out his hand to him. "I know, and I thank you once more."

"Lord! but you nearly frightened me," the sailor replied. "You looked more like a brigand than an honest man with your beard six inches long and your hair a foot in length."

Dantès suddenly recollected that neither his hair nor his beard had been cut all the time that he had been at the Château d'If.

"Once when I was in danger," he cried, "I made a vow to the Madonna of Piedigrotta not to cut my hair or beard for ten years. The time is up this very day, and I nearly celebrated the event by being drowned."

"Now, what are we going to do with you?" asked the skipper.

"Alas! do with me what you will," replied Dantès. "The bark I sailed in is lost, my captain is dead, and I nearly shared the same fate. Fortunately I am a good sailor. Leave me at the first port you touch at, and I shall be sure to find employment in some merchantman."

"Take the helm and let us see how you frame."

The young man did as he was bid. Ascertaining by a slight pressure that the vessel answered to the rudder, he saw that, without being a first-rate sailor, she was yet tolerably obedient.

"Man the lee-braces," he cried.

The four seamen, who composed the crew, obeyed, whilst the skipper looked on.

"Haul away!"

They obeyed.

"Belay!"

This order was also executed, and, instead of tacking about,

the vessel made straight for the Isle of Rion, leaving it about twenty fathoms to starboard.

"Bravo!" said the captain.

"Bravo!" repeated the sailors.

And they all regarded with astonishment this man whose eye had recovered an intelligence and his body a vigor they were far from suspecting him to possess.

"You see," said Dantès, handing over the tiller to the helmsman, "I shall be of some use to you, at any rate during the voyage. If you do not want me at Leghorn, you can leave me there, and with the first wages I earn, I will pay you for my food and for the clothes you lend me."

"Very well," said the captain. "We can fix things up if you are not too exacting."

"Give me what you give the others," returned Dantès.

"Hallo! What's the matter at the Château d'If?" exclaimed the captain.

A small white cloud crowned the summit of the bastion of the Château d'If. At the same moment, the faint report of a gun was heard. The sailors all looked at one another.

"A prisoner has escaped from the Château d'If, and they are firing the alarm gun," said Dantès calmly.

"What is the day of the month?" he presently asked of Jacopo, the sailor who had saved him and who now sat beside him.

"The twenty-eighth of February."

"What year?"

"Have you forgotten that you ask such a question?"

"I was so frightened last night," replied Dantès, with a smile, "that I have almost lost my memory. What year is it?"

"The year eighteen-twenty-nine," returned Jacopo.

It was fourteen years to the very day since Dantès' arrest. He was nineteen when he entered the Château d'If; he was thirty-three when he escaped.

Howard M. Brier

FOOLS WALK IN

ILLUSTRATED BY *DeWitt Whistler Jayne*

ENGINE 16, exhaust barking and siren rising to a trembling wail, rolled over the rain-soaked ramp at midnight and thundered down Commerce Street in the direction of the waterfront.

Bud Draper, five months in service and the youngest pipeman in the outfit, rode the tailboard of the pumper. At his side, Mack O'Toole, veteran fireman, clung to the slippery rail.

"Tough night to roll," Mack shouted from the corner of his mouth.

Bud's tight lips twisted in a grin. Rain beat against his face, dripped from his chin. He clutched the box brace with purple fingers, A raw wind slashed at his cheek.

As far as Bud was concerned, any night was a tough night to roll. Fire service was no picnic, and he had learned it early in the game. It takes about three good alarms to knock the eagerness out of a rookie. After that he either turns in his badge or finishes the six months' probation on the chance of becoming a fireman.

With five months of the trial period gone, Bud was beginning to wonder if he wanted to be a fireman. Already the fascination, the thrill, had vanished. Fire fighting was reduced to a dirty, hazardous job.

As Engine 16 swerved on to King Street, Bud caught a flashing glimpse of a big, spotted dog cutting across the sidewalk. It was Smokey, Engine 16's mascot.

Bud grinned. Rain or snow, heat or cold never stopped Smokey. For twelve years the old fellow had been answering the bells.

"An' he'll keep answerin' 'em till his legs buckle," Captain Danny Gilready would say, with a proud shake of his gray head. "There's a smoke-eater, if there ever was one. An' don't tell me he ain't got brains. He's a Dalmatian coach dog, an' you kin trace his ancestors back to the seventeenth century."

Every man in the department knew that Smokey was smart, but there were some who questioned his lineage. Around quarters he looked like any other sleepy dog. He had large black and white spots and floppy ears. Most of the time he dozed in a corner of the apparatus room, but let an alarm crack the circuit and he was on his feet in a bound. With Engine 16 leading the way, he displayed uncanny speed and endurance. Seldom was he far behind when the gleaming red pumper took a hydrant.

Smokey and Captain Danny were inseparable. Both were old-timers, and they looked it; and you couldn't fool them much about fire. They knew what it took to make a good fireman, and each could be as stubborn as a three-alarm blaze.

When fighting fire, Captain Danny never knew when he was whipped. Let a building burn to the basement, and Engine 16 would be the last to pick up.

"Licked 'er that time," he would gloat, and though the smoking ruin might be a total loss, triumph would gleam unquenched in his watery eyes.

It was Captain Dan Gilready who had persuaded Bud to take the civil-service examination for fire service.

"The department needs young fellows like you," he said.

303

"Young fellows with steady nerves an' a stomach for smoke. I can remember your dad, 'fore he died in the oil-dock fire, boastin' as how you cut your first tooth on a toy fire engine."

Bud had qualified for service. Now he wondered if it was a mistake. He was vaguely conscious of a strange feeling that swept over him at times for which he found it difficult to account. Every time an alarm hit the register, every time a call came chattering in over the joker system, something welled up in his throat. He felt jittery. His heart began to pound.

He tried to hide this feeling, tried to cover it up with a blustering jauntiness which might have deceived some of the men in his company. But it didn't fool Smokey. Only two nights before, when Bud was wiping down the rig after a hotel blaze, he had reached down to pat the dog. Smokey had drawn back into his corner, curled a flabby lip back from his teeth, and growled gutturally.

Smokey knew what was the matter with Bud, and though Bud had a faint suspicion, he was not ready to admit it.

Now, as Engine 16 roared down King Street, Bud was aware of that strange feeling flooding over him again. He tightened his grip on the rail till his knuckles stood in a white row across the back of his hand.

Other equipment was rolling. A lumbering water tower from Third and Hastings swung in behind. Pumpers from head-quarters were racing down Spring Street, led by the screaming roadster of a battalion chief. High pressure batteries, hoist aerials, and combination ladder trucks joined the parade. Tires squealed, sirens moaned, motors roared, for this was fire in the Eighth Warden District, warehouse area.

Suddenly, unexpectedly, a passenger sedan nosed out of a side street like a frightened jack rabbit. Tony, driver of Engine 16, jerked on the big wheel. The engine swerved onto the car tracks and started to skid on the wet rails. For half a block the seven-ton pumper slid out of control. Tony fought the steering gear, heels digging into the floor-boards. Captain Gilready, riding the high seat forward, clawed for the dash rail. A sickening nausea waved over Bud.

With a thud the rear wheels struck a traffic button. The heavy machine jolted in the opposite direction and tilted crazily on two wheels. The impact broke Bud's grip. He was tossed against Mack, who had an elbow hooked over the box brace.

Instinctively Mack threw an arm round Bud's body, shoved him forward over the hose bed. With feet locked behind pipe stands and arms hugging the rail, he clamped Bud's body to the box, saved him from being thrown under the wheels of a trailing ladder truck.

The tires got traction. Tony tramped on the gas. The pumper leaped ahead. When Bud came out of it, Mack was grinning down at him.

"Ride 'er rookie," he shouted. "Don't let this old coffee pot throw you."

Somehow Bud managed to hook an arm over the brace. Panting with exhaustion, he clung there and shut his eyes to blot out the dizzy whirl of buildings and lights. A confused jangle of sound beat on his ears. He knew that Tony had the pumper under control and that they were racing through the night, but he was too weak to be conscious of anything but speed and noise.

Mack slapped him on the shoulder.

"Snap out of it, kid. Almost there. She's a smoker."

Bud opened his eyes slowly. Engine 16 was rolling to a corner hydrant, her siren fading to a hoarse groan. Bud knew they were on Harbor Avenue. Across the wide thoroughfare he could see bleak pier heads rising out of the gloom.

Black smoke was pouring down from a four-story warehouse across from the docks. It surged in a billowing cloud to hide street lamps and trolley wires.

"Take that hydrant," Gilready was shouting from his seat beside the driver.

Automatically Bud reached for the lead section of hose that lay coiled in front of him. He leaped to the curb, dragging the slack with him.

Mack jerked a combination hose wrench and spanner from the rack and tossed it at Bud's feet. Without stopping, the squat pumper snorted away, laying white line like a giant spider spinning a monster web.

With hose coupled, Bud fitted the spanner over the hydrant valve, waited for orders. Captain Gilready's command came drifting through the smoke.

"Charge sixteen! Pressure . . . sixteen line!"

Bud twirled the spanner. As the pent-up torrent sought the tip, the line bulged and writhed like a serpent.

An eighty-five-foot hoist aerial truck swung around the corner, the tillerman straining at the heavy wheel that steered her rear trucks. A searchlight battery rolled to the curb, turret floods swinging into position. The thin scream of a department ambulance rose above the clamor of the bells.

Bud lingered a moment at the hydrant on the pretense of having difficulty loosening the spanner. When he turned, he saw the shaggy form of Smokey standing in the gutter. Smokey stood with forelegs apart, eyes fastened on Bud accusingly. Bud spoke to him, but the dog backed away.

"So you don't like me, Smokey," Bud said. "That's too bad, old fellow. We could be pretty good friends."

Smokey's throat rumbled.

Bud started toward the burning building. There was no sign of flame, but glass tinkled, and he knew that the fire was mushrooming through the spacious lofts of the warehouse. A going blaze, held in check by four walls and a roof, has the wild fury of a caged animal, and minutes count.

The lieutenant of a ladder company was shouting at his men.

"Extend ladders!"

A battalion chief strode through the maze of hose and barked at the lieutenant.

"Ventilate that building. Open 'er up."

Captain Gilready whirled around when Bud arrived at the pumper.

"Take up the drag on that line," he snapped. "Stub and O'Toole are workin' the head. Keep the hose clear of the door jamb, and don't snuff smoke."

Bud knew what that meant. The warehouse held merchandise

306

that would give off a deadly gas. Woolens or silks, perhaps—the smoke would be heavy with hydrogen sulphide. Bud had never been gassed, but he had helped pack out firemen who had.

Two rescue squads and a gas company crew rolled in. Quickly, efficiently they went to work.

Bud kept his body low and tried to take advantage of the fresh-air stream that flowed along the sidewalk. A division chief brushed past. He was wearing a white coat and helmet, and a pug-nosed fume mask. The smoky doorway swallowed him up.

Bud kept Engine 16's line free. When a cloud of smoke engulfed him, he stumbled out of it, choking and coughing. With fresh air in his lungs, he returned to his post.

He could tell that this was no ordinary fire. A half dozen pumpers were churning in the street near by. Two of them were feeding a fourteen-ton water tower. Four lines were coupled to her intakes, and the pumpers were booting a stream up her mast sleeve that crashed from the two-inch tip of her turret nozzle with a pressure of 300 pounds. That's pressure!

Now and then a cascade of water would pour over Bud—black, sooty water, spilling out of the burned window sills above. His bunkers were full, and the stream dripped from the vulcanized hem of his rubber coat, but he stuck close to the line, gave Mack play on the hose.

He could hear the rumble of the flames inside, the sweep of the draft, the crackle of burning timbers. He sensed the danger that lurked there and shuddered. Mack O'Toole and Stub could have the job. As for Bud, he was content to take up drag. That was as close as he wanted to get to that fire. It was a dirty, rotten business and—

Bud looked up. Captain Danny Gilready was pushing through the smudged doorway with the limp form of Stub dangling from his shoulder. The captain turned Stub over to an inhalator crew, whirled to Bud.

"O'Toole's workin' this line at half pressure. Get a mask, an' take Stub's place."

Bud hurried to a squad wagon, called for gas equipment.

He strode back toward the doorway, fitting the mask over his face. He found 16's line. With shoulders down, he groped along it falteringly, until his hands touched Mack O'Toole's crouched body. The stream was sloshing half-heartedly, with only sixty pounds pressure.

Bud's fingers closed over the butt handles of the three-foot pipe. Mack sensed his presence, kicked the shut-off valve wide open. The stream crashed. It was like holding a lashing python, but Bud and Mack braced themselves to the task.

Engine 16's line was pumping a thousand gallons a minute into a blazing inferno. The whole center of the building was

308

a twisting mass of flame, but Bud knew that overhead the fire was spreading out. Heat rises. The top floors would go first, provided the basement was free of oil or explosives.

Through the whirling smoke Bud could see other engine company crews at work. They were pouring torrents into the blazing pit. The streams sizzled, and clouds of white steam went dancing as if some genii were at work. The threat seemed to lie in this infernal crater that had eaten its way through the floor, but Bud kept glancing up. The real danger was there. When the supports were burned out, when the walls began to buckle, then it was pick up line and run for your lives. Stab at the heart of it while it had a heart, but get out when the devil cut loose.

Burning brands fell about them; hot sparks slapped them in the face. The rubber in their coats grew oozy from the heat, and Bud and Mack kept their chins down, held their ground.

Bud felt a hand on his arm. He turned to find Captain Gilready crouching behind him.

Gilready was pointing to the north wing of the building, motioning them to follow him. The flames were sweeping in that direction, and Bud knew that something would have to be done about it. He hoped that somebody else would take up a position under those crumbling rafters, but there was nothing to do but follow Captain Danny.

Bending low, they made their way through a dark and smoke-choked corridor. Tony was giving them play now, and the line moved as they jerked it along.

They came to a barred door. Captain Gilready felt of it to see if it was hot. Satisfied, he pulled out a hand axe, hacked at the thin panel. He reached inside, drew the bolt.

Bud pushed against the door with his shoulder. It opened into a low-ceilinged room that was piled high with smoke-blackened bolts of cloth. Bud brushed his hand against one of the stacks. The material felt soft and warm. Woolen.

No wonder Captain Gilready had told him not to inhale the smoke. High gas content. Once in the lungs, smoke from burning wool can prove fatal in ten minutes. The drillmaster was

309

forever cautioning beginners about gas, and Bud had taken his lessons seriously.

They crept on their hands and knees between the piles of cloth. Captain Gilready kept feeling the floor, running his hand in under the stacks.

At the far end of the room the fire was eating through the wall. Bud could see it glowing dull red and ominous.

Captain Danny pointed, and Mack whirled the shut-off valve. The stream hammered against the wall, tore boards loose, and cannoned over the fanning flames. As the hole widened in the partition, heat surged through, beat against them like the blast from a steel furnace. Bud ducked, but kept a grip on the butt handles. If Captain Danny was looking for trouble, he found it, and found more than he bargained for.

It came with a flash—a boom. The floor behind them was blasted to slivers. The whole building seemed to shake. Piles of woolen cloth went toppling. The dark room was plunged into mad confusion.

Bud had the sensation of white light exploding in his face. Sparks spread like the shower from a bursting rocket. He felt the hose jerk from his hands, felt his body lifted, thrown head over heels. For a wild moment he was in mid-air, and then his knees slammed against a wall post. He crumpled in a heap on a pile of cloth.

Numbed by the shock of the unexpected explosion, he lay trembling and groping for the parted strands that held his thoughts together. His first sensation was one of pain in his leg. His head throbbed, and a shoulder blade stabbed when he moved his arm.

Reason returned as suddenly as it had left, and he found himself staring at a sheet of flame that was spreading over a whole wall, licking out between the girders of the ceiling with pointed fangs.

His oxygen mask hung useless from his chest. The strap was broken.

Fire was spouting through a hole in the floor to the left of the door. Bud knew that minutes were precious. If he could

310

make the door before the fury of those flames reached their height, he still had a chance. He would have to hurry, or the gas would get him first.

Bud tried to move, tried to claw his way over the pile of cloth. His muscles felt paralyzed. He sank back, helpless.

It was in that frantic moment that Bud realized his own failing. It struck him like a blow in the face. This feeling that was gripping him—this strange sensation that left him numb—this —this was fear. His heart was pounding in his throat. His hands were shaking. His body was trembling. A frenzied cry broke from his parched lips. Panic flooded over him. He was afraid, deathly afraid. And yet, he could feel new forces mustering within him. The very fear that threatened to destroy him was churning power into his arms, his legs; driving him to rise up, to flee from the danger that was hemming him in.

A new distraction rose to confuse him. Whipping about his feet, tripping him up, was the lashing hose of Engine 16. He knew from the savage kick of the line that nobody was on the pipe. Where was Captain Danny? Where was Mack O'Toole?

The questions flashed in his mind, but he brushed them aside and lunged for the door. He stumbled to his knees, staggered to his feet. He was groping for the opening when a cry reached his ears.

"Bud! Bud!"

He stopped, befuddled. His head felt hollow, like a drum, and the voice kept pounding there.

"Bud! Bud!"

He whirled like a blind man, arm across his eyes.

"Captain Danny!" he shrieked. "Captain Danny! Where are you?"

"Here, Bud." The answer came from a corner of the smoke-filled room. "To your right. Can you make it?"

The flames were beating through the burning floor. They seared his skin. His face was blistered. He wanted to run, to run from this death trap. Fear told him to run. He could save his own life. He cringed for a moment, blubbering senseless sounds.

311

"Bud!" The voice was fainter. "Hurry!"

But Bud had turned his back on Captain Danny, had started down the corridor.

He had only gone a few steps when a bewildered form brushed against him. He heard a plaintive whine.

"Smokey!" Bud gasped. Captain Danny's dog had sensed trouble, was coming to help. Bud sank to his knees, ran his hand through the shaggy hair. Smokey was trembling, but he kept straining toward the door.

"If you're game, Smokey," Bud mumbled, "I'm game. Come on."

Together they crawled back toward the doorway.

"Captain Danny," Bud shouted. "We're coming."

"This way, Bud." The captain's words were scarcely audible.

Crawling over the hot boards, feeling their way cautiously, Bud and Smokey moved toward the sound.

Captain Gilready was slouched in a corner, and across his lap was the unconscious body of Mack O'Toole. A heavy timber pinned them to the floor.

Smokey nuzzled the captain, yapped joyously.

"Tried to move it," Gilready muttered. "Too much for me. It got Mack."

Bud tugged at the timber and felt it give an inch at a time.

When the old fire captain was loose, he hobbled to his feet, swayed uncertainly.

"Legs sorta haywire. Give us a hand here, we'll make it."

They lifted Mack between them and started for the door. With smoke beating into their lungs, with flame darting at them from the burning walls, they moved down the long corridor. Every foot of the way was torture to Bud. His knee was swollen stiff, and his shoulder was hammering with pain. The captain threatened to cave in with each step.

Smokey ran ahead, stopped, waited for them.

"Where the blazes is everyone?" Captain Danny muttered as they neared the door. "Well, I'll be a bowlegged ladderman, if they haven't picked up hose an' run."

The front wall was beginning to buckle. It had swollen in a

312

bulge at the third floor, and brick mortar was starting to pelt like the first drops of a cloudburst.

When Captain Danny and Bud came stumbling out of the deserted doorway, carrying Mack, there was a wild shout from the men clustered around the equipment. With helmets gone, faces streaked with soot, bunkers ripped and slit, they looked like men who had just shaken hands with death. Smokey tagged at their heels, bedraggled but happy.

Firemen ran to their aid. The department physician went to work on Mack.

"Gave you up when the heating plant blew," the chief of department said, slapping Captain Gilready on the back. "How'd you do it, captain?"

Danny Gilready nodded at Bud and winked at his commanding officer.

On the way back to quarters Bud rode the tailboard alone. He was certain he would never make a good fireman. He knew the reason why.

With the rig wiped down, he sought Captain Gilready in his cramped office.

"I hate to do this, captain," Bud said, "but here's my badge. I didn't realize it before, and it's hard to admit—but I was scared stiff when that oil plant blew. I'm afraid of fire."

Captain Danny's lips twisted in an understanding grin.

"Who isn't," he said, pushing the badge back toward Bud. "I've been afraid of it for thirty years. Only fools are never afraid. Courage and fear work together sometimes. When they do—that's fire fighting."

Bud felt something cool brush against his hand. He looked down. Smokey was standing there, licking his fingers.

"You can't fool Smokey," Captain Gilready said. "He hasn't much use for rookies, but he knows a good fireman when he sees one."

314

S. T. James

FOLLOW YOUR LEADER

ILLUSTRATED BY *Walter R. Sabel*

ANY moment now," said Barry Frost, and I glanced at him to see how he was feeling. It was the first real job our fire-fighting team had been out on since he had been appointed captain, and it threatened to be a difficult and dangerous one.

Barry looked back at me calmly. He even grinned a little, and I grinned back. I should have known that, even if he was worried, he wouldn't give any sign of it. We both looked down again at the dense yellow smoke billowing up towards us. The plane was flying 3,000 feet above the forest fire, but even so it looked uncomfortably fierce. And every minute thousands of pounds worth of timber were being destroyed.

We selected our spot and pushed out our 'chuted fire-fighting equipment. The pilot took us round again, and this time it was our turn to go.

Phillips went first, padded, helmeted, and masked. The remaining four of us followed him at precise intervals.

Down among the smoke we picked ourselves up and ran over to join Barry. Even as I hurried over to him my heart sank. It's all very well to be dropped into a clear space in the middle of an encircling fire, *if* you stand a reasonable chance of stopping

315

the flames at their weakest point. But what had looked, when we first flew over it, like a narrow strip of flame, now seemed to be an impenetrable and unconquerable inferno. To make matters worse the wind seemed to be increasing.

Barry saw me coming, but he didn't start bellowing orders as Big Bill Regan, who sometimes acted as his deputy, always did. He waited till we were all assembled and then gave his directions quietly.

"Phillips, Regan, Belton, start collecting the tackle. Johnny, get the radio working while I scout round for water."

"There's nothing effective we can do," said Regan.

We ignored him, but we all noticed it because it was the sort of unhelpful thing Regan had been saying ever since Barry's promotion. Regan had expected to be captain because he'd been with the team longer than anyone else, and Barry was a comparative newcomer. The rest of us bore no grudge; it was easy to see that Barry was one of those people who just took naturally to leadership. Only Regan wouldn't see it. He was resentful and he showed it in a dozen small, stupid ways. Now it looked rather as though he were going to show it in larger ways.

The fire had started quite near the edge of the forest, and when we had realized that it seemed to be running round the edge rather than blazing itself a straight trail, we had decided to come down in a clearing and try to save the precious timber in the middle. We didn't expect to be cut right off because a river flowed along the other side of the forest. Several of its tributaries ran through the trees, and we didn't think for a moment that the flames would be able to jump all the water-courses. Now that we were down on the ground we could see that they had leapt so high that they had simply jumped from the trees on one side of the streams to the trees on the other. What was more, the unusually hot weather had dried the smaller streams. Our only hope now was to get reinforcements to start working towards us from the outside while we pushed our way towards them from the clearing. Once we had broken the fire ring we might be able to save at least the center of the forest.

"Get the radio going, Johnny," said Barry.

I had already tried to get the walkie-talkie going and I'd failed. Now I tried again and once more I failed.

"Can't get a sound," I admitted. "Something must have broken as we dropped. But I've a few spares, and if we've time—"

"We haven't," said Barry. "We'll just have to give up the idea of meeting the others."

The fire was getting so close that we'd had to shout, and Big Regan heard us.

"We're wasting our strength and risking our lives," he shouted. "This job needs fifty men, not five."

Barry ignored him. "We'll defend the river line," he said, and led us, with axes and shovels, to the far side of the dried-up watercourse. We spread out at twenty yard intervals and began cutting down the bushes and stripping the grass to leave a patch three feet wide and absolutely bare, in the path of fire.

A spruce a hundred yards away burst into red splinters, and flames shot to the left and right like wingers in a football field. Another near-by tree burst into flames, and this time the flames jumped the stream and outflanked the earthwork we had built.

We waited for Barry's orders. Outwardly, he was cool and unruffled, as always. What he felt within, I could only guess. He must have known that the situation had changed. We now had to save ourselves—not the timber.

"I know the lie of the land, an' we're far from being trapped yet!" he told us. "This way, single file!"

Fallen logs and tangled undergrowth made a straight course difficult. Dense smoke, racing ahead through the treetops, dimmed our vision, and though Barry had a compass on his wrist, I didn't see how he could read its wildly swinging needle accurately. Burning twigs jumped ahead of us: the smoke made breathing difficult. Without looking back, we knew that the fire was gaining, just as surely as it was closing in on our flanks.

Suddenly, Barry flung out an arm, to point to the left. Here the ground rose sharply, almost into a wall, and the timber thinned.

"Hard rock!" Barry bellowed. "There's a tunnel—not far away!"

317

We panted on, crouching, crawling, staggering. We had abandoned most of our equipment, clinging only to our water bottles and to the radio, which weighed only a few pounds. Somehow, we reached the foot of the rising ground and began our ascent. Miraculously, it seemed to me, Barry found the entrance he had mentioned, and we crawled one by one into the round black mouth of a cavity where damp coolness reached out to soothe us.

"Nice work, Barry!" Bert Phillips gasped, after a few glorious minutes.

"Don't gloat!" Big Regan's voice was harsh and rasping. "The place will soon fill up with smoke. The fire's big enough to jump over us and put us in an oven to bake like potatoes!"

He was a veteran of the forest-fire service, and he knew what he was talking about.

"How far does this tunnel go?" Regan demanded. All the courtesy, all the respect had gone from his voice. "Can we get right through to the other side of the ridge? Or don't you know?"

He was taking over the leadership—mutiny, if you like, but he had the physical strength to do it, and maybe the knowledge too.

"I found the place while we were on a hunting trip. We didn't explore thoroughly!" Barry explained.

"I thought so!" Regan's voice was a savage snarl. "The shaft rises, you'll notice. The smoke'll rise, too. So we've the choice of suffocating or roasting! But not me! I can run out over the ridge, to the far side, with a bit of luck! There's still water in the big river, maybe, an' safety beyond!" He glared around with bloodshot eyes. "Who comes?"

It was now or never for Barry. "Nobody goes with you!" he said. "We couldn't possibly make the distance in time—we've had all we can take, for the present."

"Not me, I can make it!" Regan said, turning away. His bulk darkened the mouth of the cave for a second; we heard, faintly, the thump of his retreating feet.

Barry turned to me.

"Here you are, Johnny, now's your chance to take another look at the radio. I'm going to see where this tunnel goes to."

I began work upon the radio, hampered by the bad light, but desperately anxious to succeed. Outside the tunnel, there was now nothing but a world of thick smoke backed by a dull red halo. The heat and the smoke were growing stifling, but at least the fire seemed to have passed us for the moment.

Barry returned. "Cul-de-sac," he reported briefly.

From sheer exhaustion, we slept fitfully during the night. When dawn came, we ventured outside, but the world was still a mystery of smoke and dully glowing stumps, with hot ash ankle deep all around. Barry came over to where I was struggling afresh with the radio.

"We need to have help fairly quickly, Johnny!"

Something in his voice warned me.

"The wind's changing?" I guessed.

"Veering fast," he confessed. "We'll have the fire back this way very soon, I'm afraid."

Could we possibly expect to live through it a second time? I

319

turned again to my fumbling task, desperate, and somehow managed to make use of a spare part that hadn't fitted before.

"Working, Barry!" I shouted, ablaze with sudden new hope.

Almost at once, we established communication. There was a search plane out, invisible because of the smoke, inaudible amidst the crackling and roaring of wind and fire. At Barry's dictation, I described our position.

"Only a helicopter can lift us clear," I told the investigating pilot. "There isn't time for reinforcements."

"Keep your party together. Don't scatter!" The voice was fainter now, and we heard no more.

Barry turned to the rest of us. "You heard. Keep together: don't scatter. And if I don't get back to you in time, don't wait for me!"

We knew he was going to look for Regan. We even made an effort to stop him.

"He won't have gone far," said Barry. "And I'm responsible for Regan as well as for the rest of you. I wouldn't care to go home without him."

"Look after the radio, Tommy," I said, and followed Barry. He tried to send me back, but I could be obstinate too.

We heard the fire coming back. Tree stumps, half burned yesterday, exploded like bombs. Blazing fragments whipped across our path, but against all odds, we found Regan lying face downwards between two fallen trunks, half buried by charred bracken and bramble, but alive. The fire had leaped above him, from crown to crown of the tall trees, dropping burning branches and red hot ash which had burned his coat and his back, without quite taking the life from him. The thick smoke had rolled over him, but the air was just that little bit cooler and thinner where his mouth and nose lay.

Barry took the head end, leaving me with the feet. There was no time for any first-aid. Even now, the race was going to be close—closer even than yesterday.

I thought once or twice that I heard an aero-engine above us, but could not be sure: the roar of wind-driven flames was too loud. Hot gray ash settled on us. Tears ran down our faces.

We breathed harshly, and our faces grew stiff with heat and smoke, but just as we reached the point when I had no hope left and little endurance, the mouth of the tunnel loomed at our feet.

We crawled inside; time passed; the torture in our lungs eased. A little water from a canteen helped us.

"We're alone!" Barry said. "Belton and Phillips have gone!"

He began giving artificial respiration to Regan.

"Try for radio contact, Johnny," he urged.

Almost at once, I heard the voice of a pilot patrolling above the forest. "Belton and Phillips were picked up. Can't take any more until the fire passes. There's a dozen fallen trunks blocking the place we used half an hour ago!"

I saw Big Regan stirring: heard him groan.

"We'll walk out," Barry said. "Don't worry! We'll walk out as soon as we've picked up a little strength."

A little later we walked together to the tunnel mouth. Black smoke palled everything, punctuated by burning stumps. Ugly puffs of flame arose from the ground here and there. But the roar of destruction, the pressure of wind, was definitely lessening.

The circling pilot spotted and pin-pointed a clear patch for us; he asked if we could be there in exactly one hour, to meet the helicopter.

"A mile to walk. What about it, Regan?" Barry asked.

"We'll make it, skipper!" Regan said, and I breathed a sigh of relief. From now on, I knew, we'd *all* be following our leader.

As THE two exhausted men about whom you are to read in this story crept up the steep, wind-swept slope of Annapurna, one of the highest peaks of the Himalayas, they were hoping desperately to reach the top. No man had ever climbed this high before.

Herzog, the author of this story, was the leader of the French expedition which included Lachenal, Rébuffat, Terray, and others. Preparations for the final assault on the peak included hazardous explorations for the best possible way to approach it and the back-breaking task of establishing a chain of camps leading to the top like stepping stones.

The final assault began early on the morning of June third. They would soon know whether their preparations had been made in vain or whether their efforts would be crowned with success.

Maurice Herzog

THE THIRD OF JUNE ON ANNAPURNA

ILLUSTRATED BY *Hardie Gramatky*

ON THE third of June, 1950, the first light of dawn found us still clinging to the tent poles at Camp V. Gradually the wind abated, and with daylight, died away altogether. I made desperate attempts to push back the soft, icy stuff which stifled me, but every movement became an act of heroism. My mental powers were numbed: thinking was an effort, and we did not exchange a single word.

What a repellent place it was! To everyone who reached it, Camp V became one of the worst memories of their lives. We had only one thought—to get away. We should have waited for the first rays of the sun, but at half-past five we felt we couldn't stick it any longer.

"Let's go, Biscante," I muttered. "Can't stay here a minute longer."

"Yes, let's go," repeated Lachenal.

Which of us would have the energy to make tea? Although our minds worked slowly we were quite able to envisage all the movements that would be necessary—and neither of us could face up to it. It couldn't be helped—we would just have to go without. It was quite hard enough work to get ourselves and our boots out of our sleeping-bags—and the boots were frozen stiff so that we got them on only with the greatest difficulty. Every movement made us terribly breathless. We felt as if we were being stifled. Our gaiters were stiff as a board, and I succeeded in lacing mine up; Lachenal couldn't manage his.

"No need for the rope, eh, Biscante?"

"No need," replied Lachenal laconically.

That was two pounds saved. I pushed a tube of condensed milk, some nougat and a pair of socks into my sack; one never knew, the socks might come in useful—they might even do as Balaclavas. For the time being I stuffed them with first-aid equipment. The camera was loaded with a black and white film; I had a color film in reserve. I pulled the movie-camera out from the bottom of my sleeping-bag, wound it up and tried letting it run without film. There was a little click, then it stopped and jammed.

"Bad luck after bringing it so far," said Lachenal.

In spite of our photographer, Ichac's, precautions taken to lubricate it with special grease, the intense cold, even inside the sleeping-bag, had frozen it. I left it at the camp rather sadly: I had looked forward to taking it to the top. I had used it up to 24,600 feet.

We went outside and put on our crampons, which we kept on all day. We wore as many clothes as possible; our sacks were very light. At six o'clock we started off. It was brilliantly fine, but also very cold. Our super-lightweight crampons bit deep into the steep slopes of ice and hard snow up which lay the first stage of our climb.

Later the slope became slightly less steep and more uniform.

323

Sometimes the hard crust bore our weight, but at others we broke through and sank into soft powder snow which made progress exhausting. We took turns in making the track and often stopped without any word having passed between us. Each of us lived in a closed and private world of his own. I was suspicious of my mental processes; my mind was working very slowly, and I was perfectly aware of the low state of my intelligence. It was easiest just to stick to one thought at a time—safest, too. The cold was penetrating; for all our special eiderdown clothing we felt as if we'd nothing on. Whenever we halted, we stamped our feet hard. Lachenal went as far as to take off one boot which was a bit tight; he was in terror of frostbite.

"I don't want to be like Lambert," he said. Raymond Lambert, a Geneva guide, had to have all his toes amputated after an eventful climb during which he got his feet frost-bitten. While Lachenal rubbed himself hard, I looked at the summits all around us; already we overtopped them all except the distant Dhaulagiri. The complicated structure of these mountains, with which our many laborious explorations had made us familiar, was now spread out plainly at our feet.

The going was incredibly exhausting, and every step was a struggle of mind over matter. We came out into the sunlight, and by way of marking the occasion made yet another halt. Lachenal continued to complain of his feet. "I can't feel anything. I think I'm beginning to get frostbite." And once again he undid his boot.

I began to be seriously worried. I realized very well the risk we were running; I knew from experience how insidiously and quickly frostbite can set in if one is not extremely careful. Nor was Lachenal under any illusions. "We're in danger of having frozen feet. Do you think it's worth it?"

This was most disturbing. It was my responsibility as leader to think of the others. There was no doubt about frostbite being a very real danger. Did Annapurna justify such risks? That was the question I asked myself; it continued to worry me.

Lachenal had laced his boots up again, and once more we

324

continued to force our way through the exhausting snow. The whole of the Sickle glacier was now in view, bathed in light. We still had a long way to go to cross it, and then there was that rock band—would we find a gap in it?

My feet, like Lachenal's, were very cold, and I continued to wriggle my toes, even when we were moving. I could not feel them, but that was nothing new in the mountains, and if I kept on moving them it would keep the circulation going.

Lachenal appeared to me as a sort of specter—he was alone in his world, I in mine. But—and this was odd enough—any effort was slightly *less* exhausting than lower down. Perhaps it was hope lending us wings. Even through dark glasses the snow was blinding—the sun beating straight down on the ice. We looked down upon precipitous ridges which dropped away into space, and upon tiny glaciers far, far below. Familiar peaks soared arrow-like into the sky. Suddenly Lachenal grabbed me,—

"If I go back, what will you do?"

A whole sequence of pictures flashed through my head: the days of marching in sweltering heat, the hard pitches we had overcome, the tremendous efforts we had all made to lay siege to the mountain, the daily heroism of all my friends in establishing the camps. Now we were nearing our goal. In an hour or two, perhaps, victory would be ours. Must we give up? Impossible! My whole being revolted against the idea. I had made up my mind, irrevocably. Today we were consecrating an ideal, and no sacrifice was too great. I heard my voice clearly,—

"I should go on by myself."

I would go alone. If he wished to go down it was not for me to stop him. He must make his own choice freely.

"Then I'll follow you."

The die was cast. I was no longer anxious. Nothing could stop us now from getting to the top. The psychological atmosphere changed with these few words, and we went forward now as brothers.

I felt as though I were plunging into something new and quite abnormal. I had the strangest and most vivid impressions, such as I had never before known in the mountains. There was something unnatural in the way I saw Lachenal and everything around us. I smiled to myself at the paltriness of our efforts, for I could stand apart and watch myself making these efforts. But all sense of exertion was gone, as though there were no longer any gravity. This diaphanous landscape, this quintessence of purity—these were not the mountains I knew: they were the mountains of my dreams.

The snow, sprinkled over every rock and gleaming in the sun, was of a radiant beauty that touched me to the heart. I had never seen such complete transparency, and I was living in a world of crystal. Sounds were indistinct, the atmosphere like cotton wool.

An astonishing happiness welled up in me, but I could not define it. Everything was so new, so utterly unprecedented. It was not in the least like anything I had known in the Alps, where one feels buoyed up by the presence of others—by people of

whom one is vaguely aware, or even by the dwellings one can
see in the far distance.

This was quite different. An enormous gulf was between me
and the world. This was a different universe—withered, desert,
lifeless; a fantastic universe where the presence of man was not
foreseen, perhaps not desired. We were braving an interdict,
overstepping a boundary, and yet we had no fear as we continued upward. I thought of the famous ladder of St. Theresa
of Avila. Something clutched at my heart.

Did Lachenal share these feelings? The summit ridge drew
nearer, and we reached the foot of the ultimate rock band. The
slope was very steep and the snow interspersed with rocks.

"Couloir!"

A finger pointed. The whispered word from one to another
indicated the key to the rocks—the last line of defense.

"What luck!"

The couloir up the rocks though steep was feasible.

The sky was a deep sapphire blue. With a great effort we
edged over to the right, avoiding the rocks; we preferred to
keep to the snow on account of our crampons and it was not
long before we set foot in the couloir. It was fairly steep, and

we had a minute's hesitation. Should we have enough strength left to overcome this final obstacle?

Fortunately the snow was hard, and by kicking steps we were able to manage, thanks to our crampons. A false move would have been fatal. There was no need to make handholds—our axes, driven in as far as possible, served us for an anchor.

Lachenal went splendidly. What a wonderful contrast to the early days! It was a hard struggle here, but he kept going. Lifting our eyes occasionally from the slope, we saw the couloir opening out on to . . . well, we didn't quite know, probably a ridge. But where was the top—left or right? Stopping at every step, leaning on our axes we tried to recover our breath and to calm down our racing hearts, which were thumping as though they would burst. We knew we were there now—that nothing could stop us. No need to exchange looks—each of us would have read the same determination in the other's eyes. A slight détour to the left, a few more steps—the summit ridge came gradually nearer—a few rocks to avoid. We dragged ourselves up. Could we possibly be there?

Yes!

A fierce and savage wind tore at us.

We were on top of Annapurna! 8,075 meters, 26,493 feet.

Our hearts overflowed with an unspeakable happiness.

"If only the others could know . . ."

If only everyone could know!

The summit was a corniced crest of ice, and the precipices on the far side which plunged vertically down beneath us, were terrifying, unfathomable. There could be few other mountains in the world like this. Clouds floated halfway down, concealing the gentle, fertile valley of Pokhara, 23,000 feet below. Above us there was nothing!

Our mission was accomplished. But at the same time we had accomplished something infinitely greater. How wonderful life would now become! What an inconceivable experience it is to attain one's ideal and, at the very same moment, to fulfill oneself. I was stirred to the depths of my being. Never had I felt happiness like this—so intense and yet so pure. That brown rock, the

328

A fierce savage wind . . . We were on top of Annapurna!

highest of them all, that ridge of ice—were these the goals of a lifetime? Or were they, rather, the limits of man's pride?

"Well, what about going down?"

Lachenal shook me. What were his own feelings? Did he simply think he had finished another climb, as in the Alps? Did he think one could just go down again like that, with nothing more to it?

"One minute, I must take some photographs."

"Hurry up!"

I fumbled feverishly in my sack, pulled out the camera, took out the little French flag which was right at the bottom, and the pennants. Useless gestures, no doubt, but something more than symbols—eloquent tokens of affection and goodwill. I tied the strips of material—stained by sweat and by the food in the sacks—to the shaft of my ice-axe, the only flagstaff at hand. Then I focused my camera on Lachenal.

"Now, will you take me?"

"Hand it over—hurry up!" said Lachenal.

He took several pictures and then handed me back the camera. I loaded a color-film and we repeated the process to be certain of bringing back records to be cherished in the future.

"Are you mad?" asked Lachenal. "We haven't a minute to lose: we must go down at once."

And in fact a glance round showed me that the weather was no longer gloriously fine as it had been in the morning. Lachenal was becoming impatient.

"We must go down!"

He was right. His was the reaction of the mountaineer who knows his own domain. But I just could not accustom myself to the idea that we had won our victory. It seemed inconceivable that we should have trodden those summit snows.

It was impossible to build a cairn; there were no stones; everything was frozen. Lachenal stamped his feet; he felt them freezing. I felt mine freezing too, but paid little attention. The highest mountain to be climbed by man lay under our feet! The names of our predecessors on these heights raced through my mind: Mummery, Mallory and Irvine, Bauer, Welzenbach, Tilman,

Shipton. How many of them were dead—how many had found on these mountains what, to them, was the finest end of all?

My joy was touched with humility. It was not just one party that had climbed Annapurna today, but a whole expedition. I thought of all the others in the camps perched on the slopes at our feet, and I knew it was because of their efforts and their sacrifices that we had succeeded. There are times when the most complicated actions are suddenly summed up, distilled, and strike you with illuminating clarity: so it was with this irresistible upward surge which had landed us two here.

Pictures passed through my mind—the Chamonix valley, where I had spent the most marvelous moments of my childhood; Mont Blanc, which so tremendously impressed me! I was a child when I first saw "the Mont Blanc people" coming home, and to me there was a queer look about them; a strange light shone in their eyes.

"Come on, straight down," called Lachenal.

He had already done up his sack and started going down. I took out my pocket aneroid: 8,500 meters. I smiled. I swallowed a little condensed milk and left the tube behind—the only trace of our passage. I did up my sack, put on my gloves and my glasses, seized my ice-axe; one look around and I, too, hurried down the slope. Before disappearing into the couloir I gave one last look at the summit which would henceforth be all our joy and all our consolation.

Lachenal was already far below; he had reached the foot of the couloir. I hurried down in his tracks. I went as fast as I could, but it was dangerous going. At every step one had to take care that the snow did not break away beneath one's weight. Lachenal, going faster than I thought he was capable of, was now on the long traverse. It was my turn to cross the area of mixed rock and snow. At last I reached the foot of the rock-band. I had hurried and I was out of breath. I undid my sack. What had I been going to do? I couldn't say.

"My gloves!"

Before I had time to bend over, I saw them slide and roll. They went further and further straight down the slope. I re-

330

mained where I was, quite stunned. I watched them rolling down slowly, with no appearance of stopping. The movement of those gloves was engraved in my sight as something irredeemable, against which I was powerless. The consequences might be most serious. What was I to do?

"Quickly, down to Camp V."

Rébuffat and Terray would be there. My concern dissolved like magic. I now had a fixed objective again: to reach the camp. Never for a minute did it occur to me to use as gloves the socks which I always carry in reserve for just such a mishap as this.

On I went, trying to catch up with Lachenal. It had been two o'clock when we reached the summit; we had started out at six o'clock in the morning, but I had to admit that I had lost all sense of time. I felt as if I were running, whereas in actual fact I was walking normally, perhaps rather slowly, and I had to keep stopping to get my breath. The sky was now covered with clouds, everything had become gray and dirty-looking. An icy wind sprang up, boding no good. We must push on! But where was Lachenal? I spotted him a couple of hundred yards away, looking as if he was never going to stop. And I had thought he was in indifferent form!

The clouds grew thicker and came right down over us; the wind blew stronger, but I did not suffer from the cold. Perhaps the descent had restored my circulation. Should I be able to find the tents in the mist? I watched the rib ending in the beaklike point which overlooked the camp. It was gradually swallowed up by the clouds, but I was able to make out the spearhead rib lower down. If the mist should thicken I would make straight for that rib and follow it down, and in this way I should be bound to come upon the tent.

Lachenal disappeared from time to time, and then the mist was so thick that I lost sight of him altogether. I kept going at the same speed, as fast as my breathing would allow.

The slope was now steeper; a few patches of bare ice followed the smooth stretches of snow. A good sign—I was nearing the camp. How difficult to find one's way in thick mist! I kept the course which I had set by the steepest angle of the slope. The

332

ground was broken; with my crampons I went straight down walls of bare ice. There were some patches ahead—a few more steps. It was the camp all right, but there were *two tents*!

So Rébuffat and Terray had come up. What a mercy! I should be able to tell them that we had been successful, that we were returning from the top. How thrilled they would be!

I got there, dropping down from above. The platform had been extended, and the two tents were facing each other. I tripped over one of the guy-ropes of the first tent; there was movement inside, they had heard me. Rébuffat and Terray put their heads out.

"We've made it. We're back from Annapurna!"

DEEP-SEA diving is dangerous and exciting. This is the story of the man who has spent more time fifty fathoms below the surface than any other man —Alfred Pahlberg. Pahlberg was born in Sweden, and came to America intending to return home, but after he began to work for Capt. Scott, who raised ships from the bottom of the sea, he decided to stay here.

Margaret Norris

DOWN IN
DAVY JONES'S LOCKER

ILLUSTRATED BY *John Merryweather*

IT WAS during the building of Race Rock Lighthouse that the young Swede took his first dive. Race Rock, near the west end of Fishers Island, had long been a graveyard for ships. It lies at the point where Long Island Sound meets the Atlantic Ocean. In angry seas the tides sweep over it at terrific speed. The authorities had long desired to mark this point with a lighthouse, but to build one seemed a superhuman feat. At last, however, the government contract was given to the daring engineer Francis Hopkinson Smith, who was also an artist and a writer. The contract for the submarine work was given to Captain Scott.

Now began a battle with the sea that made engineering history. The laying of the foundation alone took three years. The top of the rock had to be cleaned off smooth and leveled by means of boulders which weighed from five to seventeen tons each. The stones had to be shaped, conveyed to the rock, and lowered in chains under water, where they dovetailed together like wooden joints. Sheet-iron bands, three feet high, were lowered into place around them, bolted together, and filled with concrete poured below the surface. And so on, layer after layer, until the surface was reached.

Again and again angry seas swept away derricks, huts, everything man-made. The divers struggled against all odds which the elements could devise. F. Hopkinson Smith has immortalized the venture in his book, *Caleb West, Master Diver*. The character of Caleb is drawn from Captain Scott, and Pahlberg is one of the heroes.

"When the job started I was a surface man," says Pahlberg. "Captain Scott was doing most of the diving, assisted by his half-brother, a man too old and too slow for the work. One day the old man gave out and was hauled up exhausted. Skies were clear, seas favorable, and Scott anxious to push the job. He looked up from the prostrate diver and caught my eye.

"How about it, Al? Want to put on a suit?"

"To be truthful, it was the last thing I wanted to do. I was scared to death, but, with the Cap'n looking at me like that, 'All right,' I said half-heartedly. Once they'd strapped me into that airtight contraption all blown up like a balloon with nothing but a tube to breathe through, only the thought of how the boys would guy me kept me from tearing it off. Next thing I knew I was under the water jerking up signals to the tender."

Things went all right the first day, and the Captain praised the young man's work; but next day seas were rolling. Pahlberg, standing on the rock under only fourteen feet of water, had just sent up the signal to lower a stone when a big swell lifted the derrick boat. The chain with the giant boat hook in the end of it came crashing down on his helmet and smashed the glass in the front of it. The blood spurted in his forehead, and water poured into his suit. Yet, like a case-hardened diver, the young Swede held his breath while they hauled him to the surface. They rolled him over a barrel and shook out several quarts of salt water.

"How about it, Al?" said Captain Scott. "Got your bellyful of diving, or do you want to go down again?"

"Vell, Captain," he said, "I tank I better have a coupla cups of coffee; then I'll go down and place that stone."

Then Old Man Scott knew he had found a diver. But even Scott did not know he had found the Neptune of divers, one who would keep on going down for hundreds—it may be thousands—of dives. The veteran has never counted the times he has been lowered over the ship's bow. In his slow, modest way he confesses that for ten years his help was required on an average of thirty vessels a year in both northern and tropical waters, and that some dives took him down a hundred feet.

"But that's nothing," he says quietly. "I've heard of men who went down two hundred feet. I don't know how they did it. One hundred feet was enough for me."

At my request the old man led me to the small, outlying shed where is stored the diving equipment he now keeps spick-and-span for younger men. Suspended from the ceiling hangs a row of suits—great, lanky, shapeless affairs like ghastly specters from another world; such things as Bluebeard's wife may have seen when she opened the forbidden closet. One look at them is suggestive of the dangers the diver is up against. They are gray, dull gray like the unexplored waters and as all-enveloping as a child's cold-weather sleeping garment. The old diver seemed dwarfed beside them. When I asked him to put one on, he shook his head; but to show good feeling he tucked his whiskers inside a helmet—and ceased to look like a human being. As he fingered the ungainly things lovingly, he explained their intricacies.

Next to his skin the diver wears two suits of woolen underwear of the good old red flannel variety. Body warmth must be conserved. The undersea man works in all seasons. Not long ago a pipeline three-quarters of a mile long was laid in Lake Erie while parts of the lake were frozen under twenty-seven inches of ice. And when Lake Erie freezes twenty-seven inches! Next comes the clumsy waterproof suit made of rubber and cloth through many plies and a pair of ankle-length rubber boots with thick iron soles. The shoes weigh twenty-four pounds each and keep him feet downward in the water. Around his chest is strapped a band of iron weights, adding eighty pounds more. Over his shoulders is a corselet of metal rings to which his helmet is screwed. The helmet is metal with two thick glass eyes in front, through which he gropes for the light he seldom sees a few feet below the sunlit surface. Altogether the diving dress weighs close to two hundred pounds—an exhausting encumbrance on land, but scarcely felt in the buoyant depths.

Air is pumped down to him through a rubber hose attached to the back of his helmet. It enters by a non-return safety valve which admits incoming air, but stops any outgoing flow. But what is breathed in must be got rid of; so on the right side of his helmet is an automatic escape valve which allows the air to leave when the pressure inside the suit exceeds the water pressure without.

As the diver works below, the escaping air shows itself on the surface in a stream of bubbles. By these bubbles the tender, the diver's topside mate, keeps tab on his companion. If the diver is working away at ease, the bubbles come up steadily. If he is nervous, excited, struggling, the bubbles come in intermittent puffs—the tenders cue to grow uneasy and do something.

Every diver has his tender, whose sole job it is to look after him, dress him, help lower him, maintain communication with him, and see that he is hauled up in time. Incased in a little world all his own, the diver works below. Suppose the job assigned him is to examine and report on a wreck. He has only his sense of direction to guide him, and this must be uncannily sure. A sunken ship lying on one side is a topsy-turvy affair. Stairs don't run up and down but crosswise. Hatchways are higgledy-piggledy. Doors are not upright but sideways. To open one is like raising a dropped shelf. This crazy-quilt architecture he explores in the dark, and he must find his way out again by the route over which he came. One misstep and his lines are fouled. The slam of a door and his air is cut off.

Like a gnome he gropes in the blackness until he finds the jagged hole that has caused all the trouble. This he measures with his hands and arms—just how long it is, just how wide, just how thick by the thickness of his fingers. Stuck in his pocket may be a lath on which he nicks out the measurements. On the surface he draws a diagram of that hole. A patch is made to correspond, and when he carries it down to put it on he knows it will fit to a quarter of an inch.

"You couldn't tell Pahlberg's patching jobs from one made by an expert on land, in the light," said one of the men in his firm.

Usually he carries two tools in his pocket—a clasp knife with a ring in the end and an eight-pound hammer like a baby sledge, mere extensions of his sensitive fingers. Or the job may call for the oxyacetylene torch, a fantastic tool that reverses the land-man's process and fights water with fire. It cuts through steel as a saw cuts wood. He may have to burn through the steel decks of a ship to the strong room, to recover valuable papers. Or perhaps the diver must guide a steam drill, a slender rod like a long pencil.

"We had a good wrecking job in Maine some years ago," said Mr. Pahlberg. "We had to blast out a ledge of rock to widen the channel of the Kennebec River. I drilled holes in the rock and put in dynamite in long cans, attached by wires to the boat. Then we set them off. The water shot up fifty or sixty feet in the air. Like Old Faithful geyser, I suppose, though I've never seen it. Yes, the water there was pretty cold, but if you work hard enough you keep warm."

To work at all in such conditions requires a sturdy physique and magnificent heart and lungs. No carousers or wasters need apply. The suit is rigid as a vise. The diver cannot turn his head without turning his entire body. He cannot lift his hand to his face or to any other part of his person. In any physical emergency, such as an attack of coughing or nausea, he would strangle before he could help himself. His sole link with the blessed air is the tender, truly his friend in need. Between the two a close firendship often grows.

"I had one tender ten years," said Pahlberg. "He had been a pearl diver down South, and when he got too old to dive he turned tender. He worked with me till he died. His name was George Brown—a first class man. And say—you should have seen him make the other men stand round when he wanted anything done! I felt safe with him, all right."

The diver has two connections with the tender—his airline, a rubber hose; and his lifeline, a rope. Nowadays there is also a telephone. Earphones are inside the helmet; the transmitter is in front of the mouth, and the wires go up the lifeline to the tender.

"I dived for years without a telephone," says Pahlberg, "and even the modern diver depends on his lifeline for most of his communications. There is a code of signals by jerkings on the line almost as extensive as the telegraph code, which both diver and tender understand. In all there are more than fifty signals.

Two pulls means "More slack." Two pulls repeated again and again is an SOS, "I'm fouled; send help!" Three pulls means, "I'm coming up." Four, "Haul me up." The same signal may mean different things depending on circumstances. For instance, one pull by the diver may mean, "More air." One pull by the tender means, "Are you all right?" This time the diver's answer of one pull is, "Yes, all right." When derricks are used there is a new code of signals to distinguish between the use of the boom fall, the main fall, the side fall, the trimmers. One shake and a jerk; two jerks and a shake—it is a language all in itself which each one must know as he knows his name.

Once Pahlberg almost lost his life because a green tender misunderstood, but since it smacks of heroism he doesn't talk of it glibly. "Only my big feet saved me," he says.

The once proud yacht *Iolanthe* had sunk in Long Island Sound under forty feet of water, and was buried almost to the deck in mud and silt, the backwash of the tides from farther out in the channel. Tons and tons of that shifting mire must be pumped away before Pahlberg could reach the nasty hole in her bottom. The intake hose from the suction pump, working on shore, was guzzling up mud like a giant boa constrictor—"swallowing the rabbit," they call it. As Pahlberg slogged round on the oozy bottom, suddenly his foot slipped and he tobogganed into the hole that was being torn in the ocean's floor. His left leg was jerked sideways and, with a shiver of pain, he realized his foot was caught in the intake.

"I should have been torn in two," he said, "except for the

fact that my big iron shoe wouldn't go all the way into the pipe. Yet I couldn't pull it away. There I was, anchored to the intake as though I was nailed there. With my rope I jerked out the signal to stop the pump, but the tender was new and green. He mistook it for the signal to haul me up—the worst thing the boys could do. Their pull threw me off my balance; I fell with my weight on my left leg and I could feel the tendons snap and the bones of my ankle fly out of joint. Vell, yes, it hurt pretty bad but I held onto my rope and jerked out again, 'Stop the pump.' This time Old Man Scott got the signal, and the Old Man always understood. I wasn't much good when I got to the surface, but one of the boys picked me up and carried me over his shoulder to the hospital. No, it didn't lay me up long."

"Ever had the 'bends'?" I asked him.

The old diver shook his head. "Cap'n Scott once had a touch of them, and I had to finish the job alone. And once I worked over two other boys who had 'em—pretty bad. But myself, I've been lucky."

"The bends," or caisson disease, is the malady caused by being hauled up too quickly after being far down for a long time. The victim suffers excruciating pains that bring on convulsions and may end, if not in death, in "diver's palsy," or paralysis for life. It is this which has caused the failure of many expeditions for sunken treasure. Vessels laden with cargoes of gold, unclaimed beneath fathoms of water, tempt the diver. Cupidity is stronger than fear. He goes after the prize and may bring it up—but at the expense of his life or his health. Many a diver has lived to curse the treasure that lured him down.

Why is this true?

Nothing that the ingenuity of man has devised is as unnatural as the diver working in deep water. The sea imposes a crushing punishment on any land creature who entrusts his body to the deeps. Water is heavy. The deeper one goes, the heavier it is. For every two feet a man descends, the water pressure increases about a ton over the surface of his body. The diver 100 feet down must resist a weight of almost fifty tons.

This would crush him to a jelly were not his airtight diving

341

dress blown out like a rubber tire to withstand the weight of the column of water. It supports him just as a pneumatic tire supports a heavy car. The pressure from without and the pressure from within must be kept in equilibrium. As the diver goes deeper, the pressure in his suit must be increased, or the weight of the water will squeeze him to death.

If a diver, working on the deck of a sunken ship, slips and falls the twenty-odd feet to the ocean's floor, the additional ten tons of pressure will cause his suit to collapse, and he will be crushed to a pulp. Although no drop of water may have entered his lungs he is in diver's parlance "drowned." To exist at all, the diver must breathe air under heavy pressure. At the depth of 100 feet, the air fed to him is compressed to about one-fourth its normal volume. He is always working under forced draft, like a furnace fed only with oxygen. The excess oxygen consumes his tissues at a rate much more rapid than normal, and with overlong exposure creates an oxygen poisoning.

Yet it is not the oxygen, but the excess nitrogen that causes the "bends." Nitrogen is the inert component of the air; it forms about four-fifths of our atmosphere. Under normal conditions we exhale it with each breath we give off, but conditions change when the air is compressed. The nitrogen, instead of being exhaled, dissolves in the blood stream and remains there in solution. While under water, the diver notices nothing. It is when he rises that the trouble begins. As the water pressure is reduced, the excess nitrogen bubbles out in the blood stream, clogs the arteries, and impedes circulation, causing extreme pain. If the bubbles gather in the spinal column they affect the nerve centers and cause paralysis. No wonder the diver dreads the "bends"!

The first preventive is to bring him to the surface slowly— not in one long haul but in a series of short rises with a pause at each stage, to permit the nitrogen to escape gradually. Then no bubbles of great size can form. The period of decompression varies with the depth at which the diver has been working and the length of time he has been there. From an extreme depth of 200 feet, two hours is required for rising.

As a further preventive, government surgeons have experimented with feeding the diver an artificial atmosphere composed of oxygen and helium gas. The substitution of helium for nitrogen has been found to produce an atmosphere as respirable as that provided by nature. It lessens the hazards of caisson disease for the following reasons: helium is less soluble than nitrogen; it diffuses more rapidly in the body fluids and tissues, and for this reason is eliminated more rapidly during decompression.

"Have you ever dived for sunken treasure?" I asked Mr. Pahlberg.

"Oh, yes, of course, when I was young. I suppose every diver has. But never on my own account. I was always too busy for that. It must be fifty years ago that a man from Pennsylvania, a big, handsome, strapping fellow, claimed he had located the spot where Captain Kidd's treasure lay buried. He had with him rangers who had charted off the area, and they knew within two or three feet exactly where that fabled chest of gold lay. He wanted a hardy diver to go after it and came to me.

"The spot he had fixed upon was not far from Gardiner's Island. The reward, if I brought it up, was enough to dazzle any man. Even so, he paid me ten dollars a day while I worked for him—but all I found there was mud. He had other divers working for him, sometimes seven days a week. That venture must have cost him plenty! But was he discouraged? No sir-ee! When he left he told me he'd find it yet. Poor fellow—he was slightly crazy.

"I'll undertake to raise anything if I am sure it's there. A good tough rock, for instance—that's a nice job for a diver. Such a rock lay in the midst of one of the most valuable oyster beds in the country, just off New Haven, a big, ugly rock that was in everybody's way. I had been sent after it and was kneeling down slipping the hoisting chain under it, when a sharp piece of oyster shell ripped a hole four inches long in my suit. It was an old suit, anyway, and I'd been cautioned not to wear it; and now it filled up good and fast. They hauled me up with the rock still there. The owner of the oyster bed was pretty well discouraged, so after I'd had my coffee he came up to me and said: 'Look here, Al: if you bring up that rock I'll give you an extra ten-spot.' So right away I borrowed another suit, adjusted the chain and pulled it up."

"What did you do with the ten dollars?"

"Treated the boys, of course."

"Ever had any encounters with sharks?"

"Vell, close enough," said the old diver. "It's funny," he added with a chuckle, "our closest meeting was right up here, where it's bitter cold. A coal barge had sunk just offside Bridgeport and lay heaved over on one side. I wanted to see what the natural bottom of the ship looked like from the outside and was just letting myself down by the bow chain when I felt something grab my foot. I looked round to see a baby shark some four or five feet long so close we could have shaken hands. He'd seen me moving and was hungry, I guess, in those cold, lonesome waters. He must have been as scared as I was, for he swam away pretty fast. But I thought I'd better go up just the same. I knew the boys up top wouldn't believe me, but it happened I carried up unmistable evidence of our meeting. On the iron sole of my shoe was the mark of his teeth. If he'd nipped me higher, I'd have left my whole foot with him. But it's down South where the sharks aren't lonesome. There you see them by the hundreds and so close you get to know their faces."

"When was this?"

"Let's see"—puckering his brows. "It must be twenty-five years ago, right after the Florida hurricane. I'd been given the job to raise a schooner off Key West. We were working just off the course followed by the cattle boats from the Gulf ports on their way to Europe. By the time these boats get as far as Key West, a good many of the steers are dead, and in times of strong currents every dead steer tossed overboard came floating right over the job. That was a banquet for sharks. They gathered for it as though for a family reunion. At first it made me a little nervous, but I soon learned that a shark prefers a good steer to a diver. They didn't bother us at all."

But sharks are only a part of the story of that job down near Key West. How Pahlberg, a diver from New London, chanced

344

to be away down there, was told me by a man in the office who had tipped me off in advance with the warning, "Al never tells any story that reflects credit on himself."

The story starts in the North and goes back to August, 1905, when the United States ship *Nero* was wrecked off the south side of Block Island. Wreckers say Block Island must have been named from the blocks of jagged granite that line the floor off her coast. The *Nero* didn't have much bottom left when the seas had done their work. But Pahlberg went into the dark hull of that ship and placed bag after bag of cement until the sunken craft had a new bottom almost four feet thick. Then she was pumped out and floated. Uncle Sam was pleased, and one more notable job was credited to the Swedish diver.

The next month, the Pensacola hurricane played havoc with shipping and towns. More than fifty ships were foundered or driven ashore in that big blow. Among them was a valuable gunboat which went on the rocks and sank just outside Pensacola harbor. One Navy diver after another went down, took one look at the nasty gashes in her hull where the boulders had stuck their teeth—and gave her up as a bad job. But Uncle Sam doesn't give up valuable property like that without a struggle. Navy folks at Washington scratched their heads—and suddenly remembered the *Nero* and the patching job done on her by that diver—"Let's see, what was his name?"

The result was a telegram from a high-ranking naval official to Captain Scott:

345

"Can you send the diver who patched the *Nero* to Pensacola today?"

Pahlberg took the next train south. When the gunboat had been mended, he was dispatched to the rescue of the little schooner sunk near Key West. The only comment I could draw from him on the Pensacola job was:

"It was nice diving down there. The water was clear and warm, and the bottom clean. But I think work in cold water is healthier. Once off the coast of Maine I ran into a great nest of eels. They came up and ate out of my hands like chickens."

What landlubber would make pets of eels?

But while the old case-hardened diver remains silent over stories of heroism, he loves to tell those that involve a joke. Here is a real fish story.

"Now and then we had a little fun under water, when we weren't too busy," he said. "We had a cook on the diving barge who spent every free moment fishing. He never had much luck, so we loved to kid him. Once I bet him a quarter I could catch a fish before he did. We shook hands on that bet, and I took a piece of meat down with me. I practically stuck the hook in the mouth of the first fish I saw swimming by. It was too easy, and I knew it. Then I picked up a piece of iron from the wreck weighing about eight pounds, tied a rope round it, and carefully hung it on old Dutchy's hook. Meanwhile I sent my own fish up to the surface on a line.

"When Dutchy started hauling in his line he thought he'd caught a whale. But it takes a lot of good nature to laugh at a trick like that. The coffee he gave me when I came up was weak and not very hot."

Stories like this are fast dimming in the memory of accumulated years. Pahlberg is the dean of divers, but his underwater work is done. He has an hour or so in the office every day, friends among the younger men, and in the evening cribbage or checkers. No, life is not over yet. And many a time when cries of distress are heard and there's skillful diving to be done, the wrecking crews would be glad to wrap a helmet around Neptune's whiskers.

346

Charles Nordhoff

THE PEARL DIVER

ILLUSTRATED BY *Robert Sinnott*

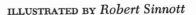

THE lagoon was calm that morning, calm as an inland lake, its surface ruffled at intervals by faint cats-paws from the north. Looking back toward the pass, there was no land in sight—the blue water met the sky in an unbroken line. Ahead of us, at the northern end of the atoll, the sea beach was little more than a mile away, and the thunder of the breakers was borne to our ears, now loud, now soft, on flaws of air.

My uncle stood in the stern, and I sat beside him; Fatu was in the bow, Ivi and Ofai at the oars. Once or twice Fatu motioned my uncle to change his course, to avoid the coral mushrooms rising to within a few inches of the surface, but in general the depth of the lagoon varied from six to twenty fathoms. Gazing down through the blue translucent water, I could see the strange forms of growing coral far beneath us; and sometimes, as the bottom turned sandy and the water shoaled, the lagoon shaded to purest emerald green. Clad only in a scarlet *pareu*, with his bronzed back and shoulders bare, Uncle Harry was leaning over the side, gazing intently at the bottom through a waterglass. He had given the word to go slowly, and the men were resting on their oars.

"This is the place," he said; "we'll anchor here and let Ofai go down for a look."

While Fatu was paying out the anchor line, I took the glass and leaned over to see what I could make out. The water was about twelve fathoms deep, and far down beneath the whale-boat's keel I could distinguish the purple coral on the floor of the lagoon. Ofai, the Rangiroa boy, was preparing himself to dive. He coiled a long cotton line in the bottom of the boat and

347

made fast to one end of it a thirty-pound bulb of lead, like an enormous sinker. Then he adjusted his goggles and went over the side. While he lay in the water, drawing a series of deep breaths, Fatu passed him the weight. He allowed it to sink a yard beneath him, seized the rope between the toes of one foot, and took a grip, high up on the line, with his left hand.

"Go ahead!" ordered Fatu.

The diver filled his lungs with air, grinned at us like some goggle-eyed creature of the sea, and let go the gunwale. Coil after coil of line flew over the side, and a train of bubbles rose to the surface, hissing faintly. When the line ceased to run out, Fatu pulled in the slack till it stood taut from the bottom and made it fast to a cleat. Gazing downward through the waterglass, I found that I could see Ofai dimly, in the twilight of the depths. He was swimming close to the bottom, with strange slow motions of his arms and legs; at times he stopped as if examining something, and finally—after what seemed a longer time than any man could hold his breath—I saw him approach the rope, pull himself upright, and heave strongly with one hand. He seemed to shoot upward faster than he had gone down; an instant later his head broke water, and he was expelling his breath with the eerie whistling sound I was to know so well. Then he shouted—the long-drawn yodeling cry which announces a lucky dive.

"Never have I seen shell of such a size!" he exclaimed, as he

handed up a great coral-encrusted oyster and came clambering over the side. "It grows everywhere—the bottom was covered as far as my eyes could see!"

My uncle was opening the oyster with the blade of his clasp knife. It was a rough, roundish thing, uncouth to the eye, and a full eight inches across. He cut the muscle, felt skillfully but vainly for pearls under the fringe, tossed the soft body overboard, and handed the shells—still attached to the hinge—to me. Craning their necks to see, the natives exclaimed with wonder. When closed, the oyster might have been mistaken for an ugly lump of coral, picked up at random on the floor of the lagoon; when open, it displayed the changing opalescent shades of mother-of-pearl, fringed with a band of gold.

"Get up the anchor," ordered Uncle Harry; "we'll try again, a hundred yards farther on."

"There would be a sensation on Tahiti," he went on, turning to me, "if you showed the traders that shell! It's worth twenty dollars a ton more than the black-lipped variety, and the books say that it produces a great many more pearls. We'll do a bit of prospecting today, mark the best places, and let the men begin diving in the morning."

We wandered on for several hours, examining the bottom at each halt and marking the more likely spots with a small buoy, moored to the coral with a few fathoms of line. By midafternoon, our work seemed finished—we had found more shell than our men could bring up in all the months ahead of us. Our final halt was close to the reef, and there, in about ten fathoms of water, Ofai went overboard for the last time that day.

The coral was light-colored at this place, and I could see every motion of the diver beneath us. Suddenly, when he had been about a minute under water, I saw him crouch and disappear in a crevice of the rock, and an instant later a long moving shadow passed beneath the boat.

"A shark!" exclaimed Fatu. My uncle sprang to the side.

I leaned over with the rest, watching with acute suspense to see if the shark would move away. No—he had seen Ofai and was turning back toward the deep crevice in which the diver

349

had taken refuge. Then the shark rose toward us and we saw him clearly—longer than our boat, livid-brown and hideous. An exclamation of horror went up from the men. There seemed nothing we could do. Thirty seconds passed; Ofai had been under water a minute and a half. My uncle had reached the limits of his endurance. He spoke to Fatu sharply:

"Your goggles! That knife! The other weight!"

The shark had approached the surface again, and as he turned to go down, before any of us could utter a cry of protest Uncle Harry went over the side, plunging downward with all the impetus of the heavy leaden bulb. It was an act of the most reckless courage; for in spite of the stories one reads, men do not attack the great sharks of the South Pacific in their own element.

Half sickened with suspense, I watched what followed: a drama played out in the limpid water beneath our boat. Grasping in his right hand a keen broad-bladed knife, my uncle shot down so fast that halfway to the bottom he overtook his monstrous antagonist. The shark was still intent upon Ofai; I saw him start and turn with a sweep of his tail as the man's body struck him and the thrust of a powerful arm sent the knife deep into his side. A pink cloud of blood gushed from the wound, and at that moment I saw Ofai emerge from his hiding place, seize the rope, and bound toward the surface of the lagoon. The diver's lungs must have been nearly bursting, and he mounted the rope with desperate speed. Now he was close to my uncle. The shark had circled, turning on his side with a livid gleam of his under parts, and was coming straight at the native. The monster reared—again I saw Uncle Harry raise his arm, saw the long knife sink home and the water reddened by a cloud of blood. The respite had been enough for Ofai; his head broke water with a gasp, and before a hand could be raised to help him he had seized the gunwale and was over the side of the boat.

My uncle was in desperate straits. He had been under water nearly a minute and was still eighteen or twenty feet beneath the surface. Fatu and Ivi were brave men and devoted to him, but it would have been insanity to think of going to his rescue now. I heard Fatu's voice, unreal and far-off, shouting to the

351

men to move to the other side of the boat; I felt the boat list, and saw, out of the corner of my eye, the gigantic figure of the mate standing on the seat beside me, bent almost double as he watched the scene below.

Uncle Harry had dropped the weight at the first attack, and now, still grasping his knife, he made for the rope and seized it with his left hand. The shark had darted away as he felt the steel for the second time, but now he was returning straight for the antagonist he seemed to recognize at last. Moving with horrid deliberation, he reared almost vertically beneath the swimmer, and opened his great jaws. My uncle stopped himself with his left hand on the rope, gathered his body together, and drove the knife into the broad rounded snout beneath him—the shark's most vulnerable point. For a moment the monster lay stunned and motionless, and in that moment Uncle Harry nearly reached the surface of the lagoon. Fatu was bent double, his hands already in the water.

Then the shark seemed to regain his senses and came rushing upward grimly. I saw the muscles of the mate's arms standing out as though cast in bronze, I saw the swimmer's goggled face within a yard of the surface, and the great fish charging with open jaws, fearfully close behind. Then the whaleboat lurched as Fatu plunged his arms deep into the water, seized my uncle and swung him up and inboard with a single mighty heave.

The shark came crashing against the side of the boat—a blow that nearly stove in the planking and started a dozen seams.

A minute passed before my uncle sat up and lifted the goggles from his eyes. "Get the oars out," he gasped, "and pull for the shallow water yonder. Bale, you two, and look lively—that fellow means mischief!"

The shark was at the surface now, swimming in swift zigzags like a hound at fault. While Ofai and I baled and the others began to row, I glanced over my shoulder and saw the tall dorsal fin heading straight for us, so swiftly that the water rippled away on either side.

"Pull hard—he's after us!" shouted my uncle, standing in the stern with a twelve foot oar in his hand.

352

We were making for the shallows over a large coral mushroom, a hundred yards away, and the men were rowing at top speed, for they realized that our light boat gave little protection against such an enemy.

The shark drew rapidly abreast of us and as his head ranged alongside, Uncle Harry raised the oar and thrust down with all his strength. The blow was a glancing one, and before he recovered his weapon, the three-inch shaft of tough wood was between a pair of formidable jaws. My uncle's eyebrows went up as he raised what was left of the oar, sheared off as a child bites through a stick of candy. Next moment Ivi cried out as the monster seized his sweep and wrenched it from his hands. I saw it float to the surface with a splintered blade—felt our boat shaken violently as the shark took the keel in his teeth. Then the bow grated on coral, and we leaped out in the shallows to pull the boat into the safety of a foot of water.

AT THE AQUARIUM
Max Eastman

Serene the silver fishes glide,
Stern-lipped, and pale, and wonder-eyed.
As, through the aged deeps of ocean,
They glide with wan and wavy motion.
They have no pathway where they go,
They flow like water to and fro,
They watch, with never-winking eyes,
They watch, with staring, cold surprise,
The level people in the air,
The people peering, peering there:
Who wander also to and fro,
And know not why or where they go,
Yet have a wonder in their eyes,
Sometimes a pale and cold surprise.

THOR HEYERDAHL had an unusual theory. He thought that the people of South America are related to the people who live on the South Sea Islands, and that there had once been a great migration to the South Seas across the Pacific Ocean. In an attempt to show that his theory was possible he and five brave men built a balsa raft, which they called the *Kon-Tiki*, and actually sailed across the Pacific Ocean! For this was the way in which the original migrants must have traveled long, long ago. On the *Kon-Tiki's* first day out a strong trade wind came up, and it took all the crew's strength and courage to handle the raft. . . .

Thor Heyerdahl

A KON–TIKI ADVENTURE

ILLUSTRATED BY *Armstrong Sperry*

BY THE late afternoon the trade wind was already blowing at full strength. It quickly stirred up the ocean into roaring seas, which swept against us from astern. For the first time we fully realized that here was the sea itself come to meet us; it was bitter earnest now—our communications were cut. Whether things went well now would depend entirely on the balsa raft's good qualities in the open sea. We knew that, from now onward, we should never get another onshore wind or chance of turning back. We were in the path of the real trade wind, and every day would carry us farther and farther out to sea. The only thing to do was to go ahead under full sail; if we tried to turn homeward, we should only drift farther out to sea, stern first. There was only one possible course, to sail before the wind with our bow toward the sunset. And, after all, that was the object of our voyage—to follow the sun in its path as we thought Kon-Tiki and the old sun-worshipers must have done when they were driven out to sea from Peru.

We noted with triumph and relief how the wooden raft rose up over the first threatening wave crests that came foaming toward us. But it was impossible for the steersman to hold the oar steady when the roaring seas rolled toward him and lifted the oar out of the tholepins, or swept it to one side so that the steersman was swung round like a helpless acrobat. Not even two men at once could hold the oar steady when the seas rose against us and poured down over the steersmen aft. We hit on the idea of running ropes from the oar blade to each side of the raft; and with other ropes holding the oar in place in the tholepins it obtained a limited freedom of movement and could defy the worst seas if only we, ourselves, could hold on.

As the troughs of the sea gradually grew deeper, it became clear that we had moved into the swiftest part of the Humboldt Current. This sea was obviously caused by a current and not simply raised by the wind. The water was green and cold and everywhere about us; the jagged mountains of Peru had vanished into the dense cloud banks astern. When darkness crept over the waters, our first duel with the elements began. We were still not sure of the sea; we were still uncertain whether it would show itself a friend or an enemy in the intimate proximity we, ourselves, had sought. When, swallowed up by the darkness, we heard the general noise from the sea around us suddenly deafened by the hiss of a roller close by, and saw a white crest come groping toward us on a level with the cabin roof, we held on tight and waited uneasily to feel the masses of water smash down over us and the raft.

But every time there was the same surprise and relief. The *Kon-Tiki* calmly swung up her stern and rose skyward unperturbed, while the masses of water rolled along her sides. Then we sank down again into the trough of the waves and waited for the next big sea. The biggest seas often came two or three in succession, with a long series of smaller seas in between. It was when two big seas followed each other too closely that the second broke on board aft, because the first was still holding our bow in the air. It became, therefore, an unbreakable law that the steering watch must have ropes round their waists, the other ends of which were made fast to the raft, for there were no bulwarks. Their task was to keep the sail filled by holding stern to sea and wind.

We had made an old boat's compass fast to a box aft so that Erik could check our course and calculate our position and speed. For the time being it was uncertain where we were, for the sky was overclouded and the horizon one single chaos of rollers. Two men at a time took turns as steering watch and, side by side, they had to put all their strength into the fight with the leaping oar, while the rest of us tried to snatch a little sleep inside the open bamboo cabin.

When a really big sea came, the men at the helm left the steering to the ropes and, jumping up, hung on to a bamboo pole from the cabin roof, while the masses of water thundered in over them from astern and disappeared between the logs or over the side of the raft. Then they had to fling themselves at the oar again before the raft could turn round and the sail thrash about. For, if the raft took the seas at an angle, the waves could easily pour right into the bamboo cabin. When they came from astern, they disappeared between the projecting logs at once and seldom came so far forward as the cabin wall. The round logs astern let the water pass as if through the prongs of a fork. The advantage of a raft was obviously this: the more leaks the better. Through the gaps in our floor the water ran out but never in.

About midnight a ship's light passed in a northerly direction. At three another passed on the same course. We waved our little paraffin lamp and hailed them with flashes from an electric torch, but they did not see us, and the lights passed slowly northward into the darkness and disappeared. Little did those on board realize that a real Inca raft lay close to them, tumbling among the waves. And just as little did we on board the raft realize that this was our last ship and the last trace of men we

356

should see till we had reached the other side of the ocean.

We clung like flies, two and two, to the steering oar in the darkness and felt the fresh sea water pouring off our hair, while the oar hit us till we were tender both behind and before, and our hands grew stiff with the exertion of hanging on. We had a good schooling those first days and nights; it turned land-lubbers into seamen. For the first twenty-four hours every man, in unbroken succession, had two hours at the helm and three hours' rest. We arranged that every hour a fresh man should relieve one of the two steersmen who had been at the helm for two hours.

Every single muscle in the body was strained to the uttermost throughout the watch to cope with the steering. When we were tired out with pushing the oar, we went over to the other side and pulled, and when arms and chest were sore with pressing, we turned our backs while the oar kneaded us green and blue in front and behind. When at last the relief came, we crept half-dazed into the bamboo cabin, tied a rope round our legs, and fell asleep with our salty clothes on before we could get into our sleeping bags. Almost at the same moment there came a brutal tug at the rope; three hours had passed, and one had to go out again and relieve one of the two men at the steering oar.

The next night was still worse; the seas grew higher instead

357

of going down. Two hours on end of struggling with the steering oar was too long; a man was not much use in the second half of his watch, and the seas got the better of us and hurled us round and sideways, while the water poured on board. Then we changed over to one hour at the helm and an hour and a half's rest. So the first sixty hours passed, in one continuous struggle against a chaos of waves that rushed upon us, one after another, without cessation. High waves and low waves, pointed waves and round waves, slanting waves and waves on top of other waves.

The one of us who suffered worst was Knut. He was let off steering watch, but to compensate for this he had to sacrifice to Neptune and suffered silent agonies in a corner of the cabin. The parrot sat sulkily in its cage, hanging on with its beak and flapping its wings every time the raft gave an unexpected pitch and the sea splashed against the wall from astern. The *Kon-Tiki* did not roll excessively. She took the seas more steadily than any boat of the same dimensions, but it was impossible to predict which way the deck would lean each time, and we never learned the art of moving about the raft easily, for she pitched as much as she rolled.

On the third night the sea went down a bit, although it was still blowing hard. About four o'clock an unexpected deluge came foaming through the darkness and knocked the raft right round before the steersmen realized what was happening. The sail thrashed against the bamboo cabin and threatened to tear both the cabin and itself to pieces. All hands had to go on deck to secure the cargo and haul on sheets and stays in the hope of getting the raft on her right course again, so that the sail might fill and curve forward peacefully. But the raft would not right herself. She would go stern foremost, and that was all. The only result of all our hauling and pushing and rowing was that two men nearly went overboard in a sea when the sail caught them in the dark.

The sea had clearly become calmer. Stiff and sore, with skinned palms and sleepy eyes, we were not worth a row of beans. Better to save our strength in case the weather should

358

call us out to a worse passage of arms. One could never know. So we furled the sail and rolled it round the bamboo yard. The *Kon-Tiki* lay sideways on to the seas and took them like a cork. Everything on board was lashed fast, and all six of us crawled into the little bamboo cabin, huddled together, and slept like mummies in a sardine tin.

We little guessed that we had struggled through the hardest steering of the voyage. Not till we were far out on the ocean did we discover the Incas' simple and ingenious way of steering a raft.

We did not wake till well on in the day, when the parrot began to whistle and halloo and dance to and fro on its perch. Outside the sea was still running high but in long, even ridges and not so wild and confused as the day before. The first thing we saw was that the sun was beating down on the yellow bamboo deck and giving the sea all round us a bright and friendly aspect. What did it matter if the seas foamed and rose high so long as they only left us in peace on the raft? What did it matter if they rose straight up in front of our noses when we knew that in a second the raft would go over the top and flatten out the foaming ridge like a steam roller, while the heavy threatening mountain of water only lifted us up in the air and rolled groaning and gurgling under the floor? The old masters from Peru knew what they were doing when they avoided a hollow hull which could fill with water, or a vessel so long that it would not take the waves one by one. A cork steam roller—that was what the balsa raft amounted to.

Erik took our position at noon and found that, in addition to our run under sail, we had made a big deviation northward along the coast. We still lay in the Humboldt Current just 100 sea miles from land. The great question was whether we would get into the treacherous eddies south of the Galapagos Islands. This could have fatal consequences, for up there we might be swept in all directions by strong ocean currents making toward the coast of Central America. But, if things went as we calculated, we should swing west across the sea with the main current before we got as far north as the Galapagos. The wind was still blowing straight from southeast. We hoisted the sail, turned the raft stern to sea, and continued our steering watches.

Knut had now recovered from the torments of seasickness, and he and Torstein clambered up to the swaying masthead, where they experimented with mysterious radio aerials which they sent up both by balloon and by kite. Suddenly one of them shouted from the radio corner of the cabin that he could hear the naval station at Lima calling us. They were telling us that the American ambassador's plane was on its way out from the coast to bid us a last good-bye and see what we looked like at sea. Soon after we obtained direct contact with the operator in the plane and then a completely unexpected chat with the secretary to the expedition, Gerd Vold, who was on board. We gave our position as exactly as we could and sent direction-finding signals for hours. The voice in the ether grew stronger and weaker as ARMY-119 circled round near and far and searched. But we did not hear the drone of the engines and never saw the plane. It was not easy to find the low raft down in the trough of the seas, and our own view was strictly limited. At last the plane had to give it up and returned to the coast. It was the last time anyone tried to search for us.

The sea ran high in the days that followed, but the waves came hissing along from the southeast with even spaces between them and the steering went more easily. We took the sea and wind on the port quarter, so that the steersman got fewer seas over him and the raft went more steadily and did not swing round. We noted anxiously that the southeast trade wind and the Humboldt Current were, day after day, sending us straight across on a course leading to the countercurrents round the Galapagos Islands. And we were going due northwest so quickly that our daily average in those days was 55 to 60 sea miles, with a record of 71 sea miles in one day.

"Are the Galapagos a nice place to go to?" Knut asked cautiously one day, looking at our chart where a string of pearls indicating our positions was marked and resembled a finger pointing balefully toward the accursed Galapagos Islands.

"Hardly," I said. "The Inca Tupak Yupanqui is said to have

360

The sea ran high in the days that followed.

sailed from Ecuador to the Galapagos just before the time of Columbus, but neither he nor any other native settled there because there was no water."

"O.K.," said Knut. "Then we won't go there. I hope we don't anyhow."

We were now so accustomed to having the sea dancing round us that we took no account of it. What did it matter if we danced round a bit with a thousand fathoms of water under us, so long as we and the raft were always on top? It was only that here the next question arose—how long could we count on keeping on top? It was easy to see that the balsa logs absorbed water. The aft crossbeam was worse than the others; on it we could press our whole finger tip into the soaked wood till the water squelched. Without saying anything I broke off a piece of the sodden wood and threw it overboard. It sank quietly beneath the surface and slowly vanished down into the depths. Later I saw two or three of the other fellows do exactly the same when they thought no one was looking. They stood looking reverently at the waterlogged piece of wood sinking quietly into the green water.

We had noted the water line on the raft when we started, but in the rough sea it was impossible to see how deep we lay, for one moment the logs were lifted out of the water and the next they went deep down into it. But, if we drove a knife into the timber, we saw to our joy that the wood was dry an inch or so below the surface. We calculated that, if the water continued to force its way in at the same pace, the raft would be lying and floating just under the surface of the water by the time we could expect to be approaching land. But we hoped that the sap further in would act as an impregnation and check the absorption.

Then there was another menace which troubled our minds a little during the first weeks. The ropes. In the daytime we were so busy that we thought little about it, but, when darkness had fallen and we had crept into bed on the cabin floor, we had more time to think, feel, and listen. As we lay there, each man on his straw mattress, we could feel the reed matting under us

361

heaving in time with the wooden logs. In addition to the movements of the raft itself all nine logs moved reciprocally. When one came up, another went down with a gentle heaving movement. They did not move much, but it was enough to make one feel as if one were lying on the back of a large breathing animal, and we preferred to lie on a log lengthways. The first two nights were the worst, but then we were too tired to bother about it. Later the ropes swelled a little in the water and kept the nine logs quieter.

But all the same there was never a flat surface on board which kept quite still in relation to its surroundings. As the foundation moved up and down and round at every joint, everything else moved with it. The bamboo deck, the double mast, the four plaited walls of the cabin, and the roof of slats with the leaves on it—all were made fast just with ropes and twisted about and lifted themselves in opposite directions. It was almost unnoticeable, but it was evident enough. If one corner went up, the other corner came down, and if one half of the roof dragged all its laths forward, the other half dragged its laths astern. And, if we looked out through the open wall, there was still more life and movement, for there the sky moved quietly round in a circle while the sea leaped high toward it.

The ropes took the whole pressure. All night we could hear them creaking and groaning, chafing and squeaking. It was like one single complaining chorus round us in the dark, each rope having its own note according to its thickness and tautness.

Every morning we made a thorough inspection of the ropes. We were even let down with our heads in the water over the edge of the raft, while two men held us tight by the ankles, to see if the ropes on the bottom of the raft were all right. But the ropes held. A fortnight the seamen had said. Then all the ropes would be worn out. But, in spite of this consensus of opinion, we had not so far found the smallest sign of wear. Not till we were far out to sea did we find the solution. The balsa wood was so soft that the ropes wore their way slowly into the wood and were protected, instead of the logs wearing the ropes.

After a week or so the sea grew calmer, and we noticed that

362

it became blue instead of green. We began to go west-northwest instead of due northwest and took this as the first faint sign that we had got out of the coastal current and had some hope of being carried out to sea.

The very first day we were left alone on the sea we had noticed fish round the raft, but we were too much occupied with the steering to think of fishing. The second day we went right into a thick shoal of sardines, and soon afterward an eight-foot blue shark came along and rolled over with its white belly uppermost as it rubbed against the raft's stern, where Herman and Bengt stood barelegged in the seas, steering. It played round us for a while but disappeared when we got the hand harpoon ready for action.

Next day we were visited by tunnies, bonitos, and dolphins, and when a big flying fish thudded on board we used it as bait and at once pulled in two large dolphins (dorados) weighing from twenty to thirty-five pounds each. This was food for several days. On steering watch we could see many fish we did not even know, and one day we came into a school of porpoises which seemed quite endless. The black backs tumbled about, packed close together, right in to the side of the raft, and sprang up here and there all over the sea as far as we could see from the masthead. And the nearer we came to the Equator, and the farther from the coast, the commoner flying fish became. When at last we came out into the blue water where the sea rolled by ma-

jestically, sunlit and serene, ruffled by gusts of wind, we could see them glittering like a rain of projectiles which shot from the water and flew in a straight line till their power of flight was exhausted and they vanished beneath the surface.

If we set the little paraffin lamp out at night, flying fish were attracted by the light and, large and small, shot over the raft. They often struck the bamboo cabin or the sail and tumbled helpless on the deck. Unable to get a take-off by swimming through the water, they just remained lying and kicking helplessly, like large-eyed herrings with long breast fins. It sometimes happened that we heard an outburst of strong language from a man on deck when a cold flying fish came unexpectedly, at a good speed, slap into his face. They always came at a good pace and snout first, and if they caught one full in the face they made it burn and tingle. But the unprovoked attack was quickly forgiven by the injured party, for, with all its drawbacks, we were in a maritime land of enchantment where delicious fish dishes came hurling through the air. We used to fry them for breakfast, and whether it was the fish, the cook, or our appetites, they reminded us of fried troutlings once we had scraped the scales off.

The cook's first duty, when he got up in the morning, was to go out on deck and collect all the flying fish that had landed on board in the course of the night. There were usually half a dozen or more, and once we found twenty-six fat flying fish on the raft. Knut was much upset one morning because, when he was standing operating with the frying pan, a flying fish struck him on the hand instead of landing right in the cooking fat.

Our neighborly intimacy with the sea was not fully realized by Torstein till he woke one morning and found a sardine on his pillow. There was so little room in the cabin that Torstein had to lie with his head in the doorway, and, if anyone inadvertently trod on his face when going out at night, he bit him in the leg. He grasped the sardine by the tail and confided to it understandingly that all sardines had his entire sympathy. We conscientiously drew in our legs so that Torstein should have more room the next night, but then something happened which caused Torstein to find himself a sleeping place on top of all the kitchen utensils in the radio corner.

It was a few nights later. It was overcast and pitch dark, and Torstein had placed the paraffin lamp close by his head, so that the night watches could see where they were treading when they crept in and out over his head. About four o'clock Torstein was awakened by the lamp tumbling over and something cold and wet flapping about his ears. "Flying fish," he thought and felt for it in the darkness to throw it away. He caught hold of something long and wet, which wriggled like a snake, and let go as if he had burned himself. The unseen visitor twisted itself away and over to Herman, while Torstein tried to get the lamp lighted again. Herman started up, too, and this made me wake, thinking of the octopus which came up at night in these waters.

When we got the lamp lighted, Herman was sitting in triumph with his hand gripping the neck of a long thin fish which wriggled in his hands like an eel. The fish was over three feet long, as slender as a snake, with dull black eyes and a long snout with a greedy jaw full of long sharp teeth. The teeth were as sharp as knives and could be folded back into the roof of the mouth to make way for what was swallowed. Under Herman's grip a large-eyed white fish, about eight inches long, was suddenly thrown up from the stomach and out of the mouth of the predatory fish, and soon after up came another like it. These were clearly two deep-water fish, much torn by the snakefish's teeth. The snakefish's thin skin was bluish violet on the back and steel blue underneath, and it came loose in flakes when we took hold of it.

Bengt too was awakened at last by all the noise, and we held the lamp and the long fish under his nose. He sat up drowsily in his sleeping bag and said solemnly,—

"No, fish like that don't exist."

With which he turned over quietly and fell asleep again.

Bengt was not far wrong. It appeared later that we six sitting round the lamp in the bamboo cabin were the first men to have seen this fish alive. Only the skeleton of a fish like this one had been found a few times on the coast of South America and the

Galapagos Islands; ichthyologists called it *Gempylus*, or snake mackerel, and thought it lived at the bottom of the sea at a great depth because no one had ever seen it alive. But, if it lived at a great depth, it must have done so by day when the sun blinded its big eyes. For on dark nights *Gempylus* was abroad high over the surface of the sea; we on the raft had experience of that.

A week after the rare fish had landed on Torstein's sleeping bag, we had another visit. Again it was four in the morning, and the new moon had set so that it was dark, but the stars were shining. The raft was steering easily, and when my watch was over I took a turn along the edge of the raft to see if everything was shipshape for the new watch. I had a rope round my waist, as the watch always had, and, with the paraffin lamp in my hand, I was walking carefully along the outermost log to get round the mast. The log was wet and slippery, and I was furious when someone quite unexpectedly caught hold of the rope behind me and jerked till I nearly lost my balance. I turned round wrathfully with the lantern, but not a soul was to be seen. There came a new tug at the rope, and I saw something shiny lying writhing on the deck. It was a fresh *Gempylus*, and this time it had got its teeth so deep into the rope that several of them broke before I got the rope loose. Presumably the light of the lantern had flashed along the curving white rope, and our visitor from the depths of the sea had caught hold in the hope of jumping up and snatching an extra long and tasty tidbit. It ended its days in a jar of Formalin.

The sea contains many surprises for him who has his floor on a level with the surface and drifts along slowly and noiselessly. A sportsman who breaks his way through the woods may come back and say that no wild life is to be seen. Another may sit down on a stump and wait, and often rustlings and cracklings will begin and curious eyes peer out. So it is on the sea, too. We usually plow across it with roaring engines and piston strokes, with the water foaming round our bow. Then we come back and say that there is nothing to see far out on the ocean.

Not a day passed but we, as we sat floating on the surface of the sea, were visited by inquisitive guests which wriggled and waggled about us, and a few of them, such as dolphins and pilot fish, grew so familiar that they accompanied the raft across the sea and kept round us day and night.

When night had fallen and the stars were twinkling in the dark tropical sky, a phosphorescence flashed around us in rivalry with the stars, and single glowing plankton resembled round live coals so vividly that we involuntarily drew in our bare legs when the glowing pellets were washed up round our feet at the raft's stern. When we caught them, we saw that they were little brightly shining species of shrimp. On such nights we were sometimes scared when two round shining eyes suddenly rose out of the sea right alongside the raft and glared at us with an unblinking hypnotic stare. The visitors were often big squids which came up and floated on the surface with their devilish green eyes shining in the dark like phosphorus. But sometimes the shining eyes were those of deep-water fish which came up only at night and lay staring, fascinated by the glimmer of light before them. Several times, when the sea was calm, the black water round the raft was suddenly full of round heads two or three feet in diameter, lying motionless and staring at us with great glowing eyes. On other nights balls of light three feet and more in diameter would be visible down in the water, flashing at irregular intervals like electric lights turned on for a moment.

We gradually grew accustomed to having these subterranean or submarine creatures under the floor, but nevertheless we were just as surprised every time a new species appeared. About two o'clock on a cloudy night, when the man at the helm had difficulty in distinguishing black water from black sky, he caught sight of a faint illumination down in the water which slowly took the shape of a large animal. It was impossible to say whether it was plankton shining on its body, or whether the animal itself had a phosphorescent surface, but the glimmer down in the black water gave the ghostly creature obscure, wavering outlines. Sometimes it was roundish, sometimes oval, or triangular, and suddenly it split into two parts which swam to and fro under the raft independently of each other. Finally there were three of these large shining phantoms wandering round in slow circles under us.

They were real monsters, for the visible parts alone were some five fathoms long, and we all quickly collected on deck and followed the ghost dance. It went on for hour after hour, following the course of the raft. Mysterious and noiseless, our shining companions kept a good way beneath the surface, mostly on the starboard side where the light was, but often they were right under the raft or appeared on the port side. The glimmer of light on their backs revealed that the beasts were bigger than elephants but they were not whales, for they never came up to breathe. Were they giant ray fish which changed shape when they turned over on their sides? They took no notice at all if we held the light right down on the surface to lure them up, so that we might see what kind of creatures they were. And, like all proper goblins and ghosts, they had sunk into the depths when the dawn began to break.

We never got a proper explanation of this nocturnal visit from the three shining monsters, unless the solution was afforded by another visit we received a day and a half later in the full midday sunshine. It was May 24, and we were lying drifting on a leisurely swell in exactly 95° west by 7° south. It was about noon, and we had thrown overboard the guts of two big dolphins we had caught earlier in the morning. I was having a refreshing plunge overboard at the bow, lying in the water but keeping a good lookout and hanging on to a rope end, when I caught sight of a thick brown fish, six feet long, which came swimming inquisitively toward me through the crystal-clear sea water. I hopped quickly up on to the edge of the raft and sat in the hot sun looking at the fish as it passed quietly, when I heard a wild war whoop from Knut, who was sitting aft behind the bamboo cabin. He bellowed "Shark!" till his voice cracked in a falsetto, and, as we had sharks swimming alongside the raft almost daily without creating such excitement, we all realized that this must be something extra-special and flocked astern to Knut's assistance.

Knut had been squatting there, washing his pants in the swell, and when he looked up for a moment he was staring straight into the biggest and ugliest face any of us had ever seen in the whole of our lives. It was the head of a veritable sea monster, so huge and so hideous that, if the Old Man of the Sea himself had come up, he could not have made such an impression on us. The head was broad and flat like a frog's, with two small eyes right at the sides, and a toadlike jaw which was four or five feet wide and had long fringes drooping from the corners of the mouth. Behind the head was an enormous body ending in a long thin tail with a pointed tail fin which stood straight up and showed that this sea monster was not any kind of whale. The body looked brownish under the water, but both head and body were thickly covered with small white spots.

The monster came quietly, lazily swimming after us from astern. It grinned like a bulldog and lashed gently with its tail. The large round dorsal fin projected clear of the water and sometimes the tail fin as well, and, when the creature was in the trough of the swell, the water flowed about the broad back as though washing round a submerged reef. In front of the broad jaws swam a whole crowd of zebra-striped pilot fish in fan for-

370

mation, and large remora fish and other parasites sat firmly attached to the huge body and traveled with it through the water,
so that the whole thing looked like a curious zoological collection crowded round something that resembled a floating deep-
water reef.

A twenty-five-pound dolphin, attached to six of our largest
fishhooks, was hanging behind the raft as bait for sharks, and
a swarm of the pilot fish shot straight off, nosed the dolphin
without touching it, and then hurried back to their lord and
master, the sea king. Like a mechanical monster it set its ma-
chinery going and came gliding at leisure toward the dolphin
which lay, a beggarly trifle, before its jaws. We tried to pull
the dolphin in, and the sea monster followed slowly, right up
to the side of the raft. It did not open its mouth, but just let
the dolphin bump against it, as if to throw open the whole door
for such an insignificant scrap was not worth while. When the
giant came close up to the raft, it rubbed its back against the
heavy steering oar, which was just lifted up out of the water,
and now we had ample opportunity of studying the monster at
the closest quarters—at such close quarters that I thought we
had all gone mad, for we roared stupidly with laughter and
shouted overexcitedly at the completely fantastic sight we saw.
Walt Disney himself, with all his powers of imagination, could
not have created a more hair-raising sea monster than that which
thus suddenly lay with its terrific jaws along the raft's side.

The monster was a whale shark, the largest shark and the largest fish known in the world today. It is exceedingly rare, but scattered specimens are observed here and there in the tropical oceans. The whale shark has an average length of fifty feet, and according to zoologists it weighs fifteen tons. It is said that large specimens can attain a length of sixty feet; one harpooned baby had a liver weighing six hundred pounds and a collection of three thousand teeth in each of its broad jaws.

Our monster was so large that, when it began to swim in circles round us and under the raft, its head was visible on one side while the whole of its tail stuck out on the other. And so incredibly grotesque, inert, and stupid did it appear when seen fullface that we could not help shouting with laughter, although we realized that it had strength enough in its tail to smash both balsa logs and ropes to pieces if it attacked us. Again and again it described narrower and narrower circles just under the raft, while all we could do was to wait and see what might happen. When it appeared on the other side, it glided amiably under the steering oar and lifted it up in the air, while the oar blade slid along the creature's back.

We stood round the raft with hand harpoons ready for action, but they seemed to us like toothpicks in relation to the mammoth beast we had to deal with. There was no indication that the whale shark ever thought of leaving us again; it circled round us and followed like a faithful dog, close up to the raft. None of us had ever experienced or thought we should experience anything like it; the whole adventure, with the sea monster swimming behind and under the raft, seemed to us so completely unnatural that we could not really take it seriously.

In reality the whale shark went on encircling us for barely an hour, but to us the visit seemed to last a whole day. At last it became too exciting for Erik, who was standing at a corner of the raft with an eight-foot hand harpoon, and, encouraged by ill-considered shouts, he raised the harpoon above his head. As the whale shark came gliding slowly toward him and its broad head moved right under the corner of the raft, Erik thrust the harpoon with all his giant strength down between his legs and deep into the whale shark's gristly head. It was a second or two before the giant understood properly what was happening. Then in a flash the placid half-wit was transformed into a mountain of steel muscles.

We heard a swishing noise as the harpoon line rushed over the edge of the raft and saw a cascade of water as the giant stood on its head and plunged down into the depths. The three men who were standing nearest were flung about the place, head over heels, and two of them were flayed and burned by the line as it rushed through the air. The thick line, strong enough to hold a boat, was caught up on the side of the raft but snapped at once like a piece of twine, and a few seconds later a broken-off harpoon shaft came up to the surface two hundred yards away. A shoal of frightened pilot fish shot off through the water in a desperate attempt to keep up with their old lord and master. We waited a long time for the monster to come racing back like an infuriated submarine, but we never saw anything more of him.

Index

Alligator up the Bayou, Steve Benedict, 60
At the Aquarium, Max Eastman, 353
BENEDICT, STEVE, Alligator up the Bayou, 60
BENÉT, LAURA, Climb High, 8
BRADLEY, MARY HASTINGS, Gorillas and Lions, 158
BRECK, VIVIAN, A Touch of Arab, 178
BRIER, HOWARD M., Fools Walk In, 302
BUCK, PEARL S., Little Red, 68
CANFIELD, DOROTHY, Down in the Wolf Pit, 38
Climb High, Laura Benét, 8
Dantes' Escape from the Chateau D'If, Alexander Dumas, 291
DAVIS, L. R., Why Bother with Ladders, 134
Down in Davy Jones's Locker, Margaret Norris, 334
Down in the Wolf Pit, Dorothy Canfield, 38
DUMAS, ALEXANDER, Dantes' Escape from the Chateau D'If, 291
EASTMAN, MAX, At the Aquarium, 353
ENRIGHT, ELIZABETH, Oliver at the Circus, 26
EVANS, HUBERT, A Trust Fulfilled, 125
Follow Your Leader, S. T. James, 315
Fools Walk In, Howard M. Brier, 302
Gorillas and Lions, Mary Hastings Bradley, 158
Guides with Wings, Clay Perry, 228
HERZOG, MAURICE, The Third of June on Annapurna, 322
HEYERDAHL, THOR, A Kon-Tiki Adventure, 354
HEYLIGER, WILLIAM, Steelman's Nerve, 144·
JAMES, S. T., Follow Your Leader, 315
KING, KENNETH M., The Mystery of the Bay, 190
Kon-Tiki Adventure, A, Thor Heyerdahl, 354
LINDGREN, ASTRID, Pippi Acts as a Lifesaver, 94
LINDQUIST, WILLIS, Yukon Trail, 1, Storm Tide, 51
Little Red, Pearl S. Buck, 68
McSWIGAN, MARIE, Secret in the Snow, 101
MONROE, HARRIET, A Power-Plant, 143
Mystery of the Bay, The, Kenneth M. King, 190
NORDHOFF, CHARLES, The Pearl Diver, 347
NORRIS, MARGARET, Down in Davy Jones's Locker, 334
Oliver at the Circus, Elizabeth Enright, 26
Pearl Diver, The, Charles Nordhoff, 347
PERRY, CLAY, Guides with Wings, 228
Pippi Acts as a Lifesaver, Astrid Lindgren, 94
Power-Plant, A. Harriet Monroe, 143
PYLE, HOWARD, Tom Chist and the Treasure Box, 247, Trial by Battle, 278
Round Up, The, Kate Seredy, 80
ROUNDS, GLEN, Whitey and the Rustlers, 16
Secret in the Snow, Marie McSwigan, 101

SEREDY, KATE, The Round Up, 80
Steelman's Nerve, William Heyliger, 144
Storm Tide, Willis Lindquist, 51
STREATFEILD, NOEL, Understudy, 200
Third of June on Annapurna, The, Maurice Herzog, 322
Tom Chist and the Treasure Box, Howard Pyle, 247
Touch of Arab, A, Vivian Breck, 178
Trial by Battle, Howard Pyle, 278
Trust Fulfilled, A, Hubert Evans, 125
Understudy, Noel Streatfeild, 200
Whitey and the Rustlers, Glen Rounds, 16
Why Bother with Ladders, L. R. Davis, 134
Yukon Trail, Willis Lindquist, 1